THE RACE

The Off World Chronicles Book I

WRITTEN BY
STEVEN LAKE

THE RACE

The Off World Chronicles Book !

Copyright © 2025 by: Steven Lake

Book Cover Design by: Donald Semora

Edited by: Steven Lake

ISBN 978-1-94015-59-06

PROLOGUE

A man in a jet black business suit, black tie and sunglasses, looking more like a holdover from a Blues Brothers concert than a government agent, walked into the office of the director of the CIA's offworld black operations command and stared at a man in his mid 60's sitting at a desk on the far side of the room.

"Where's Senator Kennedy?" he asked.

The man behind the desk looked up and studied the agent with muted curiosity. Despite all of his years in the CIA, he was still amazed at how so many of the regular field agents looked more like the typical Hollywood stereotype than what one would expect a top secret government field agent to look like. And these weren't the deep cover types either. They were the normal, bureaucratic, pencil pushing, put a knife in your back while shaking your hand types. The man behind the desk narrowed his eyes slightly as he studied the man in black.

"In a closed door session of congress the last I knew. Why?" he said.

The agent glared at him with disdain.

"Don't get coy with me, Jack," he said.

The man behind the desk snorted.

"That's Mr. Roberts to you, agent," he said pertly.

If the agent was gonna get snippy with him, Jack would get snippy right back.

"I don't have time to play games, Jack. Where is Senator Kennedy!?" barked the agent.

Jack looked at him incredulously.

"I told you already. He's in a closed door session of congress."

"No he's not! I just came from there and he's nowhere to be seen!"

Jack cocked his head slightly.

"Then I don't know where he is," he said flatly.

The agent huffed angrily, spun on his heels and then stormed out of the office and down the hallway sounding like an angry bull on a rampage. About a minute later a younger man stepped over to the desk, glanced briefly over his shoulder and then back at Jack.

"What was that all about?" he asked.

Jack grunted.

"Agent 2751 is angry because he can't find Senator Kennedy," he said pertly.

The younger man grinned. Anytime Jack was feeling offended or upset with one of the numerous field agents, the infamous "men in black" who worked in his section of the CIA, he always addressed them by their commission number rather than their name, or even their code name.

"Well, what do you expect from them? They've been drinking the top secret Kool-aid for far too long," he quipped.

"Yeah, it's Kool-aid alright, with a dash of cesium," muttered Jack.

The younger man laughed.

"So what brings you in here, despite joining me in my mockery of the rather horrible excuse for field agents they hire these days?" asked Jack.

The younger man tossed a folder on his desk. On it's cover were the words "Terran 2 Project." Jack perked up slightly.

"This is that project that Section 17 has been looking into, isn't it?" he asked.

"Not looking into. They've been a part of this whole thing since before the CIA ever existed. In fact, the only reason we're any part of this is because we absorbed the Govian group back in 1951. Prior to then, this was their baby. So if we hadn't taken them aboard, we wouldn't be dealing with any of this right now," replied the man.

Jack was intrigued by this.

"Oh, so this is a pre-agency project?" he asked.

"More like pre-American. It was started back in the early 1500's."

Jack leaned back in his chair and folded his hands together as he contemplated this.

"So are you saying that this is part of the work the Syndicate is doing?"

The young man nodded.

"It's been their project for centuries, and it's still ongoing. Section 17 is only one half of that crazy mess. The Alien Brotherhood is the other half. It's been a joint project of theirs for some time. It's where all of this got started in the first place."

Jack seemed confused by this.

"So why are you bringing this to me?"

"Because I thought you might be interested in tossing your hat into the ring on this one."

Jack's eyes narrowed.

"Whatever for? Our interests are strictly Terran in nature. I have no interest in what Section 17 or the Alien Brotherhood, or whatever those demons want to call themselves, have to offer."

"Hey, don't brush them off so quickly. They gave us the ability to travel to the stars and do things that most people can't even begin to imagine. Cripes, Jack, the most technology the average person has seen is the smart phone that sits in their pocket. The Syndicate, and the technology they've brought us, has made it possible for us to travel to the stars, seed planets with life, and so much more! What they've given us makes Apollo 11 look like monkeys with a match stick."

Jack crossed his arms and frowned.

"I wouldn't care if they served the world's best espresso. They're demons, and I want nothing to do with them!"

"Only the Brotherhood is made up of demons. Section 17 is all human."

"Half demon? Whole demon? What's the difference? Really, what's the difference? It doesn't make me trust them anymore."

The younger man studied Jack for several moments, and then smiled.

"To be completely honest, I trust them less than you do."

"Then why bring this up to me?"

The younger man flipped open the front cover of the folder and showed Jack what was inside. Jack studied it briefly, and then looked up in surprise.

"You're kidding, right?" he said in disbelief.

The younger man shook his head.

"That's been their plans since the beginning. Even though they have Section 17 believing that this is for the betterment of mankind, it's really been nothing more than a gigantic roach motel since the start and will continue to be unless we do something to stop it. All of the participants who have been a part of this project from the outset have been checked in against their will. But once they're on planet, the 'Syndicate' makes sure that none of them ever check out. Like I said, it's a gigantic roach motel; and I think that needs to stop."

"So what happens if one of them completes this race and wins?"

The younger man shrugged.

"According to the rules, everyone goes home and the project ends."

Jack folded his hands, and then rested his chin on his fingers as he thought.

"So why are you bringing this to me? You said you thought I should toss my hat into the ring on this. Why?" he asked.

"I thought you might want to help bring this to an end once and for all and save a bunch of lives in the process. Section 9 is already busy trying to bring this to an end. But I'm sure they could use some extra help, if you're interested."

Jack pondered this for a few moments, and then smiled.

"Well, since you put it that way, what are we waiting for?"

Chapter 1

Simon looked up from his computer screen and rubbed his eyes. He'd been staring at code for the past nine hours, and it was quickly becoming a blur to him. He wondered if he should call it a day. But with deadlines looming, he didn't dare. Just then his manager leaned in the door of his cubical.

"Hey, Simon. You still here?" he asked.

"Yeah. Got a couple modules I need to fix before I knock off for the night. I should be done soon," said Simon.

His boss laughed.

"Well, don't stay too long. We've got a new client coming in tomorrow and I need you fresh and alert so we can blow their socks off. They're talking about contracting with us for a big point of sale system; and we're talking *big*."

"You're having me start a new project!? I'm not even done with this one!"

"How close are you?"

"It'll be at least two more weeks before it's ready for beta testing, and that's assuming I don't hit anymore snags along the way."

"Can someone else take over your work so you can start on this new account?"

Simon shook his head.

"Not a chance. I'm the only one left on this project. My supervisor already reassigned everyone else to the McDermit account last month. That's why I'm so far behind," he protested.

His manager blinked in surprise.

"Really!? Well, that shouldn't have happened. The McDermit project isn't *that* important. At least, not compared to this one. So I'll see what I can do to get you some help. In the meantime, just shut down and head home for the night."

"I will, as soon as I finish this module."

"How long will that take you?"

"A couple more hours."

"Nah, head home now. There's no point killing yourself over a management screw-up."

Simon frowned.

"Eh, alright," he grumbled.

His boss laughed.

"Thanks. See you in the morning."

He then waved 'goodbye' and left. Simon looked back at the code he was working on, sighed, saved the open work files and then shut his computer down for the night. He grabbed his coat off the back of the chair, stepped out of his cubical and strolled out of the office. The next thing he knew he was sitting on a chair staring at the wall of a small, metallic cell. He looked around in confusion as he tried to make sense of what'd just happened. One moment he was walking to his car; and the next, he was here. Wherever "here" was. As he was pondering this, he looked down at his body and realized that he was wearing an unusual brown outfit. It felt like it was made of heavy canvas, like a pair of Carharts. Just then, the door to the cell hissed open to reveal two strong, gray skinned men standing outside. Their bodies were humanoid, but their faces were twisted and evil looking. They grabbed him by the arms and violently yanked him out of his cell. Simon tried to fight against them, but it felt like he was a small child fighting against giants. As he continued to struggle, the two men dragged him down a long, battleship gray hallway towards a large black door at the end.

"Hey, what are you..." said Simon.

"Shut up, worm," growled one of the men in a dark, almost demonic voice.

As soon as they reached the large black doorway, it hissed open to reveal another room behind it. The two gray-skinned men shoved Simon through the door which hissed shut behind him. Another gray-skinned man near the door then grabbed Simon roughly, and shoved him towards a line of people standing in front of a tall desk on the other side of the room.

"Get in line," he growled in a deep, demonic voice.

Simon stumbled slightly, but complied. He didn't know where he was, or why he was here. He only knew that this was certainly not home, nor was it a dream. And while he wasn't scared, he was certainly growing very concerned at his strange predicament. As he studied the others in line, he noticed that one of them looked to be from India, and another from China. Two more in front of them looked Polynesian. Even so, regardless of their ethnicity, they all looked as nervous and confused as he was. Slowly the line moved forward, one step at a time, as each person in front of him took their turn talking with a stout, gray skinned woman who sat behind the desk. He watched as they were each handed several items and then escorted through a nearby door. As the line moved along, others came in behind him. Eventually, Simon found himself standing before the lady at the desk. She motioned for him to lean towards her. He obeyed and watched curiously as she waved a small metallic orb over his head. She then took his left wrist and examined it with the orb as well.

"Good, all inserted components are functioning as designed," she said flatly.

"All inserted components?" he asked.

"You have been fitted with a universal translator node, a micro mainframe, a tracking device, and an identifier chip. Please do not try to extract these devices. Your survival depends on them."

Simon cocked an eyebrow in confusion, but said nothing. The lady then handed him a backpack and flipped open the top to reveal its contents.

"This is your basic provisions pack. Don't lose it. You'll need it to transport any items you acquire along the way. Inside you will find three days' worth of food, a spare pair of hiking clothes, a canteen full of water, a water filtration kit, your instruction manual, and a map of the course. You will need each of these if you wish to complete the race."

Simon blinked slightly.

"What race!?" he asked.

But the woman said nothing. She simply closed the pack, grabbed his left arm and raised his sleeve. Just above his wrist was a small, red dot embedded in his skin.

"Take good care of this device. It's the key that will get you access to the resource nodes all along the course. Without it, you won't be able to get your allotted provisions at each checkpoint. Lose it or have it stolen, and you forfeit the race."

"Wait, checkpoints? Resource nodes? What are you talking about?" asked Simon in surprise.

"All of that is explained in your instruction manual. Now please, take your pack and exit out that door. You will be told what you are to do next," said the woman as she pointed to her right.

"But I..." protested Simon.

But before he could say anything else, one of the guards grabbed him roughly by the arm and shoved him through the door. On the other side was a small room, inside of which stood a short metal post and a child sized blue-skinned man in a gray jumpsuit who hovered above the floor.

"This is a resource node," he said, pointing at the metal post.

His body then flickered erratically before freezing. Simon cocked an eyebrow slightly.

"A hologram?" he thought.

A moment later, the image seemed to reset and then begin its instructions again.

"This is a resource node. Memorize its appearance so you know how to identify this and others like it in the future. To activate it, place the red dot on your arm against the node. When it responds, you may request whatever you wish within the limits of your available funds at this, and every other node you encounter along the course. However, choose wisely. Once you've acquired an item, you will not be allowed to return or exchange it for something else. As you complete each checkpoint you will be awarded a predetermined amount of credits based upon varying criteria along the route. These credits can in turn be used to acquire additional items above and beyond your base allotment. Earned credits or allotments that are not used at one checkpoint may be saved and used at another further down the course," he said.

Simon pointed at the dot on his arm.

"So basically this thing acts like a giant piggy bank. I earn credits, and they're stored here for later use, right?" said Simon.

The man shook his head.

"The device in your arm is merely used to identify you to the system, which in turn tracks all of your achievements and the total credits you have on account that are available for making purchases at this or any other resource node along the course. Now please, interface with the node before you, and then begin by choosing your first three items. When you are done, two hundred credits will automatically be added to your account as a reward for completing this stage of the course."

Simon squinted slightly as he thought about this. He still wasn't certain what was going on, but he had a feeling that he needed to act wisely, as his survival depended on it. He waved the red dot on his arm near the node and watched in amazement as a holographic image of a book appeared above it a moment later.

"Welcome, Simon, to node zero, checkpoint home. You are allowed to choose three items from this node to begin your journey," came a voice from the node.

As he stood there, Simon quietly wondered what the best things would be for him to get. Just then images of his Boy Scout years flashed through his mind.

"I would like a compass, a survival knife, and a study Bible," he said.

A small, smart phone like device, appeared next to the node.

"A compass has been awarded, but more information is required to fulfill the remaining two requests," said the node.

"That's not a compass," replied Simon.

"This is the only compass allowed for this course. It is a digital track finder that will aid you in keeping to the trail, and locating it again should you become lost or find need to leave the trail for any reason. It will also allow you to locate resource nodes, wintering grounds, and other important resources," said the node.

"Ah, so it's a GPS of sorts. Alright, fair enough. Now what about the other two items?"

"Further information is required to process these requests. Please specify the type of survival knife," said the node.

"Give me the kind the US Army uses."

"Please specify the era of issue."

"Current era."

A heavy duty survival knife and sheath appeared next to the compass.

"Please specify language and translation of book known as 'Bible'," replied the node.

"English, King James please."

A large book in a heavy leather carrying case appeared next to the other two items.

"Thank you. Please take your acquisitions," said the node.

Simon grabbed all three items and slipped them into his pack. The holographic man then gestured towards a nearby door as it hissed open.

"Please exit this way," he said.

Simon nodded, and then walked to a door on the other side of the room. As soon as he'd stepped through, he paused and began to take in the world around him with awe and wonder. In the sky above him hovered three moons: Two large and one small. Off in the distance, a brilliant yellow sun rose over a placid and tranquil forest. Nearby, several deer like creatures grazed at the edge of a large grassy knoll that surrounded rows of wooden structures that resembled picnic tables. Beyond them stood row upon row of trees that looked very similar to those found back home. Even the flowers looked surprisingly Earth like; even though, they clearly were not. He then got the strange feeling he was being watched. He looked all around to see who might be staring at him. His eyes soon fell upon a large tower that stretched upward from the center of the reception center. Several stories above him, standing in front of a large, plate glass window on the side of that tower, were two skinny, blue-skinned men who stared down at him with hatred and contempt.

"This Toto's definitely not in Kansas anymore," he thought.

As he continued to study his surroundings, he noticed that there were quite a few other people in the area, some of whom looked American. The majority, however, were not. If he wasn't already slipping into survival mode, he might have been 'geeking out' at the fact that he was almost certainly on an alien world of some kind with real life aliens.

Or at least, as best he could determine. Even so, he was still not certain how he'd gotten here, or why he was brought to this world. Or how for that matter. But at this point the "how" seemed less important than the "why". Even so, figuring out those little details would have to wait. He had bigger things to worry about for the moment. He sighed, and then made his way to a nearby table where he sat down and began to pray.

"Dear God, I don't know why I'm here, or even where *here* is. I, also, have no idea what's happening to me; but I know that You know, and that You're in control. Guide me, and show me what I must do. Use me in whatever way You see fit, be it to show Your love to others, to be a witness, or whatever You will for me. I pray for courage and wisdom on this journey and for Your strength. In Jesus' precious name I pray, Amen."

When he opened his eyes, he retrieved the instruction manual from his pack, and began to study it. If he was going to do this right, he needed to know the rules of the race and what was expected of him. It didn't take him long to find out. The first words in the manual told him all he needed to know. It read, "The purpose of this race is to test your ability to survive at all costs."

"A survival race!?" he thought.

He read further. After a bit he blinked in surprise.

"Great Scott! This thing's six thousand miles long!" he cried.

He quickly calculated the total time it would take to travel it's entire length and groaned. Even at a realistic pace, assuming everything went well, it would take him at least three years to reach the end of the course. This bothered him a lot. Whatever happened, there wasn't going to be a quick and easy solution to this. Just then, a young man strolled up to him.

"What'cha reading?" he asked.

Simon looked up and studied the young man intently. Clearly he was not what one would consider a model, upstanding citizen. Even without his street clothes, the tattoos and the look of darkness in his eyes told Simon everything he needed to know about the young man. This wasn't someone you'd trust, ever, even at high noon surrounded by a thousand police officers, let alone a dark alley. He smiled awkwardly.

"It's the instruction manual for this race," he replied.

It was then that he noticed the young man was wearing a media player.

"Where'd you get that?" he asked.

"Oh, this? I got it from that requisition thing in there," he said, pointing over his shoulder at the door Simon had just come through.

Simon cocked an eyebrow.

"You chose a music player for one of your items?"

"No, it took everything I had to get it. But I just can't be without my tunes, man. Gotta have my jams, yo."

"You chose *that* over survival gear?" said Simon incredulously.

"Bah, who needs that stuff. This race will be easy. Just walk to the end, cross the finish line, and go home. If you hike, like, really fast, you can reach the end in, like, no time, man. I'll even get some mad toys along the way too while listening to some phat jams, yo."

Simon frowned slightly.

"I don't want to seem impetuous or anything, but when the batteries on that thing run down, what will you do then?"

The young man waved dismissively.

"Whatever, old man. Later."

"Hey, wait! Before you go, what's your name?"

The young man stopped, turned and smiled.

"Trevor Thompson."

Simon watched as the young man then strolled away, completely absorbed in his music.

He sighed, and said, "Lord, be with that boy. He's going to need Your help, a *lot*."

The morning soon grew into afternoon, and Simon felt his stomach begin to yell at him. He reached into his pack and found numerous square packages, as well as several cans. He took one of each and opened them. The can contained a very sweet, nectar like drink that burned slightly as it went down. It tasted so good that he finished every last drop and considered drinking a second one, but decided it best to conserve his food stores. He would need everything he could get for the trip ahead. He then opened the square package and found a cookie like wafer inside. He bit into it and was amazed at the explosion of flavor that filled his mouth. It tasted like one of the best tuna casseroles he'd ever eaten! Then the flavor changed and it tasted like he was eating beef stroganoff. Then it changed again and became like a cheeseburger. He quickly surmised that the flavor depended on what he was thinking about at the time. He grinned. It now no longer mattered what he was hungry for. He could have all of them at the same time if he wanted. He would have to remember to sneak a few of these back home with him when he was finally let go.

Something like this could make a person a small fortune back on Earth. Quickly feeling full, despite not having actually eaten much, he picked up his manual and read some more. A while later he looked up and noticed that it was already late afternoon. He pulled out his map and found that the first checkpoint was just ten miles away. That would be an easy three hour walk for him. But he wasn't sure how long the days were here, so he felt it best to get going now so that he didn't get caught trying to navigate the trail in the dark. He packed up his manual and map, put on his pack and began heading towards the two posts that marked the start of the trail. As he did, he looked back towards the staging area and noticed that the people he'd seen earlier were gone, and a much larger group of new faces had gathered. Some seemed confused, some scared, and others anxious to get going, ready to conquer any challenge they might face with bright eyed enthusiasm.

"God, be with all of them. They're going to need all the help they can get," he thought.

He soon passed the two markers, and heard, "Course started. Enjoy your journey. Your first checkpoint is ten standard miles ahead."

He smiled and continued walking. As he did, the two blue-skinned men looked down on him from the tower with contempt and disdain. One of them then hissed angrily.

"Why was this one brought here?" he growled.

"I do not know. But it should not have happened," growled the other.

"I agree. As a Christ follower, he will be a grave problem for us."

"Then let us solve that problem now by destroying him."

Just then a man in a brown business suit and fedora hat walked up behind them and looked at them with curiosity.

"What is it you two are grumbling about?" he asked gruffly.

The two blue-skinned men turned and glared at him.

"Our course is threatened by a new arrival. He is a follower of the way," hissed one of them.

The man in the brown suit tilted his head slightly in confusion.

"What way are you talking about?" he asked.

One of the blue-skinned men muttered a number of obscenities in Aramaic. The man in the brown suit studied him slightly before walking up to the window and looking in the direction the two blue-skinned men were. He soon spotted Simon and quickly realized what the two men were so upset about. He frowned.

"I see," he said flatly.

One of the blue-skinned men then waved his hand in front of him causing the thick glass window that spread out before him to shimmer and vanish. He then stepped to the edge as though to leap off, but paused as the man in the brown suit cleared his throat. The blue-skinned man turned his head like a possessed toy, and glared at him. The man in the brown suit furrowed his brow.

"What!?" hissed the blue-skinned man.

The man in the brown suit pulled a thin cigar from his suit jacket, lit it, and then took several long puffs on it.

"Why are you so obsessed with him? I believe he should be allowed to proceed, just like all the other new arrivals," he said with a calm that surprised the two blue-skinned men.

"Even though he is a Christ follower?"

The man in the brown suit studied the two blue-skinned men incredulously.

"I wouldn't care if he was Buddha. He should be allowed to complete the race, in its entirety, just like everyone else."

"Why?" hissed one of the blue-skinned men.

"To see what he does. I very much wish to observe how this particular individual handles himself on this course in comparison to the others. After all, that *is* why this place was created, was it not? Therefore destroying him before he has a chance to show us his abilities seems foolish. Do you not agree?" said the man in the brown suit.

The two blue-skinned men glared at him briefly before turning and looking at each other while having an extensive conversation with their eyes. They then relaxed.

"Very well. We will do it your way....for now," said one of the blue-skinned men.

The man in the brown suit took a long draw on his cigar and then nodded in return.

"That is all I ask," he replied.

After a few hours of hiking, Simon reached the first checkpoint and quickly found the resource node located there. Upon identifying himself, he was told that he had a choice between a one day ration of food, or one additional item for his inventory. He was a little disappointed, but decided that it might not be a bad idea to have a poncho in case it rained during the night. What he got surprised him. It felt as strong as steel, yet light as a feather. He slipped it into his pack, and then found a small patch of open ground around a nearby tree where he could setup camp and build a fire. It was quickly growing dark, and he'd soon need the fire for both light and warmth in the growing cool of the evening. Using some of the survival training he'd learned as a child, he soon had a crackling fire going. He then pulled out his Bible and began to read by the firelight as the more sinister sounds of the night began to replace the gentle music of the daytime. About an hour after dark, a skinny, human form appeared from the shadows and plopped itself down in front of the fire, working desperately to shake off the cold that was now permeating it's bones. Simon looked up at it, and smiled.

"Evening, Trevor. You're welcome to stay here and share my fire tonight if you'd like," he said.

Trevor nodded, and then spewed a series of expletives under his breath as he complained about everything from the cold air to his tired feet. Simon furrowed his brow.

"You're not a Christian, are you?" he asked.

"No, I'm not. So if you're selling, I'm not interested. I got enough of that from the Bible thumpers on my block. So I don't need to hear it from you too," said Trevor gruffly.

Simon shrugged.

"Alright, fair enough," he said.

He then went back to his reading. This surprised Trevor.

"You're not going to, like, throw the book at me, or beat me over the head with it?" he asked.

Simon looked up and shrugged.

"Why should I? You're obviously not interested in hearing about God, so I won't bother you with it. If at some point you decide you're interested, I'll be happy to share what I know, but only so far as you'll allow me. When you say stop, I'll stop."

"That's it? No forced conversions or anything like that?" replied Trevor in surprise.

"Why? God is love. To 'throw the book at you', as you're suggesting, would not be very loving, and therefore, not Christ like."

Trevor grinned.

"You're the first Christian I've met who hasn't tried to shove their religion down my throat."

"Christianity is not a religion. It's a relationship with God. Religion is--"

"Whoa, whoa, whoa, stop right there. I don't want that little compliment going to your head and getting you all preachy or anything. I just wanna warm myself by your fire and try to keep from freezing to death. Okay?"

Simon nodded.

"Alright. Fair enough. But if you have any questions or need anything, just let me know."

Trevor nodded, and then went back to warming himself. Simon soon felt exhaustion getting the better of him. So, he marked his place in his Bible, packed it in his bag, pulled out his poncho, and put it on to help keep him warm. It wouldn't do much, but it was better than nothing. Trevor saw this and was surprised.

"Where'd you get that?" he asked.

"I got it at the resource node over there," said Simon as he pointed into the darkness.

"There's one over there?" said Trevor in surprise.

"Didn't you see it when you arrived?" asked Simon.

"Dude, I was walking in the dark the last couple of miles."

"Well, grab yourself one then. You should have enough credits by now to request one."

Trevor nodded, slipped away into the darkness, and reappeared a few minutes later with a poncho of his own. He quickly put it on, curled up on the ground next to the fire, and was soon fast asleep. Simon awoke the next morning and found that Trevor had left already. So he sat up, stretched, and then checked the fire. It was cold as stone. So he grabbed a ration pack out of his backpack, read his Bible as he ate, and then made his way out onto the trail. He made good time to the second checkpoint where he stopped and requested one extra day's ration of food. While he really didn't need it, he wasn't sure how much longer he'd be able to get these ration packs, so he felt it best to keep his food stores well stocked for now until he could hunt for his own food.

As he walked, his mind divided itself between thinking about the trail ahead, and of things at home. What would be in his email? What would his boss say about his continued absences? His mind then turned to other things. Would anyone come looking for him? Would they even know where he was, or that he was light years away from home on an alien world? The more he thought about this the less it made sense. He eventually reached the third checkpoint late that afternoon and was surprised to find that he was allowed to request two items this time. So he chose some heavy duty rope and a hat. The rope would allow him to climb things, or even hang stuff. The hat would be useful for protecting his now balding head from the sun, as well as provide his neck and shoulders with a bit of shade during the heat of the day.

This was important because, even though he was walking along under the shade of numerous large trees, he could still feel the heat of the sun beating down on him through small breaks in the thick canopy above. As darkness settled in, he found a new place to camp alongside the trail. He then started a fire, grabbed something to eat, and settled in to read his Bible before going to sleep. But shortly after sundown, Trevor appeared out of the darkness and attached himself to the campfire. Simon smiled and nodded, but the young man said nothing. Instead, he pulled a small game console out of his pocket and began playing. Simon rolled his eyes, but said nothing. If Trevor wanted to survive, he'd need to learn to make wiser choices on his own. There was nothing Simon could do to change his mind. Hopefully, after going cold and hungry for a few days, he'd wake up to the reality that lay before him. The rest of the evening went by without a single word being said as Trevor absorbed himself in his game, and Simon read his Bible. Eventually, both men fell asleep. But this time when Simon awoke in the morning, he was surprised to find that Trevor was still around.

"What are you doing here? I figured you'd have left already," said Simon.

"Eh, I wanted to. But I figured it wouldn't hurt to travel with you for a while. Well, if you'll let me, that is," replied Trevor.

Simon smiled.

"Of course I would. I'd enjoy the company."

"Thanks."

The two then quickly secured their campsite and soon struck out on the trail again.

Chapter 2

"Where's the next checkpoint?" asked Trevor.

"About fourteen miles ahead. We should be able to reach it by lunchtime," said Simon.

"How far have we traveled already?"

"About thirty one miles. According to the map, the first three checkpoints are each ten miles apart. They then spread out into fifteen mile increments for a while. At some point further down the trail it will, eventually, stretch to weeks between checkpoints."

Trevor was surprised at this.

"You learned all that from reading a map?" he said in surprise.

"Well, some of it. The rest comes from what I read in the manual."

"The manual?"

"You did get one in your pack, right?"

"I did, but I didn't think it was all that important to read. So I haven't opened it yet."

"You really should. There's a lot of important information in it."

Trevor waved dismissively.

"Meh, I'll figure it out as I go. I always do."

Simon shook his head, but said nothing. They then walked on for a ways in silence before a thought crossed Simon's mind. Trevor picked up on this immediately.

"What's on your mind, old man?" he asked.

"I'm just thinking about the trail ahead. We may need to hunt for our food soon, so I'm just considering all the ways we can go about that."

Trevor snorted.

"You're not talking about going native, are you? Ya know, picking flowers, eating grass and that sorta nonsense."

Simon grimaced slightly.

"Hopefully it doesn't get that bad. Although, a salad right now would be nice."

Trevor grunted.

"Dude, I ain't eatin' no greens. We've got these cookie things that fill my stomach just fine."

"Maybe so, but what do you plan to do once they run out? I doubt you can dial up Donnie's Pizza out here. We're in the middle of a survival race on an alien world light years from home. If either of us plans to make it through this race alive, we're gonna need to play it smart, and not just waste our allocation slots on garbage items."

Trevor waved his media player, and said, "Dude, these ain't wasted items."

"Can you eat them? Can they start a camp fire? Can they bandage a wound? If they're not survival items, then you don't need them and should never have gotten them in the first place. Common sense would have told you to get something practical, like a compass."

Trevor pursed his lips and fidgeted angrily as he stopped in his tracks and pointed at Simon.

"Hey, you're not my dad, so don't tell me what to do!" he shouted.

Simon stopped and turned back towards Trevor.

"I'm trying to help you survive!" he replied.

Trevor stuck his nose in the air and swore at him.

"Well, I don't need your help, old man. I can do just fine on my own," he said defiantly.

Simon gestured politely down the trail.

"Well then, you're free to go on ahead by yourself if you want. However, if you're gonna stay with me, we need to work together so we can make it to the end alive; not to mention healthy and hopefully in one piece. Or at the very least...alive. The healthy part, we can work on when we get home. Again, hopefully. Either way, the point is, we can't do this alone. We have to work together."

"So what? You think I can't take care of myself, fatty!?" cried Trevor.

Simon frowned.

"Actually, yes."

Trevor shook his head.

"You're really whacked, old man."

"What makes you say that?"

"Dude, I lived in Chicago. If I can survive there, this place'll be cake."

"Actually, it won't. Surviving in the woods is entirely different from surviving in the city. You'll need a whole other skill-set for that, which I can gladly teach you," said Simon flatly.

"Look, old man, I'm not a kid," growled Trevor.

"I'm not saying you are."

"Then stop treating me like one!"

"I'll treat you in whatever way you let me."

Trevor glared at Simon.

"Fine. If you're gonna be a punk, I'm leaving. Later, geezer," he said, gesturing rudely.

Simon grunted with frustration as he stood and watched Trevor storm away down the trail.

"Lord, give me the grace not to strangle that boy," he muttered.

He then looked around and studied his surroundings. As he did, the thought of fresh food crossed his mind. He might not need it just yet, but it would certainly be a good idea to find some to augment his ration packs. Especially given the amount of time they'd have between nodes. He thought about Trevor again, shook his head and then continued on. If God wanted them to travel together, then he'd send Trevor back to him. In the meantime, food was the item of importance for the afternoon. He could always trap his dinner the old fashioned way. Deciding to let Trevor get further ahead of him so that the young man had ample space to cool off, Simon stepped off the trail, sat down under a tree, and opened his race manual. Finding the index in the back he began looking up a variety of details about the trail and the area around it. But what intrigued him the most was all the work that must have gone into compiling this book and all the information in it.

Even more interesting was that the book didn't seem as though it'd been produced by the same strange gray and blue colored people he'd met at the start of the race. In an odd way, given how it was written, it almost seemed like someone at the US Government had written it. He laughed and shook his head. Nobody on Earth had the required level of technology to bring him here or do any of the many highly advanced things he'd seen already. Yet, he couldn't shake the thought that someone obviously had to; otherwise, why would he and all the other fellow humans be here? After all, aliens weren't real. Or at least not that he knew. If they were, that'd be quite the shock to him. He shook his head and pushed the thought out of his mind. He had bigger fish to fry at the moment; the biggest of which was determining how to hunt and forage in the local landscape. He continued reading the instruction manual, and slowly began to realize that, if he played his cards right, figuratively speaking, he could rely fairly heavily on the nodes for the first part of the journey.

However, the further into the course he went, the less this would be true, and the more he would be on his own for his supplies. He wondered if that might not extend the amount of time he'd need to be on the trail from three years to perhaps twice that, if not more. It was entirely possible that he might even have to "go native", as Trevor had said, to a much greater degree than he wanted. As he thought about this, he looked up and noticed two hikers passing by him on the trail. They seemed hyper focused on what was ahead of them and didn't notice him. In fact, they were a little too oblivious to what was around them for his taste. He simply shook his head, and then went back to his reading. He would need to team up with someone eventually. However, those two would be a disaster waiting to happen. So he let them go on ahead while he continued reading the book.

Eventually, after deciding that he'd absorbed enough information for one day, he got up and continued down the trail. He reached the next resource node in the early evening and stopped for a break. Not far away sat two of the groups who'd passed him earlier in the day while he'd sat by the side of the trail reading his instruction manual for the race. He considered talking with them, but decided instead to grab whatever supplies he could from the resource node before continuing. He didn't want to be anti-social. However, after watching how they'd handled themselves so far on the trail, as well as how they were acting here, he wasn't sure it would be safe staying with them, let alone joining their group. Especially since one of the travelers appeared to have already eaten something they shouldn't have and was now very sick. He even considered walking over and witnessing to them, but felt constrained from doing so. It made him cock an eyebrow slightly. Evidently, even God, was telling him to keep his distance from these guys. So Simon instead turned his focus to the resource node. He swiped his arm past the node and heard a welcome beep.

"Greetings traveler. Please state your request," said the node.

"Hey, do you have some kind of HUD or menu system I can use? I'm getting tired of this voice activated stuff. I'd really prefer to shop using a visual interface, if possible," said Simon.

To his surprise a holographic menu appeared above the node.

"Your request has been granted," said the node.

Simon studied the interface for several moments and was surprised at all it did. He was even more impressed with the data it showed him, such as his current position on the trail, the categories of supplies he could choose from, his available acquisition slots, his accumulated credits, and much more. This would make it far simpler and easier to not only manage his account, but also choose what things he wanted to purchase as well. In fact, he might even find a few things on the list he hadn't thought of asking for. Wasting little time, he selected a bow, a quiver full of arrows, and some string. He was a little disappointed that guns weren't available on this part of the course; yet he was pleased to know that they would be later on. As soon as he finished his shopping, the node flickered and went dark. He then picked up his items and studied the woods around him eagerly.

"Alright, I think it's time to grab dinner."

Trevor leaned against a tree with his arms crossed as he cursed quietly under his breath.

"Stupid old man. I know what I'm doing. He's nuts if he thinks he's gonna just boss me around like that. I can do just fine without him," he muttered to himself.

He then glanced around and noticed another group of travelers coming up behind him. He was surprised to see them since Simon had been the only other traveler he'd met since starting out on the trail. He knew there were a lot of others out there, but so far he hadn't met any, much to his surprise. He looked at the small group of assorted individuals and studied them briefly. They glanced at him as well as they passed. After a bit, he sat down on the ground, turned on his music player and began listening to some deaf metal tunes as he played several rounds of a rather captivating game on his console. But it wasn't long before the music player shut down and began blinking a battery warning. A half hour later his game console did the same thing. Muttering several profane curses, he got up and hiked down the trail a short ways to a resource node.

"Hey, you. Node guy. My batteries are dead, so juice em' up, man."

"The cost to charge your devices is twenty five credits per unit. However, your account currently has zero credits available," said the node.

Trevor swore loudly.

"And what am I supposed to do with these? I can't use them if they got no charge! Now either charge them, or I'll shove them down your throat!" he shouted at the node.

"Once an item has been acquired, it cannot be returned," replied the node flatly.

"You worthless piece of..." shouted Trevor as he kicked the node.

But to his dismay, not only did it not affect the node, it nearly broke his toes. He collapsed to the ground and swore loudly and repeatedly as he cradled his injured foot. Finally, after several minutes he got back up, spewed several more colorful expletives at the device, and then limped off. After walking a short ways, his foot began to feel better as the pain slowly subsided. Eventually, he stopped and plopped down angrily on the ground.

"Great. So now each time I want to listen to my tunes or play my games, I need to get to another one of those stupid checkpoints. Gah! I hate this planet!"

He then reached in his pack for one of his ration packs, but found that he'd eaten them all. Even all of the juice cans were used up. Returning to the node he requested more food, but was dismayed when he was told that he only qualified for one ration. It was just enough for the evening meal, but not enough to get him to the next checkpoint. He cursed profusely, but ultimately was forced to accept the single food ration as he was getting hungry. After requesting the food ration, he sat down by the side of the trail and began to eat. As he did, he looked down the trail behind him and noticed another group of hikers coming. He watched as they stopped at the checkpoint, requested several items, and soon continued down the trail past him. He looked down at his game system and media player, and then over at the acquisition node.

He swore loudly as he felt cheated and tricked, like he'd been mugged by his best friend. After a bit, he picked up the player and the game console, and with all his might, threw them into the woods. They crashed through the trees with a clatter before coming to rest in some bushes. If the puppeteers who ran the race wanted to play him for a fool, then he'd just have to express a little civil disobedience. After a bit he got up and hiked down the trail until well after dark. Eventually, he stumbled onto several small groups camped alongside the trail not far from the checkpoint marker. But instead of joining them, he slipped off into the shadows, put on his poncho, and curled up next to a tree. Within a few minutes, he was sound asleep. But his sleep was not restful, as the coolness of the night chilled him to the bone. Then, as if to add insult to injury, it began to rain. It soon turned into a raging downpour accompanied by strong winds that whipped the trees into a frenzy and drove the rain into every crack and crevice of his body. Great streaks of lightning ripped apart the sky as thunder tore through the forest with ear splitting power, threatening to destroy everything in its path. One bolt of lightning nearly blinded and deafened him as it struck; and subsequently shattered a tree on the other side of the trail, blowing it apart like confetti. He covered his face as pieces of bark and wood glanced off his poncho. A cold fear echoed through his body as he found himself quietly praying that he would survive the storm. Eventually, the storm passed, and an eerie stillness settled over the forest. He shivered heavily as he drew his legs in closer in an effort to keep warm.

The next morning he awoke cold, stiff and groggy. As he looked around, he noticed that the groups from the previous night had already gone on ahead. He climbed slowly and painfully to his feet, and made his way over to their campfires. But to his dismay, they'd all been completely smothered and extinguished, possibly by the previous night's storm or by the campers themselves. There would be no warming himself by a fire this morning. So, he strolled back over to the tree again, opened his pack, and quickly remembered that he was out of food. He glanced over at the resource node, and glared at it. He could request another ration of food, but after the way he'd been treated, he wouldn't give his captors the benefit of seeing him beg. He would just sit there, wait, and hope that Simon would be along soon to help him; or at the very least, provide a campfire to warm himself by. As the sun climbed higher into the sky, the air grew warmer, and he began to feel better. But, he still remained where he was...defiant, and not willing to budge or give one ounce of ground. Finally, his defiance gave way to the urge for sleep; and he drifted off into a troubled and disturbing series of dreams and nightmares. He awoke after dark to the smell of something delicious. He lifted his head and was surprised to see Simon sitting next to a tree not far from him tending a campfire over which hung two sizable, rabbit like animals. He slowly got up, walked over, and plopped himself down in front of the fire where he absorbed any and every ounce of heat he could get. Simon chuckled.

"Well, hello again. Hungry?" he asked.

Trevor nodded.

"Starving. What are they?" he asked.

"Well, according to the manual, they're called 'trovets'. They're apparently similar to the brown rabbits we have back home on Earth. They were listed as edible by humans, so I decided to snag a couple. Believe it or not, they're surprisingly numerous and easy to catch."

Trevor eyed one of the trovets as his mouth began to water. He would've given his right arm for some of that meat right then, but he didn't want to seem too eager after the fight they'd had just the previous day. In some ways he wished he hadn't been so rude and condescending to Simon before. Now he felt as though he'd end up paying for that mistake, and it'd be a well-earned retribution if he did. It was the least he deserved.

"You're welcome to have one if you'd like. I figured we'd meet again, so I grabbed enough for both of us," said Simon.

Trevor paused in the middle of his self-imposed chastisement and looked at Simon with both surprise and curiosity. Here he was anticipating the worst, and yet he'd received exactly the opposite of what he was expecting.

"You got one for me? But how did you know you'd even see me again?" he asked.

"God told me. He said you'd be hungry, so He supplied these two big, fat trovets for us today. You're welcome to take the larger one if you'd like."

Trevor cocked an eyebrow. He'd never experienced kindness of this magnitude. He studied Simon intently, trying to determine if this was real, or if he was just being played. Or worse yet, if he was being bribed. But the look in Simon's eyes told him it was none of those.

"God told you I'd be hungry?" he said in curious surprise.

"Well, yes and no. While He didn't speak to me audibly, I know Him well enough that He didn't have to. He just impressed it on my heart and I listened."

Trevor looked at the trovet roasting over the fire and gulped hungrily. He then broke a leg off the larger of the two animals, examined it briefly, and eventually took a bite. It tasted a little gamy, but he was hungry enough that the flavor no longer mattered. He hungrily wolfed it down, followed by the rest of the trovet, and soon found himself full, much to his pleasure. After a bit, he turned and glanced at Simon before looking down at the ground.

"Thank you for the meal," he said sheepishly.

"Don't thank me. Thank God. He's the one who provided it."

Trevor stared at Simon curiously.

"But...you're the one who caught these...rabbit things," he said.

Simon smiled.

"My mother once taught me that, unless God provides, you'll never receive anything. It's only through His provision that you have food, clothing, and the things you need to live. So, from my point of view, these came from God."

"Does it matter that I don't believe in Him?"

Simon shook his head.

"Not at all. God loves you unconditionally, so it doesn't matter what you think of Him, or if you even believe He exists. He still loves you. He'd very much like you to come to know Him. But even if you don't, He'll still go on loving you."

Trevor looked down at the ground in shame.

"How could anyone love me? My parents never did. They just threw me out on the street and left me to fend for myself. Even the boys from my crew didn't love me. They just used me to get stuff. I did a lot of crazy, evil things just to win their acceptance. But in the end, I was just a commodity; something to be exploited, and then dumped, when I could no longer deliver."

He glanced up at Simon and frowned.

"Why am I even telling you this!? You don't need to know that! You'll just think I'm some loser and ditch me, just like everyone else."

Simon looked at him with compassion.

"Why would I do that? You may not know this, but I've been praying for you ever since we met," he said.

A tear appeared in Trevor's eye.

"You've...been praying for me?" replied Trevor, his voice quivering slightly.

Simon nodded.

"I have."

"But...why? After the way I treated you, I'd think you'd want nothing to do with me."

"How can I be unloving and unforgiving after the amazing things Christ has done for me? He's forgiven me for so much that I would be ungrateful if I didn't forgive others who offend me."

Trevor blinked in surprise as he noticed tears forming in Simon's eyes as well.

"What did you do that was so bad? Did you kill someone?" he asked.

Simon nodded.

"I did. It was my sin that caused Him to die, blameless, in my place."

This surprised Trevor.

"Who was it?" he asked.

"Jesus, my Savior," said Simon through a growing stream of tears.

Trevor felt his anxiety crash into mocking disbelief.

"You killed Jesus. Alright, real funny, old man."

Simon shook his head.

"I'm not joking. Because of my sins, Jesus had to die in my place, and He did so willingly, for me, over two thousand years ago to pay for my sins."

"You're cracked, old man! The whole Jesus story is just a fairy tale! Even if He was real, there's no way He died for your sins all those centuries ago!"

"Jesus is the son of God. In His infinite knowledge and wisdom, He knew my name, my parents, and everything there is to know about me long before I was ever born. That's why He knew what I would do, the sins I would commit, and the salvation I would need long before I ever knew I was in need of saving. God loved each and every one of us so much that He sent His Son to die for us, so that we could be forgiven and live with Him forever."

Trevor studied Simon intently. He'd heard this mantra a thousand times before, but this time it was different. It seemed real and sincere. He could clearly see that it wasn't just words. There was something more there; a deep authenticity he hadn't seen before. Most of the so-called Christians he'd met in the past seemed so shallow, and their words hollow and lifeless, as though they were merely regurgitated or vainly repeated and not from the heart as Simon's were. They all spoke the words, sang the songs, and even dressed the part in some cases; but their actions were a billboard that advertised a life that was anything but redeemed.

"So He'll forgive me, no matter what I've done? Even if it was unspeakably evil?" he asked.

Simon nodded.

"He will. And I can show you how to find that salvation, if you're interested."

Trevor looked back at the ground and thought for a bit.

After a few moments, he said, "Not right now, man. I need time to think about it."

Simon nodded.

"Alright. Take your time. God will gladly wait for you with open arms."

Trevor nodded solemnly.

"Thanks," he said, an expression of great apprehension growing across his face.

All that night, he lay awake by the fire and pondered everything that Simon had said. He couldn't sleep a wink. There was too much going through his mind. One side of him cried out, wanting a piece of the love that Simon displayed. And yet, the other argued that he was being duped again; and all Christians were just well dressed hypocrites.

Finally, out of desperation, he looked up at the stars, and said, "God, if you're real, show me You really exist, and that You're actually there and not just some stupid fairy tale told by a bunch of losers trying to feel better about themselves."

Then he blinked. What was he doing? This was silly! God didn't exist! Yet he couldn't shake this feeling. What if God was real? What if He really did love the miserable excuse for a human Trevor knew himself to be? If God was real and did love him, it would be the first time he'd ever truly been loved by anyone. A tear trickled down his face. Finally, as morning was starting to break, he got up and shook Simon awake. Simon looked up at him curiously through sleep soaked eyes.

"Ugh, what is it?" he groaned sleepily.

"Can you...teach me how to meet your Jesus?" asked Trevor sheepishly.

Simon smiled, and said, "I'd be glad to."

He then pulled his Bible out of his pack, flipped through several pages, and then pointed at a verse on the page.

"The first step in meeting God is to believe you're a sinner. Romans 3:23 says, 'For all have sinned and fallen short of the glory of God.' It means that no matter who you are, great or small, if you're human, you've sinned. It's like trying to jump across the ocean. Do you, as a human being, believe you could do that?"

Trevor shook his head.

"Nah, man. That'd be something only Superman could do," he said.

Simon nodded.

"Exactly! In the same way that we can't jump across the ocean, we're also unable to achieve or maintain perfection, which is what God requires of us. So, if we're not perfect, then that means we're sinners. Do you believe you're a sinner?"

Trevor nodded.

"Yes, I do. It doesn't take much looking at my life to see that," he said.

"Good. Then you've taken your first step. The next is to believe there's a penalty for sin. Namely death. If you sin, you die."

Trevor blinked.

"You mean I've gotta die because of what I've done!?"

"You do."

"But why!?"

"Everything has a wage to it; something you receive in exchange for what you've done. Sin is no different. Romans 6:23 says, 'For the wages of sin is death; but the gift of God is eternal life through Jesus Christ our Lord.' God is holy; and as such, He requires payment for the sins we commit. In our case, that's death. However, God also provides a way out; a way to gain eternal life through His Son Jesus Christ, and it's a free gift that all can receive."

"You mean, even though my sins require that I die, He'll let me off the hook?" asked Trevor in amazement.

"He will."

"So how does that work? What do I have to do?" asked Trevor.

"Romans 5:8 has the answer to that question. It says, 'But God commendeth His love toward us, in that, while we were yet sinners, Christ died for us.' In other words, even before we knew we needed saving, He provided a way by which we could be. It's His gift to us. Jesus died in our place, so that we wouldn't have to."

"Wait, God let His own Son die so that a thug like me could get off the hook?"

Simon nodded.

"Wow, that sounds like some whacked justice. Even a crooked judge wouldn't do that. He'd just dismiss the case and send you home as though nothing happened," said Trevor.

"But God *is* just. He can't be bribed, and His justice is always perfect. If payment must be made, He'll exact it one way or another. Without God's gift of salvation, that payment is death. But with His gift of salvation, there's life. So do you believe that Christ died for your sins?"

Trevor nodded.

"I'm still blown away by the idea; but yes, I believe. But you still haven't told me how to get this gift. What do I have to do or say?" said Trevor.

"Well, there's one more verse that answers that question for you. It's Romans 10:9-10. 'That if thou shalt confess with thy mouth the Lord Jesus, and shalt believe in thine heart that God hath raised Him from the dead, thou shalt be saved. For with the heart man believeth unto righteousness; and with the mouth confession is made unto salvation.' Since you believe that you're a sinner, and that Christ died for your sins to give you eternal life, all you need to do now is put your entire faith and trust in Him; and then ask Jesus to come into your life and save you."

"That's it? It's that easy?" asked Trevor in surprise.

Simon grinned.

"It's that easy."

Trevor blinked in amazement.

"Wow. That's awesome!" He then bowed his head, and said, "God, you know how much of a thug I am. I've sinned against You and done some pretty hideous things. But I believe You gave Your Son to die in my place. Wow, that still blows my mind that you'd do that. I don't deserve it, but thank you. And God, I need You to come into my heart. Give me Your gift of eternal life. If Your Son died in my place so that I could have eternal life, I want some of that. I want that precious gift You did so much to secure for me, and thank you for forgiving a black-hearted thug like me."

Simon smiled.

"Amen."

Tears began pouring down Trevor's face.

"So that's it? I'm saved?"

Simon nodded.

"You are. Welcome to the family."

Trevor threw his arms up in the air, and said, "Yes! Oh, this is incredible! It's like this...this huge weight has been lifted off of me."

"That weight that's left you is you're sins. You're now forgiven," said Simon.

Trevor grinned like a Cheshire cat.

"Dude, that's tight. So what else has Jesus done for me?"

Simon smiled and opened his Bible.

"Why don't I show you," he said.

They then talked through the rest of the day as Simon opened the scriptures to him.

Chapter 3

Early the next morning, Simon went out hunting for their breakfast. When he returned, he was surprised to see Trevor reading his Bible, seemingly oblivious to everything around him. Simon smiled, and then went about preparing the food he'd collected.

Finally he sat down next to Trevor, and asked, "Find anything interesting in there?"

Trevor looked up and then blushed slightly.

"Sorry about taking your Bible. I just felt compelled to read it."

"No, no. That's good. I'm glad you are. Do you have any questions yet?"

"I'm not sure. It's not easy reading; and I don't understand some of the words, but I'm getting the general gist of what's there."

Simon chuckled.

"You'll have to forgive me. I was raised in a church that only preached from the traditional King James Bible. It's a bit of a tough read for someone new to the word; but for me, it's pure gold. For you, I would recommend the American Standard Version. It still keeps all of the power of the original word, but is considerably easier to read. The NASB is good too."

"NASB?"

"New American Standard Bible."

"Oh."

Trevor glanced over at the resource node not far away and pondered his options. He had a couple allocation slots available to him again; and as such, he was strongly considering using them to get himself a Bible. He grinned sheepishly as he thought about how that would be the first intelligent choice he'd made so far on the trip.

He then handed Simon his Bible, and said, "I'll be right back."

"Where you going?" he asked.

"To get a Bible!" cried Trevor as he trotted away.

Simon smiled. Trevor returned a few moments later with a Bible tucked under his arm and a smile as wide as Texas on his face. Simon grinned in return.

"Now you've got your own treasure of God's word."

Trevor nodded, and was surprised, when he realized how it felt like he was holding onto the most precious thing in the world, rather than a simple book. It was an odd feeling, but for some reason he liked it. The two of them then ate breakfast as Simon again opened the word to him. Finally, after finishing, Simon got up and began preparing to leave camp. But Trevor didn't want to budge. He wanted to learn more about Jesus. He didn't know why, but he just couldn't stop thinking about Him. He thought it odd that only a few days earlier he didn't care at all about Jesus; and yet now, he couldn't keep his mind off Him. Simon soon realized that God was doing something special with the young man and decided it wouldn't hurt to stay in camp an extra day. They had enough food to keep them going, so he sat down again and continued his teaching. Later on that afternoon, as Trevor was reading through the book of Acts, having blazed through the four gospels already, he stumbled onto several stories that talked about baptism.

"Hey, Simon? What's all this stuff about baptism?" he asked.

Simon, who was weaving a light rope from grass fibers, looked up at the young man curiously.

"Where are you reading that?" he asked.

"Well, that John the Baptist guy talked about it, Jesus did too, and then I see it here several times in Acts. It's almost like it's super important, but I'm not sure how. Can you explain this to me?"

Simon paused for a moment, and then said, "Well, baptism is both a commandment and a symbol of your faith. You're only ever required to do it once, and typically within a short time after you're saved. However, if you feel compelled, you're free to do it as often as you like. But again, you're only required to do it once. I was actually going to ask you about that later today. But I didn't want to interrupt your reading."

"So...it's part of being a Christian?"

Simon nodded.

"It is. It's related to the Jewish Mikveh, or ritual bath. The idea is that it symbolizes our death, burial and resurrection with Jesus at salvation. Basically, it's another way of confessing your faith before God and others and showing that you've indeed given your life to Christ."

This drew a smile and a twinge of excitement from Trevor. He marked his place in his Bible, set it aside and then stared at Simon with a smile.

"Can we do that right now? I wanna be baptized! If Jesus said to do it, then I want to do it!"

Simon laughed. It was refreshing to see someone so excited about it.

"Absolutely, I can. I just wish there were more witnesses to this than just you and I."

Just then, several large deer like animals appeared at the edge of the camp accompanied by a host of birds, trovets, and other animals, both large and small. At first, the two men didn't quite know what to make of it. But after a moment, Trevor perked up as he smiled.

"Um, Simon? I think God just answered your prayer," he said.

Simon laughed.

"Ya know, I think He did. So, shall we get to it?"

"Absolutely!"

The two men then made their way down to a river, which was not far from the camp, and waded in. As they did, the birds and the animals all followed them.

Simon stood next to Trevor like a proud father, and asked, "Trevor Thompson, do you confess Jesus Christ as your Lord and Savior?"

"I do!" said Trevor happily.

"Then, Trevor Thompson, in obedience to our Lord and Savior Jesus Christ, and upon your profession of faith, I baptize you, my brother, in the name of the Father, Son, and Holy Spirit."

And with that, he submerged Trevor in the water and then drew him out again. Despite being dripping wet, Trevor raised his hands in the air and praised God. Simon smiled proudly at the young man; and then noticed that the animals and birds who had gathered also appeared to be celebrating. They then proudly escorted the two men back to their camp before dispersing into the forest. The rest of that evening, while drying off by the fire, the two men spent many hours together reading and discussing God's word at length.

The next morning Trevor was wide awake just before dawn and was already busy reading his Bible when Simon finally stirred. They chewed on several pieces of cold trovet for breakfast as they both studied their Bibles, and then broke camp shortly after finishing. They spent the first hour of their walk in near silence. Simon studied Trevor's face, but couldn't quite make out what the young man was thinking. He could tell that God was working overtime on him; but what all was happening in his mind and heart, he couldn't tell.

Finally, as they stopped for a break, Trevor turned to Simon, and said, "Hey, I've been thinking about this as we've been walking, and I've got something to say. I know I treated you like a complete dirt bag back there when you were only trying to help me. So I just want to apologize for being such a jerk. I had no right to be that way to you."

"Where did that come from?" thought Simon.

"If you want to hate me for what I did, that's fine. But I just wanted to say, I'm sorry. You've only shown me kindness, and I've treated you like trash," continued Trevor.

Simon smiled kindly.

"I forgive you, and I'm most thankful and blessed to see that God has made a new man out of you. The changes I'm already seeing are profound."

Trevor smiled sheepishly.

"Thanks."

Simon's smile then grew wider. Even though Trevor was a brand new Christian, Simon could already see God working powerfully in the young man's life. Normally, he didn't see such rapid growth in new converts. But he suspected that God had a reason for maturing Trevor so quickly. It was very possible that he'd need to lean on the young man at some point in the near future just as much as Trevor was leaning on him right now. As they hiked together over the next several days, they talked constantly. Through these conversations Simon learned more about Trevor.

"So, what were some of the things you did back home?" asked Simon.

"A lot of things, none of which I'm proud of."

"Such as?"

"Well, a lot. I feel ashamed even talking about them," said Trevor.

Simon chuckled.

"You haven't even really told me anything."

Trevor squirmed slightly as he walked.

"Well, I was what they called an arranger; a middle man of sorts. I specialized in arranging and overseeing exchanges, transfers and the sale of goods and contraband between gangs, mafia families, businesses, and even individuals. Some of it was legal stuff. But the majority of it was highly illegal, such as guns, drugs, hookers, sex slaves, stolen goods and much more. I even worked as an enforcer periodically whenever someone needed one."

"An enforcer? Did you break any kneecaps?" chided Simon.

But Trevor wasn't amused.

"I did a lot more than that. Most of the guys I enforced ended up in the hospital. I was one step short of a mechanic most of the time."

"A mechanic? You mean a hit man?" said Simon in surprise.

Trevor nodded sadly.

"Did you kill anyone?" asked Simon in concern.

Trevor sighed.

"I'm not sure, but I definitely put holes in several people. I even hit one guy square in the chest at point blank range. Amazingly, he survived, although he was quite a mess afterwards. Most of the time, though, we tried not to kill anyone; because it was really bad for business if they actually died, as our employer wouldn't get paid. So, we'd just rough them up really good; and then let them go with a warning to pay up or get buried."

"Wow, you really did have a hard life," said Simon in amazement.

But Trevor only nodded.

"What about the contraband stuff. Did you ever get caught?" asked Simon.

Trevor shook his head.

"I came close quite a few times, but never actually got busted. In hindsight, I think God did that to protect me, because there's no way I should've gotten away with half of what I did. Of course, given who my clientèle were, they probably bribed the right people on my behalf and made stuff go away. Happened quite a few times as I remember."

"Sounds like God certainly was watching out for you, even before you got saved."

"Yeah, He had to have been. Given all the crazy stuff I went through, I should be dead and six feet under by now. Yet, here I am, saved, forgiven and alive. I certainly don't deserve it," he said.

"None of us do. Yet, God loved us so much that He gave His Son to die for us. Only if He loved us unconditionally, which He does, could He ever do that. By rights, we should all be in hell right now for our sins. I know I certainly should."

Trevor sighed sadly.

"Yeah, I know what you mean. I'm all new to this, and yet I feel like a complete animal because of the stuff I've done. If God wanted to strike me dead right now, I'd totally deserve it."

Simon smiled.

"Yes, but He hasn't. That's called grace. It's getting something you don't deserve, and I know none of us deserve eternal life. From the least to the greatest, all have sinned and fallen short of the glory of God. It's written all throughout the Bible."

Trevor thought about this.

"Speaking of which, how do you know so much about the Bible? Did you go somewhere to study and learn all about it?" he asked.

Simon shook his head.

"If you mean seminary, no. I was a small town kid. Grew up on a farm outside of the little town of Marshall, Michigan, not far from the village of Marengo. We raised corn, wheat, oats and soybeans. We also milked cows and raised chickens to supplement our income during the summer when most of our money was tied up in the fields. I left the farm when I was eighteen to go to college. I, initially, went up to Michigan State to learn agricultural science in hopes of finding better ways to raise the crops my family depended on. Oddly enough, while I loved my classes, I didn't stay past the first semester."

"Why not?" asked Trevor.

"Because I fell in love."

Trevor grinned wide like a Cheshire cat.

"Oh, and what was her name?" he asked as he playfully jabbed at Simon.

"Actually, it wasn't that kind of love. It started one day when I went down to the information technology department to pick up some things for one of my professors. I was immediately struck with the big hulking machines in their NOC."

"NOC?" asked Trevor curiously.

"Network Operations Center. It's where companies or organizations house all of their servers and terminate their network infrastructure. Think of it like a Grand Central Station of information. Well, anyways, when I went in, I was immediately infatuated by the huge mainframes and servers they had. Some of them were the size of a VW bus! It was amazing! I couldn't stop talking about it for weeks! Eventually, my profs advised me to consider switching to a career in computers."

"But you said you grew up on a farm. Didn't you love farming?"

"Oh, I loved farming. Still do. In fact, I even have my own little truck farm."

"So what made you switch, other than your prof telling you that you should?"

Simon pondered this for a while.

"Well, I can't really explain it. I just felt led to make a schooling change. In fact, I ended up making a complete venue change and switched my enrollment to the University of Michigan after the first semester."

"So why'd you switch schools?" asked Trevor.

"Well, for two reasons. First, UofM had the best computer science course in the region, and two, MSU didn't have one at the time. Or if they did, it wasn't even half of what UofM had. Besides, MSU was, and still is in many ways, the top agricultural college in the nation. It's why I went there to begin with. But for science and computers, UofM was the better choice."

"So what happened after that?"

"Well, I graduated at the top of my class, got a job first with IBM, then Techsys for a while; and finally with a little software startup in Lansing. It's been fun."

"So you've been through all that, and you've never had any formal Bible training?"

Simon shook his head.

"Nope. Never. Although I did sit under the teaching of a couple pastors in Texas while working for Techsys, no pun intended mind you, who were teachers at Dallas Theological Seminary. I even got to sit under the direct teaching of Chuck Swindoll for a while. So, in many ways, I did receive formal Bible training. Just not in the traditional way."

"Wow. I bet that was a treat. I never finished school myself. I dropped out shortly after my parents kicked me out. Since then, I've spent my time doing all the illegal stuff I told you about."

"So how did you learn after that? I ask, because you sound like you at least finished high school if not a bit more than that."

Trevor shrugged.

"I taught myself. Been doing that since third grade, as our local schools were completely worthless. I learned more in one year of teaching myself than in four years with them. Got my GED when I was fourteen. Of course, then I went and wasted it all gang banging on the streets."

"Wow, you really have had an interesting life," replied Simon.

Trevor looked at the ground and sighed.

"Yeah. But it was a lonely one too."

"Why do you say that?"

"Because, you and God are the first people who've ever truly loved me. I've had plenty of friends in my life, but none of them ever cared for me beyond what I could get for them. So I did a lot of bad things in order to keep them around as so called friends; things I now regret."

"I can imagine. But, at the same time, there's things all of us have done that we regret. Most of the time, you just have to ask God to forgive you, and then move on with life."

Trevor looked at Simon in confusion.

"But I thought God already forgave all my sins."

"He did. But asking God to forgive you at this point isn't about having your sins purged. That was taken care of at the cross. Asking forgiveness for your sins after you get saved is about restoring your relationship with Him. Once you're saved, you can't ever lose your salvation. But you *can* lose your fellowship with God. Asking for forgiveness and repenting of what you've done helps to restore that, and brings you back together with him relationally."

"Repent? What does that mean?"

"To repent is to turn away from doing something. It could be a sin, a lifestyle, or even a simple decision. In human terms, it's like turning completely around and heading the other way. In Godly terms, it means to give up something that gets between you and your relationship with Him."

"So it'd be like making up with a friend who you'd offended. But, before you do, you're all mad at each other over something that happened; but afterwards, you're, like, buddies again."

"Yeah, something like that."

Trevor's eyes lit up.

"Ah, so if I repent of the sins I've committed, it does the same thing between God and I, right?"

"Yup."

"Oh, that's epically cool," said Trevor with a grin.

Simon smiled.

"Indeed."

Chapter 4

Simon and Trevor walked on in silence for a while, as Trevor prayed quietly to God, confessing sin after sin and asking God to forgive him. Simon could see that it was having a positive effect on the young man, and he quietly prayed that God would continue to grow Trevor's faith stronger and stronger, as it would be sorely needed on the trail ahead. As they stopped for lunch, Trevor watched with interest as Simon began preparing a fire; and then lit it in the most inconceivable way possible by striking a stone with his knife.

"Hey, Simon? How did you start that fire? Actually, how have you started any of the fires we've been using? I mean, they never gave us anything to light them with," said Trevor.

Simon grinned widely.

"Ah, it's interesting you should mention that. There's two ways I've been doing it actually. The first couple nights I used an old Boy Scout trick where you take a stick, some tinder and a chunk of wood to get the fire going. The last couple of nights, I've been using my knife and a piece of flint I found alongside the trail."

"Flint?" asked Trevor curiously.

Simon reached into his pocket and produced a little black and brown colored stone.

"I just strike this against the back edge of my knife and it produces sparks that can be used with dry, delicate tinder to start a fire. It doesn't always work, especially if the tinder or wood is wet; but it works often enough to get the job done."

"Well, what do you do if there's no dry tinder available?" asked Trevor.

"I'd use some of the tinder I've collected for just such an occasion."

Trevor looked at him in surprise.

"You're carrying tinder!? How are you storing it?"

"I've been saving the wrappers from the food wafers and using them to keep the tinder dry. They seem to work pretty well."

"Wow, that's interesting. It wouldn't be too much to ask if I could try starting the fire next time we make camp, would it?"

"No, not at all. It'll be good for you to learn how to do it. You never know when that might come in handy in the future."

"Sounds like a plan to me!" exclaimed Trevor joyfully.

They quietly ate lunch; and then continued down the trail through the afternoon, talking and sharing with each other until they eventually reached a resource node just a few minutes before dark. After acquiring a few more items, they began searching for a campsite near the checkpoint; but quickly found that several other groups had already taken all the good spots.

Simon pointed down the trail, and said, "Let's go a bit further and see what's available. We'll want to find somewhere else that's not so crowded."

"Why not camp here? It seems like a good spot."

Simon shook his head, and said quietly, "I sense a rather strong tension between these groups. I don't want to be anywhere near here if things turn ugly during the night."

Trevor studied the groups curiously, and soon realized what Simon was seeing. He wasn't sure why he hadn't noticed it before, but he saw it now. So they continued on for a ways, and eventually found an open patch of ground not far from the trail that was a perfect camping spot. Simon quickly dug a small pit as Trevor gathered some wood and tinder. Simon then showed him how to start a fire in several different ways. Within minutes, they had a crackling fire going, over which Simon hung a small pot and began fixing an improvised stew. However, not because of anything Trevor did, because, try as he might, he couldn't get the fire lit. So Simon eventually intervened and did it himself, much to Trevor's frustration and discouragement.

"Hey, don't get yourself down. It takes time to learn this stuff. I mean, when I first started out, I was so bad at fire starting, I just about couldn't rub two sticks together," said Simon.

"Yet, you're so good at it now."

Simon laughed and pointed at his forehead.

"That's because I've had practice, and a lot of it. You can't just master every skill on the first try, regardless of how smart you are. Some you can, but the majority takes time and practice before you get good at them. So don't give up just yet. You'll get it in time. Just be patient."

Trevor nodded.

"I will." He then looked over at a small pile of vegetables laying next to Simon, and asked, "Where'd you find those at?"

"In the forest."

"But, how did you know how to find them?"

Simon chuckled.

"I read the manual. According to page one seventy two, there are numerous wild fruits and vegetables that grow in abundance along the edge of the trail and in the nearby woods on either side that are perfectly edible. So I decided yesterday, while I was out setting my traps, to go wandering around and see if I couldn't find some. I ended up finding quite a few, surprisingly enough. Given all the people who've been through here already, I almost expected the area to be stripped clean. But, so far, that hasn't been the case, thankfully."

"It's probably because they don't have your pimp survival skills."

Simon laughed.

"Yeah, either that or they don't know how to forage for themselves."

Trevor laughed.

"Or they're not reading the manual like you are."

"Yeah, it could be that too. In fact, I don't think I've seen anyone reading the manual yet, which is kinda concerning considering that their survival depends on it."

"Yeah, you ain't just kidding. By the way, speaking of survival, do we want to keep pushing ourselves again tomorrow until after dark? If what you told me is true, the checkpoints will keep getting further apart, which means we'll have to work twice as hard to get half the resources."

Simon thought about this for a bit, and then nodded.

"It probably wouldn't hurt to do that for at least a while. Although I wouldn't suggest pushing ourselves too hard to start with, as we'll need to build our stamina over time. Even so, it'll still be useful to have some extra stuff at our disposal. The only thing I worry about is letting our packs get too heavy too soon. I've worked as hard as I could to keep mine as light as possible. But as we get farther along we'll need to start humping a lot more stuff just to survive, which will really tax our energy and endurance to it's limits. So the longer we can keep things lite, the better it'll be for us."

Trevor grinned.

"Hey, that shouldn't be a problem for me. Especially since I don't have to walk with a cane like you do, old man," he chided.

"A cane?" said Simon in surprise.

Trevor pointed to Simon's walking stick.

"Yeah, that thing."

Simon laughed and held up his walking stick.

"This isn't a cane! It's my scepter!" he replied in jest.

Trevor laughed and, pointing at Simon's hat, said, "And I suppose that's your crown?"

"Only the best, good sir," replied Simon with a fake British accent.

"Well, if you're royalty, then I'm your captain of the guard!" said Trevor as he bowed playfully.

"Hey, wait. I thought you were the chief bottle washer," quipped Simon.

Trevor laughed and slapped him playfully. The next day the two men got up early and pushed themselves all through the day, clearing two more checkpoints as planned before nightfall. Upon arriving at the second checkpoint, they requested a few more supplies; and then continued on down the road several miles before making camp for the night. They got up early the next morning and continued on through much of the day until they reached the end of the forest. What lay ahead of them surprised both men. Where once there had been thick, nearly impenetrable forest, there was now only miles and miles of wide open, unbroken prairie. Even Simon was surprised at the suddenness of the change in scenery. He hadn't expected this to happen so soon. He knew it was coming. But for it to be here already, caught him off guard.

So, realizing they likely wouldn't see anymore trees for some time, Simon decided to collect a supply of wood and bring it with them to use in making fires for cooking. He knew they wouldn't be able to carry enough to keep them warm, but at least they'd have hot food. Now, all he had to worry about was the extra weight of the wood; and how they'd go about finding food along the way. In the woods, it'd been easy to gather all they needed. However, that was likely to change once they were out on the prairie. So he chose to deviate from the trail a short distance, setup camp, and build up a supply of food for the journey. If it turned out they didn't need it, then the two of them would eat really well. If they did, however, they'd be very grateful later on for having stocked up beforehand. As they built up their supplies, the groups that'd been behind them appeared from the forest, one by one, and continued on, not stopping to stock up on food, nor showing any concern for the trip ahead. As they watched the last one disappear into the distance, Simon thought about Trevor.

"Where did you live in Chicago before coming here?" he asked.

Trevor shrugged.

"Anywhere I could get digs. Usually it was with whoever I was working for at the time."

"So you didn't have a house of your own?"

"Nah, man. Wish I had. But that worked to my advantage. If I'd had somewhere permanent to call home, a lot of people would've shown up at my door and taken me out, including the cops. Being mobile like I was saved my skin countless times."

"I bet it did. By the way, you mentioned before this that you were good at getting things. What specifically did you get people? I know you mentioned some of the illegal things you could get for your clients. But what were some of the legal things you'd get them?"

Trevor pondered this for a moment.

"Well, actually, I could get you pretty much anything and everything you'd ever want. I've even found stuff most people don't even know exists. It was actually a lot of fun. It was like the world's greatest, most lucrative scavenger hunt in history."

"Like what?"

"Well, cars, rare antiquities, jobs, that kinda stuff. I even helped out one of the boys from my crew by getting him some food and a place to hide while he was recovering from being shot. He botched a bank robbery uptown and took one in the leg while escaping. I ended up putting him in Kepo's place for a couple months so that the cops wouldn't find him while he healed up. And the only reason they didn't look there was that Kepo was in jail for possession. So they didn't know that anyone was living there. And by the time Kepo was out, my boy was long gone. So nobody ever found out. Not even Kepo. I made sure the place was immaculate when he returned so that he wouldn't suspect. So far he's never found out."

Trevor paused a moment to think about this, and then laughed.

"To think I was the grocery dog for that boy for a while. Man, the things I did for money."

Simon shook his head.

"That's amazing. So who were some of your clients? Besides your friend, of course."

Trevor snorted.

"It was more like, who *wasn't* my client. My reputation for finding the impossible netted me customers of every class and kind. Even the chief of police and the mayor hired me from time to time. You should see all the crazy stuff the mayor asked for, including drugs and prostitutes."

Simon cocked an eyebrow.

"I bet that'll go over well once people find out about that."

Trevor shrugged.

"Meh, you're talking about Chicago. It doesn't matter what you do, or how illegal it is. Just throw enough money at the right people, and you can get away with anything."

"Wow, that's messed up. I mean, the mayor I can see doing those kind of things, but the chief of police? That one's kinda disappointing."

"Oh, the chief? Nah, the mayor was the pot head. The chief was a straight shooter. Probably the only one in the city."

Simon seemed surprised at this.

"I thought you got him drugs and prostitutes too?"

"Nah, just the mayor. The chief kept his nose clean. Plus, he was always really cool with me, even though he knew all the things I did. Usually, he hired me when he needed to find something special that nobody else could. Thankfully most of it was pretty benign stuff. But, if I could get the really hard to find things for him, he usually looked the other way when I was dealing the heavy stuff, which was a blessing in itself."

"What did you usually get for him?" asked Simon.

Trevor pursed his lips slightly.

"Believe it or not, he was big into antique porcelain figurines. Especially eighteenth century stuff. Given his tough guy personality, you wouldn't take him for someone who'd be into that kinda stuff. But evidently he had a real eye for them. He knew every bit and detail about each piece he sent me looking for. The crazy part is, I only ever failed to find two of the figurines he was looking for; but certainly not for any lack of trying on my part."

Simon smiled.

"Huh, you learn something interesting ever day."

Trevor snorted.

"Totally."

Several days later, having completed all of their preparations, Simon and Trevor broke camp and made their way out into the prairie. As they walked, Trevor continued to ask Simon questions about the Bible much as he had over the past week. Simon was surprised how hungry the young man was for the word of God. He also noticed that Trevor seemed to be mellowing significantly, changing from a hardened, street smart, punk kid, to a responsible young adult who actually showed legitimate concern for his spiritual mentor and elder. He also noticed that it'd been well over four days since Trevor had uttered a single curse word, either intentionally or accidentally, despite previously having a mouth so filthy it would make a sailor blush.

He praised God for doing such an amazing transformation in the young man's life. And, even though he was green in the ways of woodsmanship, Trevor had proven a valuable companion on the journey so far. In many ways, he considered the young man to be a gift from God. As they continued walking across the prairie, Simon noticed that the trail was beginning to fade away, becoming harder and harder to find until it utterly vanished. It was at this point that he was glad he'd picked up a compass early on. It quickly proved invaluable as they struggled to keep to the path. On the third day of their hike across the prairie, Simon decided to stop early and get some extra rest. The added weight of their packs was beginning to wear on both of them, and it'd slowed their pace considerably. To make matters worse, they'd been forced to dig for their water each day. Up until recently, there had been a cool flowing river alongside the trail.

However, shortly after they'd entered the prairie, the river had turned away from the trail and headed north. So now, the only way to get water was to dig small pits in search of ground water, or wait for the rain to come where they could catch it in their ponchos and pour it into their canteens. But their struggles for food and water would soon be the least of their worries, as something unusual happened that night which would change their little group forever. Shortly before sunset, after setting up camp, Simon was sitting by the glowing remains of the evening cook fire, struggling to read his Bible in the dimming evening light as Trevor stirred the remnants of the small pot of stew that'd been their dinner. He'd wanted to heat it up a bit more before finishing it. However, he wouldn't get that chance. To his complete and utter surprise, a young woman, her eyes fiery, and her hair wild as a windstorm, appeared out of nowhere and snagged the pot out of the coals before rushing off into the darkness.

Simon looked up in surprise as Trevor jumped up from where he'd been sitting, vaulted over the fire like an Olympic track star, and tackled the girl. It was all over before Simon even knew what'd happened. But the young woman wouldn't be so easily defeated. She'd have her meal, one way or another. She rolled over and drove her elbow as hard as she could into Trevor's gut, causing him to release her, after which she leapt to her feet. But Trevor pushed through the pain, jumped up, wrapped his arms around her waist and pulled her to the ground. They wrestled for several more minutes as she tried to get away from him, but repeatedly failed to do so. Even so, Trevor was surprised at her strength. She felt like a professional wrestler trapped in a tiny little body. For as petite as she was, she had an incredible amount of fight in her. Eventually, Trevor managed to put her in a full body lock that prevented her from moving at all. The problem was, neither could he. Simon soon trotted over to where the two were lying in the grass and stared in disbelief at the scene before him.

Chapter 5

"Let me go!" she screamed.

"Not a chance! You tried to steal my dinner!" shouted Trevor.

"Arrgh, let me go!" she screamed, and then bit down hard on his arm.

He cried out in pain, and then grabbed his arm in response, allowing her to break free. But when she reached for the pot, she got a surprise she didn't expect. Despite the incredible pain in his arm, Trevor's mind was still clear and sharp, and his body immediately went into full battle mode. He rolled over, pushed off the ground, and landed a powerful kick to the girl's face. It sent her spinning like a top before crashing limply to the ground in a heap. He hadn't meant to hit her so hard. He'd simply acted out of instinct, a trait born from years of living and fighting on the streets of Chicago. But it'd been effective, immediately knocking her unconscious.

"Geez, you didn't have to hit her like that!" cried Simon.

"She nearly bit my arm off, and you're worried about how hard I hit her!?" replied Trevor.

Simon trotted over to the girl and began to examine her for injuries. At first, Trevor was raging mad. But after a bit, he began to calm down and grow concerned for the young woman.

"Is she alright? Really, I didn't mean to hit her that hard. I just...well, reacted. I hope she's okay," said Trevor anxiously.

"Yeah, she's fine. She'll have quite a headache when she wakes up though."

Trevor sighed in relief.

"Well, that's good. Even though she stole my dinner, I don't want to hurt her if I can help it. I did enough of that back home, ya know, busting people's skulls and all."

Simon nodded, and said, "I understand." He studied the girl for a bit; and then said curiously, "I wonder who she is."

Trevor shrugged.

"No idea. But I say we tie her up and wait till she comes too. Then we'll get some answers."

"Good idea," said Simon.

He picked up the young woman, tossed her over his shoulder and headed back to the campsite as Trevor retrieved the pot and followed him. Simon then laid her down on the ground next to the fire before carefully tying the young woman's hands and feet together, but not enough to hurt her. The two men then sat down and waited for the young woman to wake up again. She eventually awoke a few minutes later, and began to thrash around in a panic as she tried to escape her bonds.

Trevor quickly pinned her to the ground, and said, "Whoa there, girlie. You're not going anywhere until you tell us who you are and why you tried to steal the rest of my dinner!"

But she just screamed as she struggled to free herself. Finally, after a few minutes she stopped fighting and fell silent. Trevor noticed that she was panting hard and appeared to be shivering.

"What are you going to do to me? Are you planning to rape and torture me?" she asked.

"Say what!? No! We're just trying to find out who you are and why you tried to steal his dinner," said Simon.

"Then get this big goon off of me! He stinks!" she cried.

"Hey, you don't exactly smell like a spring rose yourself, woman," said Trevor.

"Arrgh! Get off me!" she cried.

"Calm down and tell us your name, now!" said Trevor.

But the young woman said nothing as she struggled to free herself. However, her strength was quickly coming to an end, and after a bit, she stopped and lay still as she worked hard to catch her breath. It was at this moment that Simon thought about the pot, and then realized that she may have stolen it because she was hungry.

He knelt down next to her, and said kindly, "Do you want something to eat? Is that why you stole our pot of stew?"

She glared at him for a bit, and then said angrily, "Yes, I'm starving! What's it to you?"

"We have extra food, if you want something to eat."

Trevor looked curiously at Simon, but decided to wait and see what the girl would do. He helped her sit up as she glared at Simon, who examined her briefly, and then picked up the pot of stew, which surprisingly hadn't spilled, despite all that'd happened. He took a spoon out of his mess kit, dipped it into the pot and held it out to the girl. She studied him suspiciously for a moment, and then hungrily took the food, chewing it quickly before swallowing. Simon, then fed her the rest of the stew, which she greedily consumed. After she'd finished, he went to his pack and pulled out a ration wafer and one of the juice cans.

"Untie her," he said.

Trevor looked at Simon as if he was insane.

"WHAT!?" he cried.

"Just do it. She only attacked us because she's hungry."

Trevor sighed in frustration, and then complied. Simon handed the ration wafer to the girl and watched as she ripped open the packaging and inhaled it before quickly guzzling down the can of juice. She then sat there for several moments, breathing hard, but enjoying the feeling of fullness that permeated her stomach. Eventually, she thanked Simon for his kindness.

"What's your name?" asked Simon.

"Ariana. But everyone just calls me Aria," she replied.

"I'm Simon, and this is my partner Trevor. Are you out here all alone?" asked Simon in concern.

She looked away as though in shame, and said, "I wasn't, until recently. My group ditched me, because I couldn't keep up."

"How long ago?"

"About a week."

"How much have you eaten since then?"

"Almost nothing. I had a few rations left in my pack, but those are gone already."

"Well, we don't have much to spare, but you're welcome to join us if you like. You'll need to travel with a group if you want to survive this race."

"What!? You're just gonna let her join us, after what she did!?" said Trevor in surprise.

Simon held up his hand in a gesture for silence. Trevor thought he was nuts asking Aria to join them, especially after what she'd done. But he held his peace anyways.

"Why should I join your group? You'll just ditch me the moment I lag behind or can't keep up," said Aria.

"What!? No way! Simon's not like that! If he ditched people every time they screwed up or weren't able to pull their weight, I'd have been gone a *long* time ago, woman," said Trevor.

"Or so you claim," said Aria snidely.

"Hey, I'm not lying. I have absolutely no reason to have you in our group after you went and stole my dinner. But Simon here seems intent on helping you. So I wouldn't take that lightly. He's one of the kindest, most caring people I've met in my entire life."

"Oh, so in other words, he's keeping me around until such time when he needs a 'special favor', at which point we find out just how dirty an old man he is. Is that it?"

Trevor did a double take and was half tempted to smack some sense into the young woman, but chose not to, as he felt it better to hold his peace until Simon had spoken. But to the surprise of both Aria and Trevor, he said nothing. He just sat there and studied her.

After a few minutes, he asked, "What gives you the idea that I'm a dirty old man?"

"Well, your trunk monkey over here did a pretty good job of grinding my face into the ground," growled Aria.

"Well if you hadn't stolen my dinner, I wouldn't have needed to!" protested Trevor.

He then turned to Simon for confirmation, but saw that he was once again silent, instead choosing to study the young woman carefully. Aria studied him in return for a few seconds before blushing and looking away.

"You're welcome to join us if you like. If not, you're free to continue on your own. The choice is yours," said Simon after several minutes.

Aria looked up at him curiously.

"You're not going to force me to come with you?" she asked.

Simon shook his head.

"No, not at all. You're free to go right now if you'd like, no strings attached."

Aria looked at the darkened, moonlit prairie around her, and then back at Simon.

"And if I come with you, it'll be alright to eat your food?" she asked.

Simon chuckled and patted his sizable belly.

"Of course it will be! Besides, I could stand to miss a few meals."

This drew a grin from Trevor. Aria looked down at the ground for a few moments, and then gave a quivering sigh.

"Can I think about it tonight?" she asked.

"You're welcome to take as long as you like. But we're breaking camp and moving on in the morning. So if you take too long, you might have to run to catch up to us," said Simon.

"Thanks," said Aria sheepishly.

She then got up and vanished into the growing darkness of the night.

Simon watched her go, and then said, "Let's pray for her."

Trevor nodded, and the two men bowed their heads.

"Dear Lord, we put Aria in Your care tonight. Keep her safe and warm, and help her to choose wisely. If it's Your will that she join our group, then bring her to us in Your timing. If it's not, then take care of her, wherever her path may lead. Amen," prayed Simon.

"Amen," replied Trevor.

"Well, let's pack up our things, and then lay down for the night. We're going to need our rest for tomorrow," said Simon.

Trevor squinted slightly.

"You sure that's alright? She might come back and try to rob us again," he said.

Simon looked off into the darkness and shook his head.

"Nah, I have a feeling we won't see her again until morning, if ever."

Simon and Trevor quickly tidied up their camp site for the night, and then laid down to sleep. But while Simon slept soundly, Trevor stayed awake and alert just in case Aria returned. But as the night wore on, exhaustion got the better of him, and he eventually melted into a deep sleep. The next morning he awoke to the sound of approaching footsteps. He immediately leapt to his feet and looked around in panic, assuming the worst and expecting it to be too late to respond. But, to his surprise, all he saw was a frazzled, yet surprisingly beautiful young woman approaching them across the grass, her nearly empty backpack slung awkwardly over one shoulder. It was just slightly past sunrise, and Simon hadn't stirred yet, but instead appeared to be enjoying a rather entertaining dream.

Aria approached the camp, sat down across from Trevor, and hugged her pack as she studied the still smoldering ashes of the fire in front of her. She didn't say anything, nor look up for quite some time. Trevor studied her with suspicion as he too remained silent. Finally, he reached over, grabbed a bundle of wood and some dried grass and, using the still hot coals from the night before, started the morning fire. Aria continued to ignore him as he went about fixing a pot of stew in the same way Simon had taught him. As the pot began to simmer, the savory odor made Simon stir. He sat up, stretched, and then blinked in surprise when he noticed Aria sitting next to him.

He motioned to her, and asked, "When did she..."

"About half an hour ago."

"Ah, okay," replied Simon. He turned to Aria, and said, "Do you want some breakfast? It's nothing special, but it'll put some meat on your bones."

Aria didn't smile or even look up. She just sat quietly on the grass, hugging her pack. He shrugged, pulled out his mess kit and held it out to Trevor, who scooped a sizable serving of stew into it. Simon then turned and held out the plate to Aria. The tempting aroma caught her nose and she looked up.

"Here, this is for you," he said kindly.

She looked up at him in both surprise and curious suspicion, trying to determine if what he was offering came with any strings attached. However, seeing nothing but kindness in his eyes, she took the plate and began to eat hungrily. Simon smiled. Trevor took his portion and ate it quietly as Aria finished the entire plate in record time. She then stared at the pot and the remaining stew inside. Her stomach growled, despite having already eaten an entire plate full of stew.

"You're welcome to have the rest if you like," said Simon as he read her expression.

Trevor sighed slightly. He'd wanted the rest of it for himself, or at least for Simon, but decided that she needed it more than either of them. So he reached over, took her plate, filled it with the remaining stew, and then handed it to her. She looked at the heaping plate of food in surprise.

"You don't want it?" she asked.

"You need it more than I do," he said.

A tear formed in the corner of her eye. She then smiled and ate it with a gratefulness that beamed from her face. During most of her life, she'd been treated as a bother; a person who was always in the way. There were even many nights she'd gone to bed hungry, having come from a dirt poor family of seven, of which she was the third of five children, who could barely put food on the table. But here were two selfless people who cared more about her than themselves. She wasn't quite sure what to make of them, but their kindness had already done so much to quiet the fear in her heart. She emptied the plate of stew, and then handed the empty dish back to Simon. He took a little bit of water and a small towel, cleaned up his plate and spoon, and then put them back in his pack. Trevor, in turn, cleaned up the pot and put it, and his mess kit, into his pack. They then both pulled out their Bibles and read while Aria looked on. She didn't say anything while they did, but merely observed how they acted, and how their whole attention was on the books in front of them. Finally, both of them finished their reading, packed up their things, and made ready to hike. Aria quietly got to her feet, put on her pack, and followed silently behind them.

Realizing that she was being a lot quieter than he'd expected, Simon said, "If you need to take a break at any point, just let us know and we'll stop and rest for a while."

Aria nodded, but said nothing. They hiked for several hours before Simon finally decided to stop. When they did he pulled out his navigator compass and examined it briefly while also studying the expansive prairie around them.

"Where's the next checkpoint?" asked Trevor.

Simon pointed off into the distance.

"Just a couple miles that way. But that's not why I stopped. Do you smell that?" he asked.

"Smell what?" asked Trevor.

Simon put away his compass, pulled out a pair of binoculars, and began scanning the horizon.

"When did you get those?" asked Trevor in surprise.

"At our last checkpoint. I figured they might come in handy," said Simon.

"Ah, good idea," replied Trevor.

Aria looked curiously at Simon as he studied the horizon.

"What are you looking for?" she asked.

"Rain. I can smell it in the air," said Simon.

"You can smell rain!?"

"Yeah, and it's quite strong too."

Aria sniffed the air as well, but couldn't smell anything out of the ordinary. Whatever Simon was smelling, it had to be different than what she was used to. Although she could smell a strong odor of raw fish in the air, which seemed odd to her.

"Do you see any?" she asked.

"No, not yet. That's what bugs me. The strength of the odor in the air would seem to indicate that there's a storm somewhere nearby. However, I'm not seeing anything. Of course, given that we're on an alien world, of which we have an incomplete understanding, it would be silly for me to assume that the weather works the same here as it does back home. As such, we could easily have a storm come out of nowhere and hit us without warning. Then again, the storms could work the exact same way as they do on Earth too. I just don't know yet."

"So how do you know for certain a storm is coming?" asked Trevor.

Simon lowered his binoculars, and said, "Around here I don't. But back home, whenever a storm was coming, you could smell it long before it ever arrived; and the stronger the storm, the stronger the odor and the sooner you could smell it. Assuming that the weather here behaves the same way as it does on Earth, we're in for a real gully washer based on what I'm smelling. As such, I think we'll need to stay alert for the next couple of hours. If there is, in fact, a storm coming in, we'll need to find some shelter before it hits."

Trevor looked around at the miles of empty prairie around them, and frowned.

"Out here?" he said in muted disbelief.

"Yeah, I know. There's not much to work with, but we'll have to make do if something comes our way," replied Simon.

"What if it passes us by?"

"Then we'll consider ourselves blessed. But being in the open like this bothers me, as we'll have no protection should it decide to hail."

"Hail!? How's that even possible? We're on an alien planet."

"Just because you're not in Kansas doesn't mean you can't get tornadoes," said Aria.

"She's right. This planet is Earth like enough that I'm certain we can safely make plenty of assumptions about how things work here without being too wrong. So let's get moving. God willing, the storm will miss us. If not, we're gonna be in a lot of trouble," said Simon.

"Won't God protect us?" asked Trevor.

"He will, but it's best not to do anything that will purposefully put us at risk. He loves to keep us safe, but hates it when we do something stupid and force Him to act."

"Right, gotcha," replied Trevor.

The group then continued walking, constantly watching the horizon for any sign that storms were approaching. About half an hour later, Aria spotted something.

"Hey, guys? Has anyone noticed that the horizon's getting blacker?" she asked.

Simon stopped and pulled out his binoculars. He soon spotted what she was seeing, and it was definitely a storm, and a powerful one at that.

"Well, well, there it is, and it looks like a beast. I can see almost continuous lightning coming from it's base. I can't tell where it's going; but if this wind is any indication, it might still miss us. Either way, we need to keep moving until we're sure where it's gonna go."

The group continued on, moving quickly in an effort to possibly outrun the storm. But as they did, Aria became faint and fell to the ground. Trevor was the first to notice this.

"Oops, we just lost our tag along," he said.

He turned and hurried over to her.

"You alright?" he asked.

Aria nodded.

"I'm fine. Just got light headed all of a sudden," she replied.

She then tried climbing to her feet, but found she couldn't.

"Trevor, give me your pack. You take Aria and carry her on your back. It'll allow us to keep moving," said Simon.

Trevor handed Simon his pack, and then put Aria on his back. He blushed slightly as her arms wrapped around his neck and her body pressed in against his. It made his heart skip a beat. He was also surprised at how little she weighed, even with her pack on. He wondered if this was an illusion brought on by adrenaline, or if she really was that lite.

"You all set back there?" he asked.

"Yeah, I'm fine. Let's get going," she replied.

The three of them then hurried off again. It wasn't long before they began to hear distant thunder. Simon stopped again and studied the blackening horizon. He didn't like what he saw. The storm was huge, and there would be no way they could get ahead of it. It was approaching far too quickly, and was too wide to escape on foot. Even worse, they had nowhere to hide.

"God, I need some help. I need a place to shelter these two," he prayed quietly.

To his complete surprise, he felt something telling him to stay put. He wasn't sure what to think of this. So he asked what he should do, and got the same answer. He paced back and forth briefly, and then turned to Trevor.

"I think God's telling us to stop here and setup a tent."

Trevor looked at him in surprise.

"But we don't have a tent. At least not yet anyways."

"No, but we can make our ponchos into one."

Trevor shrugged.

"Alright, works for me."

He quickly set Aria down and dug his poncho out of his pack. Simon pulled his out as well, and then helped Trevor in putting together an improvised tent. As they did, Aria sat in the grass and nervously watched as the storm approached rapidly. She quietly hoped they would survive this. Suddenly a lightning bolt ripped across the sky and struck just a few hundred feet from them. A second bolt followed not far behind it that was even closer. This caused Aria to slip into a near panic state.

As Trevor helped Simon finish securing the ponchos, he asked, "Now what?"

"Build a berm around the leading edge of the tent. It'll keep the wind from catching the material and possibly throwing it!" shouted Simon as the winds grew stronger.

Trevor immediately began to dig with all his might, carving up large chunks of earth and stamping them down around the edge of the ponchos. Moments later, it began to pour, the rain coming down in thick, nearly horizontal sheets of sharp, stinging water.

"Get inside! Both of you!" shouted Simon.

Trevor grabbed Aria, pushed her inside, and then leapt in behind her. Simon soon followed, securing the door of the improvised tent as soon as he was in. It wasn't long before the storm turned day into night. The three hikers soon found themselves sitting in near total darkness as the wind whipped the little tent around as though trying to tear it to shreds. The lightning was almost continuous now, creating a flickering, strobe like luminescence as thunder boomed with ear splitting ferocity. All three of the frightened hikers plugged their ears. As they did, Simon and Trevor prayed frantically for protection, while Aria sat and listened in sheer, unadulterated terror. It was during this frantic praying that both Simon and Trevor felt an incredible peace fill their hearts. Simon smiled and thanked God for His kindness, while Trevor marveled, uncertain of how he could feel so at peace, even though the world was coming apart around them. Then, despite all odds, the storm increased in intensity.

By now, Trevor was absolutely certain their improvised tent would be torn apart at any moment. Yet it remained firmly affixed to the ground, and in one piece. Then, as if the storm had suddenly run out of gas, the thunder and lightning quickly tapered off as the winds sharply slackened. Curious to what was happening, Trevor peeked his head through the flaps and looked up in wonder as the blackness of the storm rolled back like a scroll, gradually revealing a placid and peaceful blue sky behind it. Eventually, the rain stopped, the sky cleared and the winds grew silent.

"It's safe to come out again," he said as he slipped out of the tent.

But as he put his foot down on the grass outside, he was surprised to feel the ground give way like a soggy sponge. He bounced up and down on it several times; and then glanced out across the prairie around him. What he saw next blew his mind.

"Whoa. Guys, come check this out," he said in awe.

Simon and Aria emerged from the tent a moment later, and then paused. At first, they weren't sure what they were looking at. But then, slowly, reality began to dawn on them. They were standing on a small island in a vast sea of water. But theirs wasn't the only island. Stretching out in all directions, other little islands just like theirs peeked up out of the water like little bastions of refuge among a sea that would've otherwise drowned them.

"What in the world..." said Aria in surprise.

"What do you make of it?" asked Trevor.

"I have no idea. I've never seen anything like this before. It's like the whole prairie floor just collapsed under the weight of the rain," said Simon.

"Yeah, and we just happened to be standing in one of the few places that didn't get flooded. How's that for luck?"

"It wasn't luck. That was God's doing. He told us right where to stop so that we'd be safe when the flooding came. He's pretty good about those kind of things," said Simon with a smile.

"Yeah, I'm starting to learn that," said Trevor with a chuckle. He tested the ground again, and said, "Hey, Simon? There's something weird about this ground. It's like we're standing on a sponge rather than dirt."

He slipped off his hiking boots and socks, and waded into the water until it was just over waist deep on him.

"Hey, what are you doing?" asked Simon.

"Just testing a theory," said Trevor.

"What theory?"

"I'll tell you in a moment."

"What!?" replied Simon in surprise. "Wait a second! Come back here! It may not be safe! Trevor! Get back here now!"

But Trevor ignored him. He kept wading further and further as the water began to climb above his waist, and then his chest.

"Wow, it's deep out here," he said.

Simon frowned slightly at Trevor's seeming lack of common sense. There was no point in him putting himself in any kind of danger if he didn't have to. Trevor then dove under the water and had a look around. He quickly realized that the water got deeper for a ways before the ground began to climb back up again towards another nearby island that rose out of the prairie floor the same as theirs.

He returned to the surface, and shouted, "Hey, you guys should come in here! This place is amazing, and the water feels great!"

Simon was hesitant at first, but soon stripped off his boots and socks and dove in.

"Oh wow, you're right! This does feel good!" he said as he bobbed back to the surface.

"Hey, Aria, come join us!" shouted Trevor.

But she was hesitant to go in.

"No thanks. I'll just stay here," she replied nervously.

Trevor shrugged, and then began to playfully splash Simon who promptly returned fire, starting an all out water fight of comical proportions. As she watched from the shore, Aria began to smile as the two men played like little children. After a bit, she decided to join them. Within a few minutes, all three were splashing and playing and having a great time. They swam, dove, and just horsed around for almost an hour until they noticed that the water was beginning to get shallower.

"Hey, what's happening to the water?" asked Trevor.

"It looks like it's draining off, causing the prairie floor to rebound," said Simon.

"I guess that means we'll be on dry land again soon."

"Probably," replied Simon.

"Bummer. I was kinda enjoying this."

The water continued to grow shallower over the next hour until it was just barely above their knees. Realizing that they were running out of time, the three quickly grabbed their canteens and filled them before all the water was gone. When the land finally dried out, they packed away their ponchos and began hiking again. They found the ground under them was still a bit spongy; but it was considerably more solid than it had been just a few hours earlier, and was growing more so by the minute. They also watched with interest as the last of the bumps that'd formed during the rainstorm vanished away, once again leaving the prairie completely flat and featureless.

Chapter 6

Several days later the group found themselves near the end of the prairie as tall, beautiful green trees rose up to meet the sky in front of them. But as they drew closer, Trevor noticed something.

"Hey, Simon, get a load of that over there," he said, pointing off into the distance.

Simon stopped and looked where Trevor was pointing. He soon raised his binoculars and began to scan the horizon. It wasn't long before he spotted a small herd of deer like animals grazing in the tall grasses of the prairie about a mile away.

"Well, I'll be. I saw some of those at the departure point and when you got baptized," he said.

"What are they?" asked Aria.

"According to the manual, they're called a stagnatier. They're a local grazing animal similar to the white tailed deer we have back home."

"They sound like they'd make some good eating," said Trevor.

"They will. In fact, I think we should stop and harvest a few. We could use the hides and meat to supplement our supplies."

It was at this moment that Aria suddenly realized what the two men were talking about.

"Can I see your glasses?" she asked Simon.

He handed them to her and pointed towards where the animals were standing. She panned the area carefully until she spotted them, and was fascinated at what she saw.

They weren't quite what she'd imagined them to be, but they were still beautiful to watch.

"Are these the animals you're talking about killing?" she asked.

"Yeah. Why?"

She looked sternly at Simon, and said, "You can't kill them! That would be horrible! They're just defenseless little animals!"

Simon and Trevor both blinked in surprise.

"Umm, I wouldn't exactly call them defenseless. That king buck over there likely weighs in at better than two hundred and fifty pounds. He could use you as a sharpening stick for that huge rack of his. The only good thing about him is that he'll make for some really good eating," said Simon.

"You want to eat him!? You're sick!" cried Aria.

"Hey, if it's a choice between going hungry, or having a full belly, I'll take choice number two. Besides, one of those deer would feed us for at least the next two weeks or more," said Simon.

"Will the meat hold that long?" asked Trevor.

"Well, it will if we dry it into jerky. It'll hold for probably three or four weeks that way. Well, as long as it stays dry anyways."

Trevor thought about this for a few moments, and then said, "Ya know, it's strange. A couple weeks ago, if I was hungry, I'd just go grab a burger. Now we're standing here talking about killing and eating a deer, and the stuff actually sounds good to me. How weird is that?"

"When you're hungry, even dirt tastes good."

"I've had to eat a little of that myself," said Aria sheepishly.

"Really?" said Simon in surprise.

Aria nodded.

"Before I found you, I was so hungry that I was eating grass just to survive."

"Wow. That makes the worst things I've been through pale in comparison. Of course, that now makes me wonder why you'd turn down something like this after what you've been through."

Aria looked at the ground, and blushing slightly, said, "Well, I don't like hurting animals, so it just seems cruel to eat them."

"Well, like I said, if it comes down to either surviving or starving, then I'll eat pretty much anything. But if I don't have to hurt them, I won't. Just because I'm a hunter doesn't mean I get a thrill out of killing things."

"Did you hunt animals for food back home?" asked Trevor.

Simon shrugged.

"Eh, sometimes. I ate mostly store bought meat, or whatever I raised on my farm. But on occasion, we'd go out and grab either deer, squirrels or rabbits and have them for Sunday dinner. The flavor is a bit strong, but they're still good eating. However, that's for another discussion. In the meantime, we need to get our camp setup so we can start replenishing our supplies. However, I suggest we do that further north of here."

"Why's that?"

"Well, because there'll be other hikers coming through here behind us. I don't think any of them will try to rob us, but I'm not willing to take that chance if I don't have to."

"What? Are you kidding? I'm not afraid of someone trying to mug us! I could take them out easily!" boasted Trevor.

"Maybe so, but the rest of us aren't trained fighters, so it automatically puts us at a disadvantage in any confrontation. Besides, what would you do if one of us was taken hostage? How would you resolve that situation without getting us hurt?"

Trevor cocked an eyebrow slightly as he looked between Simon and Aria and deeply pondered Simon's question.

"Huh, I hadn't thought of that. I guess it *would* be a good idea to duck out for a while then."

Simon nodded.

"Yes, it would. Now let's get going. I'm eager to bag one of those deer."

The group soon turned north and followed the tree line until they were well out of sight of the main trail. Simon then showed them how to setup drying racks and a smoking shed out of local materials, after which he helped them gather firewood. Once their work was done, they sat down around a small campfire and cooked up the last of the trovet and vegetables they'd brought with them, enjoying every bite of it, knowing that they'd have nothing else, save for the few ration packs they had with them, until they'd gathered some more food.

Simon rose early the next morning, along with Trevor, and slipped out into the prairie in search of one of the stagnatiers that wandered the area. Half an hour after they began their trek, they stumbled onto a small herd grazing in the nearby prairie. They knelt quietly in the grass for several minutes studying the herd intently. But the stagnatier didn't pay any attention to the two men. So Simon quietly notched an arrow and took aim at the largest of the group; a king buck who sported a very sizable rack. With a twang the arrow was away, and with a thud it found it's target. But the animal didn't go down initially. Instead it bolted in fear and ran wildly across the prairie towards the two men as the rest of the herd scattered. Simon notched another arrow, popped out of the grass, and fired at the animal as it passed by him. The arrow pierced its throat and brought the buck crashing to the ground.

"Wow, great shot!" cried Trevor.

The two men then bounded over to the animal as it thrashed wildly and cried out in pain. As they drew close, it tried to climb to its feet a few times, but was unable to. Eventually it stopped moving and lay still as it breathed heavily. Simon remained back several paces as he tried to catch his breath. The animal wasn't going anywhere fast, so he was in no hurry to approach it. Trevor, on the other hand, couldn't wait, and immediately leapt on top of the animal like a champion mounting his prized stallion, whooping and hollering as he did.

"We got one! We got one!" he cried.

"Be careful! It's not dead yet!" shouted Simon.

"Are you kidding!? This sucker's down for the count!"

Just then, to Trevor's complete and total surprise, and Simon's horror, the large buck rocketed to its feet, lifting him up with it, and then began running around like a rodeo bull. Trevor held onto the stagnatier's body for dear life as Simon watched in fear for Trevor's life. He felt helpless knowing that the buck was going to throw the young man at any moment and then maul him to death. He notched another arrow and took aim, but reluctantly held his fire.

"Shoot him!" cried Trevor.

"I don't have a shot!" replied Simon.

"So what!? Shoot him anyways!" cried Trevor desperately.

Simon drew his bow several times, hoping to get a clean kill shot, but was unable to as the buck kept turning and putting Trevor in the line of fire. Simon prayed quietly that God would protect the young man, and continued to watch anxiously as the animal seemed to fight on with impossible strength. Tired of waiting for Simon, Trevor let go of its horns with one hand, grabbed hold of the arrow in the animals throat, and shoved it in deeper. The buck grunted loudly and immediately skid to a dead halt, nearly throwing Trevor to the ground in the process. It then stood there, without moving for several moments, as it gurgled and gasped for breath before falling to the ground with a thud. Simon bolted across the grass towards Trevor as he and the deer lay motionless on the ground. As he came to a stop next to them, Simon heard what sounded like snickering coming from Trevor.

"Are you alright?" cried Simon.

To his complete surprise, Trevor began to roar with laughter.

"Dude! That. Was. Awesome! I haven't had that much fun in years!" he cried.

Simon chuckled and shook his head.

"You're really something, aren't you?"

"Dude, that was, like, the best ride ever!! You should try it some time," laughed Trevor.

"No thanks, I'll pass," laughed Simon in return.

"Dude, you are so missing out," chided Trevor.

However, when he tried to get up, he found his left leg pinned under the buck's heavy body.

"Hey, while you're standing there, can you pull this thing off me? I'm stuck."

Simon laughed, grabbed the animal by the horns and lifted it just enough to allow Trevor to escape. After catching his breath, Simon recovered his two arrows, but found one of them damaged beyond use. He then proceeded to show Trevor how to field dress the animal and clean it. It disgusted the young man, but he managed to do it without hurting himself. After they finished, they dragged the animal back to camp and surprised Aria, who'd been napping by the campfire waiting for them to return. They hung the animal in a nearby tree, skinned and butchered it; and then hung the meat to dry. Once that was done, Simon began scraping the hide.

"What'cha doing with the skin?" asked Trevor.

"I'm tanning it. We'll likely need it for something later on."

"Where'd you learn how to do that?" asked Trevor.

"An old Chippewa man taught me. He ran an old fashioned leather shop just down the road from our farm. My dad was a frequent customer of his. I even got to work in his shop a few summers while I was growing up. While I was there, he showed me how to tan all kinds of leather, not to mention a lot of the other old Indian skills."

"Wow, that's not bad for a computer geek."

"Computer geek?" asked Aria curiously.

"Yeah, before I came here, I worked as a software developer. But before that, I was a farm kid. So I've learned a lot of stuff in my meager forty two years of life. And you know what? I wouldn't give up a single minute of it for anything," said Simon.

"So you know quite a few things?" asked Aria.

Simon shrugged.

"I can't claim to know everything, but I do know a lot. So if you're willing to trust me, and stick with me till the end, I'll do my best to get all of us home as quickly and safely as possible."

This intrigued Aria.

"So you're not going to just dump me when it's no longer convenient for you?"

Simon chuckled.

"No, not at all. God made sure we crossed paths for a reason; and whatever that reason is, I'm sure it's important."

"God? You're not one of those religious nuts, are you?" she asked with a mocking tone.

Simon smiled.

"I'm a dyed in the wool believer in Jesus Christ, washed in His blood and saved from my sins. Not perfect by a long shot, but most definitely forgiven by the grace of God. Trevor's one too; although, he doesn't have quite as much milage on his faith as I do."

Trevor chuckled sheepishly.

"Yeah, I only got saved a couple weeks ago. It was Simon's kindness that made me realize what he had was real. He showed me the way, I said the prayer, and here I am. Now don't ask me to quote scripture just yet, as I'm still new to all this; but it's been the most amazing time of my life so far."

"And it just gets better as you get older," said Simon.

"Well, if it works for you, that's fine; but I'm happy with just trusting in myself," said Aria.

Simon shrugged.

"Eh, that's fine with me. If you have any questions about God, I'll gladly answer them the best I can. But if you don't want to talk about it, I won't push you."

Trevor grinned. Simon had said almost the same thing to him.

"Well, that's good. I'll just stay a heathen, and you go ahead and remain a holy roller. So, as long as you keep your religion to yourself, we'll be just fine," said Aria defiantly.

Trevor was blown away by this! He may have been a young Christian, but he couldn't believe she would so callously throw away the chance to be saved! He looked at her with great concern and considered pleading with her to reconsider. He then watched Simon and studied him for clues. To his surprise, Simon continued on with his work, seemingly unaffected by Aria's brushoff. He wasn't sure why this was, but he assumed he'd understand in time. But, even though Simon wasn't bothered by all this, Aria seemed very agitated. He wondered if she'd wanted to pick a fight in hopes of bringing out the "real Simon" instead of the "goody two shoes wannabe Christian" she believed him to be. In some ways, he wondered if she wasn't trying to destroy the reality of Simon's faith as a way to salve her guilty conscience. But, try as she might to find something to "draw him out", she was coming up with nothing but a gigantic blank. After a while, she decided it was best to just move onto something else. She then turned her attention to Simon's work.

"How long will it take to tan that skin?" she asked.

"It depends on how you do it. Normally, it takes a month or more to make a good piece of buckskin. But the old man showed me a way to get a usable skin in about two weeks if you needed it in a hurry," said Simon.

"Won't we run out of food by then?" asked Trevor.

Simon chuckled.

"If you keep rodeo riding bucks like that, we'll have all the meat we need!" he chided.

"Rodeo riding?" asked Aria in confusion.

Simon laughed.

"Yeah, old genius over here thought it would be a good idea to jump on a buck before it was dead. He ended up getting the ride of his life, and nearly died because of it."

"Hey, don't knock it till you've tried it. That was seriously fun," laughed Trevor.

Aria snickered.

"Wow, you need to get out more," she quipped.

Trevor smirked.

"Oh, har, har."

Aria grinned, which for some reason made Trevor's heart skip a beat. He wasn't sure why this was, but considered exploring it a bit more at a later point in time.

"So what do you plan to use that buckskin for?" asked Aria.

"clothes, shoes, hats or anything else we might need. It's a very useful material. Later in the year, I intend to tan some trovet skins as well, if we get the opportunity. We'll need them to make coats in order to stay warm this winter."

"Winter? This place has a winter!?" said Trevor in surprise.

"Yeah. At least that's my understanding."

"What made you come to that conclusion?"

"The manual. Since it mentions wintering grounds, I have to assume that this planet has a winter. And, although I can't be sure of that, as I haven't found anything in there so far that mentions anything about seasons, it's the only conclusion I can come to. But, then again, I haven't finished reading the whole thing yet. So that might be listed in a later chapter."

"Where'd you see the mention of wintering grounds?"

Simon put down his knife, pulled out his manual and opened it to show them a section titled "Wintering Cabins".

"Again, it doesn't specifically mention winter. But, as the old saying goes, where there's smoke, there's fire. So in this case, if they're talking about wintering cabins, then there must be a winter. I mean, why else would they exist if there isn't one?"

Trevor nodded slightly.

"Sounds like I need to crack that thing open and do a little reading. So what season do you think we're in now?"

"Given that it started out a bit chilly and has been slowly warming up ever since, my best guess would be that we're probably near the end of spring which, assuming they have a typical cycle of seasons here, gives us about five or six months to reach our first wintering grounds. I don't know how things will work once we get there, but I'm sure we'll figure that out sometime before the middle of summer, or early fall at the absolute latest."

"Are we going to do more of this leather tanning before winter?" asked Trevor.

"Well, yeah, assuming we can get more material to work with. It's just that I don't know how much we'll be able to collect before then."

"Why is that?"

"Well, given that I haven't found any information on seasons in the manual just yet, I have no idea how much longer we actually have until winter. So all I can do is make an educated guess until I have better information to go on.

That's why we'll want to keep moving as quickly as we can to reach at least the first wintering grounds before the snow flies. If we get there early enough, and the weather's still warm, we could try moving on to other camps further down the trail to try and get as far as we can before it becomes impossible to travel. But if not, then we at least want to reach the first of the camps before it gets too cold to travel anymore."

"Huh, I guess that makes sense. So how long are we gonna stay here?"

"Eh, just long enough to rebuild our food supplies and get at least one piece of leather started. After that we'll want to get moving again."

Over the next two weeks, Simon and Trevor bagged several more stagnatier, as well as numerous trovets and wild vegetables; allowing them to both eat well, and also stock up on as much food as they could carry. Eventually, Simon and the others broke camp; and then headed south towards the trail again. But, unbeknownst to them, as they did, several dark, unsavory characters began stalking them from the shadows of the forest. About the middle of the second day, when it was beginning to get a bit warm and sticky, Simon noticed that the river had begun paralleling the trail again. This was the first time he'd seen it in a while, and he was glad it was there. They were getting tired of digging for their water, and all three of them were long overdue for a bath.

"Pee-yoo! Simon, I don't mean to be rude or anything, but you've got an aroma about you that'd scare away the dead," said Trevor as he hid his nose under his shirt.

But as he did, the stench of his own body assaulted his nostrils. He immediately pulled down his shirt and plugged both sinuses. Simon smelled his shirt and recoiled slightly himself.

"Ugh, you're right. We are a little ripe. Well, thankfully I've got a hygiene kit I picked up a couple checkpoints ago that comes complete with soap. How about we go down to the river, scrub ourselves up, and wash our clothes."

Aria stopped short, nearly causing Trevor to plow her over.

"You're not actually considering taking a bath in the river, naked, with me watching, are you!?" she cried in horror.

Simon blinked in surprise.

"What!? No! Not at all! That would be rude and indecent. We can, however, allow you to go first while we wait on the trail beyond sight of you. We'll come down and take our turn after you finish," he said.

"You won't spy on me, ogle me, or secretly watch me bathe from the bushes, will you?"

"Nope, you'll have complete privacy. The only way we'll break that promise is if you scream for help. Otherwise, Trevor and I will stay up here, out of sight, and wait patiently for our turn."

Aria looked at Trevor, and said, "You gonna stay with him?"

Trevor shrugged.

"Of course I will. Even if I didn't want to, I doubt I'd have a choice. He's got a bow, remember? He'd probably shoot me in the back if I tried," he said with a wink and a grin.

Aria grunted.

"That's not funny!" she groaned.

Simon handed her his hygiene kit, and then pointed towards the river.

"You should be able to reach the river by going through there. Just scream if you need us. We'll be waiting over here by the edge of the trail. Have a good bath."

Aria looked at Simon briefly, before hugging the bag and blushing slightly. She then turned and started to walk away, but paused when Simon shouted after her.

"Hey, leave your pack here. You don't want to risk that falling in the river and getting washed away," he said.

Aria slipped off her pack, handed it to Trevor, and then hiked for several hundred feet until she found the edge of the river. The water wasn't moving very fast, but she would still have to be careful as it was very deep. She looked around the area suspiciously as she continued to hug the hygiene bag. After a few minutes of checking the area for spies, she finally put the bag down, bent over and cautiously probed the water. It was cold, yet it felt very refreshing. But just as she began to do this, a pair of large, burly men stepped out of the woods, snatched her and the hygiene kit, and then spirited them both away as she screamed at the top of her lungs.

Simon leaned quietly against a tree with his eyes closed and listened to the sounds of the forest around him. As he did, he thought about the trail ahead of him, the obstacles they would encounter, and the trials that would almost certainly be there. He wondered why he was there, and why God had put him in charge of this tiny band of travelers. It wasn't that he hadn't been enjoying the journey so far. He absolutely was, and the exercise was having a noticeably positive effect on his waistline, requiring him to pull in his belt to take up the slack. Even his hiking clothes had become looser. If he kept this up, he'd need new ones before midsummer. However, he was still confused as to the purpose for why God had brought him there. But, just as he was contemplating this, he suddenly felt an overwhelming fear rush over him. Something was wrong. He immediately sat up and instinctively reached for his bow. Trevor appeared to sense it as well as he was already on his feet, his walking stick cocked in a strange martial arts like defensive stance. A moment later, a terrified scream pierced the quiet solitude of the forest like a knife.

Simon leapt to his feet and was about to rush to the river when six men jumped out of the shadows and rushed towards them. At first, he wasn't sure what was happening. But when he saw the clubs and knives the men were wielding, he immediately knew. He quickly drew and fired an arrow, burying it deep in the chest of the man closest to him. The man grunted, stumbled, and then collapsed to the ground dead. Simon immediately notched another arrow and fired again, dropping the man behind him as well. But a third man was on top of him before he could fire again. He ducked as the attacker swung his club, and then turned and buried his fist in the man's face. However, to his great dismay, all he heard was knuckles crack. He recoiled in pain, and then saw his world go black as club met skull in a backhanded swing. Trevor, however, lasted longer, putting first one, then another down, leaving just two more who were still able to fight. Both men then jumped him at the same time in hopes of overwhelming him. However, Trevor saw this coming and took advantage of it.

As the two men rushed at him, he held out his walking stick in front of him like a barrier and allowed them to slam into it at full speed, pushing him backwards. Thinking they'd gotten one up on him, they continued to push until Trevor stumbled and fell backwards to the ground. However, unbeknownst to them, this had all been part of his plan. As Trevor was falling backwards, he yanked on the walking stick, dragging both men off balance and to the ground with him. As they fell, Trevor drew his knife and, drawing on an old street tactic, used the first man's momentum to drive the blade up through his chin and into his skull, killing him instantly. Trevor then gave the second man a crowbar left hook, sending him tumbling to the side. Trevor then took this moment of opportunity, dislodged the knife from the first man's head, and quickly leapt to his feet. By this time, the second man was on his feet as well. Trevor quickly readied himself, knife in hand, and prepared for the man's attack. A moment later, the man lunged at him, fists swinging.

Trevor instinctively ducked the blows, causing the man to miss and then stumble past him. Trevor, using this brief opening, then spun on his heels and threw his arm backwards, burying his knife deep into the man's chest as he passed by. The man grunted in surprise as he partially doubled over in pain. However, what Trevor hadn't anticipated was the man's next response as he reached out with his left arm and backhanded Trevor like a sledgehammer, knocking him unconscious. The man then stumbled forward several paces, swaying like a drunken sailor as he did; the knife still embedded in his chest. He swore several times, yanked out the blade and tossed it on the ground. He then turned and headed for the woods, bleeding profusely from the wound in his chest as he did. It wasn't long before he collapsed in a heap alongside the trail. He then let out several desperate, gurgling gasps before expiring. A few moments later, a man dressed head to toe like a gigantic bush stepped out onto the trail and surveyed the carnage. Six bandits lay either dead or unconscious nearby, as well as two racers, who were their unfortunate victims. He walked up to the two bandits who were still alive and, drawing his pistol, put one round into each of their heads, killing them instantly. He then bent down over Simon and Trevor and examined them.

Much to his relief, he only found them unconscious; but otherwise no worse for wear. Not wanting to waste any time, he gathered up them, and their things, and dragged them off the trail into the woods where he hid them in a line of bushes. Afterwards, he returned to the trail, dragged the bandits off onto the other side, and hid their bodies by covering them with leaves and other forest debris. He then sprinkled dust on the trail to cover up the blood and other signs of activity before vanishing back into the woods where he'd taken Simon and Trevor. When he finished, he left behind no evidence that anything had happened, nor that someone had once been there. To anyone else coming through the area after this, they would be none the wiser to what had transpired there that day.

Chapter 7

Simon awoke several hours later, his head pounding as though the entire world were exploding around him. He tried to sit up, but felt a strong hand holding him down.

"Lie still, mate. You're pretty banged up," came a voice next to him.

"Ugh, who are..." he groaned as he tried to sit up again.

But the hand continued to hold him down.

"Just lie still. It's not safe for you to move yet."

Simon grabbed his head and took several deep breaths as pain echoed down from his head throughout his entire body. As the pain subsided, he turned to see who'd spoken to him, only to find what appeared to be a bush with eyes. This puzzled him, but his head hurt too much for him to contemplate this in more detail. He squinted slightly, and then shut his eyes tight as he tried not to cry out in pain as his head throbbed like a base drum.

"Alright, it's clear, mate. You can sit up."

Simon tried to crawl to his feet, but stopped as a flood of pain and nausea poured across his body. He sat back down and tried to fight through a severe flash of vertigo.

"Here, chew on this. It'll relieve the pain," said the bush.

Simon took what looked like a sticky lump of grass and chewed on it. To his surprise, his entire mouth began to tingle, and eventually became numb. Within a few minutes, the pain in his head and body went away.

"Wow, whah was thaa?" mumbled Simon in surprise as he tried to speak, despite a numb tongue.

"It's a little painkiller concoction I came up with while experimenting with some of the local plants around here. Given that knot on your head, I thought you could use it."

Simon nodded, and said, "Than's, I appwecia' it."

The bush laughed, and then said, "Hold out your tongue."

As soon as Simon did, the bush rubbed a reddish compound onto it. A moment later, Simon's tongue was on fire! He spit frantically trying to get it out of his mouth.

"Arrgh! What did you do that for!?" he said.

"The painkiller causes your tongue to go numb when you eat it. This fixes that."

"I wish it didn't burn so much."

"True. But it's better than the alternative."

"Yeah, good point. So, may I ask who you are?"

An arm appeared from the bush, and then pulled back it's top to reveal the painted face of an older man.

"Alexander Baker. You can call me, Alex," said the man.

"What's with the getup. You look like a walking bush," said Simon.

"Ah, this. Yes, it's my field uniform."

"Field uniform? Are you with the army?"

"SAS actually. Cobra regiment."

Simon cocked an eyebrow as he studied the man.

"So you're British then, right?"

"Aye, mate. It's jolly nice to meet you," said the man as he shook Simon's hand.

"Just a silly question, but if you're SAS as you say you are, why did you tell me you're part of the Cobra regiment? There is no such thing as far as I know."

The man shook his head.

"Not officially. It's a secret branch assigned to the really tough missions. Officially, at least for the sake of the public eye, I'm part of the twenty second regiment. But for logistical purposes, I'm with Cobra regiment. There's not many of us, but we'll give your Seals a run for their money."

"So wait a second. If you're part of a secret branch of the SAS that doesn't officially exist, why are you telling me? Wouldn't operational secrecy be paramount?"

"Aye, mate, it would be, assuming we were home and all. But I figure, what's the harm in telling you? It's not like we're ever getting home. At least, not in my lifetime."

"Hmm, alright. So how'd you get here?"

"Likely, the same way as you, I suspect. Before I came here, we'd just gotten back from a mission; and my entire squad and I were on holiday. I went to sleep one night, and woke up here the next day. I suspect you have a similar story."

Simon nodded.

"Yeah, I do. Except the last thing I remember was leaving work. I never even got out of the parking lot the day I got snatched."

"If you don't mind me asking, what do you do for a living?"

"I'm a programmer. I develop software applications."

"Ah, interesting. I've heard about these computers, but I've never seen one before. I might have to search one out when I get home."

Alex then went silent and turned his attention back to the woods around them. As he did, Simon looked over and noticed a rifle propped up against a nearby tree.

"Where'd you get that?" he asked.

"It's a custom design me dad created. We used it quite a lot in our regiment. I made this one myself."

"You made that? Here!?" said Simon in surprise.

"Aye, mate," said Alex.

"We're barely scraping by on supplies with a minimum of technology, and here you are with a state of the art rifle. How's that even possible!?"

"I've got a cabin about a hundred miles from here. I've built meself a workshop there complete with all the tools needed to make my own rifles and ammunition, as well as a bunch of other fine bits 'n bobs that I use regularly."

"You know how to make those things?" asked Simon in surprise.

"Of course I do! Me dad was a gunsmith. Made all of his own gear. He always said you don't have a real gun until you've owned one made by hand."

"So he builds handmade rifles?"

"Aye, mate. The best in all of England!"

"I thought they outlawed guns in your country."

"Outlawed them? When?" said Alex in surprise.

"I thought you knew," said Simon in equal surprise.

"No, mate. I've been a captive here since the early eighties. What did I miss?"

Simon looked curiously at Alex, but wasn't sure what to say.

Finally he said, "The best I understand it, after a few high profile massacres, almost all weapons in England were banned."

"Ah, bloody hell. I wonder what me dad is doing now. I doubt he would just give up his shop without a fight."

Simon sighed.

"He may not have had a choice. But that's not important right now. At this moment, I'm more concerned with finding the rest of my teammates and making sure they're alright."

"Well, the young man who was with you is over there against that tree sleeping off a rather nasty knock to his head."

"What about Aria?"

"Are you talking about the young lady the blaggards took with them?"

"Someone took her!?"

"Aye, mate. They nabbed her about the same time they gave you that bump on your head. If I hadn't been in the area, you'd likely be another body in a hole somewhere."

"Do they do this often? I mean, mug hikers like this?"

"All the time, I'm sad to say. That's why I'm here."

"But aren't you a racer like me? Why aren't you further down the trail trying to complete the race yourself?"

"I tried that once, mate. But it was too difficult. So, I came back here where the scoundrels are to see if I couldn't level the pitch a little."

"Well, how many of these bad guys are we talking about?"

"Twenty, maybe more. They have a small outpost not far from here. Their main lair is further up the trail."

"Is this nearby outpost where they would've taken her?"

"Aye. She'll be kept there until they've gathered enough resources to transport up to the big boss. Which, given the haul they've taken lately, may be soon."

"Then we need to get to her quickly!"

"Now hold on, mate. You're in no shape to go running into that outpost and busting your friend out of captivity. You're just one man against a small army."

Simon grunted.

"I've got Trevor. He's a street smart kid with plenty of gumption, and I've got you. If you're truly SAS, you could likely hollow out a dime at two hundred yards. As such, you could cover us while we went in and rescued her."

"Now I must protest, lad! You'd be bloody mad to do what you're suggesting! Two of you against twenty is not realistic odds. There's no way it could work. You're best to just let her go."

"I will *not* give up my friend to imprisonment, torture, and who knows what else! I'm going to save her whether you want to help or not!" shouted Simon.

Alex waved apologetically.

"Alright, alright. I don't see what your devotion to this woman is; but if she's that special to you, I'll help. But I still think it's a bad idea."

"Hold on a second. The more we talk, the less I'm convinced you're SAS. You're trained never to leave one of your own behind, and yet you're advising me to just leave her!? Is that right!?"

Alex sighed.

"Listen, mate. You're dealing with hardened thugs here, and the odds are firmly stacked against you. If I had a proper squad of fellow SAS, I'd go in, bust her out, and be back before you could say tea and crackers. But neither of you are soldiers, and I doubt you have any combat training."

"Don't count on it. I'm an expert woodsman, and I know how to deal with problems like this. I may never have been a soldier, but I've had more than my fair share of hostile predators to deal with, and animals don't play by the rules like humans do. Now, are you going to help me or not? If you won't, I'll just grab my bow and break her out myself!"

Alex sighed.

"Alright, mate. I'll help you. But we need a plan. You can't just go off half-cocked and expect this to succeed. Now, the first thing we need to do is wake up your friend. The second is to decide how we're going to go about this."

"Do you know the terrain around the outpost and what we're dealing with?"

"Aye, I do," said Alex.

"Then show me."

Alex scratched out a quick model of a small, square collection of buildings in the dirt, and then began pointing at different things on it.

"There's a small guard tower here. Someone stands watch there at all hours of the day and night. We'll need to take him out first so he doesn't warn the others. Once he's down, you'll have a clearing of about twenty yards you'll have to cross before you reach cover among the buildings."

"So in other words, I'm exposed until I get into the camp."

"Aye. That's why I need to take out the guard before you go in. Once he's down, all you'll have to watch for is his mates. They'll likely be in the main cabin here enjoying some ale and a good laugh. The building where she'll be kept is here. You'll need to break the lock and free her without the others hearing you. After that, you'll need to quickly make your way back here."

Simon pointed to a building near the edge of the camp.

"What's in here?" he asked.

"Supplies and confiscated materials. But don't waste your time going in there. You need to get in and out quickly, or you risk being caught."

"Alright. Let's go wake Trevor and get moving. I don't want to wait any longer than I have to. Especially since it's getting dark."

Aria sat in one corner of the small prison cell she'd been tossed into and cowered in fear as a large, heavily built Nigerian man sat on the far side of the cell across from her. Well, if you could call it far. The cell barely measured five feet by five feet, and left little room for personal space, or even proper sleeping. She anxiously studied the man next to her, but said nothing. To her surprise, he showed no fear, nor any sign that he was aware of his impending fate. She wanted to scream, to run away from him. Yet she couldn't. She heard laughing and shouting from a nearby building and shivered even more. She feared that it wouldn't be long before they'd come to have their way with her. She could only imagine what things they would do to her. Then her thoughts went back to Simon. He'd been so kind to her, had taken her into his group without question, and had seen to her daily needs. She would give anything to be free again, to be back with him, to hug him...and kiss him? She shook her head in denial. No, that wasn't possible. She would be nice to him, but she could never kiss him. Yet her mind couldn't shake this feeling. She thought it odd that she'd be thinking of Simon that way, and yet she longed to be with him again in more ways than one.

"Do not fear young one. I will not harm you. I am the servant of Olumide, and he has told me that I am to protect you, and keep you safe," said the man.

Aria's heart nearly exploded with fear. The man's eyes popped open, and then looked over at her briefly, his dark brown eyes seeming to pierce through the darkness and into her soul. He then turned his attention to the door as he grew tense.

"Someone comes," he whispered.

"Is-is-is it them? The b-b-bandits?" asked Aria nervously.

"No, it is another. I sense that they are an honored brother."

Aria's mind reeled at the thought of another person like him showing up. One was enough. She hoped the man was wrong.

Chapter 8

Simon studied the camp below them carefully, and then lowered his binoculars.

"You're right. There's a guard in that tower over there. But I don't see anyone else."

"You won't. They're all in the cabin for the night drinking themselves sick," said Alex.

"Well, that's good. It should make things easier for us."

"I pray you're right."

Simon looked over at Trevor, and asked, "How you doing?"

Trevor nodded.

"I'm fine. I'll be a little slow, but I'll manage. I can't believe that guy jacked me like that. I feel like an idiot for getting punked when I knew better than to stick my face where it could get hit."

"Well, we'll worry about what you did wrong later. For now, let's just focus on this."

"Whatever you say, boss," replied Trevor.

Simon then turned to Alex, and said, "Alright, we'll start out by positioning ourselves along the treeline and wait for your shot before we go."

"That's fine and all, but my rifle is silenced, so you won't hear anything. So I'll whistle twice once it's clear," said Alex.

"Even a silenced rifle makes some noise."

Alex smiled.

"Not mine."

Simon shrugged.

"Alright, fair enough."

Alex nodded and began climbing a nearby tree to get into position. Simon then turned his attention back to Trevor.

"You ready with that sidearm Alex gave you?" he asked.

Trevor nodded.

"It's a funky pistol, but I think I can use it."

"Alright, but remember, you only have nine rounds, so don't use it unless you have to. Got it?"

Trevor gave him a silly salute, and said, "Crystal clear, boss."

The two men then slipped quietly through the woods and stopped at the edge of the clearing as they waited for Alex. He raised his binoculars and trained them on the guard tower. One man with an odd shaped weapon stood in it. Suddenly, he flinched and then vanished. Moments later, they heard two sharp whistles. Simon lowered his binoculars.

"I think that's our cue," said Trevor.

Simon nodded, and then both he and Trevor ran as fast as they could across the clearing and into the middle of the camp. So far, they hadn't been seen, and Simon was thankful for that. They soon found the shed that Alex had told them about. Simon signaled to Trevor to watch his back. Trevor nodded and anxiously scanned the area as Simon quickly glanced inside the shed. He immediately spotted Aria shivering in fear in one corner. But what he saw next to her surprised him. In the other corner was a dark skinned Nigerian man who appeared easily twice her size. He wasn't sure what to make of this. However, if Aria was alright, he couldn't be too dangerous. Either way, he needed to get her out of there. He pulled the small bolt that secured the door and swung it open. Aria and the man both perked up as they heard the door swing open.

"Simon!" cried Aria with joy.

"Shh! We're here to get you out," whispered Simon.

But Aria wasn't thinking. She immediately leapt up and threw her arms around him, nearly knocking him to the ground in the process.

"I'm so glad to see you!" she squealed as quietly as she could.

"I'm glad to see you too. But who's your cellmate?" asked Simon.

Aria's mind immediately went from joy to pure terror. She squeezed Simon's neck so tight that he felt as though she would crush it. Trevor glanced over at the man, and then aimed his pistol at him as he stood up, easily towering over the young man.

"Whoa, stay right there, buddy. We don't want no trouble from you," he whispered.

The man strolled slowly, but purposely out the door, and stopped near Simon.

Trevor cocked the pistol, and said, "Don't even think about it."

"Simon, protect me," said Aria, her voice quivering in fear.

"Who are you?" asked Simon.

The man bowed slightly.

"I am Birash, servant of Olumide. I am in your debt," he said.

He then walked past Simon and made his way over to a nearby building. As he did this, Simon struggled to peel Aria off of his neck before she choked him to death.

"Aria, let go of me. I can't breathe," gasped Simon.

"Protect me, Simon. I'm scared," said Aria.

"I can't while you've got a death grip on my neck. Let go so we can get out of here."

"Hey, what's he doing?" asked Trevor as he pointed at Birash.

Simon pried Aria off of him; and then watched with interest as the man opened a nearby shed, went inside, and appeared a few moments later with four large packs of supplies and a tiger who followed him out. This was now too much for Aria, and she immediately fainted to the ground.

"Ah, great. She passed out. Trevor, grab her while I see what our guest is up to," said Simon.

Trevor nodded, secured his pistol, and then tossed Aria over his shoulder.

Simon trotted up to Birash, and whispered, "What are you doing!?"

"Saving my compatriot," said Birash.

"I am not your compatriot," growled the tiger.

Simon's mind nearly exploded trying to make sense of the fact that the tiger had just spoken. But he didn't have time to think about that. He would deal with it later. First, he had to get Aria out of there. He motioned for everyone to follow him, and then trotted out of the small outpost and into the woods. The sun was already setting; and it was quickly becoming hard to see, so speed was important. Hearing a few short whistles in front of him, Simon trotted to a stop.

"Where are you?" asked Simon.

"Right in front of you, mate," came the whispered reply.

Simon looked around him, but saw nothing.

"Straight ahead, mate," whispered Alex.

Simon trotted forward a short ways and soon found Alex squatting next to a tree.

"You got everyone?" asked Alex.

"Yeah, plus two strangers," said Simon.

"Are they friendly?"

"I think so. They were prisoners of the bandits."

Alex looked past Simon at Birash and the tiger.

"Are you sure you want to bring them along?" he asked.

"I'm certainly not going to leave them for the bandits, if that's what you mean."

"Right then, follow me. We'll be able to move faster if we walk along the main trail."

The small band then slipped quickly through the darkening woods, barely able to see each other, or the trees in front of them. Even so, they soon found their way back to the main trail. Once there, Simon was able to make a headcount and found everyone accounted for, including the two strangers they'd brought with them.

"Alright, so where to next?"

"Your packs are just up the road a ways. I put them there after I rescued you. We'll pick them up on the way through."

"I also have four more packs filled with supplies, if that is of any help to you," said Birash.

"You're carrying four full packs? Bloody hell, mate. That's a lot of weight to carry. Are you sure you'll be alright?" said Alex.

"I'll be fine."

"Right then. Let's get moving."

"But Aria's still out!" protested Trevor.

Just then, Aria stirred. Trevor set her down against a tree and checked her over.

"You alright?" he asked.

Aria nodded, weakly. She then spotted Birash and his tiger friend standing nearby. She immediately froze. Trevor spotted this and realized what was up.

"Hey, hey, calm down. They're not gonna hurt us, alright?" he said gently.

Aria shook her head in fear as she searched desperately for somewhere to hide.

"Calm down. I'm not gonna let anything happen to you, alright?" he continued.

Aria took several deep, nervous breaths, and nodded. If Trevor was willing to protect her, then she would do her best to be brave. She took his hand and stood to her feet.

"Alright, Aria's back with us, so we should go. Trevor, you to take the rear and watch for those bandits. Alex, you take point and I'll take the middle," said Simon.

Trevor nodded and slipped to the back of the group. Aria, in turn, stepped in front of Simon where she felt most safe as Alex took the lead. Birash and Yurg settled into the group just in front of Trevor where he could keep an eye on them. As they walked, Alex studied Simon curiously, watching the way that he moved down the trail, and was most impressed with him.

"You seem very skilled at war craft. Were you in the military?" he said.

"No, I never got that opportunity."

"So where did you learn to move like this? You act like a professional soldier."

"I play a lot of squad based games, so I'm pretty familiar with the drill. I learned a lot of what I know from there," said Simon.

"Well, that'll come in handy then. It's good to know that we, at least, have someone other than myself who is skilled in war craft."

"Geez, you're a woodsman, a programmer and now an armchair grunt? What can't you do?" quipped Trevor.

"Let's just say that, where I lived, they took the motto 'be prepared' very seriously, and rather literally to a fault," said Simon.

Alex chuckled.

"Nothing wrong with that, mate. Better over prepared than under. I guess that explains why you were so confident going into that outpost."

"Well, it was less because of my skills, and more because I trusted in God for our protection. I knew He would allow me to keep my promise to Aria and Trevor to get them to the finish line; because I will do anything I can to keep my word."

"Well, that's a jolly good mission, mate. But can you do it? I know I couldn't."

"Speaking of which, why *didn't* you ever finish the race? I thought as SAS you could easily reach the end without a problem."

"Just because I'm SAS doesn't mean I'm superman. Even I have my limitations."

"Alright, fair enough. But we'll worry about the reasons why you never made it later. For now, we need to keep moving so we stay ahead of the bad guys."

"Aye, agreed."

The small group then continued on down the trail all through the night, and well into the next morning before they stopped. When they finally did, Simon was intrigued to see how large the packs were that Birash had brought with him. What was scarier was that, despite their obvious weight, he didn't appear to have broken a sweat carrying them.

"Are those the packs you grabbed last night?" asked Simon.

"They are," said Birash.

"Wow, they're bigger than I thought they were! Mind if I have a look at what's in them?"

Birash nodded slightly.

"You may," he replied.

However, as Simon began to approach the packs, he looked over and noticed that the tiger that Birash had rescued was a little too close to them for his comfort.

"What about your tiger friend? Will he mind if I go through them?" he asked.

The tiger looked up at Simon out of one partially opened eye.

"My name us Yurg, and I am *not* his friend. We are enemies. However, I owe him a debt for saving my life. So, for now, we are under a truce until that debt is repaid," he said.

"We are not enemies, my friend, for I was not the one who imprisoned you, nor have I done anything to bring offense against you," said Birash.

The tiger growled slightly, and then looked away.

"There is much you have done against me, and for that I will have your head for a trophy. But not until I have repaid my debt to you, for I will not soil my honor by drawing blood from one to whom I owe a life debt," he growled.

"But I have done nothing! I have only shown you kindness, and risked my life many times to save you from danger!" protested Birash.

Yurg growled angrily at him and bare his teeth, but said nothing. Birash, in turn, looked sadly at the tiger, but said nothing as well.

"Oh great, now we've got an inter-species rivalry to deal with," thought Simon.

Just then another thought struck him.

"Wait, wait, wait. Hold on here a second. How in the blazes can you understand us or even talk!? I mean, how is that even possible!?" he asked.

Yurg looked at him incredulously.

"You have been tampered with the same as I have, and yet you ask such a question?" he said.

Simon pondered this for a moment, and then perked up.

"Oh, the implants! You got the same upgrades we did?"

Yurg frowned.

"I would hardly call them 'upgrades'. They are a curse and a plague to me!"

"Perhaps, but they allow us to speak with each other, which is good."

Yurg snorted.

"You humans have a strange idea of what is good. Even so, I do admit that there are advantages to my new condition, including the new mind I was given. It has helped me understand the sheer insanity that plagues your kind. It has made me despise you even more. As such, when my debt is repaid, I shall tear your flesh and rend it from your bones as well. But not before I have exacted my revenge upon this one you call Birash. He shall be the first to feel my rage."

Simon furrowed his brow.

"Fun guy," he thought.

He then stepped towards the bags, but again paused as the tiger eyed him coldly. This made Simon nervous.

"Uh, Birash? I think I'll wait till later to go through those bags. Your friend doesn't look too keen about me being near him right now," he said.

Birash studied the tiger mutely as Yurg glared back at him with disdain. He looked back at Simon and nodded.

"Then we will deal with these later," he said.

Yurg grunted in displeasure and turned his head away in stark disapproval of his situation. Birash rolled his eyes, but said nothing. Meanwhile, Aria sat nearby with her knees pulled up to her chest as she studied the two strangers across from her. She wasn't sure what to make of them; but so far, they hadn't shown any hostile intent. Well, not Birash at least. Yurg was a different story though. Even so, it didn't do much to assuage her fears. She then turned her attention to Simon and tried to pluck up the courage to speak to him. Eventually, she did.

"Simon," she said shyly.

"Hmm?" replied Simon.

"Why did you come back for me? You could've just left me to whatever fate awaited me back there. Yet, you risked your life to come get me. Why?"

"Because, we care about you, and I made a promise that if you trusted me, I would make sure you made it to the end. I'm not going to back out on that promise, no matter what. Only death will stop me from fulfilling it."

Aria blushed and hid her face in her knees as tears formed in her eyes. After a moment, she slid over next to him and kissed him on the lips, completely to Simon's surprise.

"Thanks," she said shyly.

She blushed redder than a rose and quickly retreated back to her place. She'd liked the experience. But it was quickly apparent that Simon hadn't.

"Why'd you do that?" he asked sternly.

"I just wanted to thank you."

"That's not the proper way to do it. In fact, it's very inappropriate."

"Sorry," said Aria sheepishly.

Chapter 9

Consciousness slowly invaded the beer soaked mind of one of the bandits as he crawled to his feet and studied the room around him. It was morning already and the cabin reeked of ale, vomit and unwashed bodies. His head pounded like a sledgehammer as the intoxication of the previous night began to wear off. He grunted as he stood and then staggered to the door. As he threw it open, the light assaulted him like fire, causing him to cry out in pain and shield his eyes. After a moment, he stumbled out into the fresh air and looked around, trying to focus his eyes in the bright mid-morning light. It was at this moment that he realized something wasn't right. He looked around and saw that the doors to the holding cell and supply shed were open. He then realized that the tower guard was dead. Fear began to settle over him as he ran inside the cabin to wake the others.

Simon chewed on a piece of dried stagnatier meat while Yurg lay nearby, content with eating a freshly killed trovet he'd caught earlier that morning. It sickened the others to see him eating the animal raw. But it was what he did. Trevor soon returned from the river with a towel over his shoulder and looked at Simon.

"I'm done. Who's next?" he asked.

"Aria's the only one left," replied Simon.

Trevor looked at Aria and smiled before holding out the hygiene bag to her.

"Well, I guess it's your turn then," he said.

But Aria shook her head.

"I don't wanna," she said anxiously.

"Hey, you're going to have to take one eventually, or you'll get an infection," said Simon.

Aria shook her head again.

"Is it that you don't want to be alone? We're only a short jog from the river. Just shout if you need us," said Simon.

"I'd rather have you there watching over me, if that's alright," she said shyly.

Simon shook his head as Trevor watched him curiously to see what he'd do.

"I told you before I won't do that," said Simon.

Aria blushed, and looked away.

"Well, you don't have to watch. You could just sit there with your back to me. I just want to know you're there."

Simon sighed. He understood why she wouldn't want to be alone by the river again. Yet, deep down in his heart, Simon knew that being there with her would be wrong. Then again, if she didn't get herself cleaned up soon, he might be forced to deal with something far worse later on.

"Aria, I can't do that. I don't want the thought of seeing you naked on my conscience."

"What's wrong with that, mate? I've seen plenty of naked women," said Alex.

"I'm a Christian! It's a sin to look upon a naked woman who's not your wife!" shouted Simon.

"Oh poppycock. There's nothing wrong with seeing a little skin now and then, mate," said Alex.

"I'm sorry, but God says that the only time I'm permitted to see a woman naked is if I'm married to her. All other times are completely off limits."

"Pfft. God sounds like such a killjoy," said Alex.

Aria fidgeted shyly, and said, "So will you come down to the river with me?"

"I'll go. After last time, I think someone needs to watch over her," said Trevor.

"No, you're not. She either goes by herself or she doesn't go at all," replied Simon.

Trevor shrugged.

"What? It's not like I'm gonna look or anything," he protested.

"I don't care. You aren't going and that's final. She's not your wife; and therefore, you're not allowed near her when she's naked. Understand?" said Simon firmly.

Trevor nodded.

"Yes, sir."

He then looked at Aria, who was clearly put off by the whole thing, and pondered all of what Simon had said. He then wondered what it might be like if he actually was married to her. Strangely enough, the idea actually intrigued him. As he contemplated this, Yurg snorted and stood up.

"I will go with the female. It's apparently troubling for some among your race to see each other's hairless bodies. However, such a thing does not bother me. Therefore, I will go with her in your place if you wish," he growled.

Aria looked at Simon, as though pleading with him not to agree. Simon stood and thought about this for a moment.

"While I don't know you all that well, from what I've seen so far, I believe I can trust you. So yeah, you can go with her if you want."

Yurg cocked an eyebrow slightly, but didn't appear to take offense at his statement. Aria, however, grunted in frustration. She'd secretly hoped that Simon would come with her; and yet, he'd flatly rebuffed her. Then, reality suddenly hit her. Why was she so concerned about him? What was it that made her want to be so close to him? She wasn't sure, but it surprised her. She turned and looked at Yurg who merely studied her with muted displeasure.

"Come, young one. Let us begin your grooming ritual," said Yurg.

Aria stood up with a sigh, took the hygiene kit from Trevor, and began heading towards the river with Yurg in tow. Simon watched with interest as the two made their way through the trees and out of sight. He shrugged and then went back to eating his breakfast.

"Simon, why is it a sin to look at a naked woman you're not married to?" asked Trevor.

"Because God told us not to."

"Where?"

"It's in the Bible in several places. If you'd like, I can show you."

Trevor nodded in approval.

Aria slowly stepped into the water, and then blushed slightly as she glanced back at Yurg. But he paid no attention to her, instead preferring to study the area around him. His ears twitched back and forth as his eyes seemed to fix on one thing, drift a bit, and then fix on something else. She grinned slightly. While he was obviously intelligent and able to speak, he was still just a big kitty cat to her. A part of her worried that he might eat her. Yet another felt safe knowing he was nearby watching out for danger. Especially after she'd been kidnapped the day before.

As she began to lather up, she turned to Yurg, and said, "So where are you from?"

Yurg looked down at her briefly, but said nothing.

"You do come from somewhere, don't you?" she asked.

But Yurg paid no further attention to her.

"Gee, fun guy. Doesn't even want to talk," she thought.

She continued to wash herself, wiping away weeks of dirt from her skin before turning her attention to her sticky, matted hair. As she began to wash it, the stench of it caught her off guard and nearly made her gag. She'd need to take baths more often to keep that from happening again.

"Why is my origin so important to you?" he asked after a bit.

"Well, everyone comes from somewhere. I just thought I'd learn more about you and get to know you better," she replied.

Yurg's eyes narrowed as he studied her mutely.

"You need not know that, for it is none of your concern. Know only that your life is protected for now until I have repaid my debt of honor to the one you call Birash. Once that is completed, his life is forfeit, as is perhaps yours. Therefore, be silent and return to your bathing before you tempt me to break the sanctity of my sworn honor," he growled.

Aria was surprised at this. She could sense the anger in his voice and wondered what Birash had done to hurt him. She wanted to ask him why he was so upset with Birash, but instead wisely chose to continue bathing in silence, ensuring as best she could that every inch of her body was scrubbed as clean as possible. She then took her clothes into the river, scrubbed them clean, and eventually tossed them up on a rock to dry. As they did, she climbed out of the river, dried herself off, and picked up her clothes, expecting them to still be quite damp. But to her surprise, they were not only dry, but felt fresh again as well. She wondered how that was possible.

"Hmm, I wonder how much they'd give for a material like this back home?" she thought.

She quickly dressed, gathered her things, and then strolled back towards the others with Yurg in tow. But as she did, she suddenly heard a growl and rapid footsteps behind her. She turned curiously and watched in surprise as Yurg raced off into the treeline.

"Oh great. He's probably going after more food. Typical men," she muttered.

It was at that moment that the sound of gunfire echoed from the trail above. She froze. All she could think about now was that something horrible had just happened....again.

Simon leaned against a nearby tree as he held his Bible open in his lap.

"Wow, Jesus really said that?" said Trevor in amazement.

Simon nodded.

"Yes, he did. And then in chapter..." he said, pausing as Birash leapt to his feet.

Simon studied the gigantic Nigerian for a moment trying to see what had upset him so much. But before he could ask, a group of bandits exploded out of the bushes nearby.

"Awe, blimey!" shouted Alex as he leapt to his feet and grabbed his rifle.

Trevor looked up to see what was happening and, upon seeing the bandits, was immediately on his feet as he drew the pistol that Alex had given him. Simon was the last to stand up. When the fight was over, nine men lay dead in the road. Yurg appeared moments later from the river, and then turned and followed Birash into the treeline where they gave chase to two more bandits that'd escaped the carnage. Alex hurried after them. Several shots rang out followed by a terrified scream and a roar. Alex returned a few minutes later with Birash and Yurg in tow. Aria soon appeared behind them and immediately ran over to Simon, hiding behind him for protection.

"What in the blazes just happened!?" asked Simon.

"We were attacked by bandits," said Alex.

He then noticed the nine men that lay in the road and nodded in approval.

"Bloody nice shooting, mate," he said to Trevor.

"Yeah, well, back home, you either learned to shoot well or you ended up dead," said Trevor, reverting slightly to his old self.

Simon knew he wasn't going back on his new found faith, but rather that the circumstances had drawn out some of his old street honed survival skills. It was an odd thing to see coming from him after he'd changed so much, but at a time like this Simon was somewhat glad to see it. Especially, since it'd helped save their lives twice now.

"Hey, you got anymore ammo? I kinda emptied the clip," said Trevor.

Alex reached into a pouch on his vest and tossed him two magazines.

"Keep track of the empty ones. I'll need to reload them when we get to my next ammo stash."

Trevor nodded, changed clips and loaded a fresh round into the chamber. He then walked around the area and studied the bodies.

"Hey, I recognize that one. He's one of the guys that mugged us," he said.

"Actually, he's not. He's merely a compatriot of those who attacked you," said Alex.

"So what happened to them?"

"They're all dead, mate. I buried them myself."

Trevor kicked the dead man's body.

"Well, good riddance to all of them, and to this jerk too. Don't nobody touch this homey and get away with it. Not now. Not ever."

"So, are we gonna have to deal with more of this?" asked Simon.

"I don't believe so; although, it's still possible, as it appears they've discovered that we made off with their prisoners and some of their goods. Too bad they were able to find us so easily. That could be trouble," said Alex.

"So then, we're still in danger," said Simon.

"Most likely. As such, we should hurry. If they're after us, it won't be long before they return, and with reinforcements. But, we can escape them if we can reach the bridge at Golden Canyon."

"How far is that?"

"About eighty miles from here."

"Eighty miles!?"

"I didn't say it would be easy. I just said we'd need to get there before the bandits do."

"So why that bridge? What's so special about it?"

"They're afraid of what's on the other side. If we cross it, they're unlikely to follow. That also means they'll expect us to make for the bridge and will likely be waiting for us there."

Simon paused briefly to contemplate this.

"Hmm, that's going to complicate things. The part I find curious is that the people who run this race allow them to exist."

"This is a survival race, mate. The controllers allow them to exist because they're seen as yet another way to test your survival skills," said Alex.

"It's a bit sadistic and cruel if you ask me. But at the same time, I understand the logic behind it, as odd as it may be. Well, either way, we need to get going. Everyone, pack your gear. We don't have any time to waste. Alex, I'm going to trust you to lead us to the bridge as quickly and safely as possible."

"Aye, mate. Count on me!" exclaimed Alex.

Simon then turned to the two new members with them, and said, "Birash, Yurg, I know you've just joined us and you're welcome to leave if you like, but if it's at all possible, I'd like you to stay. We could use your help to stave off these bandits if they return. Especially if they bring reinforcements. Plus, we'd enjoy your company."

"I would be honored to assist you. I am as much their prey as you are; and, as a man of honor, I will not sit by and do nothing while you are being hunted. By Olumide, I will lay down my life to protect those I have sworn to defend. You saved my life; and thus, I am your servant until you choose to release me. I swear this by the great name of Olumide, my lord and king," said Birash.

"And I am sworn to repay the life debt that I owe to Birash for saving me before I am free to go my way as well, or perhaps even to seek my revenge. Therefore, I will also swear my allegiance to you; and will remain in your service until I have fulfilled my debt to him," said Yurg.

Simon nodded.

"Well then, welcome to the team. Now let's get out of here."

A rugged man in a ragged, weathered outfit road up to a woodland fortress on the back of an animal easily two sizes too small for his considerable frame. It struggled with every step to move forward, and eventually collapsed in exhaustion. The man kicked the animal in anger, and then stormed into the fortress. As he walked towards a nearby hut at the center of the compound, several large, burly guards stepped in front of him.

"Halt!" said one of the guards.

"Out of my way! I'm here to see the master!" shouted the man.

"You will not approach unless Master Orbus gives you leave to enter," said one of the guards.

"I don't have time to argue with you! Tell him I have an important message on which hangs the destiny of our band!" shouted the man.

The guard studied him briefly, and then said, "Wait here. I will return shortly."

He slipped away into the hut, and closed the door behind him. A few moments later, the door opened again and he signaled for the man to enter. The man stormed into the hut, and then knelt before a large, wooden throne on which sat a somewhat rotund older man with dark, piercing eyes.

"What is your message?" hissed the old man.

"Master Orbus, our outpost was attacked by a band of racers; and all but two of the men stationed there were killed," said the rugged man.

The old man leaned forward and clenched the arms of his chair tightly.

"WHAT!?" he screamed.

"Yes, my lord. Their company was devastated."

"How many of these racers were there?"

"Six, my lord. Alex, our enemy, was among them."

Orbus growled loudly through tightly clenched teeth.

"Gather our forces! We will destroy them and that infernal monster as well!"

"All of them, my lord?"

"Every. Last. One. I want the entire strength of my army searching for them immediately!"

"Understood, my lord."

Chapter 10

Simon studied the road ahead of him as he wiped the growing sweat from his brow.

"How ya holding up there, mate?" asked Alex.

"Getting a bit winded from the pace we're taking. Of course, it doesn't help that I haven't really slept since yesterday, nor does this heat. But beyond that, I'm fine," said Simon.

"Ah, understood, chap. Don't worry. There's a shelter about a mile ahead that'll allow us to hide for a while. We can stop there and rest until dark, and then continue on under the cover of night."

"Won't that make it hard for us to see anyone coming?"

"Yes, it will. But it'll also make it hard for them to find us."

"Hey, old man. You said you had an ammo dump around here. Where is it?" asked Trevor.

"It's hidden in the shelter just ahead. I'll show it to you when we get there."

The group then continued on for another half an hour until they stumbled onto a narrow path that stretched away from the trail and out into the woods. They followed it for nearly a quarter mile before it turned and began running parallel to the main path. A short ways down, Alex stopped, surveyed the area, and then grabbed a bush and moved it to the side. To everyone's surprise, a hatch appeared beneath it that led down into a fairly good sized room made of logs buried in the ground. Alex climbed down first, and then signaled for the others to join him. Once everyone was in, he pulled the shrub back into place and slipped inside.

"How'd you build something like this?" asked Simon in surprise.

Alex grinned.

"It wasn't hard. When you've been here as long as I have, you find plenty of time to build things. Even something like this."

"But what about your cabin? Don't you go back there periodically?" asked Trevor.

"Only to resupply my shelters like this one or to work in my shop making things I need."

"So where's your spare ammunition?" asked Simon.

Alex strolled across the room and opened up what appeared to be two solid logs to reveal a slide out gun rack and ammunition box. Simon, Trevor and Aria all gagged in surprise.

"Dude! That's not an ammo stash! That's a whole dang armory!" exclaimed Trevor.

"It's not a complete armory. It's only the weapons I feel are necessary to have in the field to help me protect the hikers who pass through this area."

Simon pulled out one of the guns and examined it.

"This is pretty good craftsmanship. You made this yourself?"

"Aye, mate. It's an exact replica of an SA80. Not the meanest girl in the lot, but she's a bruiser."

"What are you carrying?" asked Trevor.

"A replica L96 sniper rifle. She's got a long reach and a nasty bite."

Trevor picked up another weapon and grinned.

"An Uzi, eh? I'm surprised to see one of these here," he said.

"She's a bit messy and terribly hard on ammo, but she works in a pinch. She's best used in close quarters where a bigger rifle would be impractical. She's also good at getting me out of a pinch when things go all pear-shaped," said Alex.

"When would you ever have use for an Uzi?" asked Simon.

"Raided any compounds lately?" said Alex with a grin.

"Hmm, good point. But even so, I wouldn't have expected you to need something like this."

"I do, but thankfully, not too often. There are, however, times when it's your only option."

Trevor snorted.

"I hope it never comes to that."

"Yeah, same here. Hey, Alex, do you mind if we take some of these with us? We could use the added firepower," said Simon.

"Not at all. I can just come back later and restock the shelter with replacements for whatever you take. Right now, your safety is more important."

"And it sure beats walking around carrying my bow everywhere. It's handy for a few things, but it has it's limitations."

"Aye, that it does. Well now, if everyone wants to get some sleep while we're waiting, I'll take first watch. When it's dark, we can head out again."

Simon nodded to Trevor and Aria, and said, "You two get a nap. I'm gonna sort these packs and take only the things we need. The rest we can leave behind."

"Yeah, good idea," said Trevor.

He and Aria then each took a bunk and were soon sound asleep. As they did, Simon set about sorting and dividing up the contents of the four backpacks that Birash had brought with him. Try as he might though, despite dividing up the packs as best he could between everyone in the group, there was still enough important items left to fill two entire packs. Unfortunately, Birash would have to carry the if they wanted to bring those items along. He then looked over at Birash as he studied Simon's handiwork.

"Hey, are you still gonna be okay carrying two packs? I know you had four before, but I don't want to impose on you if I don't have to. However, I don't think I can reduce these down any further without leaving behind a lot of valuable stuff," he said.

Birash shook his head.

"I am okay with doing whatever I must to assist you."

"Okay, good. I just didn't want to overly burden you."

Birash again shook his head.

"You are not burdening me, my dear friend. I will be alright."

"Okay, cool. Well, then if you don't mind, I'm gonna crash for a bit."

"By all means, please do."

Simon then crawled in a corner of the shelter and was soon fast asleep. The next thing he knew, someone was shaking his shoulder. He sat up and looked around, but found the room to be dark, save for a small flickering candle in the corner.

"It's time to go, mate," whispered Alex.

Simon nodded, stood up, and noticed that the others were already awake. He slipped on his pack and quickly realized just how much heavier it was. The difference surprised him. Even so, he was glad for the extra supplies. He soon followed Alex out of the shelter. Outside, it was pitch black, save for the soft glow of the moons above. They then moved as quickly as they could through the shadowy darkness until they reached the main trail again. Alex stopped them briefly to check the road for signs of danger. But seeing none, they turned and hurried down the trail, traveling all through the night and not slowing for anything, including food. Periodically, they were forced to abandon the trail and hide from the roving bandit squads that raced up and down the trail in search of them. This continued on for over a week as they alternated between hiding from the bandit patrols, and continuing to hike forward. On the morning of the eighth day, they reached the bridge over Golden Canyon. But upon arriving they spotted two bandits guarding the entrance. It was just as Alex had said. He and Simon both raised their binoculars and studied the men.

"What do we do with them? If we start shooting we'll have every bandit for miles on top of us like lightning," whispered Simon.

Birash and Yurg studied the men and then each other. While they said nothing, their eyes spoke volumes to each other; and a plan was quickly formed. Birash then nudged Simon.

"Simon, we request your permission to deal with these two ourselves, and clear our way to freedom," he said quietly.

"Are you sure you want to do this? If there's more, you could bring them right down on top of you," whispered Simon.

"It is a risk we are willing to take," said Yurg.

Simon nibbled on his lip for a second as he thought about this, and then nodded.

"Alright, but be careful," he whispered in reply.

Birash and Yurg nodded in return and soon vanished into the woods. Simon then turned and watched the two guards, waiting for something to happen. Several minutes later, the two guards turned and headed towards a nearby bush as though checking out a mysterious sound. Suddenly, a pair of hands reached out and yanked the two men into the bush with a surprised yelp. A few minutes later Birash and Yurg returned.

"The problem has been taken care of," said Birash.

"Geez, remind me not to get you mad," muttered Simon.

Alex raised his binoculars again and scanned the area.

"Alright, it appears clear to proceed. Let's get to that bridge as quickly as we can," said Alex.

"Alright, chief, lead the way," said Simon.

His small group soon emerged from their hiding place alongside the trail and began hurrying towards the bridge. But before they could reach it, a large group of bandits appeared out of nowhere and surrounded them. Simon and the others raised their weapons, but quickly found that the bandits were also sporting firearms, and greatly outnumbered them as well.

"I thought they didn't have guns," said Simon.

"They only bring them out for special situations," said Alex.

"Well, apparently we must be special, because it looks like they emptied the entire armory just for us," said Trevor anxiously.

"What now? If we spray them, we're dead meat," said Simon.

"I'm fresh out of ideas, mate," said Alex.

"Surrender immediately, or we will kill you," growled one of the men.

Simon closed his eyes, and said, "Lord God, you know we're in deep trouble right now. If there was ever a time for a miracle, now would be perfect."

"What? I didn't hear you!" said the bandit mockingly.

"What are you doing, Simon?" asked Trevor nervously.

"Trusting God to dig us out of this mess," replied Simon.

"God's not going to save us. In fact, nothing will," replied Alex.

Just then, they heard an unusual buzzing sound fill the air, like the deep throated humming of a bass singer.

Suddenly, to everyone's surprise, strange black insects appeared out of the woods and engulfed the bandits, sending them screaming in pain and paranoia in every direction until they had all vanished from sight. Simon's group soon relaxed and lowered their weapons.

"Wow, thank you, Lord. It's not the miracle I was expecting, but it works," said Simon.

"You really think that was God's doing?" said Alex in surprise.

"What else could it be? Now let's get moving! We need to get across that bridge!"

"But what about the bugs!?" cried Aria.

"They're not attacking us, so we'll worry about them later. Now get moving!" shouted Simon.

The group immediately sprinted towards the bridge, stepped across the threshold, and did not stop until they were well on the other side. Once there, most of the group sat down to catch their breath. Birash and Yurg, however, were not winded; and thus, took up watching the bridge behind them in case any of the bandits tried to follow them. But nobody came. They marveled at this. Once everyone had caught their breath, they continued on down the trail until early evening where they reached a small pathway that detoured off the trail to their right. After walking down this path for a ways, they emerged into a clearing filled with a cabin and a couple small barns.

"Ladies and gents, welcome to my home," said Alex.

"This is where you live?" asked Trevor in surprise.

"Aye, that it is, mate. She's not much to look at, but she's got room enough for all of you. Come in and I'll fix you dinner."

The others followed him inside and found, much to their surprise, that Alex's cabin was no run down hovel in the woods. It was surprisingly well appointed for what it was.

"Where'd you get all this stuff!?" asked Trevor in surprise.

"I have lots of free time on my hands during the fall and winter months, since no hikers pass through here once summer is over. So I spend that time tinkering in my workshop."

"Where'd you get the materials to build all this?" asked Simon.

"The metals I mined from ore pits just west of here. The rest was collected from the woods, or purchased from Logontown."

"Wait, you're mining your own ore out of open air pits?" asked Simon curiously.

Alex nodded.

"It's strange, but there are a lot of useful ores very close to the surface around here. When I first setup this camp, I started out with a very crude set of metalworking tools, mostly just a hammer, a few stones, and some raw ore. Then, over the years, I've advanced my craft steadily, building better and better equipment and tools until I was able to create metalwork of nearly equivalent quality to what we have back home. It was a lot of hard work, but the results are gratifying," he said.

"You've been able to build up this much technology in only a few years?"

"I wouldn't call it a few, mate. I've been here over thirty years. You find you can get quite a lot done in that amount of time."

"Where are your partners; those who traveled with you? I find your seclusion to be peculiar, given the need to travel in groups on this race," asked Yurg.

"You mean my hiking group? Well, it's a long story. We started out together from the very beginning of the race and traveled together through trials and tribulations of every sort for several years until we eventually reached the last hextant."

"Hextant?"

Alex chuckled.

"It's a word the locals use to describe the six parts of the course. The bridge over Golden Canyon completes the first hextant. We are now in the second."

"Wow, now there's a major feeling of accomplishment," said Trevor.

"So what happened to your group in the last hextant?" asked Simon.

Alex sighed.

"They all died."

Simon blinked in surprise.

"What happened!?"

"We were in the final leg of the race, and the young man who was our group leader decided to press on, despite the pending onset of winter, and my warnings against attempting such a foolish endeavor before spring. They died a month later in an avalanche in the black mountains near the finish line. I only survived because I'd stopped under a ledge to adjust my pack before continuing. That moment of hesitation left me in the only place on that hillside that wasn't swept away. I never saw them again. Finding the rest of the path ahead of be impassable, I turned around and made my way back to the nearest town. I never attempted the last hextant again. Since then, I've dedicated my life to helping others successfully pass through the first and second hextants in hopes that someone would eventually complete the course."

"Has anyone succeeded in winning the race?" asked Aria.

"Not one. I wouldn't still be here if they had, nor would you, because the controllers who created this race would've had no need to collect further test subjects. Once someone completes the race, everyone who was brought here from Earth will be sent home, and no one else will be brought here to this world from that time forward," said Alex.

"Great, that just made my day. So we're stuck here until either hell freezes over or some lucky punk gets to the finish line which, apparently, nobody has," muttered Trevor.

"Now, don't go and start panicking on me. We're still in the early parts of the course, and we have God behind us. As bad as it might seem, we're never without hope," said Simon.

"Ah, it'll take a lot more than just God by your side if you want to win this race. You'll need quite a fair bit of luck besides, of which you seem to have an ample supply," said Alex.

"I don't believe in luck, and I don't believe God would put us in this race just to leave us on our own at the one moment we need Him the most," said Simon.

"Well, that's all good for you, mate. Just keep on believing that, and you'll find yourself at that finish line in no time," said Alex.

He then walked over to a cabinet, pulled out a pile of blankets, and pointed to several rows of bunks on the far wall.

"Beds are over there. Dinner will be in a few hours, so you're welcome to take a nap if you like," said Alex.

"No thanks. I'm gonna sit down and read my Bible," said Simon.

"Actually, you're not looking so hot. I think you should crash first," said Trevor.

"No, I'm fine. I'll be alright."

Trevor shrugged.

"Alright, suit yourself."

Simon smiled, pulled his Bible out of his pack, sat down at the table, and began reading. The next thing he knew, Alex was shaking him on the shoulder, trying to rouse him. Simon sat up, his head thick and groggy, and looked around the cabin in confusion. Alex laughed.

"I think you were a bit more tired than you let on, mate. You were asleep just a few minutes after you began reading," he said.

Simon stretched, smacked his lips, and said groggily, "How long was I out?"

"About twenty minutes."

"Ugh, really?"

"We've been under a lot of stress the past several days, and you've been burning the candle at both ends. You're no youngster anymore, and can't last as long as the others. So you should remember that, or else you risk killing yourself."

Simon nodded.

"Yeah, sorry. I guess I should get some sleep," he said groggily.

He closed his Bible, slid into a nearby bunk and was fast asleep. He awoke the next morning to the sound of chattering as Trevor and Aria sat at the table quietly discussing something of great interest to both of them. He climbed out of bed, stumbled across the room and plopped himself down at the table as he tried to shake out the cobwebs that filled his mind. Aria grinned widely at him and fidgeted slightly as though she had something important to say. She then glanced back at Trevor anxiously. He nodded at her reassuringly.

"Go ahead and tell him," he said.

"What are you two carrying on about?" asked Simon groggily.

He glanced at Aria who appeared to be beaming with joy.

"I got saved!" she said with such conviction and joy that Simon wondered if rainbows would start appearing in the room.

"Huh?" he replied in confusion.

He was still half asleep, and not yet totally able to wrap his mind around what she was saying. Then, as if by a miracle, his mind suddenly cleared and what Aria had said hit him with the force of a hurricane. He perked up and looked at her in surprise.

"You got saved!? When!?" he exclaimed.

"Just a half hour ago. Trevor helped me pray," said Aria.

"You!?" said Simon in further surprise.

Trevor nodded as he grinned nearly as widely as Aria.

"We got up about two hours before you did and decided to sit at the table and talk. During that time she asked me about you and I, and why we're like we are. I gave her my testimony and then showed her the verses you showed me about what Jesus did for us," said Trevor.

Aria smiled.

"I wasn't sure what to make of it at first, but after hearing him talk about Jesus, I just had to get to know Him. Trevor showed me how, I prayed, and now I feel so, so...."

"Forgiven?" asked Simon with a smile.

"Well, yes, forgiven. But it's more than that. I feel truly loved for the first time in my entire life! To think that someone would love me so much that He would do something like that is amazing! I feel ashamed for not having asked Him into my life before this."

Simon smiled even wider. Despite having tried and tried to reach the young woman, he was glad that Trevor had. He was also proud of the young man for stepping up and witnessing to her. Because of that, they now had a new sister in Christ.

"So this young man was fairly convincing in what he told you?" he asked.

Aria shook her head, and then paused, as though to think.

"Well, yes and no. He explained it to me so that I could understand it, but it was you that made it real to me. You cared enough to come get me when anyone else would've abandoned me, and you always went out of your way to make sure all of us were well fed and kept safe along the way. You even took me in and shared your food with me when you didn't have to."

"God would expect nothing less of me. We're all lost sheep gone astray. He went out of His way to find us, and bring us to Him, even dying on the cross to save us so we could live with Him forever. If He was willing to die for us, how could I not show charity to someone else in need? To send you away and let you continue suffering would be like taking what Jesus did for me, and throwing it back in His face. I love Him too much to do that; and thus, I show charity and kindness to others wherever I can. I'm glad you're now a child of God. You'll find that, while life in this family is not easy, it's the greatest thing that'll ever happen to you," said Simon.

Aria smiled widely.

"It already is."

Chapter 11

Alex awoke late in the afternoon and noticed that the cabin was empty. He stepped outside and was surprised to see Simon, Trevor and Aria sitting around a tree with books in their laps discussing something. He wasn't sure what to make of it, but decided to go see what they were up to. As he approached, Simon noticed him first and motioned for him to join them.

"Come, have a seat. We're just doing a Bible study," said Simon.

"A Bible study?" said Alex with a hint of disappointment.

"Yeah. We have a new sister in Christ, and she wanted to learn more about Jesus. Since it was so nice outside, we decided to have it here under the trees. You're welcome to join us if you like."

Alex looked at Aria, and said, "So you're one of those 'holy rollers' now, are you?"

Aria smiled and shrugged. Alex shook his head in disbelief, and then waved dismissively.

"Ah, delude yourselves. I'm fine the way I am. But if you're hungry, I'll fix something for you to eat," he said.

"Actually, that'd be great. Thanks," said Simon.

Alex nodded.

"Right, then. I'll yell when it's ready."

He turned and strolled away just as Yurg appeared from the woods with a freshly killed Trovet in his mouth. He sat down near Simon and quietly studied him as he ate his meal. Aria's stomach churned in disgust as she watched the tiger eat; and then turned her eyes away, trying not to see what he was doing. Realizing that his actions were causing her discomfort, Yurg apologized and turned away so that the others wouldn't have to see him eat. After a bit, Simon continued his teaching, laying open the scriptures as both Aria and Trevor drank them in as though they were dying of thirst. A little bit later, Birash appeared from the woods with several more trovets.

"Well, you've been productive. How come you have more than Yurg?" asked Simon.

The tiger turned and glared at him out of the corner of one eye.

"I was only hungry for *one* this morning," he said, and then returned to eating.

Simon laughed.

"Alright, fair enough." He then looked at Birash, and asked, "So what are those for?"

"I am repaying our friend for his hospitality by providing meat for his table," said Birash.

"Ah, that makes sense. Thanks for catching those. Why don't you go give them to Alex. He's working on breakfast for us right now."

Birash nodded and then headed for the cabin. He returned a minute later and sat down next to Yurg, who quietly ignored everyone there as he continued to eat his breakfast. Birash smiled happily at Yurg, who growled at him in turn before turning his attention back to his meal. Birash felt disappointed that Yurg was still angry at him, but thought nothing more of it. He then turned his attention to Simon and listened attentively to his teaching. As he did, he was surprised at how much Simon knew.

"Forgive me for interrupting," he said.

Simon looked at him, and said, "It's no big deal. What'cha need?"

"I am curious how long you have been a Christ follower."

Simon shrugged.

"Since I was a child. Probably about thirty five years by now."

"Praise be to Olumide for such a blessed faith with such age to it," exclaimed Birash joyfully.

Simon furrowed his brow.

"Forgive me if this sounds rude. But I'm curious of something. Since the day we first met, I've been watching you; and from all I can see, you appear to be a Christian just like me. However, I consistently hear you address this Olumide as your god. Why is that?"

Birash smiled.

"Because Olumide *is* Christ," said Birash.

Simon cocked an eyebrow.

"How so?" he asked suspiciously.

"Olumide is Yoruba for 'God has come'. It is roughly equivalent to the Jewish name Emanuel."

Simon perked up slightly.

"Emanuel, God with us," he replied.

"Correct. While some might say it is...a pagan name, as its roots come from long before our Savior walked the Earth, there are many who do not see it as such. While it does have secular origins, I will admit, to me, it speaks of God as...Jehovah, as the Jewish people like to say. God is always with us, as is Christ; and therefore, it is to me not at all disrespectful to address Him as Olumide. Does that make sense, or have I confused you?"

Simon pondered this briefly.

"No, I can understand what you're saying, and I guess it does make sense. I don't like that the name has secular, and potentially pagan origins. However, one can also say that the name 'God' has both pagan and divine origins as well. Of course, I'm viewing that from the English language perspective where 'God' with a big 'G' refers to Jehovah, and 'god' with a small 'G' means a deity in general, but not any one individual entity in particular."

Birash nodded hesitantly.

"Yes, that is something like what we have. Although, as you would say, some of what the name represents is 'lost in translation' and therefore, does not fully relay its original meaning. Even so, I am a strong and devout follower of Jehovah, and His Son, Yeshua, as the Jewish people call them."

Simon nodded slightly.

"Hmm, very interesting. Do you have a Bible?"

Birash shook his head sadly.

"I do not, for I cannot read. I was never taught how."

Simon seemed intrigued at this.

"Then how did you read the bible before this?"

"Audio bible," replied Birash. "A local missionary gave it to me. It's how I first came to know Christ. I listened to it for many nights until I eventually gave my heart to Him."

Trevor crossed his arms and studied Birash intently.

"Not to sound dumb or anything, but given the stuff they shoved into our heads, couldn't you like, ya know, use that to learn how to read?" he asked.

Birash cocked his head, and asked, "What do you mean?"

"Well, not to be 'Mr. Obvious' here or anything, but if Yurg could learn how to talk with us and understand things on our level, I think learning how to read should be easy enough for you to do."

Yurg perked up, and then glanced between Trevor and Birash. Eventually, he fixed his eyes on Birash.

"Even though I do not share any concern for your wellbeing, given all that I have seen, I believe it would be wise for you to learn how to read, as there seems to be much wisdom contained in the many books that I have thus far seen since entering this world."

Simon gestured to Yurg, and said, "Out of the mouths of babes...or in his case, tigers."

This drew chuckles from everyone there, except Yurg, who didn't understand the reference.

"Yurg is right, though. It wouldn't hurt for you to use your implants to learn how to read. It would be very useful to you on many levels," continued Simon.

Birash thought about this for a few moments.

"Very well, I will do that. But who will teach me?"

Just then Trevor raised his hand.

"I can do that."

"You?" said Simon in surprise.

"Hey, just because I'm a thug doesn't mean I can't teach someone how to read. You gotta remember, I got my GED at fourteen. So, I think I've got what it takes to teach him. In fact, I might even be able to teach Yurg how to read."

Yurg gave him a look of displeasure.

"I will pass," he said.

Trevor shrugged.

"Hey, suit yourself."

Just then Alex stepped around the corner of the cabin, and shouted, "Oy, mates! Come and get it. Breakfast is ready!"

Simon waved at him, closed his Bible, and said, "Alright, let's go eat."

The four humans then slipped inside the cabin, leaving Yurg outside to finish his trovet, and were greeted by a sizable meal waiting for them on the table, including bread, eggs, juice and something that looked like sausage. However, Birash's trovets were nowhere to be seen. Simon assumed that they were likely being held back for another meal. Even so, the quantity of food before them surprised everyone.

"Where in the world did you get all of this!?" asked Simon.

"Didn't you hear the cargo bird come in a while ago?" asked Alex.

"Cargo bird!?" said Simon curiously.

"Around here, there are a number of large birds of varying species that deliver small cargoes between locations as a form of express mail. One flew over earlier and came down to see if I needed anything from town. I sent him off with a few copper rings and a short list of things I needed. He returned a little while later with the supplies."

"Why did you give him the copper rings?" asked Aria.

"Ah, you *were* paying attention!" said Alex gleefully.

Simon nodded.

"I caught that too, but surmised that the rings were some form of currency."

"Aye, mate, they are. Since a common currency here is not possible, nor feasible, a system of barter is used instead. One item of great value to the locals is metals. Being that I am able to produce refined, finished metals in my workshop, and since the townsfolk have need of such metals, I trade with them periodically, offering gold, silver, copper, tin and iron in exchange for any goods and services that I am in need of that they can provide," said Alex.

"So these come from those pits you talked about?" asked Simon.

Alex nodded.

"Aye, that they do. Most around here couldn't be bothered with mining ores, so they leave it to the adventurous chaps like myself."

"So did your dad teach you how to refine and forge metal?" asked Simon.

Alex nodded.

"Me dad believed that if you wanted your metal done right, you had to do it yourself. So he also ran his own forge."

Simon chuckled.

"Your dad is starting to sound a bit like mine. It's partly how I came to know so many things."

"Yeah, he's already shown us he knows pretty much everything," said Trevor.

Simon chuckled bashfully.

"Well, I don't know *that* much. Alex actually knows more than I do."

"Not really, mate. Each of us specializes in something. Your list of specialties just tends to be a bit more well-rounded than most," said Alex.

"Alright, I'll give you that. But speaking of skills, yours will come in quite handy as we get further down the trail. As such, we'd love to have you in our group."

Alex waved dismissively.

"I really can't, mate. I can take you as far as Logontown, but then I must return."

"Why not? Don't you want to finish the race at some point?"

"I'm nearly sixty years old, mate. If I couldn't complete the journey the first time, I doubt I'll be able to do it now. Therefore, I'm better off here protecting others who might run afoul of the bandits."

"But if someone finishes the race, everyone gets to go home! Wouldn't it be more logical to finish the race, rather than spend what few years you have left trying to stop an organization that's pretty much invincible? Well, at least against your one man army. If we can finish the race, you'll be able to protect seventy times more people than you could by staying here. Besides, consider your age! Even you admit you're old. How many more years will you be able to fight on before your age either gets you killed, or you become too feeble to continue the fight? Then what?"

Alex thought about this for a while, and then shook his head.

"I'm sorry, mate, but I can't. My place is here."

"Now hold on. You're British SAS! You can't give up! What if some of the people coming down that trail in the future are British? You would be failing your duty to protect your fellow countrymen!"

"But I'm no longer a soldier! I'm just an old man who pretends to be on."

"Once a soldier, always a soldier! It's your duty to protect those under your watch, and I won't just stand by and let you hold a pity party for yourself because you're too scared to complete the race!" shouted Simon.

Fire erupted in Alex's eyes; and then was quenched only a moment later as the memory of his original team flashed before his eyes. He sighed heavily.

"Sorry, mate, but I can't. Now, you're welcome to stay a few more days if you'd like; but after that you'll need to get going. The wintering grounds are still many miles ahead; and you'll want to reach them before it gets cold, so you'll need to leave soon," he said in a sad, somber tone.

He then turned and walked outside. Simon considered following him, but decided it was best not to. He closed his eyes, said a quiet prayer for the food, and for Alex, and then began to eat. Trevor, Aria and Birash sat quietly and watched him with interest, but said nothing.

Alex walked quietly into his workshop and studied the machines and tools all around him. No matter how long he was away, he always enjoyed coming back to them. He walked over to a heavy metal box, pulled out a keg of powder, some bullets and some casings, and began assembling more rounds to replace the ones he'd used. But as he did, something began to nag at his mind. He tried to brush it aside, but it just wouldn't go away. He grunted in frustration. He didn't understand why he felt so guilty for telling them that he couldn't come with them. He'd already done his part and got Simon's team safely past the bandits. So he was officially through with them; and they were now on their own for the rest of the journey. Yet, guilt continued to poke at his mind. It wouldn't let him walk away from them. Another voice soon reminded him of how the last time he'd tried to reach the finish line his entire team had died. If he didn't want that to happen again, then he needed to go with them. Still, another voice told him not to go, and to stay behind where he belonged. His mind battled back and forth like this for a while until he eventually forced himself to go back to filling and pressing out more bullets. Even so, his conscience continued to nag at him over and over again, demanding that he go with them.

After a bit he angrily stomped his foot, and said, "NO! I will not!"

But his voice fell upon deaf timbers and silent dust. He felt stupid for making such an outburst, and yet, he couldn't shake the feeling that he needed to help them, no matter what. Then another thought, one filled with reason, echoed in his mind. Of all the groups who'd passed through the area in the past three years, very few had survived the first hextant, and only Simon's team had demonstrated any real chance of making it to the end. In fact, they'd done better at surviving the course so far than any other team in years. That had to count for something. As much as he hated to admit it, they were his best hope at this point for winning the race and going home. Finally, he sat down on a stool to think. If he didn't go with them, their chances of surviving were slim at best, and he wasn't one to just walk away and leave them to die. They were decent people after all; and despite being a bunch of holy rollers, he liked them a lot. Yet the thought of his lost hiking companions again haunted his mind, once more dividing him between his unfortunate loss and the incredible hope Simon's group brought to him. It felt good having hope again.

But, if he let them go without him, where would that hope go? He knew that, if they left, that hope would remain with him for a brief time, and then die, just like before. The only way he could think of to maintain that feeling of hope was to go with them. He sighed heavily as he looked at the equipment around him. He then looked down at his hands and remembered just how old he was. If he was ever gonna do this, he had to either do it now, or get busy dying. Because if they too failed, then dying was the only thing he had left to look forward to. Eventually, he decided that he had to try at least one more time, as it would likely be his last chance to do so. Even if he died in the attempt, so long as they crossed the finish line, it would all be worth it. He sighed heavily, stood up, walked out of his shop and made his way to the cabin. He would get them to the end, one way or another, or die in the attempt; because he would not, once again, let go of the hope that now burned within him.

Orbus pounded his fists on the table.

"What do you mean they got away!?" he cried.

"Our men were attacked by a swarm of wasps and driven away," said a soldier.

Orbus growled in anger.

"Where are they now?" he asked.

"They've crossed the bridge over Golden Canyon. They are beyond our reach."

Orbus growled again.

"They'll never be beyond my reach!" he said through clenched teeth.

"But, my lord, they've crossed the bridge! If we cross it, we will fall victim to its curse!"

"I do not care! I will not let anything, neither curse nor bridge, stand in the way of my revenge!" roared Orbus.

The soldier blinked, but showed no fear, despite being scared for his life.

"If we cross that bridge and give chase to them, a great curse will fall upon us and many of our men will die," he said.

"Then so be it! I have grown tired of that cursed Alex and his constant meddling in my plans. But no more! That will end today. Gather everyone! We will march across the bridge and destroy these insolent, arrogant travelers, and that monster, Alexander, no matter what it costs us! I will have my revenge, and their blood will run like a river through my fingers and soak the very soil on which I stand until it can't take another drop! Now go! Time is essential!"

The soldier saluted and hurried away to carry out his orders.

Alex walked into the cabin and stopped just inside the door. Simon looked up at him curiously for a moment, and then went back to his reading. Aria and Trevor were sitting in a corner sharing a Bible as they read quietly while Birash sat on the floor next to Yurg as the tiger lay curled up in a corner sleeping. Alex mustered up his courage, walked up to Simon and then sat down.

"Hey, mate. Do you have time for a chin wag?" he asked.

Simon looked up at him, noticed his expression, and then put his Bible aside.

"What's on your mind?" he asked.

"I've been thinking. You're one of the few groups I've met in a long time who has a snowball's chance of winning this race. And you're right to say that I'm getting too old to keep doing the things I've been doing. So I think it's time I finished the race. Therefore, I have decided that I want to go with you. I figure it this way. You'll need someone who knows the course ahead, and a soldier who can defend you against the many troubles you'll run into along the way. So what do you think? Are you willing to have me in your group?"

Simon smiled and nodded.

"Absolutely! But what about your hiding places and your stashes of weapons? What about this cabin and all the equipment you have here?" he asked.

"Bah, I could care less. There's a smithy in Logontown who might be interested in some of my equipment, but he's already got many of the same tools I have. So if I leave them, someone will eventually discover the place and make good use of them."

"Like the bandits?" asked Simon.

Alex blinked in surprise as he thought about that.

"Aye, I hadn't considered that. If they find this place, it would be a bad thing for anyone coming in behind us, or perhaps even those further down the trail. Hmm, well, I guess I'll have to blow it all up then. What'cha say, mate?"

Simon laughed.

"What are you thinking about using?"

"There's enough powder stored here to send this place into the next galaxy."

"Well, sounds like we've got a plan. Besides, I've been getting the feeling we need to clear out of here tonight anyways, so this is perfect timing. How far is Logontown?"

"A couple miles up the trail. We can easily reach it in an hour or so."

"Excellent! So where do we start?"

Alex looked at Simon curiously, and asked, "So, am I on your team?"

Simon chuckled.

"Of course you are! Besides, I've considered you part of our group since the moment you first met us. So yes, you're part of the team."

Alex smiled wide.

"Alright then, mate! Let's get this place wired up to blow!"

Trevor perked up, and said, "Blow what?"

Alex and Simon laughed.

"Interested in making this place fly, lad?" asked Alex.

"We're gonna blow it up!?" asked Trevor in surprise. Both men nodded.

"Well, geez. Sign me up!" shouted Trevor with glee.

Aria shook her head, and said, "Pfft. Men."

Orbus sat atop his riding beast, a creature reminiscent of a mule, and rode to the front of his forces. There was less of them now than there had been only a few days earlier; but he still had way more than he needed, even for an assault like this. His commanders had said his actions were overkill. But he'd grown tired of Alex and wanted the old man's head, regardless of what it took, or how many of his men's lives it cost. One way or another he would have his revenge.

Seeing that all were ready, he cried, "Forward!"

He then began riding towards a nearby pathway as his men followed close behind. It wasn't long before the entire stronghold, and ultimately his entire kingdom, was emptied of every single soldier in Orbus' vast army, leaving behind only his slaves, concubines, and a sizable treasure trove of supplies. They quickly followed the narrow pathway through the woods that led away from his compound and soon emerged onto the main trail. When they arrived, they found it abandoned. Orbus wondered how much prey was getting away from them because of Alex's actions. He grunted arrogantly. With Alex gone, it wouldn't matter. All travelers from now on would be his victims, and his storehouses would soon overflow with innumerable treasures. In time, he would expand his kingdom further east, not stopping until the entire world belonged to him. In the end, his kingdom would become the greatest ever seen! He gave a cry of advance, and the entire group moved up the trail towards the bridge over Golden Canyon. They arrived several hours later to find the area devoid of activity. He looked around briefly, and then signaled for two of his scouts to cross first. They galloped across the sturdy bridge and soon reached the other side. They rode up and down the trail several times, and then signaled that it was all clear.

Seeing that it was safe to proceed, Orbus cried, "Forward!"

The legion of bandits cried out in joy, and then rushed across the bridge like a plague.

Alex tied together one final wire and inspected his handiwork.

"You sure this'll work?" asked Simon.

"If I did my job right, the only thing that will be left of this place will be a sizable crater," said Alex proudly.

"So what's up with all the tripwires?"

"They're in case someone finds this place before the timer can set off the explosives. Normally I keep my powder well hidden in case someone finds my camp. But since all of its out in the open now, I'm not taking any chances."

He turned and looked at the rest of the group.

"Alright, everyone got their weapons and ammunition?"

Everyone nodded, except Aria who studied her sidearm curiously.

"Why do I need this? I don't even know how to use it," she said.

"Well, it's necessary, love. We're all carrying weapons and ammunition, and it's only fair that you carry some as well. Even if you can't use it, one of us may have need of it later on," said Alex.

"Alright, but I still don't like it," she said anxiously.

"Don't worry, Aria. Even if you never fire it, I'm sure it'll come in handy," said Simon.

Trevor stood next to the cabin grinning like a Cheshire cat.

"I feel like Rambo carrying all this stuff," he said gleefully.

"Yeah, well. Don't go blasting away at everything that moves. We've got a limited supply of ammo and few, if any opportunities to resupply. So we need to preserve every round we can."

"Pfft. Don't worry. The only thing I'll shoot at is something that wants to take a hunk out of me. Otherwise, these babies don't talk."

Simon nodded.

"Good." He then turned to Alex, and said, "Care to do the honors?"

Alex nodded, flipped over a vile, and said, "Alright ladies and gents, we have one hour to get as far away from here as we can before this place blows. I suggest we make haste or we may find ourselves wishing we had."

"You'll get no complaints from me," said Simon.

The group quickly gathered up their stuff, put on their packs and began to walk briskly up the pathway towards the trail. As they did, Alex paused and looked back at the cabin. Simon noticed this and paused as well.

"Something the matter?" he asked.

"Not really, mate. It's just that cabin. It's been my home for over twenty years. I'm really going to miss it."

"Ah, don't worry. If all goes well, a few years from now, we'll all be back on Earth enjoying the wonders of modern technology."

Alex nodded with a smile, and continued on without saying another word. They soon reached the main trail and turned towards Logontown. But unbeknownst to them, danger was approaching rapidly from behind. They had no more than vanished around a bend in the trail and out of sight when one of Orbus's scouts appeared on the trail behind them. It wasn't long before he stumbled onto the pathway to Alex's cabin. He quickly returned and reported his findings to Orbus, who ordered his men to follow the pathway to its end. They obeyed and then raced down the trail at a full gallop. But they soon returned several minutes later with perplexed looks on their faces.

"What did you find?" asked Orbus.

"There's a cabin and some other buildings there. But when we entered, the place seemed abandoned as though nobody has been there in some time," said one of the scouts.

"Show me," said Orbus.

The scouts then led him and his entire party into the clearing where Alex's cabin was hidden. Upon entering the area, Orbus growled angrily.

"This is his place! I know it! Everyone, attack!" shouted Orbus.

The men all let out a loud cheer, and charged forward. But it would prove to be a fatal mistake. As the wave of Orbus's men charged into the center of the buildings, one of them hit a tripwire, immediately detonating all of the powder in one breathtaking explosion.

Chapter 12

Alex and the others flinched in surprise as a thunderous boom shook the ground and the trees around them.

"Blimey! That went off sooner than I expected! Quick! Take cover and watch for debris!" shouted Alex as he dove behind a tree.

Everyone else quickly took shelter behind trees as well and waited for several minutes until they were sure it was safe to come out. Much to their relief, no debris fell around or near them as they'd already traveled further than any of it would fly. When they emerged again, they looked back in awe to see a large mushroom cloud rising up from the forest behind them.

"Wow, now that's what I call an explosion!" cried Trevor.

Aria said nothing, but merely stood quaking in shock and fear.

"I thought you said we had an hour," said Simon.

"We did. Something must have hit one of the tripwires," replied Alex.

"Do you think it was the bandits that were harassing us the other day?" asked Simon.

"Unlikely. They're too afraid to cross the bridge. Of course, if it was them, they got what they deserved. Bloody good riddance and all."

Simon chuckled.

"Well, if it was them, they got quite the sendoff."

"Aye, that they did. Well, we should get moving again. The only thing left now is to push forward and complete this infernal race," said Alex.

Simon and the others all nodded in agreement. A little over an hour later they entered the small, somewhat rustic village of Logontown. As they did, Simon watched curiously as an older gentleman stepped out of what appeared to be a bakery and greeted Alex with a gigantic hug. They talked vigorously for several minutes before Alex introduced the others to him.

"Gents, this is Benjamin Bernstein. He's one of the best bakers and butchers in the entire area."

"Ah, but I am the *only* butcher and baker in the area," he said in jest, with a slight Jewish accent.

Everyone laughed.

"So my young friend, what brings you here?" asked Benjamin.

"Well, it's getting late, and I was wondering if we could impose upon you for the night. Maybe, a little room to sleep in and some bread for our stomachs," said Alex.

"But of course! Anything for my dear friend. By the way, did you hear that huge noise earlier? It sounded like thunder. Shook all my windows."

Alex grinned sheepishly.

"Sorry about that, mate. I was just getting rid of some old powder."

Benjamin laughed, and said, "It's alright. Nothing's damaged, and nobody got hurt. Come, we should go inside. My wife will love having you for dinner!"

"Thank you, old friend," said Alex.

"Um, if I may intrude. You're Jewish, right?" said Simon.

"Why, yes I am. How did you know?" said Benjamin in surprise.

Simon shrugged.

"Well, your accent mostly. But I also saw the star of David in the lower corner of your window."

Everyone looked at the shop windows, and then spotted what Simon had already seen.

"Ah, you're right, mate. I'd never noticed that before," said Alex.

"Pssh, it's nothing. Just a small memento of my homeland. I long one day to return there. Hopefully, before Messiah returns," said Benjamin.

Simon nodded.

"Yeah, same here."

Benjamin's eyes grew wide.

"You're a believer in Messiah?"

"I am," said Simon with a smile.

"Mazel tov! That is great news! We shall have to talk about this more later on. For now, you should come inside, relax, eat and enjoy yourself!"

The small group thanked Benjamin for his hospitality; and then stepped inside where they were treated to a meal that would rival most kingly feasts. After they finished, they bedded down for the night and were soon sound asleep. However, as they slept, two blue-skinned men appeared on the edge of town in a flash of fire. Peering through the walls at them, as though by magic. they quietly studied Simon's team with great contempt and hatred.

Eventually, one of them said, "He has done much better than we anticipated."

"Yes, he has," hissed the second. "We should have destroyed him at the beginning before he entered the race. Now we are bound by its rules. Even worse, he has made many allies, and even brought two of them to salvation.

He then uttered several vile, profane curses as he remembered the man in the brown suit at the reception station who had stopped him from attacking Simon.

"He should not have intervened and saved that man," he continued.

"I agree. However, the race has only begun; and there are many dangers ahead that are far greater than what they have already come through."

The first blue-skinned man hissed angrily.

"Yes, there is. However, it is uncertain if those will be enough to destroy them as they have already survived many of the challenges we have poured out against them, and even were instrumental in the destruction of our ravagers. As such there is nothing that remains anymore that will block others from passing through the first stage and entering into the second. If this keeps up they will destroy all of the hazards and hindrances we have been so careful to construct to prevent any and all from winning this race. If they do, it will mean that our work of the past five centuries will be for naught. We cannot permit that for we must not allow *Him* to win."

Just then a man in a brown suit appeared behind them in a flash of light. It made the two blue-skinned men cringe and growl angrily. The man in the brown suit looked at them suspiciously.

"Why are you two here?" he asked.

One of the blue-skinned men gestured to Benjamin's house.

"Do you not see them!?" he growled.

The man looked towards the house, peering supernaturally through the walls, before looking back at the two blue-skinned men.

"Hmm, so they've made it this far already," he replied.

The two blue-skinned men looked at him in contempt.

"They must be stopped!" protested one of them.

"Why?"

"They are destroying all that we have built! If they are allowed to continue, they will make it far too easy for the others coming behind them to win!"

The man in the brown suit looked at them with muted displeasure through deep, slotted eyes.

"Patience, my friends. No one has ever completed this race in the over five hundred years that it has been ongoing, and none ever will. However, if you are too hasty, you may inadvertently hand our enemy a victory that we can ill afford. So, for now, we will stand back, observe only and in turn allow the course to do its job as it was designed to. In time, all of our problems will resolve themselves as they always do, and all will be returned to normal," he said calmly.

The two blue-skinned men hissed at him. But the brown suited man acted as though he had not heard their angry outburst. A moment later, the two blue-skinned men vanished in a flash of fire and were gone. The man in the brown suit looked over in the direction they'd been staring and again looked through the walls of Benjamin's house at Simon's group inside. He frowned as he studied each of them individually.

After a few moments, he gave a disappointed grunt, and said, "Enjoy Your victories while You can, Yeshua. No matter how hard You try, You can't protect them forever. We *will* kill them; and all those like them, just as we always have. In the end *You* will lose."

And with that, he vanished in a flash of light and was gone.

Early the next morning Aria awoke to find Simon outside praying under the trees.

"What are you doing out here so early?" she asked.

Simon turned around in surprise to see her, and then smiled.

"Well, good morning. I'm just spending some quiet time with the Lord while praying for the rest of our trip. Especially the next leg. Given what we've been through, I felt that we needed a double blessing of protection if we're going to make it out of here alive and in one piece."

Aria smiled kindly.

"A little extra protection never hurts."

She then blushed and looked away.

Simon noticed this, and asked, "Is something the matter?"

Aria walked up to Simon, grabbed his arm and tried to kiss him on the lips. Simon recoiled in surprise and pushed her away.

"Aria!" he exclaimed.

She tried again, but he immediately put her at arms length.

"What are you doing!?" he cried.

Aria appeared hurt as she stared at him in confusion.

"I just wanted to thank you for what you've done for me," she pleaded.

But Simon knew better.

"Aria, I realize you're a brand new Christian; but there are certain things you don't do as a believer, as well as protocols you have to follow."

"Like what?"

"Like, not just randomly kissing guys on the lips for starters."

Aria cocked her head in confusion.

"But what if you really like the guy, even possibly in a romantic way?!"

Simon did a double take.

"What!? Aria, we barely even know each other. You can't seriously think that I'm suddenly gonna be romantically in love with you just because I took you in as part of my team, or even saved your life. I'm not that kinda guy. Besides, even if I did like you that way, I don't feel a relationship between us would be appropriate."

Aria was shocked by this.

"But why?" she asked, a hint of hurt in her voice.

"For one, I'm over twice your age. In fact, I'm old enough to be your dad! And two, you're not looking for a romantic relationship. You're looking for a father figure, and I just happen to fit that description. I'm sorry Aria, but I just can't do this. If you really want to start a relationship, you should talk to Trevor. He's your age."

"But I love you!" she exclaimed, and then caught herself as she realized what she'd just said.

Simon's eyes narrowed.

"See what I mean? This isn't about love. It's about your desire to fulfill a need in your life that your mind is telling you can only be satisfied by getting romantically involved with the person who fills that need. In this case, that's apparently me. Now Aria, I want you to continue being my friend; and I will continue to do my best to take care of you and protect you; but I can't allow a romantic relationship to develop between us."

Tears began to form in Aria's eyes as her face screwed up in an expression of frustration as she felt rejected, and even heartlessly at that.

"How can you do this to me!? I love you!" she cried.

"Oh God, help me. This is getting sticky," thought Simon as he sighed heavily. "Aria, I won't play this game. Deep down inside, I know you want someone to love you and be your father. However, I can't fill that role. It's not my place. But if you're willing to listen to me for a moment, I will tell you someone who can be."

Tears streamed down Aria's cheeks as she tried to wipe them away with her shirt.

"Who?"

"God."

Aria seemed offended by this.

"God!?" she exclaimed.

Simon sighed again.

"One of the names of God is Father. When you accepted Jesus into your life, God became your father, and you became His child. If you need a father figure in your life, and the ultimate father of fathers at that, then you need to go to God. He loves you and wants to hold you and take care of you as a father should. All you need to do is let go of what troubles you and give it to Him."

Aria was stunned that she was getting sermoned at a time like this! Then, to her complete and total surprise, she suddenly felt a powerful love flow over her like a flood. But not a sensual, physical love. This was a deeper, truer love than she'd ever felt before; one that came straight from the heart. She dropped to her knees and began crying profusely. Simon felt the same thing and dropped to his knees as well, praising God, thanking him, and asking that He show Himself mightily to her. And He did exactly that, to the complete amazement of both of them.

"I feel so strange. Yet I feel this incredible love flowing through me," she said.

Simon smiled wide.

"That's God showing you how much He cares for you. You already know how much Jesus loves you just by His act of dying on the cross for you. So this is merely the Father's way of affirming that love; a love that is unconditional and without requirements or limitations. There is no greater love anywhere in the universe than the love that He has for you right now, in the past or in the future to come. He never changes, and always loves you, and will do so to the very end, no matter what. And since God has no end, there will never be a time when He stops loving you."

Aria nodded, buried her face in Simon's shoulder and wept. But this time Simon didn't push her away. Instead he embraced her kindly as he knew she merely needed someone now to hold her as she cried. After a moment he released her and she looked up at him. Her face was running with water, and her eyes were blurry with tears. But the feelings of romantic love she'd had towards him before had vanished.

Instead, he could now see the signs of a fragile, broken heart that'd been mended by a simple act of kindness, and a divine act of love. They then talked quietly for another half an hour as Simon shared passage after passage with her that God brought to his mind as they sat on the ground under the trees. After praying and thanking God for this huge blessing he'd given to both of them, but most especially to Aria, they got up and made their way into the house where they found Benjamin's wife fixing breakfast as Benjamin was preparing to open his store.

The smell of eggs, meat, bread and pastries filled the house with an aroma that even woke Trevor out of a sound sleep. It wasn't long before the doors opened and patrons began making their way inside. Some brought animals for butchering, others flour or milk, while yet another brought a towel. Each then left with freshly butchered meat, fresh baked bread, and numerous sweet, delectable pastries. A few even came in with nothing, but were sent away with their arms full. This intrigued Trevor.

"Why did you give bread and meat to those two, even though they didn't bring you anything with which to barter or trade?" he asked.

"Oh, we don't barter here. Each gives of their ability, and in turn receives from us as they have need," said Benjamin.

Trevor shook his head.

"That doesn't make sense. You have to give something in order to receive something in return. That's the way it works."

Benjamin shook his head.

"Not here. God has blessed us bountifully, so we do not need to ask payment for what we do. We each do what we love; and in turn, we share with all those in need from our plentiful supplies. They in turn, as they have ability, bring us the things we need."

"But how do they know what you need? Do you tell them?"

Benjamin shook his head.

"If any of us has a need, God impresses it upon their hearts to bring of their surplus so that each of us may be blessed."

"And you never go without?" said Trevor in surprise.

"Never once have we gone without. God has always supplied our needs. Now that need may only be enough for that one day, but it is always enough and sufficient for what is required."

This was a new concept for Trevor, and it amazed him. A society that didn't function on greed, or profit, or even the exchange of money for services. Instead, it was a place where you gave and received as you had need or were able. He then watched as Benjamin reached into a basket on top of the counter, pulled out a cookie and handed it to him.

"Here, have one," said Benjamin.

Trevor bit into the cookie and was amazed at the flavor!

"Wow, this is awesome! Best. Cookie. Ever!" he exclaimed.

Benjamin laughed.

"So you like it, eh? You're welcome to take more if you want. I have plenty."

Trevor gratefully took another half dozen and thanked Benjamin for his kindness. Simon appeared in the doorway a few minutes later and looked at Trevor.

"Go wake the others. We'll be leaving in a bit," he said.

Trevor nodded, and then slipped away into the house.

"Ah, so you're ready to continue on, my friend," said Benjamin.

"We have to. While we've enjoyed your hospitality, we need to reach the wintering grounds before the first snow; and we've already lost too much time as it is."

Benjamin laughed.

"I don't believe you need worry about being late. God will ensure that you get there in time, wherever it is He has planned for you."

"Thanks, I appreciate the kind thought. But I still want to get this over with as quickly as possible; so the faster we move, the sooner we can all go home."

Benjamin nodded slightly.

"Then, I will pray for your safe and speedy journey. But before you go, see my wife. She has something for each of you."

Simon looked at him curiously, and said, "What is it?"

"Just a little gift to you out of the bountiful blessings God has given us. Food will grow scarce on the trail ahead. So we want you to have something good to eat for as long as it will last. Thus, she has made up packages filled with fresh bread, seasoned meat and cheese!"

Simon was impressed by this!

"Wow, thank you."

Benjamin laughed.

"You're welcome. Now go, she is waiting for you in the kitchen."

Simon immediately went into the back of the store, and indeed found six large packages of food waiting for them on the table, one for each of them. Simon thanked her for her generosity, gathered together the rest of his group, and divided the packages between them. Simon's group then set out on the trail again and hiked for nearly an hour. But as they did, the forest began to grow thicker around them as though closing in on them. About six miles in, they noticed that the trail, which had been well manicured and maintained for the last hundred miles, was now quickly transforming into a rugged and rustic pathway. In some places, it disappeared completely.

"It looks like the difficulty level just stepped up a notch," said Trevor.

"Yeah, no kidding," replied Simon.

This bothered him. The further they went, the more rugged the trail became, greatly reducing their progress such that Simon now feared they might even find themselves barely able to go more than a few miles in a day at best. Even so they continued on for a ways through the forest before Simon called a halt. He pulled out his navigator compass and studied it. According to what it said, they were still on the trail, even though it didn't look like it. As he did this, Trevor looked over his shoulder at the smart phone like device.

"Is that thing correct?" he asked in surprise. "I mean, are we still actually on the trail!?"

"According to the compass, we are," said Simon.

Trevor snorted.

"Could've fooled me," he replied.

"So how do we stay on the trail if we can't physically see it?" asked Aria.

"It's actually not that hard. If you know what you're looking for, and keep facing the same direction, you will eventually come out of this woods and onto the trail again," said Alex.

Trevor gave him an incredulous look.

"You sure we're gonna get through here without getting lost!?" he asked.

Alex laughed.

"Of course I am, mate. I've been through here before," he said.

Trevor looked back and forth between Alex and the forest.

"So you've navigated this before?"

Alex nodded.

"Aye, many times."

"But how do you know where the trail is if it's not marked and there's no sign of the path!?"

Alex walked up to Trevor, put his hand on his shoulder, and then pointed off in the distance. Trevor carefully followed his gaze and looked where he was pointing.

"You see those trees, lad? Do you see how they form a path through the woods?" he said.

But try as he might, Trevor couldn't see what Alex did. Simon, curious of what Alex was looking at, lined himself up with the direction Alex was pointing, and then stared through the forest ahead. At first, he didn't see anything. But eventually his eyes spotted a line of trees that appeared to be far too uniform to be natural. Suddenly his eyes grew wide.

"Oh I get it! If you ignore all of the overgrowth and just focus on those trees, you can see they make what appears to be two lines on either side that mark the way through the forest!" he said.

Trevor looked at Simon in confusion and then at the trees. But try as he might, he still couldn't see what Simon and Alex were seeing. He then looked over at Birash and Yurg who both appeared to shrug as though they couldn't see it either.

"Well, I'll take your word for it, as I can't see it," he said.

Simon laughed.

"I wouldn't expect a city slicker like you to see something like that," he chided.

"Me!? A city slic...oh you little punk," chided Trevor in return.

The others all laughed. The group continued forward through the ever thickening forest, constantly finding themselves having to struggle over fallen trees or scale steep hills, in order to make any kind of forward progress towards the other side. At one point, Yurg moved to the front of the group and began acting as a guide, helping the others to find the most easily traversable paths. Come nightfall, they setup camp at the base of a gigantic tree and tended to each other's injuries, as the number of cuts, bruises, scrapes and aching joints was considerable in number and variety. If the forest didn't end soon they might have to stop for a few days just to let their injuries heal. As Trevor rubbed his tired, sore feet, he huffed in frustration.

"You'd think that by now someone would've found an easier way through here," he muttered.

"I've had to traverse this part of the course numerous times in each direction, and it's never easy, no matter what you do. But the worst part is what's coming up," said Alex.

"Such as?" said Simon.

"At the end of this forest is a wall made of solid stone that blocks our path. It's ten yards high and situated in front of very muddy, soft earth that acts much like a moat and is impossible to cross. Therefore, we must find a way over it if we wish to reach the next part of the course."

"I'm surprised Benjamin and the other villagers didn't come out here and clear the path already to make it easier to get through here," said Trevor.

"Oh, they have. But the path always fills back in within days, and all their hard work is wiped away, leaving not a trace of their efforts behind. So they've chosen to not bother anymore, as nothing they do ever lasts, or aids the hikers traveling through here."

"Why is that?"

"Many believe it's the will of the controllers. They apparently don't like it to be easy for anyone to successfully pass through this area without first suffering much tribulation."

"So this mess is the work of the controllers!?"

"Aye, lad."

"That makes this race sound a bit more difficult than I expected," said Simon.

"Oh, trust me, mate. It gets worse. This is just the warm-up."

"And you've done this part numerous times?"

Alex nodded.

"It's easier going back than it is going forward. At least up to a point. Once we surpass the difficulties here, the next challenge is endurance. The controllers set the difficulty on this part of the course as high as they did to weed out the weak, the lazy, the selfish and those wishing to go it alone. Unless you work as a team you will never complete this hextant."

"But why would they want to do that? I would suspect that difficulties like this would eliminate too many hikers."

"But that's exactly what they want. The more who are eliminated, the better."

Simon seemed shocked by this.

"That seems silly. Why would they do something like that?"

"Because they only want the best to advance. So if one cannot get through this hextant, then there is no hope of them completing the other four. Therefore, they eliminate those they consider undesirable early on in the race so that only the good subjects remain."

"So in other words, if we wimp out, we're dead," groaned Trevor.

"Aye, lad," replied Alex.

"Well, I don't know about the rest of you, but I don't plan to quit."

"Neither will I," replied Birash.

Yurg glared at him out of the corner of one eye, and then looked away with a snort.

"Nor I, for I will not suffer the shame of failing my duty to you," he said gruffly.

"That makes three of us," replied Simon.

"Count me in as well, mate," said Alex.

"And me too!" exclaimed Aria.

Yurg studied the others with curiosity, and then gave a wide, toothy grin.

"I see that there is much spirit in each of you. That will prove useful for the journey ahead."

The group continued on through the next several days until they reached a clearing, in the middle of which stood a thirty foot tall wall of solid stone that stretched away to the horizon in both directions. In front of it was a moat of boiling hot sand that was nearly as wide and deep as the wall was tall. This surprised Alex.

"This is new," he said.

"What is?" asked Simon.

"The last time I was here, the moat was filled with an extremely damp, impassable mud. This time, it's fiery hot quicksand."

Trevor grunted in frustration.

"This is really getting to be annoying. If it wasn't hard enough to begin with, now they've made it outright impossible!"

"Nothing is impossible if God is with you," said Simon.

Trevor frowned, and pointed at the wall.

"If He's able to do the impossible, I'd love to see how He plans to get us over that wall."

Just then, a powerful windstorm erupted out of nowhere, blowing everyone off their feet. A moment later, a torrential downpour exploded from an empty sky and quenched the fiery hot sand for hundreds of feet in both directions, sending an eruption of sand and steam high into the air. At the same time, the ground shook violently, causing two large cracks to appear in the wall so perfectly straight as to defy possibility. The wind then beat against the wall, causing it to fall over onto the recently quenched sand with a thud. perfectly spanning the moat as it did. A moment later, everything went silent. Simon was the first of the terrified hikers to look up. What he saw amazed him.

"Guys?" he said in wonder.

The others looked up in fearful curiosity, and then abject wonder. Where once an impossible obstacle had been, there now stood an open pathway over the quicksand and through the wall. Simon soon began to laugh and praise God for what he'd just done.

He turned to Trevor, and said with joy, "I told you nothing was impossible with Him!"

The young man looked at the wall as he shook in fear and wonder.

"You don't have to tell me twice. I believe it!"

"You have believed, because you have seen. Blessed are those who have not seen, and yet believe that God can do anything," said Simon.

"Where'd you hear that?" asked Alex.

"It's my adaptation of what Jesus told Thomas when he doubted that Christ had risen. What he said was different, but the principle can be applied to just about anything."

"I'll take your word for it, mate. But for now, we need to get across that moat and to the other side before the controllers try to stop us."

"Good idea. Come on, everyone! Let's get moving!" said Simon.

The six travelers immediately leapt to their feet and hurried across the bridge as the recently quenched quicksand began to heat up again, sending hot, scalding jets of steam high into the air. Everyone then raced with all their speed to clear the short distance across the moat to the other side. The last to cross was Yurg, who'd no more than cleared the last few feet of the fallen section of wall when it broke in half and slowly disappeared into the steaming hot quicksand moat. The travelers all let out a sigh of relief. Simon then raised his hands into the air and began to sing.

"Praise God from whom all blessings flow. Praise Him all..."

Suddenly sharp spikes of stone began to shoot up from the ground around them in an effort to impale the startled hikers.

"RUN!" cried Alex.

The six travelers immediately bolted for the tree line as one spike after another burst out of the ground around them. Despite how fast they were running, the spikes stayed hot on their heels. Several of them got so close that they grazed Simon and nearly took Alex's arm off. One of them even erupted directly in front of Aria so suddenly that she had no time to react. She hit it head on, at full speed, and nearly knocked herself out as she bounced off. Birash rushed in behind her, and yanked her to her feet, as Yurg scooped her up from beneath. He then turned to Birash, who motioned for him to go.

"Go! Get her out of here!" shouted Birash.

Yurg roared in frustration, and then bolted forward with Birash in close pursuit. Aria quickly came to her senses, grabbed Yurg tightly around the neck, and held on for dear life. The group soon made it to the safety of the nearby trees just as the spikes stopped appearing, causing everything to fall eerily silent. A few moments later, the spikes disappeared back into the ground, with the ground healing itself again as though nothing had happened. Even so, Simon's group continued deeper into the woods for a ways before collapsing to the ground, having spent all of their energy. They then lay on the ground in a heap and took deep, heaving breaths as they tried to regain their strength. Only Aria and Birash had any energy left, and thus stood watch as the others rested.

"Well...they certainly...go out of...their way...to drive home...a point," panted Trevor.

"What point...is that?" panted Simon in reply.

"That they...don't like us."

"Ugh...point taken," groaned Simon.

Eventually, Simon's group caught their breath, climbed to their feet and continued on, weary from the effort of the day's adventure. As they continued on through the forest and back out onto the main trail again, unbeknownst to them, a blue-skinned man stood on the edge of the forest and watched them with hatred, anger and disdain. Despite his best efforts, he'd again failed to end their lives. He then looked back at the area where the spikes had appeared and growled angrily. It was obvious that someone had been protecting them because the spikes had *not* come up where he'd wanted them to. He then lifted his eyes to the sky and shook his fist.

"I will defeat you, Yeshua; and I will kill Your children. Mark my words. I will see to it that they are eliminated. No matter what You do, I *will* win."

He then disappeared in a flash of fire, and was gone.

Chapter 13

"Rise and shine, gorgeous."

Simon groaned sleepily as he felt a hand shaking him. He rolled over to see Trevor leaning over him with a plate full of food. Simon sat up and felt his head swim. He knew he was tired, but not quite *this* tired. He looked over and noticed that Yurg was gorging himself on a pair of trovets as Alex was helping himself to one of several trovet carcasses that were hanging on a spit over the fire. He then turned his attention to Aria, who looked like death warmed over, as she sat half-awake in front of the fire trying to get her wits about her. He soon realized that her hair was considerably shorter, but still frazzled and disheveled.

"What happened to her?" he groaned.

Trevor looked at Aria, and then laughed.

"Oh, she asked me to cut her hair last night. It was getting too long and was starting to become a problem. She looks a lot nicer now, but her hair's still a mess." He then pushed the plate in Simon's face again, and said, "Here, eat your breakfast while it's hot."

Simon took the plate, briefly studied its contents, and then popped a piece of roasted trovet in his mouth. The flavor surprised him.

"What'd you do to this trovet?" he asked.

"That was actually Alex's doing. While we were out hunting for breakfast this morning, he happened across some herbs that he used to make a spice rub. It's surprisingly delicious."

"Yes, it is."

Trevor smiled, and then went back to the fire.

A minute later Alex stepped over to him, and said, "How ya feel, mate?"

"Like roadkill," groaned Simon.

Alex laughed.

"I suspected as much. You slept all last night and most of today. So I figured you were tired."

"What time is it?"

"It's late afternoon right now. The young lad and I have been up since dawn hunting, while our two friends watched the camp for us."

Simon groaned again and rubbed his eyes.

"Sorry, I didn't mean to oversleep."

"Oh, bother. Don't worry about it. You and the young lady were exhausted from yesterday and needed the extra rest. Since we're still making good time, I decided that it wouldn't hurt to stay in camp an extra day and let you rest."

"I don't like losing days, but thanks for thinking of us."

"Well, it's better that we lose a few days than risk you collapsing from exhaustion before we get to the wintering grounds."

Simon nodded in understanding, and then went about finishing his breakfast. Afterwards, he joined the others around the campfire where they spent the rest of the afternoon talking and getting to know each other better. Along the way, they noticed that Aria was being unusually quiet. Well, more quiet than she normally was.

"Is something the matter, young lady?" asked Alex.

Aria merely shook her head.

"Hey, you haven't told us anything about yourself," said Trevor.

Aria looked at him with a strange sparkle in her eyes that made his heart skip a beat.

"Yes, why don't you tell us where you come from, what your life was like before coming here, and anything else you want to share. The rest of us have already told everyone our life stories, or at least the abbreviated versions of them. So you should share yours as well," said Simon.

"We have not," said Birash.

"I do not wish to share my history with you, or anyone else," said Yurg pertly.

"Well then, Birash, how about you tell your story after she does," said Simon.

Yurg gave Birash a piercing look that made him frown.

"I believe that, for my friend's sake, I will abstain from sharing that for now."

The others studied the look on Yurg's face and quickly understood his reasons.

"Alright, then that just leaves you, Aria," said Simon.

But the young woman didn't seem interested in sharing her story. She merely looked at the ground and fidgeted shyly. As she did, a strange tingle went through her body as Trevor put his hand on her knee to encourage her. She blushed shyly.

"Come on, tell us. You don't have to be afraid. You're among friends," he said kindly.

Aria took a deep breath, and sighed nervously.

"I don't want to talk about it."

"Why?" asked Simon curiously.

"You'd hate me if I told you."

"You're our sister in Christ. There's nothing you can say that will make us hate you."

Aria studied the others for several moments, but only saw encouraging looks.

She quietly plucked up her courage, and said, "I'm a thief."

She then waited to see if they would immediately ostracize her. But when they appeared interested in hearing more, she continued.

"I wasn't always one, though. It became my way to survive. I grew up in a poor family on the south side of Chicago. I was the third of five siblings, and was forced out of my house when I was twelve because my parents couldn't afford to feed me anymore. I lived on the streets after that, scrounging for food wherever I could find it. Eventually, I discovered that I could steal from people and do it well enough that I'd never get caught."

"Well, I guess that explains why she stole my dinner the night we met her," quipped Trevor.

Aria glared at him, making Trevor smile apologetically.

"I only did it to survive," she said sternly.

"Hey, you don't have to get mad at me, sister. I spent a large part of my life on the streets just like you; and in the same part of town, even. So I can relate."

This seemed to make Aria relax somewhat, as she realized that there was someone else there who understood her and her soiled history, and had likely experienced many of the same things that she had. It made her smile.

"What were you doing before you were brought here? Well, besides stealing. Were you selling drugs or your body or anything like that?" asked Alex.

Aria seemed insulted by this.

"Absolutely not! I'd never do anything like that! I saw early on what those kinds of things did to other people, and I wanted nothing to do with them!" she protested.

Trevor laughed.

"Sounds like me," he replied.

Alex, in turn, waved apologetically.

"My apologies, lass. I didn't mean to offend you. I just assumed that you might have taken up those occupations as well to survive."

"I have to agree. Given that she's from roughly the same area as me, I'm surprised she didn't. Then again, I shouldn't be. After all, I can claim almost the same thing as her. While I may have gotten into some of the darker offerings of the south side, I never did drugs. I sold them, sure, but never took any myself. Nor did I sleep around or do any of the darker things that others did. Saw too many people dying or getting into some pretty serious trouble from doing those things. So I kept myself away from that stuff. I figured I could get further in life if I kept myself clean," said Trevor.

"That was very smart of you," said Simon.

Trevor shrugged.

"Perhaps. Although, in hindsight, I give God the credit for that. I think He had a big hand in it."

"He almost certainly did," said Simon. He then looked at Aria apologetically, and said, "Sorry for interrupting you. Please, continue. If I remember correctly, Alex just asked you what you were doing right before you were brought here."

"Aye, that was indeed my last question," replied Alex.

Aria sighed slightly.

"I was trying to escape the city. However, I needed money before I could do that. So I joined up with a group of other girls who were putting together a plan to scam a local kingpin out of his money. I was hoping that my part of the haul would help me start a new life somewhere else."

"Who'd you try to hit?" asked Trevor.

"He called himself Fatdog."

Trevor did a surprised doubletake.

"You tried to pull a scam on Fatdog!? Wow, you're brave. Even I'm not *that* crazy. I mean, Fatdog isn't someone you mess with! He's killed people before who merely *thought* about trying something like that, let along succeeded. So how'd you get away with it?"

"We didn't."

Trevor blinked in surprise.

"You didn't!? Then why didn't he kill you?"

"He almost did," said Aria anxiously. "He and his men cornered us in a building down in Englewood and was about to execute us when everything suddenly went black. The next thing I remember was waking up in the orientation building at the start of the race."

"Hmm, you two sound like you have similar histories," said Simon.

Aria and Trevor looked at him briefly, and then at each other. Their eyes twinkled as they exchanged glances. Aria briefly took in Trevor's young, handsome features, blushed and then looked away. Simon smiled as he saw this.

After a bit, Aria looked up at the others again, and said, "You're not going to be mad at me because I'm a thief, are you?"

"Not at all! You're part of our team, and a friend. Whatever your past was, it's behind you. All that matters now is getting home," said Alex.

"I'm with him. Whatever you've done in the past; stays in the past, and we won't hold it against you in any way," said Simon happy.

Aria smiled shyly.

"Thanks."

She then looked at Trevor who smiled very kindly and lovingly at her. As she studied Trevor's face, she felt her heart leap within her. She again looked away and blushed shyly. Trevor noticed this and smiled even wider. She looked back at him again, and once more her heart leapt within her. She didn't know why, but she liked the feeling. She would have to explore it a bit more some day.

Simon's group continued on for several more days until the forest abruptly gave way to a beautiful patch of sunrise colored wild flowers that stretched both to the right and the left as far as the eye could see. On the edge of the patch, directly ahead of them, was a single, solitary tree. Its branches spread out before them like a gigantic umbrella, which made it appear as though it were welcoming the hikers to its domain with open arms.

"Take a look at that!" exclaimed Aria.

"Okay, that's just cool," said Trevor in amazement.

Alex gestured proudly to the field, and said, "Lady and gents, I'd like to welcome you to the third hextant."

"We're there already!?" said Aria in surprise.

"We are indeed."

"So what's next? Do we have more hazards to deal with?" asked Trevor.

"We do. However, this hextant is about endurance. So you'll find yourself hiking over many hills and valleys along the way, as the path through here is in no way smooth. As such, you will quite often be forced to push yourself beyond your limits."

"How large is this next section?" asked Simon.

"About twenty three hundred miles. It's one of the longest on the course. The next one is even longer. The last two, though, are thankfully short, albeit very difficult," said Alex.

"Will we be able to keep the same pace in this section that we have so far?"

"Not likely. Even so, if we keep going and don't stop for any great length of time, we should make the wintering grounds with time to spare. And if not, then we should still arrive before the first snow falls. If we come up too short, we can just build a shelter of our own to winter in, or stay in one of the local towns along the way. The only issues with that will be gathering enough food to carry us through until spring."

"Do the controllers supply hikers with food in the cabins?" asked Simon.

"Aye, they do. And nearly any other resource you may need for the winter. That's why they're preferred by most racers for wintering over."

"In that case, we'll want to ensure that we reach the cabins before winter at all costs, as I don't want to risk starving to death if it becomes difficult to find food once the snow flies."

"We have our skills in hunting that you may rely upon," said Birash.

Simon pursed his lips.

"As useful as that is, I'd rather not place the entire burden of our survival on your shoulders because we were late reaching our destination. No offense, of course."

Birash smiled.

"None taken, my friend."

The group then continued forward into the field of wild flowers, stirring up large swarms of little black bugs that were hiding among the flowers as they did. This in turn brought out large flocks of brilliant yellow and green colored birds that flitted in and out of the flowers like little sparrows in pursuit of the bugs. Aria laughed and giggled at this as the little birds would dive into the grass or flowers all around her, and then appear moments later with their mouths full of bugs. They all marveled at the seeming symphony of colors and sounds as the birds happily devoured the bugs until they had eaten their fill, after which they flew away to their nests in the trees of the forest behind them. In the midst of this feeding frenzy, one of the birds landed on Aria's shoulder and seemed to study her curiously for several moments before flying away. This made Aria laugh and squeal with joy.

"I think one of them likes you," said Trevor.

"Their feathers tickle!" said Aria with a giggle.

Simon reached down and picked some of the flowers as he made his way through the thick canopy of color at his feet causing a large swarm of bugs to rise up and encircle him like a black fog. Immediately, dozens of the swallow like birds dove on him and began gorging themselves on the bugs before flying away again.

"Wow, I wish we had bug control like that back home," he chuckled.

One of the little birds then flew up to Aria and hovered in front of her as she studied it curiously. She then held out he hands to the bird. To her surprise, it happily landed in her hands and began grooming itself. Several more joined it, and the small group happily began to chirp and sing as they all set about making merry in her hands. This went on for nearly a minute before they all took to the air again and flew away. Aria was disappointed.

"Awe, they're so cute. I wish I could keep one!" she said.

Trevor laughed.

"I'll buy you one when we get home."

Aria's eyes sparkled excitedly.

"Would you!?" she asked.

"Absolutely!"

"Awe, thank you," she said gratefully.

The group then continued on for nearly a mile further until they crested the top of a gentle hill where everyone stopped and stared in wonder at the land that stretched out before them. It was clearly not flat in any way as the ground weaved and wandered back and forth in a beautiful, green sea of hills and valleys that rose and fell like gigantic earthen waves upon a coat of many colors. It was at this point that Simon realized that the trail had once again vanished. He pulled out his navigator and noticed that, while they were most certainly still on the trail, it appeared much wider than it had in the past. He showed this to Alex.

"What do you make of this? I've never seen the trail this wide before," he said.

"That's because the path is up to you for now; and thus, your compass is expressing that fact. So, you can choose to take whatever way you wish through here," replied Alex.

"So you get to pick your own poison in other words."

Alex shrugged.

"I wouldn't express it that way, but it would certainly be one way to look at it."

They then continued over the first hill in front of them, through the valley on the other side, and then up the next hill. While this felt easy for them at first, by the time they reached the top of the fourth hill, it was quickly becoming apparent who was in good shape and who wasn't. Eventually, Simon was forced to sit down to catch his breath.

"You alright, mate?" asked Alex curiously.

Simon nodded.

"I'll be fine. I would expect to be in better shape by now. But I guess twenty years of hugging a desk and sucking down junk food has really taken its toll. But give me a little bit to catch my breath, and I'll be fine. I hope, anyways."

"You sure you're not gonna have a heart attack, old man?" chided Trevor.

Simon laughed as he patted his gut.

"Given the shape I'm in, nothing would surprise me. Either way, even if this is a bit taxing on my body, all of this climbing is doing me a lot of good. I haven't been this skinny in years."

"Aye, mate, I've definitely noticed that you have indeed been losing weight. You've grown noticeably thinner since I met you," said Alex.

Simon chuckled.

"Yes, I have. And yet, despite how hard this is, I'm thoroughly enjoying myself. It's definitely helping to make me healthier. Too bad it took me coming here before I did anything about it. I mean, I've been threatening to lose weight for years, and yet I never did anything about it. Then

I come here, and the next thing you know, I start losing it by leaps and bounds. It's certainly a rough way to lose weight, but you can't deny the results," he said with a grin.

"I think all of us are in better shape. Heck, I'm feeling better than I ever have," said Trevor.

"Me too!" replied Aria. "What about you?" she said, looking at Birash and Yurg.

Yurg glared at her.

"Where I come from, those who grow lazy die quickly," he said flatly.

Birash said nothing, but merely shrugged, as though affirming Yurg's statement. The others looked at each other awkwardly for a moment, but said nothing else.

Simon looked up in surprise as several flashes of light flickered on the distant horizon. Trevor caught this as well. However, the others didn't see it as their eyes were fixated on the ground as they focused on where they were stepping so as not to stumble and fall in the growing darkness of late evening. Simon would've already stopped by now on most days; but today, he felt like pushing the group as long as they could hold out. The others seemed to agree with his decision. Again, more lights flickered on the distant horizon. This soon caught the attention of Trevor.

"Was that lightning I just saw?" he asked.

"I think it was," replied Simon.

Trevor began to sniff at the air just as Simon had taught him; but all he smelled was wild flowers and fresh, green grass.

"I don't smell anything coming," he said.

"We may not for a while. It depends on what direction the wind is blowing, and how far away the storm is. For all we know, it may be far enough away that all we'll see is some heat lightning. Especially since I can't see anything I could identify as cloud tops."

Trevor pondered this.

"Hmm, that's possible. I mean, we've seen that kinda thing a few times already. Even so, do you think we should stop? It *is* getting hard to see where we're going; and while I don't know how you're feeling, I'm up for stopping for the night. I know you wanted to keep pushing ahead, but my feet are killing me."

Simon looked at the others in his group, and asked, "How are you guys feeling? Myself, I want to see if we can't get at least another mile under our belts before stopping. Yet, at the same time, if you're not feeling up to it, I'm okay with just stopping here for the night. But that's up to you guys. If you wanna stop, I'm okay with that."

"Can we, please?" begged Aria.

"I would agree as well," said Yurg.

"As would I," said Birash.

Simon stopped and looked at the others in surprise.

"Are you guys really that tired?" he asked.

The others stopped and looked at him with pleading eyes.

"I'm ready to collapse. I only wanted to keep going because you did," said Aria.

"I'm a little winded too, mate; but I can continue on if you'd like," said Alex.

Just then, Yurg pressed through the middle of the group and sat down at Simon's feet.

"With all due respect, oh fearless leader," he said, with a hint of sarcasm, "Some of us do not have the same stamina as you do. So if it is of any consolation to you, I believe it would be wise if we were to stop for the night before something…unfortunate happens."

Simon thought about this briefly, and then nodded.

"Alright, then we'll set up camp here. No point having everyone committing mutiny or falling out dead because we pushed too hard," he said with a grin.

Aria gave a grateful sigh of relief and plopped down on the ground where she stood without even taking off her pack or anything. She just leaned back against it and lay quietly as she tried to catch her breath. Trevor took off his pack, set it on the ground, and then helped Aria get hers off as well. Even though she was tired, she didn't need to be wearing it all night long. Simon shrugged slightly, pulled his off, and then pulled out his tent. More lights flickered in the distance. He again turned his eyes towards the horizon and studied it. As much as his eyes told him a storm was coming, the air told him a different story. He soon returned his focus towards setting up his tent. He and Alex then set about gathering firewood, grass or anything else that would burn from the local area and brought it back to camp. But, by the time they returned, both Yurg and Aria, as well as Trevor, were sound asleep. Only Birash was still awake. Simon studied the motley bunch of sleepers and was surprised that none of them had setup their tents. They'd merely wrapped themselves in their ponchos and fallen sound asleep. But what made him smile the most was seeing Trevor and Aria laying on the ground cuddled together with Yurg in the middle as though using the tiger as a source of heat in hopes of staying warm. Either that or he made a perfect furry pillow to sleep on.

Weeks earlier Simon never would've thought it possible that he'd ever see anything like this. Before this, Yurg would've objected to this. But this time, he didn't seem to mind. In fact, he appeared to be taking somewhat of a liking to the two teenagers, even though he wouldn't admit it. This made Simon smile. Alex saw this too; and then looked off in the distance as yet more lights flickered on the horizon. He soon looked back at Birash, whose very dark complection made him almost completely invisible into the growing darkness. It was clear that he wasn't asleep yet, or even attempting to do so. But Alex couldn't tell why. He wondered if it had something to do with the incredible endurance that he'd displayed on so many occasions. It was that quiet strength that Alex so admired. It seemed like, no matter what Birash went through, he never stopped, and no one ever heard him complain. Not even once. It'd given Alex an incredible respect for the young man. People like him were rare these days. Just then, the wind picked up. He turned and sniffed at the air in search of the tell tale smell of rain or even storms in the air. However, there was still nothing that he could smell that spoke of either. He was somewhat thankful of this. He then tapped Simon lightly on the shoulder to get his attention.

"What'cha need?" asked Simon.

"Do we really need to light this fire?" he whispered.

Simon sighed.

"I've been kinda wondering that myself. I mean, half of our team is already out cold; and I'm sure the rest of us aren't that far behind," he said.

"I agree. Even if you were to light a fire, it would be wise to keep the majority of the wood we've collected for the morning meal."

Simon pondered this briefly before looking off to the west again. A brilliant spiderweb of lightning lit up the distant horizon and illuminated the outline of a tall, powerful thunderhead that peeked up over the distant hills. He pondered this for several moments, and then shook his head.

"Alright, then let's not light one right now. We had a hard enough time finding what we did. So let's cover over the wood to keep it dry in case it rains and save it for morning, unless we get so cold during the night that we need to light a fire to warm up."

Alex nodded slightly.

"I agree. I'll see to it that the wood is covered. In the meantime, you go lay down and rest. You need to sleep just as much as the rest of us."

"Thanks. Have a good night."

"I will."

Simon then made his way over to his pack and pulled out a small tarp which he used to cover his pack to keep it dry, after which he climbed into his tent. A few minutes later his eyes fluttered shut, and he drifted off to sleep. He was awoken with a start an hour later by what sounded like someone banging on a large kettle drum. He was surprised to find that the wind had picked up considerably, and there was now a strong smell of rain filling the air. However, when he looked around to see where the storm was, he was pleased to see that it was passing comfortably to their south. If they did get any rain, it would only be a small amount. Even so, the thunder and brilliantly flickering bolts of lightning made it impossible for him to get back to sleep. He soon climbed out of his tent and looked back at the others. To his surprise, despite the incredible noise, Trevor, Aria, Alex and Yurg were all sound asleep.

However, Birash appeared to still be wide awake. He was sitting quietly in the grass on the edge of the camp as he studied the storm intently, but did not appear to move at all. Simon wondered if he was actually watching the storm, or if he might have fallen asleep sitting up. After a bit, he withdrew into his tent, closed his eyes again and tried to sleep. But the continued peals of thunder, along with the roar of the wind, kept him awake. He rolled over again and looked in the direction of Birash. Eventually, he got up, walked over to where he was sitting, and took a seat in the grass next to him. However, just like before, the large Nigerian man did not move nor make any indication he was either awake, nor aware of anything around him. Simon studied him quietly for several minutes, but said nothing. Eventually Birash turned and looked at him.

"Could not sleep?" he asked.

Simon grunted.

"Not with this storm making a racket like it is," he grumbled.

Birash smiled.

"I can understand."

The two men then sat in silence for a while longer.

After a bit, Simon turned to Birash, and asked, "Is there any reason you're still awake?"

Birash nodded slightly.

"I am worried about my family," he said.

"How many are there?"

"Seventeen."

Simon blinked.

"Well, someone's been productive," he chided.

Birash laughed.

"No, my friend. We are not all from the same parents. However, we are all orphans. I am...the family leader, if you will. It is my job to protect, feed, shelter and provide for the others."

He gave a deep, heavy sigh as his eyes drifted towards the ground.

"I have been very worried about them since coming here, for without me, I do not know what will become of them," he continued.

Simon sighed.

"I can respect that. I grew up in a large family with six other brothers and sisters, as well as countless aunts, uncles and cousins. Our family reunions are usually pretty big."

"And what of your family? Your...children?" asked Birash.

"Well, that's the funny thing. The rest of my siblings all have big families of their own. Myself, I never got married for some reason. Never felt interested in it. Either that or I never found the right one for me. But if God wants me to have a wife, He'll send me one. If not, then I'm content being single the rest of my life. Even Paul said it was good to be single. But that doesn't mean I wouldn't love a few children of my own," replied Simon.

Birash smiled.

"Yes, they are a great blessing; no matter how they may come into your life."

"Agreed. Speaking of which, if you don't mind me asking, what's your connection with Yurg? You two seem to have kind of an odd relationship."

Birash nibbled slightly at his lip.

"Yurg...is hard to explain. How we came together involves several continents and a series of unfortunate events that led up to where we are today."

Simon glanced back at Yurg briefly. Just then, a powerful bolt of lightning ripped across the sky and brought with it a clap of thunder so loud that it shook the ground, as though it'd been struck with a massive hammer. Yet none of the others stirred or even roused slightly. Simon was somewhat jealous of this. He wished he could sleep just as soundly as they were. However, his conversation with Birash was proving to be quite fascinating, despite his insomnia.

"Anything interesting that might shed a little light on how you two came to know each other?" he asked.

Birash sighed.

"When we first met, Yurg was an animal in great need. One of the local warlords was keeping him as a pet. However, he abused and starved my friend nearly to the point of death. Seeing his plight, I put myself at great personal risk in order to rescue him, after which I worked very diligently to tend his wounds and nurse him back to health."

"Yet he still hates you."

"He does. But why, I do not know. It may be because of what was done to him, or because he thinks I worked for his abusers."

"Did you work for them?"

Birash shook his head.

"Never. However, to save my friend, I...lied about where my loyalties laid. I had to if I wanted to gain access to his cage. There was no other way. I believe he still remembers my conversations with the guards the day I came to save him."

"So, is that why he hates you?"

Birash nodded.

"I'm sure it is one of many."

"So let me get this straight. You risk your life to rescue him from the clutches of death and nursed him back to health; and yet he still wants to kill you?" said Simon.

Birash sighed.

"Sadly, yes."

Simon crossed his arms as he thought about this.

"That still doesn't explain how he got here. I say that because I have yet to see the controllers, or whoever they are that operate this race, bringing anyone or anything else to this planet which isn't human. Yurg seems to be the odd man out. Or in his case, the odd tiger. He's the only non-human in this entire race I've seen so far. Even Benjamin said as much. Apparently, he's the first non-human in memory to ever be entered in this race which then makes me wonder why they did it. The controllers I mean. It really makes no sense to me."

"Perhaps it was done in order to present a challenge to me that I could not overcome."

Simon thought about this for several moments before nodding.

"That's entirely possible. I can absolutely see them doing something crazy like that. I mean, after all, they are a sick, sadistic bunch of goons, if nothing else. I'm sure they don't care about Yurg, but I'll bet they want to see you fail in any way they can, and he's a good start in that direction."

Birash grinned as he gave a slight chuckle.

"Perhaps. However, I do not believe they expected him to have such great honor."

Simon laughed in return.

"No, I don't think they did either, or else they might've reconsidered their idea. And, ya' know, that might just play to our advantage."

"How so?" asked Birash curiously.

"Anyone with the level of honor that Yurg has will almost certainly be a valuable asset. As such, I think he's gonna prove to be extremely useful to us throughout the rest of this race. But even if he's not, I still want to make sure he gets home, just like us. He's part of our team, after all, even if he doesn't want to be. And, like with Trevor and Aria, if he's willing to trust me, and if the Lord permits, I will make sure he makes it to the end just like the rest of you."

Birash smiled.

"I am sure he would appreciate that."

Simon nodded.

"Oh, I know he will. And, despite how tough he pretends to be, he's actually a very nice guy. Or in his case, a very nice tiger."

Birash laughed.

"Yes he is."

The two men then continued talking for another half an hour as the storm to their south slowly began to wind down and dissipate. But as they did, unbeknownst to them, Yurg was listening carefully to each and every word they said as he lay quietly by Aria's side, even though he showed no signs that he was even awake. And, as he listened to the two men talk, he took every single one of their words to heart, and pondered them deeply.

Chapter 14

As Simon's group crested the top of one of the many hills that surrounded them on all sides, he spotted a welcome sight not far ahead of them: A gently flowing river. They'd run out of water four days earlier, and digging for water had proven nearly impossible as the rocky ground that covered the gently rolling hills around them was too formidable to dig into to any great depth. The only thing that'd kept them from dying of thirst was a freak thunderstorm along the way; as well as several foggy mornings in which the dew was exceptionally heavy on the ground. During these times Simon had made the others setup their ponchos such that they acted as dew traps, giving them at least a little water to go on. It hadn't been much, but it'd been enough. The group quickly took their fill of the cool, refreshing water; and began not only filling their canteens, but also anything else they could find that would hold water. Some of the things they chose to use weren't very practical, but they were better than nothing. The more water they could carry, the better. Especially, if water was going to become ever increasingly difficult to find along the way.

It was bad enough that each of the resource nodes were over thirty miles apart by now. That, by itself, made things difficult enough as it was. It was even worse that, in this part of the course, the nodes would not supply them with any form of drink or beverage at all. It quickly gave everyone a whole new appreciation for even the littlest things, such as a simple drink of water. Also, due to the odd way in which the resource nodes were operating, combined with their ever increasing difficulties in capturing wild game, the group found themselves low on food as well. That'd always been in short supply before. But now, it'd gotten so bad, they were finding themselves more often than not either going without or only eating one meal a day in order to conserve rations. This was having an immediate impact on their stamina, slowing them down considerably. So, unless they found significantly more and consistent sources of nutrition, it might even stop them entirely.

As the group rested by the edge of the river in an effort to gather their strength for the next part of the trail, Simon noticed several very large fish in the water. And, even though he hadn't used his bow since meeting Alex, he'd still kept it with him in case it was needed, and now was definitely one of those times when it'd come in handy. So he took an arrow, tied a piece of light weight string around it, notched it up, and very carefully and patiently looked for signs of fish in the water. Trevor came down by his side and watched him intently. He considered asking Simon what he was doing, but after knowing Simon for as long as he had, he decided to just stay quiet and watch, for there was always something new to be learned by doing so. He watched as Simon carefully panned the water's surface with a skillful, practiced eye before eventually spotting what he was after. He slowly drew the arrow back, took aim, and then let the arrow fly. It briefly hissed through the air before hitting something just under the surface of the water with a deep, solid thud.

He then dropped the bow, grabbed the string, and began trying to reel in his catch. As the fish came close to shore, Trevor dove into the water to help him land it. However, before long, he found himself in the fight of his life with a fish whose sheer size shocked him. Even Simon was impressed with how big it was. This was clearly a monster. Trevor battled relentlessly with the writhing fish as it fought desperately to free itself. But it kept slipping out of his hands no matter what he tried. This was causing the young man to grow frustrated.

"Grab him in the mouth!" shouted Simon. "Or grab him in the gills! Either one will give you a good grip on him!"

And Trevor did exactly that. Still, this didn't help him land the fish, as it fought even harder than before. Eventually, Yurg dove into the river to help Trevor. But after getting tail slapped several times he gave up and retreated back to shore. Eventually, Trevor held on long enough that the fish grew exhausted and finally gave up fighting. Not wishing to squander his opportunity, Trevor drug the fish to shore with the last of his rapidly dwindling strength and was assisted by Simon who helped him haul the catch onto dry land. Once safely out of the water, Trevor collapsed to the ground as he tried to catch his breath. Simon tried to haul the fish further onto shore, but found that his strength too was running out. Seeing Simon's dilemma, Alex and Birash rushed in and helped him drag it back to camp. After Trevor had caught his breath again, he rejoined them in the camp. But once he got a good look at the true size of the fish, he was amazed it hadn't had him for dinner.

"Man, that's a big fish!" he said in amazement.

"Yeah, it definitely is. They generally don't get this big back home," said Simon.

"So how are we going to divide this up? I mean, this is a *BIG* fish!"

Just then, Yurg stepped forward, and said, "You may choose whatever parts you wish to eat, and I will settle for whatever remains."

The others all looked at him in confusion. This was not typical of Yurg. They wondered what'd come over him that he'd suddenly become so polite and generous.

"I have to gut him out first. So if you want to start with that, I can give those to you to chew on as we won't eat them," said Simon.

Yurg nodded.

"That will be fine."

"Then fish guts it is!"

Simon then set about cleaning the fish, first by disemboweling it, and then scraping the scales off with his knife. As he scraped the fish, Yurg took the bowels that were removed, picked them up, and then trotted away a distance to eat them in privacy, not wishing to offend the other members of the team. Simon looked at Alex and Birash, and with a few body gestures, motioned towards Yurg as though asking what'd gotten into the big cat. Both men shrugged. Simon shook his head slightly, and then went back to cleaning the fish. Once it was ready he put it on a large stick over the fire that Alex had collected and left it there to cook for some time before slicing off several pieces and serving them to the others. Yurg, after finishing his meal of fish guts, returned and waited patiently for the others to finish their meals. Once they had eaten their fill, he then took only the parts that he felt they would see as unappetizing, such as the head and the tail, and ate them as well. The rest he left for his team to eat. By now, even Aria was taking notice of the changes in Yurg; but she wasn't sure why they were happening, or where this curious new attitude would ultimately lead.

The next morning, Simon awoke at sunrise to check the fish traps he'd set along the banks of the river. As he did, he met Trevor coming the other way.

"Oh, this is a pleasant surprise. Where'd you come from?" he said chidingly.

"Yurg got up just before sunrise and left camp heading north. But I haven't seen him since. So, I went looking for him," replied Trevor.

Simon waved dismissively.

"Ah, he's probably out hunting for his breakfast."

"Yeah, probably. So what are you doing?"

"Checking my fish traps."

Trevor laughed.

"No more bow fishing?"

"Pfft, after what that last fish did to my arrow, I'm going the more economical way and just using primitive fish traps to catch them. I probably won't get as big a fish this time; but at least they'll be easier to bring ashore than that last beast."

Trevor laughed and patted his belly.

"Yeah, tell me about it. I'm still stuffed from last night. That was quite a feast."

"No kidding. Too bad we don't have a way to smoke or salt some fish, or I'd be putting up a bunch of it for the trip ahead."

"Well, even if we can't, if this stuff we cooked last night lasts long enough, we should be able to bring it with us, right?"

Simon nodded.

"For a day or two, but not much beyond that or we risk getting sick. So we'll have to play it safe and not keep the leftovers for very long."

"Sounds good. Well then, I'm headed back to camp. I need to finish my morning bible study, and then get back to walking Birash through how to read."

"Cool. So how's he doing?"

Trevor nodded approvingly.

"Surprisingly well, actually. Although, I think part of that is due to the stuff the controllers shoved into our heads. But hey, if that helps make us better, then I'm all for it. The only question I have is if they'll ever take it out."

Simon shrugged.

"No idea. Although, I'm less worried about that than I am about what hidden 'gotchas' these implants might have."

"Such as?"

"Mind control, for one. If they can take control of our bodies and make us do things against our will, imagine how problematic that'll be."

Trevor crossed his arms and frowned.

"You have a point. That's especially bad when you consider Birash and Yurg. If the controllers took control of them, they'd be a two-man wrecking team."

Simon grunted.

"I know. That's why I'm praying that these implants are only limited to the couple of things that Alex has told us about so far. Because I certainly don't want to consider what the other possibilities might be, if they exist. What we're dealing with already is bad enough."

"Pfft, tell me about it."

Later that evening, Simon sat quietly on a hillside overlooking the river and chewed on a cold piece of fish as he watched Aria and Trevor talking with each other. They'd slowly gone from a pair of unfortunate strangers who more or less hated each other, to what he would now consider cordial neighbors. But they didn't appear as though they were quite ready to step into the role of friends just yet. They were still at that stage where they were feeling each other out to determine how far they wanted to go with their relationship. Although, Trevor did seem more interested in moving forward on his side of things than Aria was. She was still very self conscious and cautious about opening up much to anyone, even him, despite her clear interest in him. Nearby, Birash and Yurg lay on the grassy hillside and appeared to be talking casually with one another, even though their conversations were typically limited, with many long silences between words. Even so, it appeared as though Yurg had softened considerably to Birash. He wasn't quite ready to be friends just yet. However, their relationship had at least advanced enough to put Simon at ease about them.

Even so, deep down, he wished they would become friends. But even if they didn't, at least they were no longer bitter enemies. If nothing else, that was a step in the right direction.

He sighed as he thought about his life back home. While he was thoroughly enjoying himself here, despite the tough conditions, he missed his books, the Internet, his overly stressful job, his farm and even the annoying rooster that loved to peck at his feet every time he went to feed the chickens. One of these days, that rooster was gonna be invited over for Sunday dinner, and would be the guest of honor. That is, assuming of course, that he was still alive when Simon got back. If his family hadn't been stopping by regularly to check on his animals, most of them would likely have starved or died of thirst by now. His two Shetland pony's would probably still be alright, as they had plenty of land to graze on, and an ample supply of water nearby. But not the chickens. Unless someone was out there every day making sure the food and water was filled, they would run out of both by the end of the day.

Even so, of all the things he missed from his former life, the greatest and most important of these was his quiet time with God. Every morning before work, but after chores, and every evening after work and after chores, he would spend time in his study or the living room simply reading the Bible and praying. Sometimes, he'd only spend twenty or thirty minutes; and at other times, he'd spend the entire afternoon reading and praying. While there were ample opportunities to read his Bible whenever they'd stop for a break or for the night, and even sometimes in the early morning before everyone else awoke, he missed those quiet moments of solitude with God. Even though he could go off on his own for brief periods of time to get away from the others, it was always best to never go far. In many ways, he wished he could return to his previous life; cluttered and busy as it was, just to be able to have those moments of alone time with God once again. He missed Sundays at Church too. But his personal time alone with God was the most precious of all those. As he was contemplating this, Alex walked over and sat down next to him.

"What's on your mind, mate?" he asked.

Simon shook his head.

"A lot of things. I'm just thinking about what life was like before we came here; wishing we could all go home, and to go back to life as it was."

"Aye, I can understand that. I've thought about that many times myself. But don't focus on it too much, or you'll lose sight of the present. Because, the only way you'll get out of here alive, is to put your everything into this race with the goal of winning it."

Simon nodded.

"I agree. Which brings up another thought I wanted to run past you. It's nothing serious. Just a little advanced planning on my part. You and I are the only two 'wayfinders' of the group; you more than me, obviously. As such, I'd like to start training the others on how to do what we do. Yurg will obviously do well enough on his own. However, Trevor and Aria are both city kids without a stitch of woodland training; and Birash, well, I'm not sure quite how much he knows. I suspect he has some experience; however, I get the feeling that he's a city kid as well; although, probably not to the degree of Trevor and Aria. That's why I think we need to teach them 'wayfinding' and 'pathfinding', as both will be important skills for them to have out here. That way, if something ever happens to the two of us, or we get separated, I want them able to take care of themselves and possibly even finish the race alone if need be."

"That's a good idea, mate. But how do you propose to do that?"

"Well, I was thinking of letting Trevor do a little pathfinding for a while. It's the easier of the two skills the learn, and sometimes the more important one. But, he'll do that under our watchful eye, of course. So, I want to start out by teaching him the basics; and then let him try it for a while on his own. I figure it'll have the unfortunate side effect of making our journey considerably rougher and slower for a while. But, once he gets the hang of it, we should pick up speed again; and in the process, he will gain some valuable skills. After that comes the fun of teaching him wayfinding. Since they have no real compasses here, I'll have to teach him the old fashioned way of doing it; which really would be better for him to know anyways. After we get him trained up on at least pathfinding, I plan to start working on the others and teaching them the basics too, one at a time, until they're all proficient at it. I eventually want them able to do it in their sleep."

"That sounds like a great idea, mate. But are you going to formally train him, or do you intend to let him learn as we walk?"

"Well, I'll walk him through the basics first before I let him out on his own, so that he has a good foundation on which to begin his learning. After that, he'll learn as he goes. I also want to do this to put a little distance between him and Aria for a while. We need to give her a little room so he doesn't go and smother her. He's clearly ready to go full speed ahead with a relationship, but she's not. So rather than just letting the hormones flow unrestricted, I plan to channel all that energy into better things. Therefore, by keeping him focused on the job of pathfinding, I think it'll give her more time to come out of her shell and warm up to the group. I mean, she's already doing that now; but not as fast as she should be. So a little separation between those two, from time to time, won't hurt any. And in the end, we should hopefully have another well-trained pathfinder and wayfinder in our group."

Alex pondered this briefly.

"I'm very impressed with your idea, mate; and especially with your concern for the young adults in our group. Well, two of them, anyways. I'm unsure of exactly how old Birash is."

"Yeah, I've been wondering that too, but he won't tell me. The best I can guess is that he's in his early twenties or so. He's another one we need to work on getting out of their shell."

Alex laughed.

"Indeed we do, mate."

Chapter 15

Over the next several weeks, Simon gently took Trevor under his wing and began to teach him the art and skills of a pathfinder as they continued down the trail. To Simon's surprise, Trevor took to it a lot quicker and easier than he'd expected. He still struggled at some things. But under both Simon and Alex's careful tutelage, he slowly began to come around and learn the skills he needed. Even so his inexperience regularly showed through as he would often unintentionally lead them off course, or down a less than advantageous path. However, failure is often the best teacher, and after the first week, Simon slowly became hands off, letting Trevor learn from his own mistakes, only stepping in when necessary. Slowly, bit by bit, the young man began to figure it out. Sometimes, Yurg even helped him with pathfinding when even Simon and Alex got stumped a few times.

And while his patience with Trevor wasn't the best, and with Birash even less so, Yurg did understand what Simon and Alex were doing, and thus he did his best to help them through the process, knowing that his future might depend on it someday. At the same time, he didn't mind doing this all that much, as it had the welcome effect of slowing the pace just enough that he was better able to keep up without inconveniencing the others. Being a tiger who needed up to sixteen hours of sleep per day, it was proving difficult for him to keep up his strength without sufficient rest breaks along the way. Especially since the humans in his team were able to survive on as little as six hours of sleep a day. Even so, he didn't complain too much, as he didn't want to be left behind and lose track of Birash. But even he had his limits. If it hadn't been for Simon's kind consideration of him, allowing the tiger to take just enough breaks throughout the day to keep up his stamina, he probably would've fallen behind long ago, or even been abandoned altogether.

Yet he also liked the results that the demanding pace was producing. It'd greatly boosted his stamina, which proved beneficial to him in many ways. Eventually though, his willingness to endure paid off, as one day, the group crested a hill and found themselves facing a lush green valley that spread out before them for miles in every direction. For nearly the past month, through the growing warmth of mid summer, they'd been forced to hike over one hill after another in an arduous daily struggle in the direction of the finish line. But now the land ahead of them seemed to flatten out for a ways which would provide them with a much needed break from the constant routine of climbing and descending repeatedly. Even more intriguing was that, at the very bottom of the valley, lay an extensive series of fields that surrounded a humble little hamlet of no more than twenty houses, and modest ones at that.

"Whoa, what's that?" asked Trevor in surprise at seeing this.

"That's the village of Pongo. It's not much to look at, but they're very friendly to travelers like us. They'll even give us hot food, and a warm place to sleep for the night if we ask," said Alex.

Trevor gave an excited shout.

"Woohoo! What are we waiting for then!?"

Simon and the others laughed. Trevor then bounded down the hill towards the village with energy unbecoming of his tired and worn out state. The others soon followed, and eventually joined him at the bottom of the hill as he lay in the grass panting heavily while berating himself for his foolish over expenditure of precious energy. The others chided him about it a little, but not too loudly, as they too felt just as tired and worn out as he did. As they all walked together into the village, they were met by a kindly old lady who greeted Alex with a giant, toothy grin.

"Hello, love. How are you?" asked Alex.

"Daba boh ne! Ishtaka tara bosh ne desha?" she asked.

"Just escorting another group to the finish line."

"Dabo tin!" replied the woman.

Simon cocked an eyebrow, and then leaned over to Alex, and asked, "What did she just say?"

"She asked how we were doing," said Alex.

Simon screwed up his face, and asked, "In what language!?"

"It's Bonisi, the local dialect," replied Alex.

"That's fine, but why can you understand her and I can't? I thought the stuff they installed in my head would allow me to understand anyone?"

Alex shook his head.

"Only fellow racers. However, she's not like us."

"How so?" asked Simon curiously.

"Toka tara burah?" asked the old woman.

"Yes, we'd love to," replied Alex.

The woman beamed with joy, and then motioned for the others to follow.

"What'd she say?" asked Simon.

"She invited us to come to her house and stay for a while," said Alex.

Simon shrugged and followed him.

"So is Bonisi used a lot throughout the course?"

"Nearly everywhere. Although there are also quite a few here who speak English. But I would say that at least half or more speak only Bonisi."

Simon rolled his eyes.

"Great, something else to learn."

"Don't worry, mate. I'll teach you everything you need to know to interact with the locals."

"Good, I hope so. However, why didn't you tell us about this before?"

"It wasn't relevant at the time. I thought to tell you later when it'd be more important to know as we come into more populated areas."

"So there's more places like this coming up?" asked Simon.

Alex nodded.

"Quite a few, actually, and bigger. Although, we won't encounter all of them, as not every village or town is located directly along the trail."

"Ah, so some of them are off the beaten path."

"Exactly. Those off the main trail tend to be those who speak only Bonisi; while those along the trail primarily speak English, or some other language."

"What other languages?"

"French, German and some Spanish, as well as Arabic, Chinese and several of the African languages. However, the majority of them speak either English or Bonisi; so we will still be able to communicate with them."

"Well, that's good to know."

As the small group followed the woman into the village, an older man appeared from a nearby house, spotted Alex, and then raced over and embraced him excitedly.

"Alex! How are you my old friend!" he shouted.

"Jacob, it is good to see you! May we lodge here tonight?" asked Alex.

"Need you ask? Come, come! My home is your home!" said the old man.

Simon's group followed him inside, slipped off their packs, and then sat down around a large wooden table.

"Nyant bosh itara?" cried the old woman from another room.

"Yes, please. Thank you," replied Jacob.

"Alright, my curiosity is killing me here. We can both understand him; and you two can understand her, but I can't. Why is that?" asked Simon.

"Because, he's a first generation racer, and she's a third," said Alex.

"What do you mean by first and third generation racers?" asked Simon in confusion.

"To understand that, you need to know that this race has gone on for at least half a millennia that we know of."

"Geez, that long and nobody's won it yet!?" said Simon in surprise.

Alex shook his head.

"None that I'm aware of. If they had, we wouldn't be here."

Simon snorted in frustration.

"Well cripes, that kinda kills my hopes of winning," he muttered.

"Don't give up just yet, mate. Just because nobody has won doesn't mean that nobody will. Given that you have me as your guide, your chances of succeeding are far greater than they would be if you were to do this alone. Besides, we'll be fine so long as we don't give up trying."

Simon cocked an eyebrow.

"But you quit your first time through," he said.

Alex sighed.

"Aye, I did, and much to my shame. Even though I lost my group, I still should have completed the race, even if it meant going back and gathering another party."

"Hey, not to butt in or anything, but I'm dying to hear your answer to Simon's other question, about the language and generations thing," said Trevor.

"Ah, right. I almost forgot. The woman you met is a third generation racer. By local standards, we are all first generation racers, as we were brought here from Earth. Anyone who is second generation and beyond is someone who was born here."

"So why the funky language?"

"I'm not entirely certain. Nobody knows where it comes from, or how it came to be. Some believe it to be an adulteration or blending of languages over time, drawn from those who were brought here over the centuries. I only know it because some of the locals taught me how to speak it. It's really a simple language to learn. But our translators won't translate it into our native languages unless it's spoken by a first generation racer, and only because they too have the same embedded translator technology that we carry in our heads."

"Why is that?" asked Simon.

"I don't know. I suspect it has something to do with how the implants work. They may require two identical translators to be in close proximity to each other in order to function. Or they may purposely be forbidden from translating anything spoken by the locals as a means by which to drive a wedge between them and us."

"But why do that? What purpose does it serve?"

"The controllers hate the locals. It was never their plan for any of the racers to ever stop and build settlements, settle down, have offspring or anything like that. They also dislike the idea that the locals, through their farms and various levels of technology, are able to provide, on occasion, material support to the racers who pass through their borders. The controllers want everything that we either acquire or interact with to be under their direct control. They still allow us to interact with those of the second and later generations. However, they frown on it greatly."

"Well, that seems a bit cruel and sadistic if you ask me," muttered Simon.

Alex frowned.

"And you have just described with supreme perfection who the controllers are."

"Yeah, I'm starting to realize that. So, how far do these villages and towns go?"

"Almost all the way to the finish line. We won't encounter them very frequently, but there are many of them out there which we will pass through as we move forward."

"So, wait a second here. You're telling us that there's villages like this all the way to the end of the course?" said Trevor.

"There are."

"So why hasn't someone near the end just headed over to the finish line and completed the race already!? I mean, they're right there. Why not just cross it and get this mess over with?"

Alex shook his head.

"Unless they're a first generation racer like us, they can't. The controllers won't allow it. Anyone who did not enter the race at the reception station cannot cross the finish line. If they try, they will die, and nothing will be gained by it."

"How do you know?" asked Simon.

"Because many have tried, and all have died. There are many first hand witnesses to this fact who have been there when it happened."

"So in other words, unless you came in through the start point the same way we did, you're just dead weight?"

Alex shrugged.

"Not dead weight, per say, but most definitely unwanted by the rulers of this world, and disqualified from competing in or completing the race. They are also strongly discouraged from interacting with those like us who are participating in the race. Although, most ignore those warnings and do whatever they so please."

"So how do they know who is a legitimate racer?"

Alex pointed to the red dot on his wrist, and said, "With this. It's how they know who you are, where you are, and if you are permitted to access any of the nodes."

"What happens if someone steals it?" asked Trevor.

"The controllers will kill them on the spot."

Trevor blinked in surprise.

"Well, that'll certainly discourage theft."

"Aye, it does."

Simon looked at his, and said, "So if I lose this, I'm officially out of the race?"

Alex nodded.

"I'm afraid so. However, I believe that is the least of our worries. There has been increasing evidence over the years that the controllers may be growing as weary of this race as we are."

Simon smirked.

"Well, that's an interesting twist. Do you think they'll end it before someone finishes?"

Alex shrugged.

"I don't know. But given how they've been so benevolent to travelers of late, it may indicate that they're trying to increase the chances that someone will eventually win."

Trevor snorted.

"If you call this benevolent, I'd hate to see what sadistic looks like."

"So what about the old man? He's obviously a first generation racer; and yet, his wife isn't. Why is that?" asked Aria.

Alex grinned.

"It's called love, young lady. He met her in this village years ago as his group was passing through, and fell in love. As such, he chose to stay behind rather than continue on. In many ways, I'm glad he did. He's been an invaluable asset to myself and many others who've come through here in the numerous decades since then."

Just then, Jacob appeared from a side room, along with his wife, and set bowls of a thick, green soup, several loaves of bread, and glasses full of a thick malt drink on the table. They then gave a bowl full of fresh meat to Yurg. He cautiously sniffed at it first, and then gave it a taste. Pleased with the meal he'd been offered, he thanked them for their generosity, and began to eat. Jacob and his wife then turned and left the room. Simon took a quick second and prayed over the meal, after which everyone dug in and consumed their meals gratefully.

"So how hard is this Bonisi to learn? You said it was fairly easy?" asked Simon as he chewed on a piece of bread.

"Aye. As I said, it's not a difficult language to learn. It's like Hebrew. Once you learn the alphabet, and the meanings of the individual letters, the language itself becomes very easy to understand as the letters are the language," replied Alex.

"That's very interesting, as I studied Hebrew for a while. So if it works the same way as that, it should be easy enough to learn. Now, is it a left to right or right to left language?"

"You mean the written language?"

"Yeah."

"Well, fortunately for us, it is a left to right written language. However, I do not believe you will have to deal with anything written in the course ahead."

"Maybe not, but I still think it'd be a good idea for all of us to learn every aspect of the language so we're not left at a disadvantage at any point."

Alex thought about this for a bit, and then nodded.

"Fair enough, mate. If you'd like, we can begin with your first lesson this evening. It shouldn't take me more than a few hours to get you up to speed on the basics," he said.

"Sure, I'd love that."

The others then continued eating in silence. After a bit, they finished their meal and sat back, satisfied with having their bellies full. As they did, Aria noticed something.

"Simon, you've got some soup on your beard," she said.

Simon looked down curiously and saw she was right. Trevor laughed as Simon wiped it away.

"How long are you gonna let that grow out, Grizzly Adams," he chided.

Simon blinked, and then chuckled.

"Grizzly Adams? That show's older than you are! Where'd you hear about that?"

Trevor laughed.

"I watched late night reruns just like you did."

"Reruns? Ha! I grew up watching that show! It was one of my favorites. Oh, and speaking of my beard, what's that little bit of peach fuzz on your chin there?" chided Simon.

"I don't know about the rest of y'all, but my stash is pimp, yo," said Trevor jokingly.

"Pimp? You look more like a bad impression of King Louie," chided Alex.

Everyone laughed, except Birash and Yurg, who didn't get the joke.

"Hey, speaking of beards, why do you have one, Alex? Being SAS, I'd think you'd always be clean shaven," said Simon.

Alex shrugged.

"We only shaved while we were on base. When we were in the field, we were allowed to grow out our beards. So I haven't shaved since I first arrived here, save only to shorten my beard in the spring in preparation for the summer heat," he said as he proudly stroked his beard.

Simon nodded.

"Yeah, that makes sense, I guess."

Just then, the door opened and a very haggard old man stepped into the room. Trevor and Aria were the first to notice this.

"Hey, who's that?" asked Trevor in surprise.

Alex turned around and quickly recognized the man.

"Father Mathews!" he shouted.

A moment later, Jacob stepped into the room and was horrified at what he saw!

"Mathews! What are you doing here!?" he shouted.

He then hurried across the room and helped Mathews into a chair.

"You're supposed to be in bed," he said sternly.

Mathews pointed to Simon's group, and said, "God has sent me to speak to these travelers. He has a message for them."

Simon's group froze.

"Wh-what m-m-message?" stuttered Aria anxiously.

Mathews looked at Simon, and said, "God has brought you here for a purpose. You will be His hammer that will shatter the power of the controllers and help bring freedom to all who have been imprisoned on this world. You are also called to be a teacher to others, and a lighthouse of wisdom for those who need a word of truth from God."

Simon gagged in surprise.

"What!? I'm no teacher! Good grief! I'm lucky if I don't sweat rivers doing presentations at work! Besides, God's never called me to be one before."

"He has. You just never realized it, as you take to your gift naturally."

Trevor raised his hand, and said, "I'll vouch for that."

"Me too!" said Aria.

"I as well," said Birash.

"But-but, you must be mistaken," said Simon insistently.

"God does not make mistakes," said Mathews sternly.

"But that's not one of my spiritual gifts!" protested Simon.

"Yes, it is. As I said, you take to it naturally; thus, you would not have known you had it."

Trevor raised his hand curiously, and asked, "What are these spiritual gifts you're talking about?"

"They're gifts from God to aid you in your walk with Him. Your gift is 'helps'. You will be a great asset to your friends throughout this journey, and to all who you encounter," said Matthews.

"What about me?" asked Aria.

"Your gift is 'discernment'. While you are a quiet one, your ability to see and understand the world around you will be of great benefit to your group and to those whom you encounter."

"But how do I use it?"

Matthews smiled.

"You don't. When God has need of it, He will manifest it within you."

"What about me?" asked Birash.

Mathews studied him briefly, and then smiled.

"You have the gift of 'mercy'. God will use you to reach others, and show them the truth of His love to them, including your companion."

Yurg perked up slightly at this, uncertain what the old man meant. He looked at Birash and was intrigued at his smile. He folded his ears to the side in curiosity. Birash was his sworn enemy; one he wished to kill at his first opportunity. And yet, despite this, there was something special about him. Never once had Birash been mean or condescending to him since they'd met. In fact, he'd gone out of his way several times, even putting his own life at risk, to help him. Yurg pondered this in his heart. Even though he couldn't get past his hatred of Birash, he'd slowly begun to soften towards him and the others. While it would be some time before he could ever call them friends, he was most intrigued at how kindly Birash, and especially Simon, were treating him. They didn't see him as an enemy, or a bother, or anything less than a friend. He looked back at Mathews who studied the six intrepid travelers and began to wonder if his mission to kill Birash was actually the right thing for him to do. Even though he knew he had to, he was beginning to question that decision. He then watched as Matthews turned his attention to Alex.

"Great things await you up ahead, my friend. Be vigilant and cling to this band of friends until the very end. They will lead you to your destiny."

Alex nodded.

"Aye, I will."

Mathews then looked back at Simon.

"Take care of those in your charge. Great dangers await you. But as the Lord God says, 'I will be with you, always.' So go in peace, for your path is blessed."

And with that Mathews slumped over and died.

"Mathews!" shouted Jacob.

Alex leapt up from his seat and rushed over to Mathews. He quickly examined the old man, but found his body to be lifeless. Panic crashed over him.

"Trevor, help me get him back to his hut! We need to get him into his bed! Jacob! Call your wife! We need hot water and some medicine!" shouted Alex.

"No. There's no need for that," said Simon.

"What!? Don't just stand there! We have to help him!" shouted Alex.

"You can't help him anymore. He's gone."

"No he's not! He's..." said Alex, his voice trailing off.

But as his eyes fell on Mathews, he knew Simon was right.

"No, he can't be gone," he said in disbelief.

Simon shook his head sadly.

"I'm afraid he is."

Jacob dropped to his knees and began to wail. His wife came in moments later to see what all the fuss was, and soon joined her husband in crying as she immediately realized what'd happened. Alex turned away and began to pace anxiously as he tried to deal with the pain that was welling up inside him. He'd known Mathews for years, and his passing hurt him deeply. Every time he'd come to the village, the old man had treated him so well, even pleading with him several times to "find God" as he would say. Alex soon turned and stormed out of the house. Aria raced after him. A few minutes later, they returned, both their faces covered in tears. Even though Aria didn't know Mathews personally, she still felt sadness at his death. That evening, they dug a simple grave in the shadow of a large nut tree that Mathews had often enjoyed sitting under, and buried him there. Simon's group then spent the rest of the night in silence. Afterwards, they remained in the village for several more days, resting and recovering their strength before setting off on the trail again. They walked on in silence for most of that day, until it was time to stop and setup camp for the night. As Simon began building a fire, Alex slipped off into the surrounding hills with Birash and Yurg to hunt for dinner. Once the fire was going, Simon, Trevor and Aria sat down and began talking. It wasn't long before the topic drifted to spiritual gifts.

"Simon, that Mathews guy said I had the gift of helps. What is that?" asked Trevor.

"It means you're a helper to others. One way to look at it is that you're someone who works behind the scenes; and sometimes in the limelight, helping others to make their work better and more effective. If it wasn't for Christians with the gift of helps, a lot of work in the church wouldn't get done; or if it did, it would be of less quality, and quantity, than it is with them."

"So, does everyone get a gift like this when they're saved?"

Simon nodded.

"They get at least one for certain. Some people get a whole shopping list of them. The thing is, they normally manifest themselves within a short time after you're saved; some more prominently than others. The part that throws me is that he said I have the gift of teaching. I've never been a teacher. Even my pastor would agree with that."

"Well, I wouldn't say that. The amount of things you've taught us already is incredible! I mean, in the short time after I was saved, you've managed to teach me enough that I was able to lead Aria to the Lord. Your teachings even helped me change from an arrogant, foul-mouthed, street punk to...well, someone who now sees just how bad he was. Before this, I didn't even think about the things I did, or whether they were good or bad. Yet now, I feel like the worst sinner of all time. I mean, I'm still shocked that Jesus was willing to save me. If I'd been in His shoes, I'd have tossed my punky little butt straight into Hell years ago."

Simon smiled.

"That's called 'grace'. God loved you so much that He sent His Son to die for you so that you could be saved. In Greek, it's known as 'Agape', which means 'unconditional love.' Nothing we do can earn it. God gives it to us freely. Hence, 'grace'. If we'd earned it, it wouldn't be called grace. It'd be called restitution. Grace is giving someone something they don't deserve."

Just then, Alex returned to the camp. As he approached the fire, Trevor noticed the odd, dove like birds that he was holding.

"What are those?" he asked.

"They're a local bird called a klek. Yurg stumbled onto a nest of them just a click north of here. They're quite good eating. But, it'll take me a bit to get them cleaned and cooked; so don't let me interrupt your conversation," said Alex.

"Where's Birash and Yurg?"

"Still hunting. They should be back shortly."

Simon nodded, pulled out his Bible, and began reading verses to Trevor as he resumed their bible study from the day before. As he did, Aria watched this and smiled, knowing that Simon was, once again, very naturally exercising his gift of teaching, even if he didn't realize it. But what intrigued her the most was seeing the expression on Alex's face. Even though he appeared to be ignoring them, she could tell that deep down he was absorbing everything Simon was teaching. She smiled and quietly said a quick prayer that God would change his heart. She then turned her attention back to Simon and soaked in his teaching like a sponge.

Chapter 16

After a long, restful night's sleep, the group broke camp the next morning and continued their journey. But the further they moved from the village, the more difficult things became again. To make matters worse, it began to rain nearly every day, making travel increasingly difficult. More than once, they found themselves sliding or tumbling wildly down hillsides, or having to traverse rain saturated muddy earth that acted more like quicksand than any semblance of solid ground. It was causing Trevor no end of grief trying to find the best way forward for the entire team, and a lot of stress. Even the two experienced pathfinders in the group were finding it extremely challenging to pick the best path across or around each of the increasing number of obstacles they were encountering. But, despite this, they allowed Trevor to continue leading the group, as they knew the experience would be good for him. Still, there were times when things didn't go exactly to plan; and sometimes took a rather unfortunate turn of events. In one case, while traveling down one of the hills, Birash lost his footing on the slick, muddy hillside and began sliding rapidly towards the valley below, taking out everyone else below him like dominoes as he went.

Eventually, they all came to rest at the bottom of the hill in a giant, laughing pile of bodies. However, it wasn't always fun and games. The weather made it nearly impossible to keep up their food supplies. Hunting was challenging at best in good weather; but nearly impossible in this near constant rain. Even worse, the persistent moisture made it difficult to preserve food for later use on the trail. But through all of this hardship, no matter how bad it got, there was never a shortage of prayer. Even Yurg began to join the others in praying, not because he believed in Jesus; but rather, because he saw that it worked. He'd watched in amazement time and time again as the prayers of the others were answered, and sometimes in very amazing ways. Seeing the incredible things this simple act of faith was producing, he felt that the least he could do was add his voice to their requests. But the best part of this was that, at least to him, no matter how bad it got, they never went hungry, as there was always at least something to eat, even if it wasn't all that much, or didn't taste very good. But to him, sometimes having something edible was better than nothing at all, even if it didn't taste good. After two weeks of this constant slogging through mud, rain and endless misery, they found themselves filthy, mud caked, tired, smelly and exhausted. Eventually though, the skies cleared; and the sun came out. Soon after this, Trevor spotted something in the distance.

"Hey guys! I think I see a town!" he shouted.

Simon stopped, pulled out his binoculars and looked in the direction Trevor was pointing.

"Well, if I didn't know any better, I'd say you're right," he said.

"Let me see," said Alex.

He took the binoculars and had a look for himself.

"Well, well. It appears we made better time than I expected."

"What is it?" asked Simon.

"That is the city of Trail Point. It's the central hub in a vast network of towns and villages that dot the landscape around us for miles in every direction. It's also the gathering place for every kind of vice imaginable."

"So, are all the villages around here independent of each other, or are they part of a much larger republic or kingdom?"

"Well, it's a bit of both really. All of the villages we've been to so far are all independent. However, Trail Point, while also independent, doubles as the capital of a much larger kingdom known as the Keep of Woes. It's a demi-kingdom run by a coalition of barons who control everything that goes on inside it."

"Wow, tyranny by committee," quipped Simon.

Alex laughed.

"Something like that. As long as we only go out during the day, we should be fine. But you still need to always be aware of your surroundings. The slave trade in this area is very active; and if you're not careful, you'll find yourself on the auction block before you know it."

Simon nodded.

"I'll make note of that."

An hour later, Simon's team entered Trail Point, and made their way down to one of the local Inns where they found rooms for the night. Simon, Trevor, Birash and Alex all shared one room, while Aria and Yurg took another. After they got settled in, they wasted no time in availing themselves of the bathhouse, scrubbing off the layers of dirt and grime they'd accumulated on themselves and their clothes over the last two weeks. But, of the six travelers, only Yurg did not want to take a bath. He was content to clean himself in more traditional feline ways now that ample water was available, and the risk of once again soiling his fur was no longer an eminent danger. Aria offered to bathe him anyways, but he refused. However, after some gentle pleading from her, he relented and allowed her to scrub his back. At first, he seemed annoyed at this special treatment. But, as she worked to wash the mud out of his fur, he gradually relaxed and began to enjoy it, eventually finding it to be very enjoyable. When everyone had finished bathing, and their clothes had dried out, they dressed again and found their way downstairs to the pub where hot food and cold drinks were in ample supply. As they sat around a large table in the far corner, Simon studied the scattered collection of patrons in the room and took note of each. At first, they made him feel uneasy, as though he were being examined as a possible victim.

But in time, he realized that this was merely his imagination getting the better of him, as most in the room were more interested in their drinks than him. He then studied Aria, knowing that she had the gift of discernment, but saw no fear in her eyes as she didn't see anything to worry about either. This further put his mind at rest. If she wasn't worried, then he didn't need to be either. Eventually, a waitress came and served their food, but was a little uneasy about Yurg. Even so, she remained cordial and catered to everyone's needs, regardless of their race or species. The next morning, the group awoke late; and after checking out and eating a hearty breakfast, wandered out into the town. Song, dance, music, and the cry of merchants mingled with the voices of hundreds of people all bartering with dealers of every kind for the things they needed most. Intermixed into this cacophony of loud voices and music were dozens of unique and delicious fragrances, some of which they'd never smelled before. One especially delightful odor made Aria's mouth water.

"Mmm, what is that incredible smell!?" she asked.

"Pantia bread. It's made with a sweet local herb that's something of a cross between mint and cinnamon. It's extremely delicious. We can pick up some if you like," said Alex.

Aria squealed with glee. Alex laughed.

"Right then, we'll do that. But first, I have to exchange some of our things for the local currency. Most merchants in the market only accept money, as they prefer to leave the trading of raw goods to a handful of shop keepers."

"Don't you have some copper left over from your old cabin?" asked Simon.

"Aye, I do. But we'll need more than just a handful of copper rings if we wish to get anything of significance here."

"Alright, that makes sense. Then, we'll wait for you here."

"Actually, all of you need to come with me. You have things in your packs that I need."

"Do you want us to pull them out now?"

"No. I'd prefer it if we didn't let the locals know what we have. The more we look like poor, hungry travelers, the less likely they'll be to take interest in us."

"Well, that makes sense. Alright, lead the way."

The group soon made their way over to a large wooden building along the main street that looked reminiscent of an old frontier trading post. Inside, it smelled of fur, leather and musty earth. All across the walls were items for purchase of every shape and kind, from rudimentary tools, to advanced and complex items only available from the resource nodes. However, Alex ignored these, and instead made his way to a large counter at the back of the shop. Behind it stood a tall, burly man who smiled and greeted Alex as he approached.

"Well, howdy partner! Long time, no see! How ya been?" he said in a Texan accent.

"I'm fine. We need to convert some barter stock into the local currency," said Alex.

"Ah, I can do that as always. However, who is this with ya? Are they another party you're leading down the trail?"

Alex nodded.

"Aye, mate, they are. We're just in town long enough to get cleaned up and restocked. After that we need to be on our way."

"Ah, good to hear. So, what've you got to trade this time?"

Alex pulled a bundle of Trovet furs out of his pack and laid them on the counter. The man inspected them briefly; and then said, "I can give you twelve coppers for these."

Alex cocked his head in disbelief.

"That's less than you gave me last time."

The man nodded.

"I know. But they're not in high demand right now. In fact, I've still got some left over from last year, so I can't give you as much as I'd like."

"Fine, I'll take it," muttered Alex.

The man counted out the money and handed it to Alex. The others then brought their packs to Alex, one by one, and allowed him to pick certain items out of them. After he'd gone through them, the man studied the pile intently.

"I can give you nine silver and twelve copper for these."

Alex nodded, and said, "Done."

The man counted out the coins, and then handed them to Alex.

"Aren't you going to barter with him for a better price?" whispered Simon.

Alex shrugged.

"We've known each other long enough that I know his prices, and what he can get for things. So haggling wouldn't help, as he's already given us the best price he can."

"Ah, okay."

Alex then laid two copper coins down on the counter, and said, "Can you give me six money pouches?"

The man nodded, grabbed six leather money pouches from under the counter, and then gave one of the copper coins back to Alex.

"Aren't these a copper for three?" asked Alex.

"Consider it a discount for all the great things you've done for me," said the man.

Alex smiled, and said, "Thanks, mate."

He then divided up the money and handed each person a pouch.

"This is your spending money while we're here, and for any other towns we encounter further up the trail. So don't spend it all in one place," he said with a grin.

The six hikers walked out of the building, and soon made their way over to the marketplace. But as they did, several suspicious individuals began watching them from a nearby stall. However, none in Simon's group took notice of them. Eventually, the group split up with Alex, Birash and Trevor going one way, and Simon, Yurg, and Aria going the other, as they each were interested in different things, and thus gravitated towards different parts of the market. Trevor watched Aria go with Simon and felt a twinge of fear for her. He wasn't sure why, but something didn't feel right. He could tell that she was a bit nervous about this arrangement as well.

They met each other's eyes briefly, and soon returned their attention to their surroundings. Trevor then noticed that both Yurg and Birash were feeling anxious as well. Given what Alex had told them about the city, he half expected someone to mug them at any moment. But to his surprise, few paid any attention to him; and those that did, could tell he was not someone to be messed with, and thus gave him plenty of space. It was at this moment that Trevor realized why. He was once again carrying himself in the same way he had back on the streets of Chicago. There was a swagger in his step that broadcast a powerful confidence that deterred any would be criminals. He found this to be odd, as he hadn't acted this way in months. He could only assume that it was due to his current environment, which was bringing out some of his old street habits. Apparently, given the situation he was in, his mind had automatically switched into defensive mode.

He then turned his attention back to Alex and was surprised to see that the old man had changed as well, with his face becoming hard and frightening, like that of a well seasoned soldier who had no fear of anything. Trevor was impressed. Simon, on the other hand, appeared relaxed and caught up in the moment. He wasn't too worried about this. Yet, for some reason, he felt like Simon was about to walk into trouble. He quickly shook off the feeling, as he knew Simon could easily take care of himself, and then went about studying the various booths around him for anything of interest. Simon continued to sweep the booths as well, and was intrigued at everything he saw. It reminded him of the rustic flea markets he'd regularly attended back home. But he didn't see anything that would prompt him to buy something there. Eventually though, he came across a booth with several items that made him pause and take a second look. As he did, several of the dark figures who'd been watching him earlier took notice. They quickly began to see an opportunity for personal gain.

"These three will make a fine addition to tonight's sale," whispered one of the men.

"How are we gonna bag them?"

"The way we always do."

"What about the pussycat?"

"He won't be a problem."

"I don't know. He looks too dangerous to meddle with."

"Trust me; he won't be. We'll either bag him, or bury him."

The first man grinned lustfully.

"Well, so long as he doesn't try to keep me from that cutie in the middle, it'll be alright."

"The girl? Oh don't even think about keeping her for yourself. The boss will kill you if you try."

"Pfft. Do you think I'm foolish enough to go against the boss again? No, I'm merely window shopping. If she goes cheap enough, I might take her home. But if not, then we'll simply take our share of the profits and do as we always do."

"What if she's sold to one of the brothels?"

The first man chuckled lustfully.

"If she is, I'll almost certainly become a very frequent customer of hers."

Just then, the two men noticed Yurg looking at them; his eyes piercing deeply into their skulls like fiery hot daggers. They frowned slightly, and quickly slipped away. Yurg's eyes then darted back and forth across the marketplace in search of anything else that appeared suspicious; but he didn't see anything too out of the ordinary. His group then continued down the long row of stalls until they came across a tall, lanky man in Arabian style clothing standing between two of the booths. The man studied them intently for several moments before approaching Simon.

"Good sir, could I interest you in some things for your journey? A pile of ration packs perhaps? Maybe some flashlights? How about a lighter, or maybe some more ammunition for that lovely rifle you're carrying," said the man.

Simon adjusted the rifle on his shoulder and studied the man curiously.

After a moment, he said, "Is this booth yours?"

"Oh no, sir. I have my own shop. It's just down that narrow street over there," said the man as he pointed at a nearby alleyway.

Realizing it wasn't too far away, Simon nodded and said, "Yeah, it wouldn't hurt to see what you've got. Nobody here seems to have anything we need."

The man bowed.

"Very good, sir. Please follow me."

But before he could take a single step, Aria grabbed his arm.

"Simon, don't go with him. He's up to no good!" she whispered.

Simon studied Aria for a moment, and then looked at the man.

"What do you mean?" he asked.

Aria paused briefly, and then said, "I don't know. I think it's that discernment thing that Mathews told me about. It's like my entire body is screaming danger."

The man, having overheard this, waved dismissively.

"You have nothing to concern yourself with, young lady. I merely wish to show you some of the wares that I have for sale."

Simon pondered this for several moments as his eyes flipped back and forth between Aria and the man. Just then, Yurg stepped in between them and glared at the man.

"I must agree with the female. There is something about him that is...wrong. We should avoid following him," he said suspiciously.

Simon stood quietly and glanced carefully between Yurg, Aria and the merchant. As interested as he was in seeing what the man had, common sense told him to just walk away. Eventually, he decided to agree with its suggestions, and that of his friends.

"Ya' know, on second thought, I think I'll pass," said Simon.

The man frowned.

"That is unfortunate for you," he said.

Suddenly, Simon felt something akin to fire race throughout his body. Aria, who was standing next to him, saw a man step out of the crowd and jab him in the ribs with a stun device that looked like a cattle prod. She screamed so loudly in terror that it brought the market to an almost pin drop silence. The man grinned devilishly as Simon collapsed to the ground in a heap. Seeing this, Yurg roared loudly and charged at the man with the stun device. But before he could reach him a large, heavy rope net was thrown over him, stopping him in his tracks. Another man leapt out of the crowd and thrust a stun device at him too. But Yurg was too quick for him and easily batted it out of the way before carving a gigantic gash in the man's leg with his claws. The man screamed in agony and tumbled backwards, knocking Aria to the ground. She hit her head on the cobblestone street and was knocked unconscious. Yurg tried to turn and aid her, but found himself barely able to move because of the net.

Two other men then hit him with stun rods, causing him to roar with pain. He staggered slightly, but refused to go down, even though the world around him was beginning to spin and go dark. By this time Alex, Trevor and Birash had heard the screams and were running towards him at full speed, their guns drawn and ready. People all over the marketplace scattered in every direction, clearing a path for the three travelers as they ran. Birash was the first to reach the scene and was horrified to see Simon and Aria on the ground as Yurg, entangled in a net, struggled to stay conscious as he tried in vain to fight off his attackers. Birash roared with anger and charged the closest man, but was quickly forced to take cover as a hail of bullets flew his way. While he was brave, he knew he wasn't bulletproof. The Arabian dressed man and his slaver cohorts then quickly gathered up Simon and Aria and whisked them away, leaving behind their weapons, ammo belts and back packs.

Nearby, several more men worked frantically to finish subduing Yurg, but were having a difficult time of it. Seeing the situation unfolding before him, Alex rushed over to where Birash was taking shelter and flattened himself against a nearby building. Not wanting to cause any casualties, or possibly hurt his friends, Alex held his fire as he waited for the now panicked crowds to finish clearing. Slowly, he raised his head and was immediately forced back down as bullets sailed his way. Alex glanced over at Trevor, who'd already taken cover behind a large stone fountain, and noticed that he appeared to have taken on another persona entirely. Trevor was no longer the bouncy, fun loving teenager he'd been earlier. He was now a hardened street veteran, well seasoned in urban warfare, and unafraid to face whatever life threatening challenge awaited him. Alex was happy for this. It meant he'd have a strong and very capable ally backing him up. He whistled to Trevor; and then, using hand signals, told him how many there were, who was where, and what they were carrying.

Trevor nodded, cocked his Uzi, and then leaned out from behind the fountain. The Uzi rattled with excitement as his bullets found one target, and then a second. He immediately withdrew behind cover as the slavers returned fire. Alex was next, using the momentary confusion of the previous exchange to take another peek at what was there. To his dismay, he saw Aria's feet disappearing through a nearby doorway. Simon, however, was nowhere in sight. It wasn't long before only Yurg remained behind, and he was already halfway to the door. Alex leaned out with his rifle, took careful aim and dropped two of the men that were dragging Yurg. He immediately pulled back again as bullets danced off the cobblestones nearby, sending up a spray of metal and stone chips. He pulled a small mirror out of his pocket and eased it around the corner. He soon spotted two shooters in a set of upstairs windows not far away. They were obviously the ones providing cover for the slavers who were taking away their friends. He'd have to deal with them first if he wanted to have any chance of saving his friends. Alex then turned to Trevor and signaled to him the location of the two shooters. The young man looked up quickly in an effort to spot them, and then ducked back down. He signaled to Alex and requested a distraction, which was soon provided.

A moment later, Trevor sat up, emptied the rest of his magazine at the two gunmen; and then ducked back down as Alex popped out briefly from his hiding spot and took out the two shooters in the windows as they returned to their posts, after momentarily taking cover. Trevor quickly changed magazines, and then waited for Alex's orders. Seeing that it was now clear, Alex motioned for the others to follow. They hurried across the deserted marketplace and up to several bodies that lay in the street: The byproducts of their handiwork. They quickly frisked them for anything of value, and then took up positions on either side of the door that the others had been dragged through. Alex checked the door and found it to be unlocked. He knocked, much to the surprise of Trevor, and waited for any kind of response. But nothing happened. He then turned, kicked it open and raised his rifle to the ready, fully expecting to encounter a sizable armed resistance. But instead, he found the room to be completely empty. He cautiously stepped through the door and swept the room. But he found no one inside. He then slipped over to a nearby stairwell and ascended it to the second floor as Trevor and Birash watched the first. A minute later, he returned with several bandoleers of ammunition and two rifles. Alex looked over at Trevor, and was surprised to see the young man jumping up and down on something.

"What are you doing, lad?" he asked.

"I think there's a trap door here!" exclaimed Trevor.

Just then a disturbing shout came from the street outside.

"They went that way!" shouted a city guardsman.

"Awe, blimey. Not them," muttered Alex.

Trevor rushed over to the door, spotted several uniformed guards racing towards them and grunted in frustration. He aimed over their heads and gave two quick trigger pulls on his Uzi, immediately sending the guards scampering for cover. He then raced out into the street, followed by Birash, and policed up Simon and Aria's things. The two men then hurried back into the building as Alex slammed and locked the door behind them. He then whistled at Trevor who turned and saw that he was pointing upstairs.

"Topside, mate. Keep them busy while I check out this floor," he said.

Trevor nodded and made his way upstairs. A moment later, Alex heard several short, staccato bursts of gunfire. He was thankful that there were none answering in return. As Trevor kept the men outside busy, Alex stepped over to the spot where Trevor had been standing and noticed what appeared to be an unusually round knot of wood in the floor. He carefully pressed it and watched as part of the floor slid away to reveal a set of steps that led down into a dark tunnel below the floor. His eyes narrowed in suspicion.

"This smells like the trap to end all traps. But if they've been taken down there, we need to follow. Birash, grab Simon and Aria's gear and bring it with us. Trevor! Hurry up, mate! We need to go!" said Alex.

Trevor thundered down the steps a moment later, a look of concern on his face.

"You've got that right! Reinforcements are coming, and they don't look happy," he said.

"Are they armed?" asked Alex.

"I can't tell, but I'm not gonna take any chances."

"Alright then, mate. Into the hole," replied Alex.

The three men scurried down the steps into the tunnel under the trap door and closed it behind them. As they moved down the dark passageway, they hoped beyond all hope, that they might be able to somehow save their friends.

Chapter 17

Consciousness slowly invaded Simon's mind as a thick, damp, putrid odor burned at his nostrils. He slowly sat up and struggled to clear his head. It soon became apparent that he was sitting in a very small cage, about the size of a portable dog kennel. He quietly scanned the dim, gloomy darkness around him and could make out dozens of other people on either side of him in much the same predicament he was in.

"Lord, where am I?" he thought.

It wasn't long before a group of men appeared and began unlocking cages and hauling out their occupants one by one as they went. They eventually pulled Simon out of his cage, attached a special collar around his neck and led him away. As they rounded a corner ahead, Simon noticed a line of other people forming at the bottom of a long flight of stairs that led up to a stage. Then, to his surprise, he found he'd been put in line directly behind Aria and Yurg.

Aria turned to him, and asked in a nervous whisper, "What's going to happen to us?"

"Face forward!" shouted one of the slavers as he prodded her.

She cried out in pain and crumpled to the ground. Simon growled angrily at the man and turned as though to attack him. But the man put his stun rod in Simon's face.

"Don't even think about it, fatty. You make one move, and I'll burn your face off."

"Get up girlie!" shouted another slaver as he hauled Aria to her feet.

Yurg quietly sat through all this, his ears twitching from side to side as though he were studying his surroundings, looking for a good opportunity to break free. But, given his lack of action, Simon guessed that it wasn't the right time. He heard cheers from the steps in front of them as a man shouted something he couldn't quite make out. Over the next half hour, the others in front of them were led up the stairs one by one to the same cheers and shouting. Finally, it was Yurg's turn.

"Oh God, be with him. I don't know what they'll do to him, but put Your cover of protection over him and keep him safe," prayed Simon silently.

Yurg's four handlers led him carefully up to the stage, and then set him down in the middle of it as they remained safely out of range of his claws and teeth at the end of their control ropes. Yurg looked out over a dimly lit room full of people dressed in everything from fine linen and jewels, to dirty old rags. Some among them even appeared to be soldiers.

"Barons and baronesses! Lords and lieges of every kind, and honored underworld masters of crime, I now present to you, this fine specimen. He is a strong beast, requiring no less than four of my strongest men to keep him contained," said the auctioneer.

Yurg sat proudly on the stage and looked down on the crowd with disdain and condescension.

"You are filth and scum, creatures with no honor, and cowards unable to show your faces to the one who now stands before you," he said.

"Cowards? Cowards!? How's this for cowardice, pussycat!" came a cry from the audience.

A dagger whistled through the air and embedded itself in the stage at Yurg's feet. But Yurg didn't flinch. He simply glanced down at it, looked up again, and cocked an eyebrow defiantly.

"Oh, he's a cocky one! I like him!" came a shout from the crowd.

"Yes, he's a magnificent beast, and an intelligent one too! With enough training, he'd make an excellent guard animal for your compound or castle. Of course, if you're just looking for a little fun, he'd make a great source of entertainment as well," said the auctioneer mockingly.

"Ten silver!" came a shout from the floor.

"I have ten silver! Do I hear twenty!" said the auctioneer.

"Twenty!" came the reply.

Simon listened with sickened disgust as the bidding climbed steadily higher. But Yurg seemed unmoved by all this; because, no matter how much humiliation and torture he was subjected to, he would get his revenge in due time. All he had to do was wait for the right opportunity.

Trevor leaned around a corner and studied the hallway beyond. After a moment, he pulled his head back and grunted in frustration.

"The place is crawling with guards. If we try to shoot our way out of this, we'll end up six feet under with nothing to show for it," he whispered.

"Then, we need to find another way through this place," said Alex.

Birash pointed to a nearby ladder, and said, "I suggest we climb."

"Climb!? Why?"

"To reach the attic."

"Why there, lad?"

"Because, if what I have overheard is right, it overlooks the stage where our friends will soon be sold in tonight's slave auction. If we are to have any hope of seeing where they go, we must climb above the stage where they will be so we can watch."

Alex was both surprised and appalled at this revelation.

"The slave auctions!? Oh bloody hell! Of all the places we could possibly end up, it had to be here," muttered Alex.

"Then you've been here before?" asked Birash in surprise.

"No, but I've heard more than my fair share about it. Whatever happens, we need to keep our heads cool and our lips shut. The patrons at this place tend to be the dregs of society. One wrong move and we'll either be dead, or the next items on offer."

The other two nodded. Alex looked at the ladder, grunted in frustration, and then climbed it quickly. Upon reaching the top, he began to hear cheers and raucous laughter below. Eventually, he spotted several holes in the ceiling and crawled over to one of them. What he saw next made him angry. Yurg was currently on the stage being auctioned off. Trevor soon topped the ladder and quickly scurried over to him. He too was shocked at what he saw.

"Isn't there something we can do to rescue him?" whispered Trevor.

"Give it time, lad. Rescuing a slave takes patience," replied Alex.

He then looked around and noticed that his other teammate wasn't with them.

"Where's Birash?" he asked.

"Down at the bottom of the ladder guarding our stuff. He's too big to be up here. So, I figured he'd do better being a guard dog. I doubt anyone will want to mess with a guy his size."

"Aye, probably not."

The two then went back to watching the auction. Eventually the bidding ended, and Yurg was led off the stage. A few moments later, Aria was brought on to a cacophony of catcalls and whistles.

"Aria!" said Trevor in surprise.

He began to move, but was stopped by Alex.

"Wait! Don't do anything foolish, lad," whispered Alex.

"But Aria's down there!" cried Trevor.

"I know! Just sit and watch. I think I might know how we can save them. But we have to be patient and wait for our opportunity."

Trevor grumbled, but complied.

"And this beautiful young lady here is fresh off the trail and ripe for the pickings. She'll make a excellent addition to your household staff. Or even your bedroom," said the auctioneer with a grin.

"One gold" came a cry from the front of the room.

"Baron! You want this little sunflower too!? But you have such a large harem already," said the auctioneer with playful mockery.

"Oh, but you can never have enough flowers in your garden, if you know what I mean," said the baron lustfully.

Aria shivered in disgust and fear. She could sense the dozens of perverted eyes sizing her up as their minds imagined multitudes of illicit and terrifying things they would do to her if she were to become their property.

"Two gold!" came a shout from the back.

"Three gold!" came another reply.

"Ten gold," said another.

The baron turned to the crowd, and said, "Twenty gold, and don't one of you think you can outbid me. This pretty little thing is mine, and you would be wise to accept that."

Several groans were heard from the room as the other men realized they had little chance of winning against him. Finally, the baron turned back to Aria and gave a greedy, lustful grin. Aria felt her bones turn to ice.

"I'm going to enjoy playing with you, little girl," he said as he licked his lips.

Aria recoiled in disgust.

"Well, since you've apparently killed off any chance for a higher bid, she's yours for twenty gold," said the auctioneer.

The baron pulled a pouch out of his pocket and tossed it at the auctioneer. It thudded heavily onto the stage.

"Take whatever you need and put the rest on my account."

The auctioneer picked up the pouch, studied it briefly, and then motioned for the handlers to lead Aria out. Next up was Simon. He entered to a loud chorus of boos and hisses.

"What's this garbage? He's fat and old! Throw him out!" came a cry from the back of the room.

"Be thankful. You don't have to feed the fat ones as much. At least not right away," came a mocking cry from elsewhere in the audience.

The others laughed.

"Hey, he looks like he wants to speak! Let's hear what he has to say!" cried one of the men.

The auctioneer looked at Simon, and said, "Do you have something to say?"

Simon nodded.

"Well, there's a surprise. Alright fatty, let's here it," said the auctioneer mockingly.

Simon took a deep breath, and said, "God loves all of you."

"God loves us!? Yeah, right! And my mother-in-law is a duck!" came a mocking reply.

The whole room burst into laughter as several pieces of food were hurled at Simon. But he didn't respond to any of the taunts or abuse. This surprised several people.

"What is this guy, a preacher? Hey, why don't you give us a sermon preacher boy!" came a taunting cry from the audience.

"Everyone in this world is a sinner," continued Simon.

"Oh, thank you, Mr. Obvious! You're talking to a room full of thieves and criminals! Of course, we're sinners; and we love it!"

The room burst out in a chorus of raucous cheers.

"What's the matter, preacher boy? Think you're better than us?" came another shout.

Simon shook his head.

"I do not, for all have sinned; and all are sinners, but none worse than me."

This caused the room to suddenly fall silent. They weren't sure if he was mocking them, or being frankly honest. If he was being honest, they wondered what he'd done to make him feel this way. Curiosity soon overtook the crowd, who now sat in utter and complete silence, waiting with rapt attention for his next words.

"Every one of us is guilty of sin; a crime punishable by death. Not one of us is righteous, nor good enough, to ever deserve anything but eternity in Hell. Nothing we can do, no good work, no good deed, will ever make amends for our sins or save us from eternal punishment. That's why God sent Jesus, His only Son, to die for us. He took our punishment and forgave us of our sins so that we could be saved and live with Him in Heaven for all eternity. In return, God asks that you turn from your sin, believe that His Son died and rose again to pay for your sins, and ask His forgiveness. If you do this, you too can enjoy salvation and eternal life. God loves you with an unconditional love. No matter what you've done, He still loves you, and doesn't want to see any of you perish."

Several pieces of food, and even a partially full bottle of wine, flew at him from the crowd.

"Ah, shut up, preacher boy! We don't wanna hear anymore of yer yappin', ya lunatic!" came a cry from the crowd.

Others soon joined him, but fewer mocked him than before. Some among the crowd even appeared genuinely convicted. Those that were soon turned and left the building. Those that remained became even more belligerent.

"Where's your God now, preacher boy? Why isn't He saving you? You want to know why? Because He ain't real and He don't exist! Your God is a lie; a figment of your worthless imagination!" came a shout from the front. The man turned to the auctioneer, and said, "Get this idiot off the stage! Nobody wants a nutcase like him!"

"But someone has to take him. I can't just toss him back in the dungeon," said the auctioneer.

"Then...kill him! Be gone with the crazy fool!" shouted the man.

"I can't do that either. He must be sold today."

"Fine! Then I'll do it for you!" shouted the man.

He pulled out a knife and began to approach the stage. But before he got more than a few paces, a heavy wooden walking cane cracked him across the face, sending him sprawling to the ground in excruciating pain. A stately, well dressed baroness stepped out of the darkness and glared at him condescendingly. The man looked up at her with fiery anger in his eyes as he held his now shattered, bleeding nose.

"You busted my nose, you old hag!" he screamed.

The baroness glared at him.

"Silence your mouth, or I will add greatly to your misery," she said sternly.

He growled angrily, but said nothing more, as he slipped away into the darkness to see to his injury. The baroness then turned her attention to Simon and examined him intently for several moments. She soon pulled a copper coin out of a pouch wedged firmly in her cleavage and tossed it to the auctioneer.

"Have him put with the others," she said regally.

"You'd pay for something like that!?" came a cry from the crowd.

The baroness turned towards the man and gave him a cold, withering look that made him cringe. She soon turned back to the auctioneer, who nodded, and then motioned for Simon to be removed from the stage. As he was being dragged away, the Baroness turned, pulled out a cloth fan and began to fan herself as she walked proudly back through the crowd. The other men in the room stared at her as though she were insane. But she took no notice of them. Seeing that Simon was being led away, Trevor got up and began to make his way towards the ladder. But when he noticed that Alex wasn't following, he stopped and turned back towards him.

"Hey, Alex! We need to get going! They're taking the others outside!" he said.

Alex blinked slightly, and then looked at Trevor.

"Ah, right, mate. I'm coming."

He then lingered near the hole for a moment longer before joining the others.

Simon stood in line at the back of the stage and wondered if he'd said enough in the short time he'd been allotted. Aria stood next to him, crying as she quivered in fear. She knew her future was a bleak one; but despite this, she felt an unexplainable peace fill her heart. Several more slaves were soon led up to the stage and auctioned off before the events of the night were finished. Once it was over, the patrons were allowed into the back to retrieve their merchandise. The first one to arrive was the buyer for Yurg who came and took him away. Several more came and left before the dirty old baron who'd purchased Aria appeared.

He walked over and studied her with lustful glee. Aria recoiled in horror at the stench that emanated from his body. He slowly ran his wrinkled, gnarled hands up and down her body lustfully, causing Aria to pull away from him. But he grabbed her bonds and yanked her face close to his. She sobbed and cried as she continued to quiver in fear and disgust.

"Tonight will be fun. I will enjoy getting to know you, young lady," said the baron with evil glee. He then turned to his men, and said, "Take her to my carriage!"

As Aria was being led away in tears, Simon closed his eyes, and quietly prayed, "God, be with her and protect her. Let no harm befall her, and free her from her bonds. Do not let her be defiled by this evil, wicked man. Save her, Lord, I pray."

Alex studied the alleyway behind the auction house and noticed that there were several guards standing watch nearby. They were armed with both pistols, as well as daggers and bows. The daggers and bows were used when silence and stealth were needed, and the pistols for times when heavier firepower was required.

"Wait right here. I'll take care of this," said Alex.

He then slipped into the alleyway and vanished. He reappeared behind the first man moments later and slit his throat. He did the same with the second before they even knew what'd happened, and all without making a sound. Alex then quietly dragged the bodies into the shadows before returning to Trevor's side moments later with the men's bows and daggers in hand. He handed one of the bows and some arrows to Trevor who looked at him in confusion.

"What do you want me to do with this?" asked Trevor.

"Shoot it at the bad guys, of course," replied Alex.

"But I don't know how to use one."

"Oy, mate. We'll need to resolve that first chance we get. For now, just hold the extra bow while I use this one to take out the others who are holding our friends."

"Why not just haul out the hardware and blow them away?"

"Guns make too much noise. We want to be as stealthy as possible."

"Alright, fair enough," said Trevor. He thought for a bit, and said, "Hey, you grabbed some daggers off those guys, right?"

"I did. Do you want them?"

"If they're throwing daggers, absolutely. I'm a pretty deft shot with them."

Alex was surprised at this.

"You are? But I thought you were a city chap."

"I am. But I'm also good with knives. It saved my butt quite a few times back home."

Alex shrugged and handed him the daggers.

"Here you go, lad. Just try not to hit our friends."

Trevor nodded. Alex then turned to Birash.

"Do you know how to use one of these?" he asked.

Birash nodded.

"I used them many times to hunt food for my family," he said.

Alex then handed him one of the bows and several arrows.

"Here you go, mate. Just try not to hit our friends when they come out," he said.

Birash nodded in understanding. Just then, the rear door began to open.

"Oops, we've got company," whispered Alex as he dove for cover.

Trevor quickly slipped across the street and into the shadows along with Birash. He then studied the group exiting the building, but saw that none of them were from their party. The small group walked across the street to a waiting carriage with their new slaves in tow, and then drove off into the night. Another carriage appeared a minute later. It stopped by the door and disgorged one man who went inside. He reappeared a few moments later with four burly handlers who were struggling to restrain Yurg. As they did, the coach driver climbed up into his seat as he waited for them to load Yurg into the coach. As the men fought desperately to force Yurg through the side door and inside, Trevor carefully sized up the four handlers and prepared to throw his first dagger.

"Come on, come on. Step just...ah, right there," he thought.

But before he could release his first knife, the sound of arrows filled the air as two of them came out of the darkness and buried themselves in the backs of two of the four handlers, sending them collapsing to the ground with muffled grunts. This immediately caused two of the control lines holding Yurg to go slack, raising the ire of the other two handlers.

"Hey, hey! Keep your line tight, ya fat lumux," growled one of the men.

A moment later two more arrows sailed through the air and hit the other two handlers in the chest, sending them collapsing to the ground as well. Surprisingly, in the midst of all this, Yurg remained completely motionless and calm. If anything he was extremely confused, uncertain of what exactly was happening. All that remained alive now was Yurg and the coach driver. Trevor looked back at Birash, and then over at Alex in surprise and wonder.

"Dang, I want you two on my crew when we get back home," he said.

Birash smiled and nodded. Uncertain of what was happening, the coach driver climbed down from his perch and soon spotted the dead bodies of his compatriots laying on the ground next to a somewhat confused tiger. Suddenly, an arrow drove through his chest, killing him instantly. Alex, Birash and Trevor quietly slipped out of the shadows and quickly piled the bodies into the carriage. Once they were inside and the door secure, Yurg gave out a growl that sent the carriage animals into a panic. They immediately bolted away into the night taking the carriage with them. As they did, Birash rushed over and untied Yurg's restraints.

"You alright, my friend?" he asked.

Yurg nodded.

"I am fine. But why did you save me again? Would it not have been expedient to leave me to my fate while you escaped to safety?" he asked.

Birash shook his head.

"I would not do such a thing to you."

"Why?" asked Yurg in surprise.

"Because, even though you hate me, I consider you my friend. Therefore, I could not abandon you to suffering, torture and imprisonment, even if freeing you would cost me my life," said Birash.

Yurg blinked.

"Then, you are not concerned that I still seek to kill you, even though I am presently restrained from doing so by my honor?" he said in surprise.

Birash shook his head.

"Honor is important, but Olumide is greater than any duty our pride requires of us."

Yurg cocked an eyebrow in confusion, still uncertain why someone like Birash, who he still considered his mortal enemy, would risk so much to save him. He then looked around and saw Alex and Trevor melting back into the darkness.

"Now is not the time for this. But if your Olumide will permit me, I would like to speak to you more about this at a later time," he said.

Birash smiled, and said, "Gladly."

The two then melted into the darkness and waited by the doorway for the next participants to exit with their slaves. As they watched, and waited, several more patrons came and left with their slaves before the perverted baron, two of his servants, and Aria appeared through the door. As the baron stepped down onto the street, he smiled greedily.

"I'm eagerly looking forward to my time with you tonight. You will make a nice edition to my little collection. In fact, it will be your duty to join me in bed every day until I die, as a man needs his entertainment, and youthful warmth," he said with twisted glee.

"Never! I'd rather die!" cried Aria as she struggled against the two men holding her.

The baron grabbed her by the chin and drew his face close to hers.

"Oh, don't be so crass, little one. You'll get your wish. Because once you've spent the night with me, you'll cry for more and more until it kills you," he said sadistically.

Trevor watched this from the shadows and fought every urge to rush the baron as his blood boiled with rage. Finally, he gathered his senses together and hurled one of his daggers. It buried itself deep in the baron's neck, killing him instantly. Aria gasped in surprise as the baron's eyes went wide in terror, and then rolled back into his head as he collapsed to the ground. Trevor heaved another dagger at one of the handlers who turned just in time to catch it with his bare hands. Trevor gasped in surprise as the man cackled with glee. He'd never seen someone catch a blade mid air like that before, except in the movies, and that wasn't real.

"Nice try whoever you...ugh," he said, grunting in pain as Alex buried an arrow in his chest.

The man stumbled momentarily, and then collapsed to the ground dead. This left only one other person standing. He immediately clutched Aria close to his chest and held a dagger to her throat.

"Whoever you are, stand down, or I cut the girl's throat!" he shouted.

But before he could do anything else, a giant mouth came out of the darkness and bit down hard on his arm, causing him to cry out in pain and release Aria, who tumbled to the ground in surprise. The man turned towards the mouth that held his hand and was shocked to see the blood thirsty face of Yurg staring back at him. He quickly fumbled for the dagger that hung from his belt and reached it just as Birash fired his bow, sending the arrow through the man's skull and out the other side.

"Dang, dude! Killer head shot!" exclaimed Trevor in amazement.

The man twitched, and then collapsed to the ground in a heap. Aria, who'd been terrified and fearful for her life only a moment before, stared at the man before her in confusion. Just then, the sound of feet came rushing towards her. Immediately, fear viciously gripped her heart again. She turned and looked into the darkness in the direction of the sounds, expecting the worst; but was soon overcome with joy as Trevor, Birash and Alex appeared from the shadows.

"Aria!" cried Trevor as he raced over and embraced her tightly.

Aria buried her face in his chest and wept.

"I'm so glad to see you," she cried.

"I am, too! I was afraid I'd lost you. I don't know what I'd do without you," said Trevor.

Aria went wide eyed in surprise at this. She then met her eyes with his.

"What do you mean?" she asked.

He released her, and looked deep into her eyes.

"I'm sorry I've never said this before, but I like you a lot. I just, well, never had the courage to say it until now. But I really care a lot about you. In fact, I love you."

Aria blushed.

"Trevor, I...I didn't know," she said in amazement. "I knew you liked me, but..."

"I know. That's my fault. If you don't want anything to do with me--"

Aria put a finger to his lips and smiled.

"No, no it's alright. You've always been very sweet to me, and it was your love that brought me to Christ, and your kindness that eventually sparked a love within me for you as well. I have to confess that I too was afraid to admit it, hoping deep within my heart that you liked me as much as I liked you. Now, I know you do."

"Really?" said Trevor in surprise.

Aria smiled wide, and said, "Really."

"Hey chaps, I hate to break this up, but we need to dispose of these bodies before someone else comes as we still need to rescue Simon," said Alex as he stepped up behind them.

Trevor released Aria from her bonds; and then worked with Alex, Birash and Yurg to drag the bodies away from the door and into the shadows beyond so that the next party wouldn't see them and get suspicious. They quickly recovered their weapons, stripped the bodies of anything useful, and soon returned to the shadows to wait for the next group to emerge.

Chapter 18

Simon watched as the Baroness who had purchased him appeared from the darkness of the main auditorium and strolled slowly over to him. She fanned herself proudly as she walked slowly around him, as though inspecting a cow.

"I liked that little speech you gave back there on the stage. It was so inspiring," she said with a hint of twisted sarcasm.

She fanned herself a bit more, and then closed the fan.

"Was it real, or were you just pleading with your God to save your miserable soul from a hellish life of slavery and toil?" she said sternly.

Simon straightened himself, and said, "What I said was all true. It was not a show, and I will not deny my Lord, no matter what."

The Baroness grinned slyly.

"You certain? Because I'd hate to have you whipped for lying," she said.

"I am not lying," replied Simon.

The Baroness pursed her lips as she studied him, and then put her fan under his chin as she stared deeply into his eyes. After a moment, her features softened.

"Then praise God that I have found another brother," she whispered.

Simon cocked an eyebrow in curiosity.

"What do you mean?" he asked.

She leaned over and whispered in his ear, "As Christ has freed me, so I free you."

Simon blinked in surprise.

"You're a Christian!?" he said.

"Shhh! We don't want to let the entire neighborhood know. Now come. Your friends are likely waiting for us outside."

She then motioned to her servants who turned and followed her to the back door. But just as they stepped outside, a dagger flew at one of the men. He dodged it, and quickly took cover. The Baroness immediately stepped out into the open.

"Stop right there, whoever you are. I am not your enemy," she shouted.

Her eyes darted back and forth at the shadows, but couldn't make out any movement.

Simon stepped through the door, and shouted, "Guys, if that's you, put down your weapons! She's a friend!"

"Give me one reason that a dishonorable female such as yourself should be believed," said Yurg as he emerged from the shadows.

"Trust me, she's with us," said Simon.

Slowly, Alex and Birash stepped out of the shadows, their bows drawn and at the ready.

"You wouldn't be lying to us, would you?" asked Alex suspiciously.

The Baroness raised her hands, and said, "As God is my witness, I am telling the truth."

One of her men stepped out into the street, and said in a gruff, deep voice, "The Baroness is a woman of great honor. She can be trusted, even with your life. If she could not be, I would not willingly serve her as a free man."

Alex studied the man for several moments.

"You're not a slave?" he asked suspiciously.

The man held up his arms for Alex to see.

"As you can tell, I am not," he said strongly.

Alex studied him for several moments, but could see he was telling the truth. He lowered his bow, and then motioned for the others to stand down as well.

"Why do you serve her if you're free?" he asked.

"I do it in repayment for the kindness she has shown me," said the man.

The Baroness stepped out into the street and gave a sharp series of whistles. A minute later, a pearl white carriage appeared out of the darkness and rolled to a stop near the door.

"Come now, everyone, into my carriage. We need to flee here quickly. I suspect you've drawn plenty of blood tonight, which means that if we do not hurry, the night will become much darker than it already is," said the Baroness.

Trevor wasn't certain he wanted to trust the woman. But after studying Simon's face for a moment, he understood that she could be trusted. At least, for the moment.

He then turned to Birash, and said, "Help me grab our gear."

The two men disappeared briefly into the darkness, and reappeared moments later lugging their packs and other gear. The servants of the Baroness then helped the two men load their gear onto the top of the carriage. As soon as they were done, everyone climbed inside. It was tight quarters, but they all managed to fit. The carriage then sped away into the night. As they rode through the city streets towards the countryside, Simon sighed in relief, and then bowed his head and began to pray.

"Thank you, God, for protecting us today, despite the danger," he said.

"And thank you, Lord, that I was once again able to save a brother," replied the Baroness.

"Amen," said Simon in return.

"So you really aren't the dark and evil woman we saw back there in the auction house?" said Trevor in curious bemusement.

"*OH*, you saw that?" replied the Baroness with a chuckle. "Well, that's all part of a very elaborate act I put on as part of my ministry here."

"Ministry?" said Simon curiously.

"The Keep of Woes is a den of thieves, villains and denigrates of every kind. I arrived here about twenty years ago as a naive young traveler. It didn't take long before I was captured by the slavers and sold to an old baron who wanted to use me as his play thing and personal bed warmer. But he became deathly ill before I could provide any 'special services' to him. So, I was sent to work in other parts of the house while he healed. It was during this time that I met a young servant named Davial who witnessed to me. Thanks to him, I came to know the Lord. Then, shortly after I got saved, unusual things began to happen. The old baron, who had bought me, grew weaker and more feeble which, in turn, protected me from being defiled by him; and in time, provided me with an opportunity to take control of his small kingdom. Eventually he died and, through the grace of God, and the help of Davial, I became the Baroness of Hollow Manor. It was at that time that I realized I could use my newly acquired wealth and power to help other Christians who also were unfortunately captured by the slavers."

"Like us," said Simon.

The Baroness nodded.

"As well as each of my servants, and everyone else in my employ, who are also fellow believers, and former slaves, purchased from the markets in the same way as you."

"Aria and I are believers too!" said Trevor.

"Ah, splendid! And what about you?" she said, looking at Alex.

"I'm an atheist, madam," he said flatly.

The Baroness seemed to pout slightly.

"Awe, I'm sorry to hear that. But what of your friends?"

"I am a servant of Olumide," said Birash.

"Ah, excellent! Then we too are brother and sister; albeit from different lands," she said.

Yurg cocked an eyebrow, but said nothing. The Baroness saw this, and thus did not ask him as she knew what his answer would be. They then spent the rest of the trip discussing all that Simon's team had been through on the journey so far. Eventually, they reached Hollow Manor some three hours later and pulled up to the front door of an elaborate, expensive and lavish estate. Tired and exhausted, they piled out of the carriage, trod into the mansion and were shocked to see a brightly lit interior that glistened white as pearl, silvery as the clouds and golden as the bright morning sun. Clearly, the Baroness must be someone of great wealth and power to have a house *this* nice.

The Baroness then stepped forward, and said, "Welcome to my humble abode."

Trevor snorted.

"Humble!? Yeah, try like Beverly Hills kinda humble," he quipped.

The Baroness grinned, and then clapped her hands twice. Two servants immediately appeared from a nearby room.

"Yes, Baroness?" they asked.

"Prepare hot baths and appropriate rooms for each of our guests," replied the Baroness.

The two bowed and slipped away.

The Baroness then turned to Simon, and said, "If it's alright with you, I will have my men take your gear, clean it up, and have it ready for you in the morning if you wish to leave right away. In the meantime, you're welcome to stay the night here with me."

"Thank you. We appreciate your kindness," replied Simon.

Aria looked around the elaborate mansion with star struck wonder, and said, "Can I have a tour of your house?

It's beautiful! I grew up in a poor family and never had anything nice like this."

"Can I come too?" asked Trevor.

The Baroness laughed.

"But of course! I'd be honored to show you around this wonderful gift that God has given me."

"Sweet!" said Trevor.

A moment later, his stomach growled.

"Eh, but would it be possible if we could stop by the kitchen first? I'm starving."

The Baroness laughed.

"Absolutely!"

She then led the two teenagers over to the kitchen as Birash and Yurg were escorted away to another part of the house by one of the servants.

As soon as they were gone, Alex turned to Simon, and asked, "Can we talk?"

Simon shrugged.

"Sure, what's on your mind?"

He motioned to a nearby room and said, "Let's go in here."

Simon followed Alex into a side room and watched as he closed the door behind him, locked it, and then turned back towards him.

"You really believe this stuff, don't you?" he said.

Simon cocked his head curiously.

"Believe what?"

"This whole God thing! You really believe it's true, don't you?"

Simon smiled.

"With all my heart, soul and mind."

Alex turned away, crossed his arms and stared at the far wall.

"So this is something you'd die for, right?"

"If I had to, yes."

Alex began pacing back and forth. After a moment, he stopped and looked at Simon.

"For eighteen years my parents dragged me to the local parish to listen to the vicar spout nonsense about 'Jesus is the way' and 'You must know God if you want to see Heaven.' I even heard me parents spout that same nonsense over and over again at home; but never *ONCE* did I see them live it! Not a single word of it! Me dad went to the pub every night and drank himself under the table. Pint after pint after pint. He would also sleep around with other women and treated me mum like she was a piece of meat. And me mum was no better. The things she did are unspeakable, even to a hardened, bitter old man like myself. I hated those words. 'Live like Jesus.' 'Jesus died for you.' 'Jesus loves you.' I never *once* saw me mum or dad live like this Jesus, ever. EVER! Not even the parishioners in our parish lived those words." He turned back towards the wall, and said, "Yet, I can't get the words of the vicar out of my mind. It's like they're burned in there with a hot iron."

"Maybe God's trying to get your attention, to show you He's real."

"Real? *Real*!? When did I *ever* see this Jesus become a reality in anyone's life!? Well, except yours, of course. You're the first person I've met who actually lives like he really believes this stuff. But not a single other person I've ever known."

"Well, Aria, Trevor and Birash are all believers as well. I know Trevor and Aria are kinda new to all of this; but Birash has been a believer for some time from what he tells me. He may be a quiet individual, but he's got a very strong faith."

Alex thought about this for a bit, and then nodded.

"Aye, I believe you're right. But yours....yours is special."

"How so?"

Alex sighed heavily.

"When you talked about God in front of those scoundrels back there in the slave auction, you...you...showed a love that hit my stone cold heart like a hammer. You...said things that shined a light into the darkness of my life, revealing the evil that hides within my soul."

"God says that everyone's a sinner. No one is perfect."

"Bloody hell. Don't you think I know that!? Do you know how many people I've killed, and without even a hint of remorse? Or the number of times I've lied, cheated, stolen, and did God knows what kind of other horrible things. If this God of yours is real, He'd be silly not to throw me in Hell, lock the door, and throw away the key."

"I agree. We all deserve death. It's the punishment for sin. But Jesus died to pay that penalty so we wouldn't have to."

"Well, that's fine for you. You're all chummy with Him. I'm just a black hearted old man who's about as dirty as they come."

"Jesus died just as much for you as He did for me. He's already paid the penalty for your sins. All you need to do is believe, accept His gift, and what He's done for you."

Alex studied Simon for a moment, and then asked "So I just say some magic words and I'm in your little club? Is that it?"

Simon shrugged.

"Well, it's not quite like that. First off, you have to believe you're a sinner."

Alex snorted.

"As if that were difficult. I'm about the worst there is."

"Then, you've taken the first step. Next, you have to understand that the wages of sin is death. By what you said earlier, I suspect you already understand that."

Alex nodded.

"Aye."

"Thirdly, you must believe that Jesus died on the cross for your sins and rose again, so that you would be free, and forgiven," said Simon.

"Aye, that I do."

"Then, you only have one more step to go. You must now put your entire faith and trust in Jesus Christ, and Him alone, and confess Him not with just your lips, but your heart as well. Do you want to accept Jesus as your Savior?"

Tears began to stream down Alex's face. He nodded.

"Aye."

"Then tell God you're a sinner, that you believe Jesus died and rose again for your sins, and that you accept the gift of salvation He's given you," said Simon.

Alex dropped to his knees, tears pouring down his face, and said, "God, I don't know if you can accept someone like me, but if You will have me, I give myself to You completely and without reservation. I know I'm a sinner. Blimey, I'm probably the worst sinner ever. But I know You sent Jesus to pay for my sins so that I might be saved. Oh God, forgive me for what I've done and save me. I accept Your gift with humble gratitude. I am not worthy of such a gift, nor am I deserving of Your love, but thank You so much for saving me. Oh God, I'm sorry for being so blind. So blind. Please Lord, forgive me and let me into Your kingdom. Amen."

"Amen," replied Simon with a smile.

Alex then reached over and embraced Simon as the two wept together with joy.

"Welcome to the family, brother," said Simon.

Finally, when they separated, Alex said, "Thank you for being so committed to God. Without you, I likely would've remained the cold-hearted man that I've been for so long."

Simon smiled.

"I'm merely the vessel which God used to show you His love."

"Well, you make a fine vessel. But that now brings up another question. What happens next?"

"Well, typically I tell people to first confess to at least two or three others what God's done for them. Then, I recommend finding a Bible and a church. However, since we're here, we'll have to forgo the third item for the time being and settle for small group Bible study instead. But when we get back, we'll have to get that third item settled."

Alex smiled.

"Aye, I will, mate. You have my word on it. But for now, we need to get item one taken care of; and I know just the people I want to be the first I share this with."

He then got up and hurried out of the room.

Simon bowed his head, and said, "Thank You, God, for saving Alex. I know I've prayed a lot for him throughout this trip and have been patiently witnessing to him in any way I could. And even though he seemed to rebuff You at every turn, I thank You for finally making him a brother. Take care of him, Lord, bless him and help him grow strong in You."

Simon then heard Aria squeal with joy as Trevor shouted, "Really!?"

Simon laughed.

"And bless him, Lord, as he guides us through the rest of this race. Help him stay strong and healthy as we travel, and give him wisdom and strength all the way to the very end. In Your precious name, Lord Jesus, I pray. Amen."

The next morning Simon awoke in a soft, warm bed and was greeted by the sound of birds and the smell of breakfast wafting on the breeze. For a brief moment, he thought he'd awoken at his parents home back on the old family farm where he'd grown up. But then, memories of the past several months came flooding back to him as he looked at the small red dot on his wrist. Despite his best hopes, he was still on an alien world forced to partake in a race that he most certainly wanted no part in. Just then, one of the servants peeked in the door and smiled.

"Ah, good morning, sir. I see you're finally awake. If you're hungry, breakfast is available for you in the garden," he said with a smile.

"Thanks, I'll be right down," replied Simon.

The servant bowed, and then stepped out of the room. Simon crawled out of bed, looked around the room, and then spotted a folding wall on which hung a pair of freshly cleaned hiking clothes. He slipped them on, and then hurried downstairs to the garden. There he found the Baroness reclining in a large, plush chair as the rest of his group sat around a table full of what appeared to be bacon, eggs, toast and some strange kind of fruit. At either end were jugs of juice and milk.

"Hey, Simon! Come have breakfast with us!" exclaimed Aria.

Simon walked up to the table and examined the bowls.

"What is this?" he asked.

"Well, it's not a traditional American breakfast as we were accustomed to back on Earth. But, by using certain local foods available to us, we've been able to create something that is more or less the same thing," said the Baroness.

"Grab some, Simon. It's really good," said Aria happily.

Simon quickly fixed himself a plate and began eating. As he did, the Baroness raised her hands and clapped twice. Moments later, two maids appeared.

"Please give Ms. Aria one of our special baths," she said.

Aria looked at the Baroness in confusion.

"Why? I had a bath last night," she said.

"Oh let them pamper you, sweetie. You've been camping in the dirt for months by now. I think it's time you indulged yourself a little," said the Baroness.

Aria protested initially, but was soon talked into it by the others. As the two maids escorted her away, Simon turned and studied the Baroness for a few moments before taking a sip of juice.

"I see you enjoy your position a lot," he said.

The Baroness smiled.

"It only seems that way. As I said last night, it's part of my disguise. When living among wolves, it is wise to howl like one from time to time so you aren't mistaken for prey," she quipped.

"So is that why you live like this, even though you're inside your mansion?"

She nodded.

"I never know who may be watching. So I need to keep up appearances as much as possible. While the act may be relaxed somewhat when we're inside the compound; as I trust those who serve me with my life, I still don't feel comfortable letting down completely. Only in the chapel can any of us truly be ourselves."

Simon blinked in surprise.

"You have a chapel?"

The Baroness nodded.

"It's hidden in the basement. It would be impossible for anyone to find if they didn't know what to look for."

Alex chuckled.

"That sounds rather clandestine," he said.

"Everything we do here is clandestine. The local barons hate Christians. It ruins their business because believers don't visit the brothels, gamble, drink, buy slaves or do other illicit things that earn them money. As such, we're persona non grata with the ruling powers."

"Yet here you are in control of likely the biggest, most powerful house in the entire area."

The Baroness shook her head.

"Not the biggest or most powerful by any measure, but certainly not weak or small either."

"What do you do to make money?" asked Simon.

"Mostly, trade and farming. We own a considerable amount of land in the Keep, and on it we plant and harvest crops every single year. We also control many of the mainline trade routes in the area, and trade exclusively in necessary goods and services that either the other barons can't provide, or refuse to. Anything immoral, though, we leave that for them to partake in. It leaves us less competition to deal with, and makes our business far more lucrative and profitable than all of theirs combined. In fact, God is blessing us such that we are slowly making their businesses unprofitable. In doing so, we pray that our efforts will eventually put all of them out of business. Or if not, we at least wish to make them reconsider their business choices. And, if God should so choose, we hope that some day believers will be able to walk openly in the Keep without fear of death or persecution. But for now, it will be many more years before we see that come to pass."

"What else do you do with your money and power?" asked Trevor.

"We print Bibles and other resources and provide them to anyone who needs them. We also purchase slaves who are professing Christians, such as yourself, and either free them, or put them to work here on the estate if they wish to stay. In fact, every one of my staff is a born again believer, from the butler all the way down to the scullery maid."

"Do the locals know this?" asked Alex.

"Every one of them. They think I'm nuts. But I tell them that I like having Christians for slaves. They make good, honest workers I can trust who won't try to stab me in the back or kill me in my sleep. They've seen how dedicated and loyal my servants are; and thus, they leave me alone. A few of the local barons have even bought a few Christian slaves themselves and put them to work in their households. By following my example and treating them well, the slaves work hard, and over time they slowly convert the staff members and their fellow slaves. In fact, two of the barons east of here are believers, as well, thanks in part to the Christian slaves they brought into their houses. They, in turn, now work with me as part of the Christian underground."

"Fascinating. How many are part of this underground?" asked Alex.

"There are only a few hundred of us right now; but we're growing, albeit slowly. In time though, we should easily outnumber the unrepentant; and may even, at some point, be able to come boldly into the open, as I mentioned before. That is our prayer, anyways; to be able to reveal ourselves with no fear for our lives."

"Wow, that sounds like the first century Christians to a degree," said Simon.

The Baroness chuckled.

"Well, I'm no Polycarp; but I've come very close to being a martyr myself several times."

Trevor grimaced slightly.

"Ouch, that's gotta suck."

The Baroness nodded.

"Indeed, it can."

"Uh, ma'am, I hate to interrupt, but I remember you saying you had Bibles. Would I be able to get one from you?" said Alex.

"Bibles? Ah, yes. I heard that you got saved last night, so you would now be in need of one. Let me get one for you," said the Baroness.

She clapped her hands and a servant quickly hurried over to her.

"Go below and get our friend a Bible."

The servant bowed and slipped away, returning a few minutes later with a beautifully leather bound book with a stenciled gold fish on the cover. Simon cocked an eyebrow at this.

"No cross?" he said curiously.

"The cross too easily gives away the true nature of the book when seen from a distance. So we use the same technique for disguising our bibles as the first and second century Christians did by putting a fish on the cover to identify it to believers without giving away it's true contents to the unrepentant. So far, it's worked well; although, the fish is not the only symbol we use. Sometimes we're required to use other symbols that only the believer would know or understand."

Alex shrugged.

"Right, then. I guess that works, so long as it's the same inside."

"Yes, it is. If you would like, there are benches out in the arboretum where you can sit and study quietly without interruption. If you have any questions, each of my servants are well versed in the Bible and can help you with anything you need."

"Thanks!" said Alex.

He then leapt up and hurried off to begin reading.

The Baroness looked at Trevor, and said, "You can go, too, if you like."

Trevor smiled and then hurried off as well, leaving just Simon and the Baroness behind. It was at this moment that Simon realized that Birash and Yurg weren't around.

"Where's our two other friends?" he asked.

"Out in the back. I felt they should talk, so I sent them off together for some quiet time."

Simon nodded in understanding.

The Baroness then stood up, and said, "Would you like to join me in the garden? I'd like to take a walk and would enjoy some company."

Simon shrugged, and then followed her out into the garden.

Chapter 19

Birash and Yurg walked through the luscious gardens at the back of Hollow Manor and were amazed at their incredible beauty. Yurg soon paused and contemplated his surroundings.

"This is very much like what my childhood home was like," he said.

"In some ways, it is like my home as well. I only wish that my people would not fight each other as they do, for it destroys the great beauty that Olumide has given us," replied Birash.

Yurg's eyes narrowed.

"Why do you do nothing about it? Do you not have the power to change this?"

Birash studied his friend deeply.

"Do you have the power to change the course of rivers, or command seas, or move mountains out of their place?" he asked thoughtfully.

Yurg contemplated this.

"Is it truly that difficult?"

Birash sighed.

"I'm afraid it is, my friend. It is sin that drives men to destroy one another. Only Olumide can change their hearts."

Yurg pondered this again, as he took in the exquisite and rare beauty of the garden around him.

"May I inquire something of you?" he asked after several moments.

"Of course you may, my friend! Anything! If it is within my power to answer you, I will tell you all that you wish to know!"

Yurg pursed his lips and looked at Birash.

"Who is this 'One' you continually refer to as Olumide? You say that He is the same as the Jesus that Simon and his friends speak of."

"He is. Olumide is the Yoruban name for Him. It means, 'God with us,' much as the Jewish name 'Emanuel' does."

"Yes, you said that to the others. But, if He is God, why have I never heard of Him before?"

"Because you are an animal, and He came only to save the souls of men, not beasts," came a voice to their right.

Both of them turned and were astonished to see a short, stout, feathered creature with tiny wings and a head not unlike that of a Fennec fox, standing in the garden not far from them. He barely stood three feet tall standing upright on his hind legs; and yet, looked every bit capable of holding his own in a fight, even with the likes of Yurg.

"Who are you?" asked Yurg suspiciously.

The tiny creature quietly studied the two companions for several moments.

"I am Fallon, son of Adar, son of Zek, master of the Southern Weyr," he replied.

"Are you friend or foe?" asked Birash.

Fallon studied the two companions mutely.

"I am both, and yet neither. What I am depends entirely on what I am required to be at any given moment," he replied flatly.

"Your answer does not make sense."

"You will find, in time, that there is much in this world that does not."

Just then, a blue-skinned man appeared in the garden adjacent to Fallon and glared at Birash and Yurg. He then hissed angrily as his eyes fell on Fallon. The little creature gave him a powerful, deep and commanding glare. The man hissed again.

"Leave. You should not be here," he said with incredible authority.

"You have no power over me! You are our servant!" screamed the blue-skinned man.

Fallon cocked an eyebrow slightly. He then glanced briefly at Birash before returning his gaze back to the blue-skinned man.

"You may have authority over me; however, *he* has authority over you. Now leave, or he will make you leave," he replied sternly.

The blue-skinned man hissed at him again, his anger growing even more fierce.

"Do not tell me what to do, slave! You will obey or I will destroy you!"

Fallon furrowed his brow and then glanced at Birash. He then motioned to the blue-skinned man nearby. Immediately, Birash understood what he meant. He then turned his attention to the blue-skinned man who hissed angrily at him.

"And you. I will rip your--" said the man angrily.

"I rebuke you in the name of Olumide!" shouted Birash, interrupting the man mid-sentence.

The blue-skinned man immediately froze as though a video had been paused. Fallon looked at him and narrowed his eyes.

"I warned you," he said flatly. He then turned to Birash, and said, "You need not fear him, for He who is in you is greater than he who stands before you."

Taking that as a hint to continue what he had done before, Birash repeatedly shouted, "I rebuke you in the name of Olumide!"

The blue-skinned man's features began to slowly grow harder and darker as he did. He then let out an ear piercing, demonic scream.

"I rebuke you!" screamed Birash.

The blue-skinned man eventually gave one final, terrifying, angry hiss; and then vanished in a flash of fire. Fallon nodded in approval, and then turned to Birash.

"Well done," he said.

"What was that?" asked Yurg.

"That was one of the controllers. On this world, they disguise themselves as aliens; but in reality, they are nothing more than demons."

"They are the ones who brought us here?"

Fallon nodded.

"They are. Although, they are only half of the puzzle. There are still others, humans by birth, but demon like by nature, who follow down the same dark and evil path as they do."

"Then, they are the ones who we are truly up against," said Yurg.

Fallon contemplated this briefly.

"Partially. The entire truth is far more complex than you are ready or capable of understanding at this time. Needless to say, we are watching over you, as is your God. They seek to destroy you because you present a risk to them and their plans for this race. Your God seeks to end this abomination, and has chosen you and your friends as the hammer by which He will do that. As such, you will soon see His hand moving mightily across this land, via your team and its members, as I am sure you have already begun to witness thus far in your journeys. In turn, the controllers will do all they can to prevent this. You will, therefore, have to face them and their agents many more times in the days ahead, both in the fires of nature, and through the passions of men. Until then, I leave you this warning. Do not stray from the path. Walk wisely, and trust God for everything."

And with that, he vanished in a flash of light, and was gone. The two companions looked at each other in curiosity.

"Should we tell the others?" asked Yurg.

"I believe we should," replied Birash. "However, I am not sure they will believe us."

Yurg furrowed his brow.

"Then we will have to do our best to convince them."

Alex looked up as Trevor walked into the garden and sat down next to him.

"What'cha reading?" asked Trevor.

"The book of Matthew. It's quite humbling. What's most interesting is that I finally understand it. Before this, it never made sense. Now, it's as clear as a cloudless sky."

Trevor laughed.

"Yeah, the same thing happened to me. I heard people talking about the Bible and salvation when I was growing up, but it all sounded like idiots talking. Then I got saved, and suddenly, everything I heard and read made sense."

"Aye, that it does, mate. So. where's your girlfriend?"

Trevor blinked in surprise.

"Girlfriend!?"

"Little Ms. Aria. You two seem like an item. I'd have thought you'd have made it official by now," said Alex with a smile.

Trevor shrugged. He couldn't deny that he liked Aria, or that she liked him, the latter of which was the most surprising. His heart tingled as he thought about her.

"Well, we do like each other. But it's such an odd thing. I've never been in love before. About the only thing I loved prior to this was myself. Well, I can't call it just loving. I was so wrapped up in myself, I was my own greatest idol."

He sighed heavily as he thought about this.

"I look back on that life now and wish it'd never happened. I'm so much happier now that I'm saved. I wish I had that growing up," he continued.

"Aye, so do I, lad. Our vicar tried to convince me that I needed God for many years. But I couldn't get past my parent's hypocrisy to see my own sin. I feel like such a fool for waiting this long. The things I could've done for God boggles my mind."

Trevor snorted.

"Welcome to the club," he said.

Just then, Aria's voice tickled his ears as she called out to him. He turned to see what she wanted, and was immediately blown away by what he saw! Instead of the disheveled, trail worn young girl he'd known, before him now stood a beautiful young woman. She blushed as he stood gape jawed at what he saw. He quietly took in her simple, innocent beauty, and the brilliant golden locks of glistening brown hair that cascaded down from her head and onto the simple white sun dress that she wore. The sight of her nearly made Trevor's heart leap out of his chest! He'd known she was beautiful, but never had he seen her like this before! Even Alex was taken by her simple, youthful beauty. Were he forty years younger, he would've readily challenged Trevor for her hand. Aria studied Trevor's face for several moments, and blushed again.

"How do I look?" she asked as she fidgeted shyly.

But the best Trevor could do was shake and stutter like a man who'd been kicked in the head by a mule. Aria noticed his utter speechlessness and smiled. Even though he couldn't say it, she knew what he was thinking.

She held out her hand to him, and said shyly, "Do you want to go for a walk?"

Trevor nodded, and took her hand.

"Yes, please," he said.

The two then walked away, hand in hand, through the garden; their eyes darting back and forth between where they were going, and each other. Alex grinned as he watched the happy couple walking along, nearly on top of the world with excitement.

"Ah, to be young and in love again. Well, at this point, I'd gladly settle for young," he quipped.

He then went back to reading his Bible.

"So you worked for a software company?" asked the Baroness.

Simon nodded.

"We wrote custom applications for all kinds of companies and organizations ranging from IBM to the FBI. The job was never boring."

"And you're a former farmer as well?"

"Farm kid, actually, but yes. Believe it or not, I have my own farm; although, it's not much to talk about. I do it more because I love it, as I sure don't make a lot off it."

"Fascinating. I now see why God chose you to lead this group."

Simon shrugged.

"Well, I never asked to be the leader of anything, especially since it's not one of my skills. I simply set off on my own with God as my rear guard, and just sorta gained a whole crew of friends along the way, and most of them by accident."

The Baroness laughed.

"There are no accidents. God has a special plan for you and everyone in your group. What that exact plan is though remains to be seen."

Simon chuckled.

"Well, if it's anything like what we've been through, it certainly won't be boring."

"Indeed. Excitement always makes the trip better. So, what's your plans for the trail ahead?"

"Well, I'm not sure, other than trying to reach the wintering grounds before the first snows fly. The rest, we'll just have to discover that as we go along. Of course, with Alex on our team, it'll make our future discoveries less surprising."

The Baroness was intrigued by this.

"Why him?" she asked.

"Because he's our guide. He's also the only one of our group who knows the trail ahead and everything we'll encounter along the way."

"That does sound like he would be handy. We could've used someone like him when I first arrived here. It was our ignorance about the course, and it's more unsavory elements, that led to what you see here now."

Simon shrugged.

"Maybe so, but what happened to you is a blessing."

The Baroness looked confused.

"How so?"

"Just look at all the good God has done through you! He's used you to rescue and protect numerous Christians who've come through here, and even facilitated the salvation of many others, including a few barons. That's nothing to sneeze at."

The Baroness blushed slightly.

"Yes, God has been good to me, hasn't He?" she said shyly.

"He has, and I'd like to see Him keep using you in the future, no matter how dark and evil the Keep becomes. God put you here for a reason, and I think you're only beginning to see what that is. I suspect there are even greater things to come."

The Baroness smiled widely.

"I hope so," she said excitedly. "So how soon do you plan to resume your trip?"

"Well, if the others aren't against it, probably tomorrow if possible."

The Baroness nodded.

"Then, I will see to the arrangements."

Just then, Birash and Yurg appeared from the garden and hurried over to them.

"Simon, we need to talk with you. Something very unusual has just happened."

Alex strolled into the courtyard and noticed that his entire team, as well as the Baroness and several of her staff, were gathered there.

"I came as soon as I got the message," he said.

"Have a seat. We have much to discuss," said Yurg.

Alex thought it strange to see Yurg acting so politely; and yet, at the same time, he wasn't, given how much the tiger had changed over the past several weeks. He quickly took a seat, and then studied the others intently as he tried to discern what the meeting was about.

"So what did you call us here for?" he asked.

Birash and Yurg laid out, in detail, their entire encounter with Fallon and the controller who'd appeared in the garden with him. Everyone in the group seemed shocked, save only for the Baroness and her staff. Simon picked up on this immediately.

"You don't seem at all surprised by this," he said.

The Baroness crossed her arms and mulled things over for a minute.

"I am more intrigued than anything. It's been quite some time since Fallon has been seen around here," she eventually replied.

"Then, you know him," said Birash in surprise.

"It's not that I know him, so much as I know *of* him. However, I've never personally met him. On the other hand, some of my staff have, as well as several others outside of the manor. As for the controllers, I've had considerable experience with them."

"So what does this mean for us?" asked Simon.

"Fallon, one of the many dragons on this world, only appears when his presence is required to protect someone in whom the controllers have taken an unhealthy interest. He works for his grandfather, Zek, master of the Southern Weyr, and acts as a powerful counter force to the will and power of the controllers, sometimes also known as the Syndicate, which is one of their many names. If he has appeared before you, and especially at the same time as a controller, then it is likely that the controller came here with the intent to harm you. As such, it is almost certain that your group has come to the unfortunate attention of the controllers. If that is true, then you are in graver danger than you realize," said the butler.

Trevor snorted.

"What? And like it hasn't been dangerous already?" he quipped.

The Baroness shook her head.

"The race is dangerous in and of itself. That much I will agree with. However, to have drawn the attention of the controllers now places you in a level of danger far greater than you are likely ready to face."

"Agreed. If they're now interested in you in the way I suspect, then your lives aren't worth the very dirt on which you now stand. Therefore, it's almost certain that they will do all within their power to kill you before you get another hundred miles," said the butler.

"And is that different than any other day? The controllers want all of us dead. Thus, the only question that remains is, by what means it will happen," said Alex.

"True. However, we must also remember that, until God is done with us, we are immortal. Physically speaking, of course," replied Simon.

"Immortal, perhaps, but not beyond harm," said the butler.

Just then, Trevor stood up and puffed out his chest boldly.

"I don't know about the rest of you, but I'm not about to let a bunch of men or demons, or whatever they are, make a punk out of me. If they want my life, I say bring it, because God's got my back! And from what I've read in His word, unless He permits it, they have no power to even touch me, let alone take my life. So if they think they can scare me into hiding or quitting, then they just phat crazy, man," he said.

The others sat quietly for several moments, trading glances, as they contemplated what Trevor had said. Eventually, Aria stood up and took Trevor's hand. Even though she tended to be the most fearful of the group, at this moment, her courage was both bold and inspiring.

"I'm with Trevor. We can't let them intimidate us into quitting. To fear them is to say that God isn't big enough to protect all of us. God is bigger than them! He's bigger than everything!! Therefore, we have nothing to fear. But, if we stop now, we make a liar out of Him, and I won't do that!" she said.

Alex shook his head as he smiled widely, and then rose to his feet, clapping as he did.

"Well said, both of you. And I agree with everything you've said. However, the final decision is not ours; but rests firmly with our fearless leader," he said as he looked at Simon.

Suddenly, Simon felt like an ant under a microscope as all eyes turned to him. Slowly, he began to stand as an incredible peace washed over him, causing him to smile from ear to ear.

"I have to agree with all of you. We can't stop. Not only did I promise to take all of you to the end and get you back home, I also agree with and believe exactly as Aria and

Trevor do. God will protect us and provide all of our needs. So, unless He specifically tells us to stop, I'm going to keep going, no matter what," he said.

"As will I," replied Yurg. "While I may not know your Jesus, or Olumide as Birash calls him, I have seen enough to know that I, too, can trust Him to bring us as far as He desires, be that only a few paces, or all the way to the end."

All eyes then fell on Birash. He smiled.

"I, too, will go; for I cannot leave any of you behind, no matter what. Therefore, I will come with you for as long and as far as Olumide permits," he replied.

The Baroness nodded in understanding.

"Very well. We will respect your wishes," she said.

"But what about Fallon? If he and one of the controllers have appeared to them, then, they are in grave danger," said a butler.

The Baroness sighed slightly.

"We must leave that to God. There is nothing else we can do, save only to send them on their way with much prayer and supplication for their safety."

"As you wish, milady."

Chapter 20

The next morning the entire team rose early and hurried downstairs into the chapel for a lengthy prayer meeting with the Baroness and many of her staff where they lifted up prayers of protection for Simon's team on the journey ahead. Afterwards, Simon's team were fed breakfast, given new hiking outfits, more rations and supplies, loaded onto a waiting carriage with all of their gear, and then sent away into the countryside. It took them two days to get out of the Keep, and another two before they reached the seaside town of Donville, arriving just as the sun was setting on the horizon. The carriage made its way through the village to an inn near the seaside, where it dropped off its passengers before turning back towards Hollow Manor. The group immediately got rooms for the night and settled down to sleep. The next morning, they arose, ate breakfast, and then headed down to the docks. To everyone's surprise, save only for Alex, the port was bustling with ship and merchant traffic of every shape and kind. However, they were most intrigued at the unbelievable size of the body of water in front of them.

"Wow, that thing's huge," said Trevor.

Simon laughed.

"Actually, from what I read in the instruction manual, it's not much bigger than Lake Michigan. You should've seen that quite regularly if you lived in Chicago."

Trevor snorted.

"Not really. I stayed west of the Dan Ryan most of the time. I think I was down by the shoreline twice in my life, and neither of those times were for anything good," he replied.

"Well, you don't have anything to worry about. It shouldn't take us more than four or five hours to get to the other side, weather permitting."

"Yeah, but first we've gotta get a boat."

"Well, I'm leaving that to Alex. He's done this before."

"Aye, I have. Now come. We need to find what ships are leaving port soon," said Alex.

Simon and the others quickly followed him down to the docks where he found one of the port call boards. These were large pegboards located at various points along the docks that listed the names of all the ships currently in the port, when they'd arrived, their intended destination, captains, expected cargoes, their scheduled departure times and much, much more. Alex quickly scanned the list of ships on the board in hopes of finding the one he was looking for. Eventually, much to his delight, he found it. Even better, the ship was due to leave port within the hour. Simon found this intriguing.

"That almost looks like the flight display board at an airport," he said.

"Aye, mate. It is very similar indeed," said Alex.

"But how do the port masters know all this information?"

"Because the captains tell them. Given the amount of trade that transpires at this, and all of the other connected ports around the area, it's to the benefit of the captains and their ships to tell the port masters all of the information they have about their ships, and their destinations, so that prospective customers will know and can find them. It's proven very lucrative for them; and thus, I doubt you will see its use ended anytime soon."

Alex then led the group further down the docks towards one of the cargo ships moored there. As he walked up to it, a grizzled old sea captain turned and greeted him.

"Alex, ye old scurvy dog! How be ye?" he asked in a pirate like accent.

"Greetings mate! I'm doing well. How are you?" he said.

"Arr, I've been better. The old controllers are busting me jaw of late, though. But I and me crew are managing," said the captain.

He then turned to the others in Simon's group, and nodded approvingly.

"Are these yer latest escorts?" he asked.

"Aye, mate, they are. And they're a fine lot too, I must say."

"So, ye be needing passage to the other side as usual?" asked the captain.

"Aye. Same fare as always?"

"Nay. After the fair profit your tip brought me, this journey is on me!"

"Oh, but I must protest!"

"Nay! Nay! You deserve it. Besides, me belly is full and me coffers are overflowing. It's only fair that I treat ye to something good as me gratitude."

Alex smiled.

"If you insist, mate, I gladly accept! So, how soon do you leave?"

"As the board says, we will be leaving at ten."

Alex turned and studied the giant clock that sat on top of the massive city hall building and saw that it was a quarter til. He turned back to the captain.

"Then we will board immediately," he said.

The captain bowed slightly, and then led them onto the ship. At ten sharp, the ship pushed away from the dock, raised sail, and was off into the sea, riding the wind quickly out of the small bay and into the open waters beyond. As it did, a blue-skinned man watched them from atop a nearby house as they slowly disappeared into the distance. He soon vanished in a flash of fire and was gone.

Simon sat on the port side of the ship and poured the entirety of his breakfast over the side in sickening heaves and gags. Even Trevor and Aria were looking a little green. Only Alex, Birash and Yurg were unaffected. However, they wisely stayed in the back of the ship away from the worst of the tossing so as to avoid suffering the same fate as the others.

"Humans have such weak stomachs," said Yurg whimsically.

"Actually, we humans are fairly sturdy creatures. However, not all are properly equipped to handle the regular motion of a ship at sea," said Birash.

"Hmm. That seems like it would be a rather troublesome disadvantage."

Birash laughed.

"Yes, it is. However, if we are patient with our friends, their bodies will quickly adjust."

Yurg furrowed his brow as he twitched his ears pertly.

"I hope so. Their strength will be needed in increasing degrees as the trail continues."

"Olumide will ensure that they have all they need for the journey ahead."

"Indeed."

The ship continued across the sea at a surprisingly good speed, as the wind blew in their favor the whole way. Eventually Simon, Trevor and Aria gathered their strength and brought their stomachs under control, despite the ship's motion causing a constant resurgence of their nausea.

"I take it you're not a lover of the sea," said Alex with a grin.

"I love being out on the water. But for some reason, it doesn't like me today," groaned Simon.

Alex laughed.

"When it comes to water like this, I'll pass," groaned Trevor.

Alex laughed again. But his laugh quickly faded away when a sudden burst of wind caused the ship to lurch forward. He looked up curiously, but only saw clear blue skies. He thought this strange as there were no clouds anywhere. However, it wasn't long before a small one began to form out of nowhere. The cloud quickly grew in size and was soon joined by many others that rapidly merged together into thick, dark, menacing storm clouds. The captain, who was an expert in these waters, was surprised at what he saw. In his many years sailing these waters, he'd seen plenty of storms, but never one like this. The wind again picked up in intensity, causing the ship to creek and groan in ways that made the captain nervous.

"Strike the sails, mates! It's a sea storm!" he shouted over the ever increasing wind.

It wasn't long before Simon, Trevor and Aria's nausea returned with a vengeance. But by now, they had nothing left in their stomachs to send over the side. Lightning ripped across the ever darkening sky as though it sought to split the very veil of heaven itself. The crewmen worked feverishly to bring in the sails, as the captain and helmsman struggled to keep the ship under control. All around them, the waves continued to grow in size; eventually becoming so large that they threatened to swallow the ship whole without the slightest effort.

Seeing the growing danger around them, Alex turned to the others, and said, "I think it might be wise to take cover below deck, mates."

The others didn't hesitate a moment in following him below. It wasn't long, though, before the rest of the crew, save only for the captain and the helmsman, followed them.

The winds continued to grow stronger over the next hour, soon reaching gale force speeds. It was as though a hurricane had formed over the large, inland lake causing every timber in the great ship to creak and grown, as though crying out in fear. Still, the wind and waves continued to grow stronger, beating against the ship with every increasing ferocity. Down below, Simon and his group prayed without ceasing for the safety of the ship and the crew. But the more they prayed, the stronger the storm became. Soon, waves were coming over the ship that were so high that they threatened to capsize the boat. The sailors below manned the pumps frantically, as they struggled to pump out the water and keep the ship afloat. But that would soon prove to be the least of their worries.

As they worked frantically, a sound echoed through the ship that sent sheer, unequivocal terror through the hearts of everyone aboard. It was the ship's main beam snapping in two. Even if they somehow managed to keep the ship from flooding, with the main beam broken, the ship was doomed. So, the men abandoned the pumps and raced for the upper decks in search of the lifeboats that hung from the side of the ship. But, upon arriving, they discovered, to their complete and total horror, that the storm had stripped away every single one of them from the sides of the ship. Just then, a powerful wave slammed into the bow, causing the ship to heave violently, and then rip in half. Timbers and beams exploded in every direction sending men, tackle and cargo flying into the air.

The waves then descended upon the ship like wolves rushing in for the kill; their water hitting the hull like powerful watery hammers that further ripped it to pieces. What then remained of the ship groaned in agony, crumbled, and soon sank beneath the waves. Moments later, the storm broke and began to rapidly subside. Within a few minutes, the clouds dissipated, the wind ceased and the sky became cloudless and blue once again. All that remained of the ship was a large debris field filled with floating boards, beams, crates, casks and dead sailors. A blue-skinned man soon appeared over the field of wreckage and studied the water quietly as he floated effortlessly in the air above it. Seeing no survivors, he vanished in a flash of fire and was gone. A moment later, a man dressed from head to toe in glistening, pure white garments ascended out of the water holding the unconscious body of Simon in his arms. He floated across the lake to the far shore and deposited Simon at the door of a fisherman's home. He then gently stroked Simon's head causing him to gasp briefly in surprise before slipping back into a soft, sleep like unconsciousness.

"Live on, blessed of God, and grow strong, for there is still much work for you to do in the race ahead," he said quietly, and then vanished.

Simon groaned as consciousness slowly invaded his mind. He felt as though a truck had run him over and then backed up out of spite. He took a deep breath and was surprised to smell fish, old rope and damp wood. His ears then heard the soft crackle of a fire and the muffled sound of sea waves crashing against a rocky shore. He soon noticed that he was laying in a nice warm bed covered in several thick, woolen blankets. He slowly opened his eyes and saw a ceiling made of old, damp timbers, much like one would find on a sailing ship. Just then, images of the shipwreck flashed through his mind, and then went away. Had what he'd seen only been a dream? He slowly sat up and looked around in curiosity. To his surprise, he found himself in a tiny cottage by the seaside. Nearby was an old stone hearth, inside of which crackled a warm, inviting fire. A small, black kettle hung from a thick metal arm that stretched out over the fire, inside of which boiled a hardy fish stew. A gray haired, older man, in a thick woolen sweater and pants, sat in a rocking chair in a corner of the room and studied him through weathered, time worn eyes.

"Ah, you're finally awake, my friend," said the man.

"Where am I?" groaned Simon.

"In my humble abode on the edge of The Reaping Sea."

Simon sat up and looked around the room, but saw nobody else.

"Who are you?" he asked.

"Mathias."

"Where are the others of my group?"

The man shook his head.

"There were no others. I only found you. Well, I can't quite say I found you, as you apparently found me."

"What do you mean?"

"When I came home several nights ago, I found you laying on my doorstep. You've been unconscious since then."

Simon became anxious.

"There were five others in my group. Are you sure you didn't see anyone else?"

Mathias shook his head again.

"I thought there might be others, so I and my mates searched diligently up and down the coastline, but found no one else."

Simon sighed heavily. After months of hiking together with his five faithful companions, he now found himself alone again. He tried to get up, but his legs quickly folded under him and he tumbled back onto the bed.

"I wouldn't try to stand yet, my friend. You still need to regain your strength. From what I can best tell, the sea nearly killed you."

Suddenly, a memory of drowning flashed through Simon's mind. More images of shattering timbers, rushing water and crushing pressure appeared, followed by images of dead bodies and broken tackle as they sank down into the depths. It made him shiver.

Mathias noticed this, and asked, "Is something on your mind, friend?"

But Simon said nothing. He simply sat there on the bed and pulled the blankets closer around himself. Mathias narrowed his eyes. He'd seen that look before, and knew what it meant. He got up, filled a bowl with stew and handed it to Simon.

"Take this. You'll need it to regain your strength."

Simon studied the bowl briefly, and then gladly took the steamy hot meal. Mathias returned to his chair as Simon humbly bowed his head and began to pray.

"Thank You, Lord, for sparing my life once again, and for the kindness of Mathias, for him taking me into his house, for caring for me, and even now feeding me. Bless this food, and bless him as well. I also pray, wherever my friends are, Lord, watch over and take care of them, bring them safely to shore, and bring us together again. But, if they are with You, then I pray that their passing was swift and painless." He paused briefly, and then said, "Lord, also bring me safely to the end of this race, if that be Your will; and bring Your children back home to Earth once again as well. I pray this, Lord Jesus, in Your blessed name, amen."

He then took a spoonful of the stew and began to eat, rapidly emptying the bowl. As he did, Mathias studied him quietly for several minutes, but said nothing. Eventually, he picked up a thick, black, leather bound book that lay next to him, opened it and began reading.

"Why art thou cast down, O my soul? And why art thou disquieted within me? Hope thou in God: for I shall yet praise Him, who is the health of my countenance, and my God," he read aloud.

Upon hearing these words, Simon perked up as his eyes widened. He looked at Mathias in amazement.

"That's Psalm 42:11. How did you..."

Mathias held up the book for Simon to see.

"God's holy word. It's my treasure in this world; and the jewel that keeps this old heart of mine alive, as I await our salvation from this world of suffering," he said.

He stood up and took the now empty bowl from Simon, filled it again, and handed it back to him before sitting down. Simon sat quietly and ate as he listened to Mathias continue to read.

"The troubles of my heart are enlarged: O bring thou me out of my distresses. Look upon mine affliction and my pain; and forgive all my sins."

Simon's heart slowly began to cheer up as he heard Mathias read one verse of encouragement after another from the Bible. Soon, his sadness lifted and his mind became at ease. Even though his friends weren't with him anymore, he knew that wherever they were, God was watching over them. He hoped they were alive. But even if they weren't, his heart was at peace; because he knew that some day they would all meet again, be that here, at home on Earth, or even perhaps in Heaven. But as he thought about this, his eyes grew heavy. Mathias took the bowl from his hands, gently pushed him back down onto the bed, and pulled the blankets over him.

"Rest now, my friend, and regain your strength. God will carry you through this trial and bring you safely to the end," said Mathias.

And with that, Simon fell fast asleep with a peaceful smile on his face.

Chapter 21

Trevor awoke to find himself laying on a soft, comfortable bed covered in fancy, expensive blankets. Curious to where he was, he sat up slightly and looked around. In one corner sat a man on a chair who, upon seeing that he was awake, hurried out of the room. A few minutes later, a lavishly dressed man and his wife appeared. Both were pleased to see that he was awake.

"How are you feeling, young man?" asked the husband in a very debonair manner.

"Exhausted and starving," groaned Trevor.

"Ah, good. We expected as much and have asked the chef to prepare extra food for you."

Trevor looked around the room briefly, and then back at the couple.

"Where am I?"

"In my manor house at the eastern end of the Sheffield Republic near The Reaping Sea. I am Lord Banister, and this is my wife Lidia."

"Where's the others?" asked Trevor.

Banister looked at him in confusion.

"What others?"

"The other five members of my team. The last I saw them, we were on a ship crossing the lake to the other side."

The couple looked at each other in confusion, and then back at Trevor.

"There were no others. We only found you and your slave. Both of you were half naked and nearly dead when they brought you here."

Trevor gave the couple a strange look.

"My slave?"

"Yes, the dark-skinned man that washed ashore with you. We put him in the slave quarters where he could rest and recover."

Trevor scratched his head. He wondered if they were referring to Birash.

"So you didn't see anyone else?"

Banister shook his head.

"Unfortunately, we did not."

Trevor groaned and rubbed his face in frustration.

"Great. Not only am I shipwrecked, but my friends are gone; and I appear to have died and gone to Beverly Hills," he thought.

He threw aside the covers and jumped out of the bed. To his surprise, his new hiking clothes were gone, and had been replaced with a clean, silky pair of pajamas. He even had on clean, fresh underwear. He contemplated asking how that'd happened, but decided it was best if he didn't know. He then noticed that the couple seemed somewhat uncomfortable at seeing him this way. Trevor found it odd, but didn't ask why.

"Ah, yes. Um, there is a closet over there full of clothes you can change into. If you need anything, I can send one of the maids up here to help you," said the husband.

The couple then dismissed themselves and slipped out of the room. Trevor furrowed his brow as he watched them go. He soon walked over to the closet, threw it open, and nearly gagged.

"Dawg, what is this? Everything looks like it's a leftover from the disco era."

He began pulling outfits out of the closet, one at a time, and examined each of them briefly before tossing them on the floor in disgust.

"Nope, nope, not happening, absolutely not happening, nope, nope, burn it, nope, fail, epic fail, not even gonna comment on that one, nope, nope, not a chance, oh *absolutely* not," he said as he kept pulling items out of the closet.

After a bit, he stopped and studied the remaining outfits with dismay.

"Good grief. I may not be a thug anymore, but I'm certainly not wearing these," he muttered.

He stood there for several moments and studied the wardrobe selection. Eventually, his mind locked onto a top and pair of pants that he liked, even though they didn't match. He quickly stripped off his pajamas, changed into the new clothes, and then checked himself out in the mirror. They weren't to his taste, but at least it was better than nothing. He sighed, and then stepped out of the room. He found the hallway filled with elaborate and intricate decorations, as well as numerous pieces of very expensive looking furniture. As he walked along, he noticed that all of the lighting was electric, the first he'd seen since arriving on the planet. This surprised him. Everyone else had been using candles or oil lamps. Yet, these were good old fashioned incandescent light bulbs.

And, even though they were a bit archaic in their design, they were still more modern than anything else he'd encountered so far. He walked over to a nearby wall and played with the light switch briefly to be sure that what he was seeing was right. Sure enough, the lights turned on and off as he fiddled with the switch. He found this curious. If they had power, why didn't anyone else? He strolled to the end of the hall, down a pair of white marble steps, and into a grand gallery that led to a set of large double doors, another pair of hallways, and a library stuffed to the ceiling with books. Several maids and other staff members, in traditional, turn of the century, British style servant's clothes, were busy cleaning in a nearby hallway. He then perked up as he heard what sounded like a car outside. He turned and headed towards the front door to see what it was. Upon stepping through, he found himself face to face with a tall, gray-haired butler who stared at him in abject confusion.

"Hey, Jeeves," said Trevor jokingly.

He then pushed past the man and out onto a large, sprawling porch. Not far away sat a vehicle that reminded him of an old Dusenberg, ornate and elegant. He was again surprised. This was now two pieces of technology he'd not seen since coming to this planet. He was even more amazed that they had it in the first place. Not even the Baroness had something this modern or advanced.

"May I help you, sir?" asked the butler.

Trevor turned and studied the man.

"Oh, hey. You're the butler, right?"

"I am, sir. And who might you be?" said the butler, condescendingly.

"Trevor. I just came down from one of your bedrooms on the second floor. Nice place you got here, but the clothing is rather lame."

The butler glared at Trevor.

"Are you that drowned rat they saved yesterday?" he asked with a hint of displeasure.

Trevor shrugged.

"Probably."

He then walked over to the car idling nearby before the butler had a chance to say anything else.

"Hey there. What kind of car is this?" asked Trevor.

The driver looked at him curiously, and then studied his odd choice of apparel. After a bit, he snorted disapprovingly, jumped in the car, and drove away. Trevor frowned.

"Dude, that was cold," he muttered.

He shrugged it off, pushed past the butler as he slipped back inside, and continued exploring. As he did, he smelled something delicious wafting through the air. He followed the scent across the house, and soon found himself in a large dining room. Over on one side of the room sat the couple he'd met earlier. They appeared to be eating something he couldn't quite describe. They soon noticed him standing in the doorway.

"Come, sit down. We're just having breakfast," said Banister.

Trevor studied the couple briefly, and then took a seat across from him.

"What'cha chowing on?" he asked.

"It's a local delicacy. They call it Bantenyan. It's quite delicious."

Trevor studied Banister's plate briefly, and then shook his head.

"Meh, I'll just settle for some trovet and vegetables if you have any."

The couple seemed appalled at the mere thought of such a simple meal. Banister snorted in disapproval and gestured dismissively.

"We don't eat such things. They're food for the common people. We're better than that," he said with an air of superiority.

Trevor frowned slightly. He was liking the place less and less. A moment later, one of the maids swept into the room, plopped down a plate of food in front of him, a glass of a bluish drink, and the single nicest set of dinnerware Trevor had ever seen. He cautiously took a bite of the food and was surprised at how good it tasted. He quickly wolfed it down, followed by a second plate, and eventually a third before he truly felt full. The couple watched him in dismay as he ate his breakfast in a way that seemed almost barbaric to them. Yet, they held their peace. Despite being so different from what they were used to, he was still their guest; and they needed to treat him as such, even though he was severely testing their patience. As Trevor sat there letting his breakfast digest, a thought crossed his mind.

"Hey, you said you put my slave in the slave's quarters. Where's those at?" he asked.

"At the rear of the manor. Why do you ask?" said Banister.

"I just wanna go check on him to make sure he's alright."

"Very well. I can have one of the staff show you to where he's being kept. Just be forewarned. The slaves do not live clean lives. Therefore, you might find your sinuses assaulted upon entering the building. We always do. But then again, what do you expect from slaves?" said Banister with an air of superiority and condescension.

Trevor studied the couple mutely, his face not giving any clues to what he was thinking. If there was one thing he was good at, it was keeping up his poker face whenever dealing with either strangers or undesirables like Banister and his wife.

"I think I'll manage," he said, a smile growing across his face.

However, deep inside, he was feeling anything but joy.

"I need to get to those quarters and spring my friend, and then get out of here before the natives get restless," he thought.

Simon stirred slightly, as the first light of day broke through the windows and flooded the small cottage. He looked across the room and found Mathias curled up on the floor under a blanket near the fireplace. He slowly got up, walked over to the fireplace and found there was still some stew in the pot. He put some in a bowl, prayed, and then began to eat. As he did, Mathias sat up and looked at him.

"Ah, good morning, friend. How was your night?" he asked.

Simon shrugged as he chewed.

"Interesting. I had some really weird dreams about the ship we were on."

"Do you remember what happened to you out there?"

"Kinda. We got caught in a big storm that came out of nowhere, bashed the ship to pieces and sent it to the bottom like a rock."

Mathias sighed.

"Aye. That is a story we hear far too often around here. Most go about their days on the sea without a single trouble. Others die within hours of stepping onto its waters. It's the nature of the sea, and there are few who fully understand its whims. That is why all of us know it as The Reaping Sea, for it does well to earn its name."

Simon rubbed his beard.

"Yeah, there are a few seas like that back home on Earth."

"Aye, I have heard of them. I hope one day to see them with my own eyes, and then sail the seven seas of Earth for the first time."

This intrigued Simon.

"Weren't you a sailor before you came here?"

Mathias shook his head.

"I've always lived here, as I am native born."

Simon cocked an eyebrow slightly.

"Native born? What generation are you?"

"Fourteenth. And I see you're a first generation. You've done well learnin Bonisi, given your short time on this planet."

Simon looked at him in confusion.

"What do you mean? I'm speaking English."

Mathias shook his head.

"You're speaking Bonisi, and likely in the purest form I've ever heard. Your Bonisi is even better than mine, not that mine is all that bad."

Simon was even more confused now.

"How is that even possible? Alex has only just begun teaching us Bonisi, and we're not even conversational yet, as we're still learning the basics."

Mathias pondered this curiously.

"How odd, because I hear you very plainly speaking Bonisi. As such, I'm curious of something. Would you be willing to follow me for a moment?"

Simon shrugged slightly.

"Sure. Where are you going?"

"To see the others."

"There are others here?"

"An entire village."

"Well, let's go meet them then!"

Mathias then led Simon out of the cottage, to the center of the village, where a group of men and women sat in a circle cleaning the day's catch.

"Is this a fishing village?" asked Simon.

"Aye, it's how we make our living. It's a tough job, but we do well enough."

One of the villagers stood up and walked over to Mathias.

"Goova dep nardoc tro?" he asked.

"Yep, that's the Bonisi I remember," thought Simon.

What intrigued him even more was how much of it he understood. He had to admit that he hadn't reached the point of being conversational with it yet; but clearly, Alex's teaching, up to this point anyways, had been good enough to help him at least understand the basics.

"Aye, he is feeling better," said Mathias.

"Hoos gardroc arounase mon fooss nahchou?" asked the man.

"He will leave when he is well enough to travel again," replied Mathias.

The fisherman smiled, said, "Ba de," and then returned to the others.

Simon found this intriguing. It was definitely Bonisi; but he wasn't entirely sure of everything that'd been said, even though he'd understood some of it.

"So what was he saying?" he asked.

"He was curious how you were feeling. The others heard about your arrival and have been very concerned for you. Around here, there are no secrets; so if something happens, everyone knows. In fact, those of us who are believers have been praying for you."

"Well, that was nice of them. I just wish I understood what they were saying."

"So you really don't know how to speak Bonisi," said Mathias curiously.

"Not really. I know a little of it, like thank you, good morning, good evening, and so on, but not much more than that. Alex has been teaching us how to speak it since we left Pongo. But I'm still not fluent in it yet. Thankfully, the last few villages and towns we've been through were filled with mostly English speakers. Otherwise I'd have been screwed trying to talk with them."

"Hmm. Then, there must be something special between us that the others don't have."

"Any ideas what that might be? The only thing I know of is that we're both believers."

Mathias perked up slightly.

"Is it possible that we're speaking in tongues?" he asked.

Simon shrugged.

"I don't know. There's certainly nothing else I can think of which would explain this."

Mathias grinned.

"I must say that this is most intriguing. If it is indeed tongues, it is the first time I have actually seen it in use outside of the Bible narrative."

Simon laughed.

"Hey, anything is possible as I've seen God do some pretty amazing things over the years. So if this is actually tongues, I wouldn't be the slightest bit surprised."

"Aye, neither would I."

Simon laughed.

"Now, I'm kinda wondering, if all those people we ran into before weren't actually speaking English, but instead were experiencing the same thing we are right now."

Mathias scratched his beard as he thought.

"That is entirely possible, my friend."

Trevor wandered slowly through the extensive Sheffield mansion from hallway to hallway and carefully studied everyone and everything he saw. He soon spotted a military officer walking down a nearby hallway and thought it so unusual that he decided to follow him. The officer eventually made his way to a room on the south side of the mansion complex, inside of which where a number of other similarly dressed men who were gathered around a map table in the center of the room discussing something of apparently mutual interest. They saluted the officer as he entered, and then returned to what they were doing. Trevor stopped just outside the door and listened carefully.

"General, we've analyzed the activities of the GAK Republic, and it appears they may be planning to attack our western border soon," said one of the men.

Trevor leaned around the corner and studied the men cautiously. The one they'd addressed as "General" studied the map table carefully; and then began giving orders to move troops and reassign other resources to the front. He even sounded like he wanted them to deploy tanks. Trevor didn't like the sound of that.

"What about Thorn?" asked the general.

"We're not sure, sir. They've gone quiet of late, which is unusual for them. It may mean they don't have the resources to engage us at this time," said one of the men.

"Hmm, knowing their commander, he's probably preparing to make a surprise attack, hoping that our fight with Unity will leave us unable to repel it. Send two squads of men to spy on them. I want to know exactly what they're doing at all times, and why."

"Yes, sir!"

Trevor frowned. Whatever was happening, he didn't want to be around there any longer than absolutely necessary. Especially if there was a war going on. He turned and began to slip away when he spotted several soldiers coming out of a room in a connecting hallway. He quickly hid in a nearby closet and waited patiently for them to pass by. Once they were out of sight, he slipped over to the door they'd come from and noticed the title plate on it.

"Armory? Well, this could be useful," he thought.

He examined the lock briefly and was pleased to see that it's design wasn't very complicated. That meant it would be easy to pick. He pulled a piece of wire out of his pocket, inserted it in the lock and worked it until he heard a gentle disengagement. He then swung the door open and was in awe at the collection of guns, ammo, and various munitions inside.

"Geez, you could start a small war with this!" he thought.

He leaned out into the hallway to see if anyone was coming, and then quickly stuffed two large rucksacks full of weapons and ammo, including several compact rifles, before slipping two pistols and several magazines into his pants and covering them with his jacket. He then dragged the two rucksacks out into the hallway and before securing the door behind him.

"Now it's time to spring Birash and blow this joint," he thought.

He took the rucksacks and hurried across the complex to where the slave quarters were, and was surprised to find Birash locked up in a cage inside one of the buildings. He walked over and fiddled with the lock briefly before being interrupted by the slave master.

"Hey, what are you doing?" he asked.

"I'm just retrieving my friend," said Trevor.

The slave master shook his head.

"You can't do that. If the slave is in here, he belongs to the lord of the manor."

"He's my friend, and I'm taking him with me," protested Trevor.

"No, you're not, young man. As I said, any slave in here is the property of the--"

Trevor grabbed the man by the collar, slammed him against a wall, and then shoved a pistol under his chin. The slave master's eyes grew wide in surprise.

"What part of, 'I'm taking him with me', didn't you understand, punk?"

The slave master gulped nervously.

"Now, now, young man. No need to get hasty."

"Open the door! Now!" growled Trevor.

He then shoved the slave master across the room and pointed his pistol at him.

"Do it, or I'm gonna have to get twitchy with you," he said sternly.

The slave master fumbled nervously with his keys, found the one he wanted, and unlocked the cage. Birash stepped out quietly, glared at the man, and then with a powerful right hook, put the man on the ground like a sack of wheat. Trevor did a surprised doubletake.

"Dang dawg, you scare me sometimes," said Trevor.

Birash grinned.

"My apologies. I will leave him for you to deal with next time."

Trevor shrugged, and said, "Nah, I'm good." He put his pistol away, and said, "Hey, help me toss this guy in the pen. It'll keep him quiet for a while."

Birash gestured for Trevor to wait, and said, "Allow me."

He picked up the man, shoved him in the cage, and locked the door. Next, he took the man's keys and threw them high into the rafters where they would be hard to find. Trevor grinned.

"Dude, that's cold."

"It will keep them busy for some time," said Birash proudly.

"Yeah, no doubt. Now let's blow this joint. Given what the big dogs are proposing, I don't want to be around here any longer than I have to."

"What are they doing?"

"They're getting ready to go postal on each other, and I don't plan to be here when they do."

Birash scratched his chin in thought.

"Hmm, if that is so, then I agree that we must hurry. However, we are without our packs, and our supplies. What will we do once we resume the trail?"

"Are you kidding? This dude's loaded! He's got rooms just stuffed to the gills with supplies, ration packs, and tons of other stuff. So, we just take what we need and split. I've even put together a couple boom bags for the road ahead."

"Boom bags?" asked Birash curiously.

"Yeah, packs full of weapons, ammo, stuff like that."

"Ah, understood," replied Birash.

"Alright, let's go."

Birash gestured to the door, and said with a smile, "Agreed, my friend. Lead the way, and I will follow you wherever you go."

Trevor smiled.

"Ya know what, buddy? That's what makes you so cool. No matter what kind of 'poo pile' we get ourselves into, I know you'd always be there for me."

Birash smiled, and said, "And you as well, my friend."

Lord Banister sat quietly in his study as he read the afternoon reports from the front.

"Unit is becoming a pest," he grumbled.

"I agree, my lord. However, it may be in our best interests to seek peace with them," said one of his generals.

"Peace with the Unity Empire? Don't be absurd. It'll make us look weak to the other empires, and they will then think us easy prey," growled Banister.

"My lord, the purpose of my suggestion was not to make us appear weak. It is to ensure that no racer escapes our grasp while we are fighting with each other."

Banister waved dismissively.

"No racer has escaped our defenses in decades, and none ever will."

"If the war continues, it will only be a matter of time before one does," said the general.

Just then, one of the soldiers burst into the room.

"My lord, we've captured a spy!" he shouted.

"WHAT!?" cried Banister.

A moment later an officer and a group of soldiers came into the room escorting a prisoner. The man grinned arrogantly as Banister studied him.

"Who are you with?" asked Banister.

"The great and mighty kingdom of Thorn, my lord," said the man proudly.

Banister snorted.

"How predictable. Thorn sends us another spy to seek out our weakness so that they can overthrow us and take the entire Four Kingdoms for themselves. Isn't that right?" he said condescendingly.

The man grinned even wider.

"Oh, there's far more to it than that, my lord," he said deviously.

Banister studied the man for several moments. He'd been part of the Banister house staff for years and had never once shown any signs of disloyalty, even handing over a fellow Thorn spy who'd slipped into the compound months earlier. He'd also been instrumental in helping watch over Trevor when he'd first arrived. An eyebrow went up slightly as Banister processed this. Suddenly, a horrifying and terrible thought crossed his mind. There was a racer in their midst! The man laughed.

"Figured it out, did you?" he said mockingly.

"Why you..." growled Banister angrily.

"Say goodbye to your beautiful kingdom, Banister; because when that racer crosses the finish line, you'll lose everything."

Banister leapt to his feet in anger.

"You idiot! If they win this race, you'll lose everything too!"

The man grinned with devilish glee.

"You just don't get it, do you? Unlike you, we of the Thorn know how to make empires. Once we return to Earth, it will be but a simple effort to take the entire planet as our own, and when we do, it will be *you* who bows at our feet."

Banister roared with anger, drew a pistol and put a bullet through the man's head.

He then looked at the general, and said, "Find that racer and kill him!"

Chapter 22

Simon sat on a bench in the village square and watched as the other fishermen mended their nets.

"How much longer will you be staying with us?" asked Mathias.

"I don't know. I was planning on leaving soon, but all my gear is gone. So I don't know exactly how I'll be able to get started again."

"I think you've lost less than you realize."

"What do you mean?"

"Follow me," said Mathias.

He then led Simon over to his cottage where he produced a hiking pack that looked strangely familiar. Simon opened it and was amazed to discover it was his! He looked up in surprise.

"Where did you get this!?"

Mathias shrugged.

"I found it in the same place I found you."

Simon tried to make sense of this.

"Hmm, this is too strange."

"Indeed, it is."

"How do you think it got here?"

Mathias shrugged.

"Likely, in the same way you did."

Simon's eyes narrowed.

"Possibly. But the thing is, I don't know how I got here. The last memories I have are of the ship sinking and me drowning. The next thing I remember is waking up in your cottage. As such, it almost makes you wonder if God didn't put me here."

"It wouldn't be the first time He's done something like that."

Simon slipped on his pack, tightened the straps and pulled out his navigator compass.

"Are you leaving already?" asked Mathias.

"I have to. The others may be gone, but I still need to win this race. But the longer I stay here, the more people will die. I can't have that on my conscience."

Mathias pursed his lips.

"I applaud your courage. But this is a very hostile land. You will not be able to cross it without our help."

Simon stared at him in confusion.

"Our help?"

"Aye, my friends and I will need to escort you through this part of the course, if you wish to cross it safely."

"Why? Is it that dangerous?"

"It is. The Four Kingdoms control this area, and they will do all within their power to ensure that no racer passes through here alive, including you."

Simon blinked in surprise.

"What!?"

"Yes, my friend. They fear what victory will bring. So, it is the policy of their leaders to prevent any racer from reaching the end and winning the race."

Simon shook his head in confusion.

"Wait, that makes no sense. Why would they want to do that?"

"Here they are kings. On Earth, they would become paupers, a future they find undesirable."

Simon pursed his lips in frustration.

"So they're trying to keep everyone trapped here so they can continue to live in power and luxury? That's just not right."

Mathias shrugged.

"There's not much anyone can do about it."

"Yes there is! I'm going to finish this race one way or another, by the grace of God, even if an entire army stands in my way!"

"Again, I admire your courage, my friend; but without an escort, you will not survive this part of the course. That is why we are going with you."

"But you're fourteenth generation. You're not allowed to take part in the race," protested Simon.

Mathias waved dismissively.

"I don't intend to. However, that doesn't mean I can't help you get safely through the lands of the Four Kingdoms. That is the least I can do."

Simon smiled.

"Well, then I'd be happy to have you along. Besides, the company will be welcome, and so will the protection. Plus, it'll be nice to have someone who knows the native language, since the only member of our team who spoke fluent Bonisi is likely in heaven right now."

Mathias smiled.

"Then I will do my best, with God's help, to aid you as much as I can."

Birash slipped on his pack and adjusted the straps as Trevor continued to fill his with goodies. Finally, he drew the top shut, slipped it on, and then adjusted it on his back. Birash then picked up the other two bags that Trevor had filled with weapons and ammunition.

"Alright, we ready to go?" asked Trevor.

"I am ready. But how will we leave? It is unlikely that they will simply allow us to walk out of here uncontested," replied Birash.

Trevor thought about this for a bit, and then remembered the car he'd seen earlier. He grinned slyly, which caused Birash to furrow his brow.

"Hey, you up for a little grand theft auto?" he asked.

Birash seemed confused by this.

"I don't know what you are talking about, but I will follow your lead."

Trevor grunted.

"Well, as long as you can keep the thugs off my back, we'll be good. I just hope those cars drive faster than their ancient counterparts, or this could be a very short getaway."

"We will concern ourselves with that later. For now, let us hurry, my friend."

The two of them turned and raced down the hallway past several surprised maids and made their way over to the garages. Once inside, Birash stood guard while Trevor searched around for the best vehicle to take. Eventually, he found a very sporty looking convertible and quickly located the key for it. The car started with a roar and soon settled down to a growl.

"Oh man, that is music to my ears!" he said.

"Your taste in music is most confusing," replied Birash.

"Just get in! We're busting out of here!"

Birash tossed the two bags of weapons into the back and then leapt in as well. He held on tight as Trevor shifted the car into gear and flew out of the garage. The engine roared with excitement as the wheels spun eagerly under them. They exploded out onto the main roadway moments later and accelerated away rapidly.

"Oh, man! This car is phat, yo!" he exclaimed happily.

"I hate to dampen your enthusiasm, but we have company," said Birash.

Trevor looked in the rear view mirror and spotted four other vehicles racing after them. Inside of each were numerous well armed soldiers.

"Oh, come on! You've gotta be kidding me!" he said in dismay. "Keep them off my back, man! Lay down some fire!"

Birash pulled a rifle from one of the bags, leveled it at the cars behind them and began squeezing off one round after another. Trevor, in turn, shifted up a gear, and punched it. To his surprise, the four cars that were following him continued to gain. A moment later, bullets flew past them.

"Oh, man, this ain't good! Hang on back there!" shouted Trevor.

He down-shifted as they came up to a cross street, drifted the corner and then buried the accelerator. The engine roared with excitement as the wheels eagerly squealed with glee. The four vehicles behind them tried to follow, but one of them missed the turn and crashed into a tree. Another behind it also missed the turn and sailed into the ditch. But the last two cars successfully made the turn and were soon back on his tail. Birash changed magazines and continued to fire, hitting three different soldiers in the process. Trevor soon shifted up and pushed the engine as hard as it would go as he worked the turns in the road like a pro. The other two cars continued to keep pace with him; despite Trevor's speed and the hail of fire that Birash was throwing at them.

"Man, these guys are harder to shake than the cops," he thought.

As he came upon another turn, he cut the steering wheel hard over and managed to make a nearly impossible right turn, just barely missing a tree as he did. However, the two cars behind him didn't fair so well. The first hit the tree he'd just missed, and the second swerved to miss its companion and flew off the road into the forest. Trevor slowed down slightly, thinking he'd shaken his pursuers, but soon had to accelerate again as another vehicle joined the chase, followed quickly by a second who emerged out of the woods behind him. He powered his way down the road as fast as he could go, despite the jostling the car was taking. But his two pursuers didn't give up. More bullets flew at him, one of which shattered his right side mirror, and another punched through the windshield.

"Keep shooting, man! Get their heads down!" cried Trevor.

"I am trying, you are making it difficult for me to aim at them!" replied Birash.

Trevor soon came upon another intersection and took a sharp right turn before burying the accelerator into the floor again. It was at this moment that he saw something that might help him escape his pursuers. He quickly turned off the road at the entrance to a narrow pathway on his left and then slipped in behind some trees not far away just moments before his pursuers came around the corner behind him. He listened quietly as they sailed past him and out of sight. Once he was sure it was safe, Trevor quietly slipped back onto the road and returned back the way he came. He was soon able to navigate his way back out onto the main highway again. As they continued to drive, Birash sat in the back seat and looked at Trevor in amazement.

"Where did you learn to drive so well?" he asked.

Trevor laughed.

"When you lived the life I did, you learned how to be good at getaways. If you didn't, you either ended up dead or in jail."

"Well, your driving skills are most admirable."

"Yeah, well, let's hope that those losers don't send anyone else after us, or we could be in a lot of trouble. That little cannon ball run has already cost us a lot of gas. Hopefully, we'll have enough to reach a town where we can refuel and then go hunting for the others."

"Are you suggesting that they may still be alive?"

"Are you kidding? With all we've been through already, I'd be shocked if they weren't. Even so, I'm not giving up on them. Especially Aria. I don't even want to imagine living the rest of my life without her."

"Well, then let us pray that you are right; and they are alive. If not, then you will have to soldier on without them until you can be reunited once again before Olumide."

Trevor pursed his lips in frustration.

"Well, I'm not about to give up on her just yet. I'm not gonna give up on any of them."

A man in a light brown sweater pushed open the thick bulkhead door in front of him and stepped through. Nearby, a nurse tended to Aria as she lay unconscious on the bed in front of her. A moment later Yurg stepped through the door behind him.

"What's the prognosis? Has she awoken yet?" asked the man.

The nurse shook her head.

"Not so much as a groan or a twitch since she arrived."

Yurg looked up at the man, and said, "Do you think she's brain damaged?"

The man scratched his beard in thought.

"Given how long she was down, anything is possible. But I pray that she's alright. I would hate to see such a fine young lady die needlessly because of those cursed controllers."

Yurg growled, and then snorted.

"May their bodies rot from their bones," he said.

The man laughed.

"I can understand your hatred of them. We dislike them as well."

Yurg snorted again.

"I do more than dislike them. I hold them in great contempt given what they've done to my friends. It is the least they deserve."

The man sighed.

"Yes, it is."

Yurg then closed his eyes and began to pray.

"Olumide, I know that I am only an animal, and one whom You view as less than these before me. But I ask You, please save Aria and heal her, as she is the only friend I have left," he thought.

Just then, Aria stirred. Yurg's eyes immediately flew open and grew wide in surprise. He watched as she groaned briefly, and then opened her eyes. She looked around in confusion, and tried to sit up, but was held in place by the nurse.

"Don't move, young lady. You've had a bad accident, and you need time to heal," she said.

"Ugh, where am I?" asked Aria weakly.

"Aboard the submersible ship, Calypso," said the man.

Aria looked over at him, and groaned, "Who are you?"

"Captain Clifford Weiss, at your service," said the man elegantly.

Aria smiled.

"Hello, captain," she said weakly. She then took a deep breath, and said, "How'd I get here? I thought I was on a boat."

"You were. But it was damaged by a severe storm and sank," said Yurg.

Aria's eyes lit up as she saw the face of her tiger friend sitting at the foot of her bed.

"Yurg!" she said excitedly.

The tiger smiled.

"It's good to see you are awake. However, I believe it is best that you sleep some more. You need to regain your strength."

"How are the others?" she asked, coughing slightly.

Yurg opened his mouth, and then paused. Aria noticed this immediately. She closed her eyes, sighed sadly, and then went back to sleep. Clifford became concerned.

"Is she alright?" he asked.

The nurse examined her briefly, and then nodded.

"She's fine, just exhausted. After what her body went through, it's understandable. We should leave her alone for a while to rest. The sleep will do her good."

Clifford sighed.

"Alright, well, then let's head out."

"With your permission, I would like to stay with her," said Yurg.

Clifford looked at the tiger briefly, and then nodded.

"Take good care of her for us," he said.

"I will."

The captain and the nurse turned and left the cabin, leaving just Yurg to watch over Aria. As he did, he sat stock still, in absolute silence, for several minutes as he worried deeply about her.

Finally, he sighed, and said, "Olumide, You know I haven't been the best person, and I don't deserve the grace and kindness You've shown me. But I ask that You take my friend Aria into Your care and heal her. I can't bear the thought of losing her. She's the only friend I have left."

He then sat silently by her side and waited patiently for something to happen.

Trevor pulled into a small service station alongside the main highway and stopped in front of a fuel pump. A station attendant in overalls stepped out of a nearby building and walked up to him.

"What can I do for you, my lord?" he asked.

"You got gas?"

"Yes, we do. Whom may I ask is purchasing it?"

"House Sheffield."

Trevor watched as the attendant studied him intently for a moment. He then walked over, turned on the pump and began fueling the vehicle. Once he was done, he gestured for Trevor to follow him.

"Come with me, sir. I'll need your signature."

Trevor shrugged. He'd already stolen a car, weapons and numerous supplies from Sheffield, so it wouldn't be a big deal if he took a little gas too.

"Yeah, be right there in a second," he said.

The attendant nodded, and then walked over to the station house and went inside. As he did, Trevor cautiously turned to Birash.

"Keep your eyes pealed. If things go sideways, I'll need you to bail me out."

"I will be most alert, my friend," said Birash.

Trevor nodded, and then walked over to the station house, and up to the counter where he saw the attendant, who'd pumped his gas, eyeing him oddly.

"Alright, so where do I have to sign?" he asked.

Just then, he felt the cold barrel of a pistol press against the back of his head.

"One wrong move, mate, and you're dead," came a voice behind him.

Trevor slowly raised his hands into the air.

"Alright, Birash, I could use a little help," he said quietly.

The man cocked an eyebrow curiously at this.

"Turn around, lad," he said as he backed up slightly.

Trevor turned slowly and stared at the man before going wide-eyed.

"Alex!?" he exclaimed.

"Trevor!?" said the man in return.

The two stared at each other in surprise as Alex lowered his pistol.

The attendant looked at Alex curiously, and asked, "You two know each other?"

"Aye, we do!" said Alex happily.

Trevor then embraced Alex warmly.

"Dude, I'm so glad you're alive!" he cried.

"Oh, it's so good to see you too, lad! I didn't think anyone else had survived!"

Trevor beamed with joy as a surprised Birash stepped in the door.

"It is good to see you, old friend," he said.

"Birash!" exclaimed Alex with joy.

The two briefly hugged and then shook each other's hands.

"I am most thankful that Olumide has blessed us with this fine reunion," said Birash.

"Yes, He has! So, where's Simon and the others?"

"I don't know, but I aim to find out. If God was cool enough to save the three of us, I'm almost certain the others survived as well. I've even got a car we can use to search for them. If we drive around long enough, we might just stumble onto the others," said Trevor.

"Agreed. However, we should be careful of the locals. They're most unfriendly," said Birash.

"Aye, mate. I fully agree, as I've already had unfortunate dealings with them," said Alex.

"Well, not everyone around here is unfriendly," said the attendant.

Trevor pointed a thumb at him, and asked, "So who's this guy?"

"An old friend of mine. He's helped me take my previous teams safely through this area many times in the past. After I came ashore I worked feverishly to locate him."

"Cool, so he's a good guy?" asked Trevor.

"Aye, he is."

Trevor looked at the attendant, and asked, "So what's your name?"

The attendant shook his head.

"I cannot tell you my name, sir, as it would jeopardize my work here were you to be captured. So I will merely say that I am a friend."

Trevor shrugged.

"Fair enough." He then looked at Alex, and said, "Hey, since the natives are getting restless, I think we need to bust out of here as quickly as we can. I don't want to stay around any longer than we absolutely have to. But I'm also not leaving without the rest of the crew. So we need to get out there and find them as quickly as possible."

"What makes you think God saved them?"

Trevor shrugged.

"We're alive, aren't we? So, I'm betting they're alive as well. Especially given all the scrapes God's gotten us out of so far."

Alex studied the young man intently for several moments.

"Are you sure you want to take that chance?" he asked.

Trevor frowned angrily.

"Simon would never abandon any of us, and I'm sure as heck not abandoning him nor anyone else in our group so long as I'm alive. Especially, not Aria. She's the best thing that's ever happened to me, and I don't plan to give up searching for her until I'm sure she's dead."

Alex sighed slightly.

"Alright, mate. We'll turn around and hunt for the others. But if we don't find them by the end of the week, promise me you'll give up and continue the race."

"Deal."

"I agree to your request as well, for my friend, Yurg, still remains among the lost members of our team," said Birash.

"Yeah, we're not leaving him behind either," said Trevor.

"Alright lad, let's get going. Time is not on our side," said Alex.

"I'm on it!" said Trevor excitedly.

He hurried out to the car, jumped in the driver's seat, and started the engine. Alex soon walked up to the driver's side and motioned for him to get out.

"I'm driving," he said.

"No you're not," replied Trevor.

"Get out. That's an order."

"Fat chance, Gramps. I'm the better driver and you're the better shot. If we get jumped by more of those goons along the way, you'll need my pimp driving skills; and I'll need your mad shooting skills. So get in. You're riding shotgun."

Alex grinned. He had to admit that Trevor was right. It'd been so long since he'd last driven that he wasn't sure he'd remember how.

"Alright, lad. Then do your best," he replied.

He then hurried to the other side and got in. Trevor, in turn, threw the car into gear, popped the clutch, and powered down the road with a roar.

Chapter 23

Simon crouched down next to a tree as Mathias and his four men took cover behind him.

"Oh, this is gonna be interesting," said Simon.

"What do you see?" asked Mathias.

"Trouble, and lots of it. I'm counting seventeen, all well-armed regulars, and at least two LAV's, none of which look friendly."

"What are LAV's?"

"Light armored vehicles. We'll definitely want to avoid getting on the wrong side of those."

"So what do we do now?"

"I'm not totally sure. Alex was our combat expert. I'm just an armchair general."

"And I'm a sailor, so we're both in the same boat. No pun intended, of course."

Simon looked behind him, and said, "Are any of your men combat trained?"

"Only in fending off pirates, but nothing like this."

"Hmm, that's going to complicate things," growled Simon.

"What do you mean?"

Simon lifted his binoculars and studied the soldiers in front of them. After a bit, he sighed as he lowered them.

"In order to get where we're going, we'll probably have to shoot our way out of here; and against regulars like that, we're cannon fodder."

Just then, a whistling filled the air, followed by a boom and a shower of dirt that sent several men flying into the air. Another explosion shattered a nearby tree, instantly killing two men.

"Oh great. What else can go wrong?" muttered Simon.

"What is that!?" asked Mathias.

"Artillery! Keep your head's down!"

The two LAV's nearby immediately turned and began scrambling for cover. As the shelling continued, one of the shells landed on the top of an LAV and destroyed it. It wasn't long before the soldiers vacated the area along with the last remaining LAV. Shortly after this, the shelling stopped; although more rounds could be heard landing in the distance.

"Well, that's an improvement," thought Simon.

A moment later, two stray shells exploded not too far from his group; followed by another that shattered a tree just in front of them a second later.

"Okay, that's it! We're outta here! Everyone, follow me!" he shouted.

The six men then got up and sprinted as fast as they could through the woods as more stray shells exploded nearby. As they ran, though, they were soon spotted by two soldiers who hadn't as yet evacuated the area.

"Hey, you! Halt!" shouted one of them.

Simon drew his rifle and fired, dropping both men. He and the others then continued sprinting through the forest as best they could, despite the mass chaos around them. Suddenly, three soldiers came through a line of bushes in front of them, rifles at the ready. But before they could shoot, Simon and Mathias took them out as the others in the team knocked down another group that attacked them from behind. Moments later more soldiers appeared.

"Enemy left!" shouted Simon.

His entire group turned and decimated the enemy squad.

"Go! Go! Go!" shouted Mathias as he urged the others forward.

The group sprinted forward; and eventually made their way out onto a nearby trail where they found, much to their surprise, a unattended jeep parked near a tree.

Simon tossed his rifle in the front seat, and said, "Get in!"

The five men quickly piled in as Simon fired up the engine, threw it into gear, and then raced away as fast as the vehicle would go. Several soldiers tried to stop them, but Mathias and his men put them down with accurate and deadly fire. They then continued on for a ways, flying past one group of soldiers after another. But none of these took any notice of them, almost as though they were now invisible. Eventually though, after driving a considerable distance, the jeep ran out of gas and the six men were forced to walk again. However, it'd been enough to at least get them away from the front lines and deeper into Sheffield territory. Now it would be much safer for them to proceed from this point onward as they'd managed to leave most of the war behind. The rest of that afternoon they walked down a series of side roads and wide pathways until they reached the main highway. But, just as they stepped onto a main road, Simon spotted a vehicle approaching them at high speed.

"Car! Get down!" he shouted.

The group quickly retreated off the road and melted into the bushes. Simon then raised his binoculars to see who it was. To his surprise, he spotted Alex, Trevor and Birash all riding in what appeared to be a sports car. He rushed out onto the road and waved happily to them. The car soon pulled to a stop in front of him.

"Blimey, mate! Are we glad to see you!" exclaimed Alex.

"How did you guys survive?" asked Simon in amazement.

"By the grace of God, that's how."

"So where'd you get the car?"

"Dude, you like it? It's my new pimp-mobile. I stole it from the Sheffield mansion, so it's the hottest thing on the road right now," said Trevor in a jazzy, street thug manner.

Simon laughed.

"I love it. Is it fast?"

"It's pimp, and it moves, yo."

Alex then looked over at the edge of the road as five men appeared out of the bushes and approached the car casually.

"Hey, Simon, who are these chaps?" he asked.

Simon gestured to the men, and said, "Gentlemen, this is Mathias and his team. They took me in after I washed ashore, and gave me a place to stay for a few days. After that, they helped me get through some seriously rough territory to get here."

He then studied the others and soon realized they were missing two people.

"Hey, where's Aria and Yurg?"

"We're still looking for them. Hop in, and you can help us search," said Trevor.

Simon nodded, and then turned to Mathias.

"Thank you for all your help. But you should get back to your village. With the war escalating, your people will need you soon."

"What about you?" asked Mathias.

"Most of my team is back together again, so I'll be fine. God bless you, and take care."

Mathias smiled and patted Simon on the shoulder.

"God bless you as well, brother; and may He guide your paths, and carry you safely to the finish line, or to wherever He wishes."

"Amen," said Simon happily. He then jumped in the back with Birash, and said, "Alright, young man, let's go find the rest of our team!"

Trevor gave out a whooping cry, put the car in gear and punched the gas. As they sped away, a blue-skinned man watched them with contempt from the nearby trees.

"I may have failed to destroy them before. But I will not fail again," he hissed, and then vanished in a flash of fire.

A moment later, Fallon stepped out of the bushes alongside the road, looked to his left in the direction that Simon and the others had gone, and then over at where the blue-skinned man had been. He soon pursed his lips in displeasure. A moment later, a man dressed head to toe in glistening white robes appeared next to him. Fallon grunted.

"He is persistent, if nothing else," he muttered.

"In the name of God, he will not succeed," said the man in white.

Fallon sighed.

"No, I doubt he will. However, he will still cause them great pain and suffering."

"Maybe so, but that does not mean that God will not be victorious."

Fallon nodded.

"Agreed," he replied

He then looked to his left again in the direction of Simon's team.

"But at what cost to him and his team?" he continued.

The man in white shook his head.

"I do not know."

"Neither do I. Even so, whatever it may be, I pray that whatever they are made to suffer will not be greater than what they are willing or able to bear."

Clifford walked onto the bridge of the Calypso and studied the stations around him.

"Status report."

The first officer turned to him and shook his head.

"Nothing to report, sir. The scope is clear."

"Any word from the Odyssey?"

"They're not seeing anything either. However, they've been picking up scattered radio chatter from the Four Kingdoms all day. Apparently, they're going at it pretty hot and heavy right now."

"Any response from the controllers?"

"None yet."

Clifford's eyes narrowed.

"Yet, they sank a ship full of innocent travelers. How odd," he said as he mulled this over.

The first officer cocked his head slightly.

"Maybe they're not as innocent as you think."

"Possibly. But why would the controllers go out of their way to attack them; and yet do nothing about the Four Kingdoms. It just doesn't make sense."

The first officer shrugged.

"Perhaps because some of them were believers like we are. Given that the controllers don't like us, it's possible they were attacked because of their faith."

Clifford contemplated this.

"Possibly, but I still think there's more to it than that. But we'll determine that another day. In the meantime, take us to periscope depth. Let's see what's out there."

"Aye, sir," said the first officer.

The submarine ascended and soon leveled out near the surface. Clifford raised the periscope and looked around, but saw nothing except flat blue sea. He turned slowly as he scanned the area trying his best to see something other than open water. After a bit, he glanced over at the compass, and then back through the periscope.

"Helm, make revolutions for ten knots and set course two seven two degrees."

"Revolutions for ten knots, course two seven two degrees, aye," came the reply.

Clifford felt the gentle acceleration of the submarine under him as he continued to scan the sea for ships. It worried him that he could see nothing but empty water.

"Any sonar contacts?" he asked.

"Negative, sir. None at this time. The scope is clear," came the reply.

Clifford lowered the periscope.

"Helm, five degrees down bubble. Depth, one hundred feet."

"Five degrees down bubble. Depth, one hundred feet, aye."

Clifford thought about things for a bit, and then turned to a map table next to him. His first officer stood to the side and studied him curiously.

"What's on your mind?" he asked.

Clifford sighed heavily.

"It doesn't make sense. These lanes are normally crawling with merchant ships; and yet, we've not seen a single one of them for the past several days. At least, not since that last storm."

The first officer nibbled on his lip.

"I agree. So it makes me wonder if this mission is over with already."

Clifford looked up at him curiously.

"What do you mean?"

"Think about it. What was our only haul for this trip?"

Clifford cocked an eyebrow.

"Just the cargo of one ship, plus two unexpected passengers."

The first officer nodded.

"Right, and what have we had since then? Nothing. No new cargo, no newly sunken ships, and nothing but flat, calm seas. If you ask me, I think we're being told to go home."

Clifford scratched his beard in thought. He then narrowed his eyes.

"You don't think that our passengers were the whole reason we were sent out here, do you?"

"I don't know. But if that was the primary purpose for this mission set down by God, then we're not likely to bring home anymore cargo this trip than what we've already brought in. So it's only reasonable to assume that we'll gain nothing by staying out here any longer."

Clifford mulled this over for a bit. Finally, he nodded in agreement.

"That's entirely possible, given what I've seen. Very well, then, let's set course for home."

"Aye, sir."

Lord Banister walked into the military war room of his estate, on the far side of the Sheffield Republic, and over to a general who was standing next to a large map table akin to those used during World War 2. He leaned against the table as he studied the map quietly for several minutes as various women with headsets and large pusher sticks moved numerous wooden markers across the map like chess pieces on a gigantic Risk board. Each one represented one of Sheffield's numerous army units and their positions relative to the three neighboring kingdoms.

"What is the prognosis of the battle?" asked Banister after some time.

The general crossed his arms and frowned.

"Neither good, nor bad. As before, we are stuck in a stalemate with Unity along the western border, and have made little progress into Thorn territory beyond our initial incursion. The only good news is that, thankfully, Thorn has show little interest in fighting. They seem more concerned with GAK than they are with us," said the general.

Banister rubbed his chin as he pondered this.

"And we, in turn, are more concerned with Unity than we are with Thorn. Especially since Unity has that blasted General Amaroth commanding their best troops. If we don't keep him boxed in, he'll become a real problem for us."

The general narrowed his eyes.

"That is true. But we should not take Thorn lightly, either, as they are still a threat, even though they are relatively quiet for the moment," he replied.

"Yes, they are indeed a threat. But nowhere near as much as Unity. So long as they have General Amaroth at their disposal, the Unity Empire will remain a difficult, and potentially lethal threat to us. As much as I am loathe to seek peace with Thorn, it may be in our best interests to do so until we have dealt with Unity."

The general frowned.

"That might work *if* we were able to trust them to keep that peace, which we should not."

Banister shook his head.

"I believe we can. As you said, Thorn is less worried about us than they are about GAK. So I believe that, if we were to seek peace with them for a season, it would buy us the time and resources we need to defeat Unity, and they GAK in turn. Then, once we have each dealt respectively with those two, we can then settle our differences between ourselves."

Just then, a dispatch runner rushed into the office, saluted the general, handed him an envelope, and then hurried away to deliver other messages. Banister looked at the general as he opened the envelope and read its contents. The general's brow furrowed at what he read.

"What is it?" asked Banister.

"It would seem that the missing racers that we have been looking for were spotted no more than an hour ago about sixty miles from here," replied the general.

"Have they been captured or killed?" asked Banister excitedly.

The general lowered the letter and looked at his supreme leader.

"Unfortunately, neither has happened. The local commander who received this tip was unable to act on it quickly enough to intercept them. However, based on their last known location and direction of travel, we can safely predict their next destination."

"How?" asked Banister curiously.

The general turned to the map table, took a stick that lay in front of him and used it to point at one part of the map.

"They will soon arrive here, if they haven't already," said the general.

"And how do you know this?"

The general again furrowed his brow. He pointed at another place on the map.

"I know that because they were last seen turning down this road here. And, given the lateness of the hour, and their likely fuel situation, it is believed that they will stop here for the night. As such, that is where the commander is sending the bulk of his forces in an effort to intercept them."

A dark, evil grin drew across Banister's face.

"And then we will have them cornered before dark," he said with sadistic glee.

"Indeed we will, sir. And once they're dead, we can continue our efforts to rule this entire world uncontested," replied the general.

Banister let out a low, dark, guttural laugh.

"Even though we have failed briefly at our task to block all racers from completing the course, in the end we will still succeed; and as such, our kingdom will not fall on my watch. No, in fact, it shall never fall. Not even in a thousand years."

Yurg's ears perked up as he heard a groaning come from the bed nearby. He looked up in interest and saw that Aria was stirring.

"How are you feeling?" he asked.

"Like roadkill. It's the worst thing ever. Plus I'm hungry. Any chance you can get me something to eat?" groaned Aria.

Yurg stood up and headed for the door.

"I will see what I can do."

He slipped out of the room and returned a while later with a nurse and cook in tow. They fed her a simple meal of pottage, which she inhaled greedily as though she hadn't eaten in weeks. As she waited for it to settle, the nurse gave her another inspection and found her fit enough to move about the ship. Aria took the news gladly and immediately got to her feet. But a quick flash of vertigo sent her wheeling again. She fought through it the best she could and soon regained her balance.

"Now take it easy, young lady," said the nurse.

"I'm fine, really," protested Aria.

Yurg sat on the floor nearby and studied her with interest.

"You still appear sick," he said with a hint of concern.

"Yurg, I'm fine. I just..."

She stumbled backwards as another rush of vertigo hit her like a freight train.

"On second thought, I think I'll stay here," she said as she back down on the bed.

"That's a wise idea. You're recovering well, if I do say so myself. But, you'll still need a bit more time until you're healthy enough to go walking again," said the nurse.

She tucked Aria back into bed, and excused herself from the room. Yurg studied her with both concern and curiosity. What was it about this human female that made her so determined to get up and move about despite her condition. Her bravery and determination were admirable, even among his own species. He walked over, sat down next to her, and laid his head in her lap. She smiled happily and kindly scratched him behind the ears. Yurg purred contentedly. Aria laughed.

"You not a tiger. You're just a big, furry kitty cat, aren't you?" she chided.

Yurg grinned.

"While I am similar to your felines, I am still very much a tiger." He then raised his head slightly, and asked, "How are you feeling?"

Aria grunted.

"I'm still feeling sick. I don't know why, but I am. In fact, I don't remember much at all since the boat trip. I remember boarding with the others, we sailed for a while, there was a storm, we all went below as the wind tossed..."

She paused as terrifying memories of the storm filled her mind. She remembered seeing the ship break apart, but couldn't remember anything else after that. She looked down at Yurg curiously.

"Did the ship sink?" she asked.

Yurg nodded.

"It did," he said grimly.

"What happened after that? I don't remember anything."

"Unfortunately, neither do I."

Just then, the door to their cabin creaked open and Clifford stepped in.

"I may be able to help you with that," he said.

Yurg raised his head and looked at Clifford curiously.

"What do you know about the events surrounding our arrival here?" he asked.

Clifford crossed his arms and studied the two racers before him.

"Quite a bit, actually. Needless to say, you arrived in the strangest way I've ever seen, and I've seen a lot. It all started several days ago when a sea storm came out of nowhere. Realizing that your ship was in peril, we immediately sailed to your location expecting it to sink at any time, as we were after the cargo that would be spilled from its holds when it did. And it wasn't long before my hunch proved right. But when we began searching for recoverable cargo, my dive teams came across you and your tiger friend who were both, much to our surprise, still alive. So, I had them rescue you and bring you aboard."

"Wow. Were there any other survivors?" asked Aria.

Clifford shook his head.

"You were the only ones we found alive, and for that, you should be thankful. Both of you were half drowned when we brought you in. Normally, we don't rescue survivors of shipwrecks as there rarely are any after The Reaping Sea gets done with them. But in your case, somehow, you beat the odds. So, we took you aboard and have been tending to you ever since. I can't say so much for your friend, though. He was back on his feet in no time. It was quite the recovery."

Yurg turned away shyly.

"It was by the grace of Olumide that I am well; which is an honor that I do not deserve," he said.

Clifford laughed.

"None of us does, my feline friend. But God still loves us, despite our failings. If He didn't, we'd all be chum by now."

"For what I've done in my life, I should be," said Yurg.

Clifford bent down and gently took the tiger's face in his hands.

"Olumide has forgiven you, so you should serve Him to your fullest."

Yurg studied him intently for a moment, and then nodded slightly. Just then, one of the crewmen came racing up to the door.

"Captain, you're needed on the bridge. It's Sheffield," said the man.

Clifford glanced at him briefly, and then back at Aria and Yurg.

"Excuse me for a moment. I have something I need to attend to."

He then hurried out of the room and down the hallway. As soon as he was gone, Aria and Yurg looked at each other in concern.

"What do we do now?" asked Aria anxiously.

Yurg sighed.

"I believe we should do what our friend Birash did in situations like this."

"What's that?"

"Pray."

"But I don't know what we should pray about?"

Yurg grinned.

"Does it matter?"

Aria thought about this for a moment, and then shrugged.

"Fair point. Well then, since you suggested it, I think you should start us off."

Yurg grinned wider.

"It would be my pleasure."

Simon sat on the end of his bed and carefully went about cleaning his rifle, as Trevor and Alex sat nearby doing the same thing with their weapons.

"I have a question for you, mate," said Alex.

"Shoot," replied Simon.

"I notice you're still carrying the same weapon I gave you earlier in the race, as well as the same gear you had before. How is that possible when the rest of us lost all of ours?"

Simon shrugged.

"Beats me. From what Mathias told me, he found me and my gear completely high and dry just sitting on his porch one morning as though I'd never been in the water."

"Well, that's odd. I've never heard of that before."

"Do you believe it was the controllers who saved you?" asked Birash.

"I don't think it was. From everything I've heard, they're more likely to kill you than save you," said Simon.

"Pfft. Controllers. I'd like to bust a cap in all of them," muttered Trevor.

Simon stared at him oddly.

"You've been in a rather foul mood since we found each other earlier today. What's up?"

"Gee, I don't know. So far this week, I've been shipwrecked, shot at, my girlfriend is missing, and that's just the beginning. So, you take a guess, genius," snapped Trevor.

Simon studied Trevor for a bit, and then set his rifle aside.

"Does the thought of losing Aria bother you that much?"

Trevor looked at Simon incredulously.

"She's your friend, too; and you're not worried about her?" he said.

"Yes, of course I am. You're all my friends, and the thought of losing any of you is heartbreaking to me. But in the end, we're all believers; so we'll never really lose anyone. Those that die will just go on ahead of us to Heaven where we'll all be reunited again some day. But if they're still alive, then I believe that God will bring us back together again soon."

Trevor sighed heavily.

"And what if He doesn't? What then? What if He sends them another direction?"

Simon shrugged.

"Then, so be it."

"WHAT!? You'd just let them go like that!?" snapped Trevor.

"If it's God's will, then there's nothing we can do. But look at the bright side. If He's sent them on a different path from us, then He must have a special plan for them. So, we should be happy for them, especially if they're still alive. Either way, God has us in His hands, and nothing this world brings against us can take us away from him."

Trevor snorted.

"That's a rather lame answer."

"Well? What more can I say? Just look at where we've been and what God's done for us so far. He brought us together, got each of you saved, except of course for Birash who already was, and protected us from some pretty crazy situations. Yes, I understand that you're angry about this whole thing; but you've got to just let it go and let God handle this. If you don't, it'll poison your heart with bitterness, anger and resentment which will in turn destroy the wonderful person you are."

Trevor sighed as he thought about this.

"Alright, I'll try."

Just then, a banging came at the door.

"Who is it?" asked Simon.

"You gentlemen need to leave immediately! Sheffield troops are surrounding the village! I believe they're after you and your team!"

The four men looked at each other nervously.

"Okay, not good," said Simon.

Chapter 24

Clifford stepped onto the bridge and noticed his first officer looking through the periscope.

"What'cha got?" he asked.

"Sheffield troops are surrounding a fishing village just ahead," said the first officer.

"Come again?" said Clifford in surprise.

The first officer stepped back and gestured to the periscope.

"Have a look for yourself."

Clifford walked over and glanced through the periscope. He couldn't see much in the dwindling light of early evening, but the shapes that lined the outskirts of the town were unmistakable. Even more surprising was the sheer number of them.

"Why would Sheffield send troops to a little village in the middle of nowhere?" he asked.

"That's what I was trying to determine. But so far, I haven't been able to come up with a reasonable answer," said the first officer.

Clifford pondered this briefly, and then said, "Park us on the bottom of the river on the southern shore. I want to wait and see what this is about."

"Aye, sir," replied the first officer. He then turned to the two helmsmen, and said, "Helm, all stop. Adjust dive planes and set us gently on the river bottom."

The two helmsmen repeated and confirmed his orders. As they did, Clifford lowered the periscope and then leaned against a nearby railing as he thought about this.

"What's on your mind?" asked the first officer.

"I don't know. Sheffield wouldn't be doing something like this unless they had a really good reason to. Especially with the war in full swing as it is."

"Do you think they're after someone?"

"It's possible. The question is, who would be so valuable that they'd commit that many troops to their capture, or perhaps worse, their execution? All I saw was a lot of frightened villagers, but no Unity troops nearby. So their actions make no sense."

"Is there anything we can do?"

"At this point, no. For now, we'll just wait and observe. The Sheffield troops won't move again until first light when they can see what they're doing. So that'll give us time to discover what this is all about. However, until then we need to gather reinforcements, just in case we need them. So contact the Odyssey and the Thor. Tell them to meet us here as quickly as possible."

"Aye, sir."

Fallon appeared in a flash of light in the middle of a lush, green valley in front of a large, brilliantly red dragon and stood quietly as the elder dragon slept. However, it wasn't long before the dragon's nostrils twitched and wiggled as he sniffed at the air. He then cracked his eyes open and soon spotted the young dragon.

"Well, hello, young one," said the elder dragon with a smile.

"Greetings, Elder," said Fallon in return.

The older dragon, who was Fallon's grandfather, Zek, master of the Southern Weyr, let out a slow, deep chuckle. Even though his grandson was still just a young child by dragon standards, Fallon displayed a maturity and professionalism ten times his age.

"For what purpose do you come here today?" he asked, his voice authoritative, yet kindly.

"I have come from seeing to the safety of the one known as Simon, as well as his team. It would seem that the demon Sheobaal has taken an unhealthy interest in them," replied Fallon.

Zek pondered this for several moments.

"Hmm, you have told me about his interest in them before. Have you, as yet, determined the reason for his unhealthy interest in them?" he asked.

Fallon shook his head.

"I have not. I can only assume that he, this Simon, is hated so greatly by Sheobaal because he is a strong Christian. Thus, Sheobaal seeks to do all within his considerable power to destroy him and those who travel with him."

Zek thought about this deeply.

"Hmm, yes indeed. Such a theory does seem within the bounds of credibility. But what do you intend to do about it?"

Fallon furrowed his brow.

"I am not certain at this time. For the moment, I have quietly hindered Sheobaal from the shadows with reasonable success. However, as his anger increases, doing so will become ever more difficult. In time, I may even need to openly raise my hand against him; an action I do not wish to undertake if at all possible."

"Why?" asked Zek.

Fallon pursed his lips.

"Because, if I do, he will bring reinforcements, which will be most unfortunate, as one demon I can handle by myself. But a whole legion? Even you do not have the strength to stand against such an army. Nor would you wish to enrage our masters in doing so either. It is why I fear to push against him too greatly; lest, in his anger, he seek out others to join with him on his mission of destruction. Or, perhaps even worse, bring the wrath of our masters down upon us."

"What of Caleb? Is he not an angel?"

"He is. But even he cannot stand against an entire legion."

Zek contemplated this briefly.

"Hmm, perhaps. But, even if they can defeat one such as Caleb, should he stand alone against them, they cannot overcome the power of God. Therefore I believe you are concerning yourself too much with this trial, young one."

Fallon frowned.

"Maybe, I am. But one is not wise if he is not also cautious."

Zek smiled.

"Indeed. However, do not be too cautious. Such might be mistaken for weakness."

Fallon furrowed his brow, but said nothing.

"So, what do you intend to do about this Simon and his team?" asked Zek.

Fallon turned and began to pace back and forth. After a bit, he stopped and looked at the elder dragon, thoughtfully.

"Of all the years in which I have been a part of this race, I have never seen one such as him. It is as though there is something special about him, as well as those who travel with him. I cannot explain it; save to say that, for the first time in many years, I actually feel as though I have found someone who has a real chance of winning this race."

"But you are only barely fifty years old; a young child in my eyes. What could you have seen in such a short span of time that would give you the authority to speak on this topic?"

"I do not speak, merely, from my own experience; but also from that of nearly every other dragon on this world. Especially those who've lived since before the race began. It is through all that they have taught me, as well as my own experiences, that I have come to this conclusion."

Zek licked his teeth in intrigue.

"Hmm, interesting."

Just then, a small red dot on Zek's forearm chirped and began to blink. He cocked his head slightly in interest.

"It would seem that I am being summoned," he said.

He waved his hand over the dot and a moment later the holographic image of a man in a brown business suit appeared next to him.

"Ah, greetings, master! How may I serve you?" asked Zek.

The man took a long draw on a thin cigar and then exhaled a thick cloud of smoke.

"There's a village in hextant three, quadrant seven four five one, that is causing problems for us. Their defiance has created a situation that needs immediate rectification. Therefore, we request that you destroy it and scatter its inhabitants. We wish to send them a message that their blatant insubordination will not be tolerated," he said.

Zek gave a slight bow of his head.

"As you wish," he replied.

The image then shimmered and vanished. Fallon found this intriguing.

"So you have an assignment," he said.

"Yes, indeed, it would seem that I do. The first one in some time, in fact. It brings me a feeling of excitement to, once again, put wind under my wings and bear fire from my breast!"

Fallon narrowed his eyes.

"I pray that your adventures do not cross my path. For it is already difficult enough for me to keep them safe without you or the others getting in my way," he said with a hint of frustration.

"Hmm, as do I. However, I do not believe they will come near the place in which we will be plying our duties," replied Zek.

"I pray that you are right. So, how soon do you plan to leave?"

"There is much scouting that must be done before our battle can be set in array. So it may be several days before I will know when that will be."

Fallon nodded.

"Understood. Then, I pray that your mission goes well."

Zek smiled.

"As do I."

As morning dawned the next day, Alex studied the Sheffield troops through his binoculars as he sat in the bushes near the Inn.

"Blimey. That's a lot of soldiers," he whispered.

"Are there more than we thought there were?" asked Simon.

"Lots more, mate. At least several companies, if not more."

"Several companies!? Why so many!?"

"Given the ruckus we caused over the last few days, I'm surprised they didn't send the whole army after us," quipped Trevor.

"Yeah, well, army or not, we're still pinned down with no way out. That's going to make life *real* difficult for us," said Simon.

"Enemies of the Sheffield Republic! We know you're there! Surrender now and you will be shown mercy. Resist, and we will level this village to the ground!" shouted one of the soldiers.

"Go home you ogres! We're not scared of you!" shouted a villager.

"We're not here for you, old man! We want the racers who are hiding in your village."

"We don't have any."

"Liars! Our spies saw them enter your Inn. Now, surrender them or face the consequences!"

"You can't take what ain't here! So get lost, you worthless dirt rat!"

"Do not defy us! We have armor and an entire division of soldiers at our disposal! Surrender the racers and we will leave you alone. Resist, and we will obliterate you!" shouted the soldier.

Simon grunted in frustration.

"The Sheffield aren't exactly subtle with their demands, are they?" he said.

"They never are," said Alex.

"Eh, this isn't any worse than a few of the standoffs I've been in. Just kneecap the right guys and the rest will open a path wide enough for you to drive a truck through," said Trevor.

"I don't think that's such a good idea. On the streets that might work, but not against battle hardened infantry. So we have to be careful what we do. Especially since we risk drawing the villagers into this," said Simon.

Trevor looked at the dozens of villagers scattered around the village and took stock of their impressive collection of firepower. He snorted dismissively.

"Given what they're packing, I doubt this is the first time they've tangoed," he said.

Alex studied the others briefly, and then shook his head.

"Maybe so, but they're only civilians, not soldiers. Given the number of regulars we're facing, this will quickly become a slaughter if the Sheffield start shooting," he said.

"Eh, maybe, and maybe not," said Simon.

"What do you mean?" asked Alex.

"I'm no professional here, but I have a feeling the Sheffield aren't quite as strong as they let on."

"How so?" asked Alex.

Suddenly, he realized what Simon was getting at.

"The war," he said.

"Exactly. Given how small these kingdoms are, from what you and the others have told me, and given the fact that they're currently at war with each other, committing anything more than a company of soldiers to hunt us down would be strategically and logistically impossible. Or at the very least it'd be unrecommended. So I think they're actually committing less troops than they're saying, or making us think that they have," replied Simon.

"So, wait a second. Are you saying that they haven't jumped us yet because we actually outnumber them!?" asked Trevor.

"I don't think that's the case. If anything, it's the other way around. So I get the feeling that they're wanting to come out of this without any casualties on their side as they likely can't afford them. That's why they're playing it safe and using threats and psychological warfare to flush us out rather than bullets. They could also be under orders to bring us back alive. That means that any exchange of fire on their part risks those orders going unfulfilled or properly carried out."

"I guess that makes sense. So what do we do to extricate ourselves from this situation?"

"Could we not escape via the river?" asked Birash.

"We could, but we'd need boats for that; and we don't have any for the moment," said Simon.

"Actually, we do. Look."

Simon turned and studied the dock carefully. He soon spotted two boats tied up there. Unfortunately, neither looked to be in very good condition. He soon turned back to the others.

"That won't work. The docks are too exposed, and the boats are questionable. To make matters worse, if we tried that, they'd just cut us down before we got halfway there," he said.

"Alright, so what's our plan then? We can't just stay here forever," said Trevor.

Just then Birash heard a whooshing sound emanating from the river. He turned and was surprised to see three submarines rising out of the water behind them.

"Look! A new danger has appeared!" he said, pointing towards the docks.

The others turned just in time to see the submarines deploying their remote controlled, twin barrel, deck guns that were slowly turning in their direction.

"Oh, this is gonna get ugly," groaned Simon.

Suddenly a 'pop-pop-pop' began echoing from the guns. However, much to the surprise of Simon's team, the shells were not aimed at them, but instead buzzed over their heads and slammed into the Sheffield lines, sending men flying through the air, and scrambling in every direction.

"Whoa! Whose side are they on!?" shouted Trevor.

"Obviously, not Sheffield's," replied Simon.

He, and the others, then watched in fascination as one shell after another tore through the Sheffield troops, causing the men to dive for cover; and then eventually, scatter into the woods. After a bit, the guns fell silent. The four men looked anxiously at the river.

"Now what?" asked Trevor.

"Let's wait and see what happens," said Simon.

It wasn't long before one of the submarines turned towards shore, and then pulled up to the pier. As it did, an older man in a floppy cap and woolen sweater appeared on the conning tower.

"Ahoy, mates! Is one of you Simon?" he shouted.

"That's me," replied Simon.

"Excellent! Come aboard before Sheffield returns with reinforcements!"

"How do we know we can trust you?" shouted Trevor.

"Your friends are waiting for you below! Now come, quickly! We don't have much time!" said the man insistently.

"Do you think they're legitimate?" asked Trevor.

"Given our situation, I'm willing to take the chance. Now let's go," said Simon.

The four men immediately scurried across the village and boarded the submarine. As soon as they were inside, the man closed the hatch behind them, and then activated a nearby intercom.

"Bridge, this is the captain. Move us to the middle of the channel, and then dive to periscope depth. Radio the others to submerge as well."

"Aye, captain," came the reply.

Simon studied the man with interest.

"So you're the captain, eh?" he said.

The man tipped his hat to him, and said, "That I am. Clifford Weiss is my name, and I'm the skipper of the Calypso. It seems that God is with you today. We came up this way with plans to drop off your friends at our base further up river. However, it seems that God had other plans."

Simon furrowed his brow.

"You're a believer?" he said in amazement.

"Yes, sir, I am. Have been most of my life."

"Wow, that's incredible. We were praying that God would lead us to our other friends; and here He's not only arranged our reunion, but transportation as well," said Simon happily.

However, Trevor studied the man suspiciously.

"You said our friends were here. What's their names?" he asked.

"Aria and Yurg, according to them anyways. It's a young girl and her tiger friend, am I correct?" asked Clifford.

Trevor's jaw nearly hit the deck.

"She's alive!?" he said in surprise.

"Sure is. If you wish to see her, come this way."

Clifford then led the four men through the submarine and up to one of the cabins where they found Yurg and Aria sitting quietly on the bed.

"Aria!?" said Trevor in utter joy.

Aria turned and looked towards the door; and as soon as her eyes met Trevor's, her entire face lit up with joy! She leapt out of the bed and hugged him tightly. Tears then streamed down their faces as they held onto each other with what looked like a death grip. Clifford laughed.

"Well, they're obviously happy to see each other," he quipped.

Simon laughed.

"Eh, they'll come up for air, eventually."

The others laughed. As Trevor and Aria continued to hug each other, Birash pushed his way past them and walked over to Yurg. He stared at the tiger compassionately as tears began to well up in Yurg's eyes.

"How are you, my friend?" he said kindly.

"I am better now that I know you are alive. It gives my heart a peace it did not have before," replied Yurg happily.

"Are you still worried about the life debts?" asked Birash in concern.

Yurg looked away briefly.

"While they are still important, having your companionship means more to me than anything else. Our separation, albeit brief, has shown me how much I need you, even though I never thought so before. It is because your friendship is a blessing to me."

Birash scratched Yurg's chin kindly.

"And yours has been a blessing to me as well."

Yurg closed his eyes, smiled and purred happily. He then reached up and embraced Birash, much in the same way Aria and Trevor had each other. Even though this surprised Birash, it made him happy. He then hugged his friend in return. Simon smiled as he watched the two former enemies, now friends, so happy to see each other. Finally having them as true teammates would make things easier on the journey ahead. He then turned his attention to the two teenagers next to him. To his surprise, they were still hugging. He laughed.

"Alright, you two, breathe," he chided.

Eventually, they parted; but kept their eyes locked on each other as tears poured down their faces. Simon smiled and patted Trevor on the shoulder.

"You two stay here and talk a while. I want to go discuss something with the captain," he said.

Trevor and Aria giggled happily, and then sat down to talk as Simon and Alex stepped out of the room and closed the door behind them.

"So what did you want to discuss?" asked Clifford.

"A destination. Given the current unfriendliness of the neighborhood, and the fact that we've somehow unwittingly made ourselves serious enemies of the Sheffield, we need passage upriver to somewhere safer."

Clifford scratched his chin.

"Where specifically did you have in mind?" he asked.

Simon turned to Alex, and said, "You know the course better than any of us. Got any ideas on a good place we can put ashore and resume our journey?"

Alex shook his head.

"Sorry, mate. I have no idea. I've never taken the river before."

Simon sighed as he tried to think of a solution to their problem. Suddenly, he remembered his navigator compass. He pulled it out of his pack and studied it. It showed the river they were on, but no sign of the trail. He then fiddled with several of the buttons on it, causing the map to zoom out until he could see where they were relative to the trail.

"Alright, according to the compass, we're here. Somewhere in this area is the Four Kingdoms, through the center of which passes the trail. Since it's apparently their mission, for whatever crazy reason, to kill every single hiker that passes through their territories, we'll need a way to get around them; and hopefully, into safer territory beyond. I'm thinking this river and your submarine might do the trick for us. Can you help us?" he asked.

Clifford looked at the compass in Simon's hand.

"I think this would be better done on a larger screen. Follow me," he said.

He then led the two men to the bridge and over to a map table where a digital overview of the area was being displayed. Simon was impressed with this. The map table looked like a much, much larger version of his navigator compass.

"Where did you get this?" he asked.

"It's one of several that we salvaged it from a crashed controller shuttle we found in the woods a few decades ago."

"And the controllers are alright with this?" asked Alex.

"I doubt they are. But if they don't have a problem with us having it, then neither do we," said Clifford with a grin.

He played with the digital map for nearly a minute until he was able to produce a much larger, fully detailed layout of the area. He then pointed to the map.

"Alright, these areas here represent the Four Kingdoms. Each of them currently controls a section of the trail or its adjoining territories, as I'm sure you're aware of. To get past them, you'll need to follow the river we're on due west of this point here, which is our base at Subton, for several hundred miles. However, you'll have to do most of that on your own, as we're not allowed to go past our base, which is located here."

Simon looked at the map and nibbled on his lip in frustration.

"Yeah, but that's the problem. Your base is right in the middle of Unity territory which will still leave us in considerable danger."

Clifford shrugged.

"I wish I could help more; but as I said, we can't take you any farther than that."

"Why? Is it an operational restriction or a technical one?"

"It's actually a navigational issue. About ten miles west of our base, the river becomes too shallow for us to continue operating. So, we're not allowed up river any further than Subton. There's also tactical considerations involved with that, given that we don't have a good relationship with the Unity Empire or its leadership; who unfortunately control the entire river west of our base all the way up to their western border."

Simon sighed.

"Well, take us as far as you can; and we'll figure out what to do from there."

Clifford nodded.

"I'll see what I can do."

A Unity soldier hurried over to a colonel standing around a nearby map table and saluted. He then handed the officer a message. The colonel took it, read its brief contents, and then frowned.

"General Amaroth, it would appear that several racers have escaped from the clutches of the Sheffield Republic and are traveling our way up the river," he said.

A haggard old general looked over at him and glared.

"Once again, the Sheffield have failed to contain the racers. Well, no matter. We will succeed where they have failed. Ready two regiments of soldiers immediately. We will hunt them down and destroy them before they can escape."

The colonel saluted.

"Yes, sir!"

The End